Love's Perfect Surrender

Chiara Talluto

A & S
MERCURY
EYES
PUBLISHING

Cover design by Eddie Vincent/ENC Graphic Services
Front cover photographs young couple: © coendef/bigstock.com;
older couple: © smith/istock.com path and rose :© Shutterstock.com
Backcover photograph couple: © smith/Istock.com

ISBN: 1497492882
ISBN-13:978-1497492882

DEDICATION

Jesus, this is for you.
Years ago, you placed an idea in my head about a struggling married couple and their amazing child. No matter what I did to shake it off, you continued to keep it at the forefront of my mind. I am not worthy of being the messenger of this story. But through You, and your continued love for all my imperfections, this project has come to fruition.

To all the Isabella's in the world—girls and boys. The Bible refers to children as a blessing and heritage of the Lord. All children deserve to be given life and loved no matter their skin color, or any missing part of their flesh and bones. Remember, you are loved child…You are loved…

For all the Antoinette's who have experienced infertility and/or loss of a child. I've been there. I know your hurt. Never lose faith; God will get you through your adversities.

To all the parents like Antoinette and Vito Libero who have lost the "us" part of their relationship because of your infertility journey. It's difficult to not be consumed with something you so desperately want, but you can't have your marriage suffer as a result of it. You need to be yoked together as a husband and wife, and remove those individual perceptions. Expectations can be surrendered. Love is about surrendering those expectations.

TOGETHER LOOKING OUT

Here we stand face to face on top of the highest mountain of our marriage.

Hand in hand, we will look across the horizon in anticipation of the joys and pains yet to experience in our lives.

If what we built together, a foundation of respect and surrender, can tower above all other hills, then our love will always be solid as a rock, with its arms reaching for the horizon.

- Chiara Talluto. October, 1995.

PART 1: THE MIDDLE

"In order to understand the middle, one must accept the beginning and trust the end."

—From Antoinette Libero's Sticky Notes

CHAPTER 1

February, 2000. Near Chicago.

At the rectory of Our Lady Catholic Community Church in Villa Park, Illinois, Antoinette Libero poured coffee into two mugs. She hesitated over the third mug, leaving it empty. Her indecision reflecting her mood. Then putting the coffee pot back on the counter, she slumped into a chair next to Father Robert O'Malley.

"So, what seems to be the problem?"

She nervously brushed a strand of sandy brown hair from her face. "I'm sorry to have bothered you. Vito and I are…" Antoinette's voice squeaked.

"It's okay," he patted her hand.

"Father, we aren't as close as we once were. It's like we've fallen off the wagon, and we can't get back on. I don't know what else to do," she shivered even though she wore a wool sweater.

The priest, portly, in his mid-fifties, nodded his head and stroked his graying beard. "At least he came. That's a first step, dear," he whispered.

She and her husband had driven to the church separately after work and had met the pastor at the door. The Father had taken them back to the dining room where they could talk privately. They waited for Vito now. Five minutes earlier, he had excused himself to go to the restroom.

Taking a sip of hot coffee, Antoinette looked toward the bay window of the dining room, wondering how the meeting would go. Three inches of snow blanketed the parking lot of the church grounds, with more still falling. She and Vito had been married for nine years. Her marriage was crumbling before her eyes; the spark was no longer there. They were still childless after years of trying. She thought it had been a good idea to seek counseling with their pastor. Now she was rethinking her decision.

Looking around, she noted the interior of the rectory. Pale shades opened against dark beige walls, and made the room dull and uninviting. Two brown leather couches and a small, glass coffee table sat to the right of the window. A kitchenette stood on the other side. She and Father Robert were sitting at a large cherry-wood table, and it was smack in the center of the room.

It was already after seven on a Monday evening. She worked as a teacher at Griffen High School, and it was a fifteen minute drive to church. Tonight, it had taken almost an hour to get there with the weather.

She had spent the whole day in a daze, contemplating how to salvage her marriage. Normally, she'd head home to fix dinner but knew Vito wouldn't be there. So, she stayed late at school grading papers, avoiding a drive to an empty and lonely house. She hadn't eaten since breakfast, but food was the last thing on her mind.

Father Robert reassured her with plans of his own of what he was going to discuss with them at this meeting. She was easy to convince, but her husband might not be as open to a marriage intervention, especially if it involved a priest. Vito disliked third parties in his personal affairs. He was very protective about that.

As her husband lumbered back through the dark hallway and into the dining area, she watched as he approached them. The lines around his hazel eyes were more pronounced, his chiseled face, haggard. Even his wavy blondish hair had started to turn gray at his temples. With hunched shoulders, he appeared smaller than his 6'1" frame in khaki corduroys, blue sweater, and brown loafers.

He took a seat across from Antoinette and reached for the mug in front of him.

"What? No coffee for me?"

He shoved the mug, sliding it across the table toward her.

"I'm...I'm sorry. I'll get it."

She rose from the table and reached for the pot and quickly poured the liquid into his cup. "I didn't know if you wanted any coffee."

Vito twisted his hands together. "It's freezing out." Then he took a sip. "Damn weather. I can't wait till spring."

The priest nodded. "You're right. Last month wasn't so bad, considering those two big snow storms we had after the New Year. But late tonight into tomorrow morning," he pointed outside, "they're predicting another three inches on top of what we currently have."

Her husband peered at his watch and sighed heavily. "Driving home won't be an easy ride, either. We haven't had dinner yet, and I still have to shovel our driveway. So maybe we could get on with this meeting, or whatever this is."

Father Robert cleared his throat. "Well, first, I'm happy you both came." He looked from Antoinette to Vito. "Secondly, from what your wife has told me, you both seem to be going through a rough patch. My role is to give you tools to strengthen your marriage."

"Hmm... That's private. Why do you need to know our business?" Vito rubbed his hand down his face.

"It's standard procedure, Mr. Libero. When we work with couples who are having marital issues, we set up counseling sessions to help them uncover what it is that is straining their relationship."

"I'll tell you what's 'straining' our relationship." He pointed to Antoinette. "We can't have kids. All the money wasted, empty promises from doctors; I'm sick of it."

"So, that didn't work. What can you do? Spend your life being angry for what you didn't have, rather than what you have now," the priest consoled. "You can't let it ruin your marriage?"

"Too late for that," Vito snapped.

Antoinette glanced at the clock above the refrigerator in the kitchenette. They had been there only ten minutes and the conversation had already turned sour. She felt sick to her stomach. Could the pastor save her marriage? When she had spoken to him on the phone to set up the appointment, his concern was genuine. She wasn't comfortable talking to either Vito's parents or her own about their problems, or anyone else.

"This is just a bump in your road. I can help you and your wife."

"Give me a break." Vito stood up from the chair he was sitting in and jerked his jacket off the back of it. "I've heard enough. Get up, Antoinette. Let's get out of here."

She took a deep breath, shook her head, and held her folded hands firm on the table. "Vito, could you please settle down? Let's stay and talk this through. You haven't given *this* a chance." Her unblinking eyes locked onto his. Even with the wide table between them, the air felt thick and stuffy.

Her husband leaned on the back of the chair, "Settle down, huh?" He pointed at her again. "You say I never have any emotion, or express myself. Guess what? I'm feeling it now, baby. Strong as hell."

Father Robert coughed. "Let's not use that language around here, okay?"

"Antoinette, come on, already."

The priest stretched out his hand. "Hold on a few more minutes."

Vito spun to face Father Robert, his face flushed. "*Hold on a minute?* You're a priest, for God's sake. Don't you get it; I'm expected to carry on the family name. And now there isn't *any* family name to carry on."

Antoinette shook her head, exasperated. *Lord, how come every time I try to do the right thing, it always turns out for the worse?* She knew her husband's temper. His mother, Rosa, often reminded her of that fact. The woman had thought nothing of spoiling her only son. Vito saw things as black and white. He couldn't deal with emotional issues. He couldn't control his temper either, and recently started hitting the bottle.

Father Robert held up his hands again, and smiled cordially. "Vito. What about adoption? There are so many wonderful children who are looking for loving homes and..."

"No! I don't want anyone else's kid," he snorted, refusing to sit down.

Antoinette watched him fumble with his jacket as he put it on. Just as she expected, he blamed everything on her.

"I was only trying to help our marriage."

He threw up his hands. "I see what's really going on here. You two have some sort of plan. You're blabbing about our personal problems. Telling him so he feels sorry for you. Stay away from her," he pointed to the priest. "This is ridiculous. Let's go. Now!"

"No." She rose and marched around the table to where he stood. "I want to have our own children as much as you do. You think the only way we are going to be a real family is to have blood children?"

Father Robert stepped in between them. "Maybe this isn't the best time…"

Vito turned away, and Antoinette continued. "*I* was the one who pushed us to see an infertility specialist when we couldn't get pregnant. *I* was the one who went through all the shots and pain of IVF. *I* was the one who went through bloating and morning sickness. It was *me* who was treated for depression when Devon died. Remember him? Your stillborn son, *our* son."

"How about coming back this Thursday at seven?"

Antoinette nudged the priest out of the way. She was on the verge of tears now. "Every time I try to talk to you about it, we fight. We fight about everything, including adoption. What else do you want me to do? Can't you see? Our marriage is suffering from all this."

"Stop for God's sake."

The priest leaned forward. "Can we continue this discussion—?"

Vito barged past him. "This is bullshit, I'm outta—"

"Again with the language."

Furious and disappointed, Antoinette crossed her arms. She should have known this was the way the meeting was going to end.

Her husband headed for the door, and then stopped and turned toward her. In the dimly lit dining room, his face darkened, "I can't do this anymore." His voice was barely audible and heavy with sadness. "This whole infertility thing, the losses, has made things worse between us. I don't know if I love you anymore, Antoinette. I can't stay in a relationship without children. I'm sorry. Maybe we're not meant to be together."

Her knees buckled, she caught herself by grabbing onto one of the chairs. "You don't mean that."

"Please, think about Thursday," Father Robert said.

With a guilty look on his face, Vito stared at her. "You wanted me to say what's been eating at me. Now you know. I'll be outside."

The priest put his arm around her. "Let him calm down. Give him time to think about the issues. Everything will be fine."

CHAPTER 2

Vito hugged his overcoat as the frigid air sunk into his skin, and made his way through the shoveled parking lot. Stomping his feet on the plastic runner in the foyer entrance, he shook the cold from his bones.

It was after one on a Tuesday afternoon, and rock music blared outside of Stadiums Bar and Grill, an old, run-down restaurant and bar with little lighting. As Vito stepped inside he observed hundreds of pictures of baseball players, past and present, covering the dark green walls of the interior. The owner was a baseball fanatic, hence the name, Stadiums.

The bar seriously needed a facelift. The paneling was at least twenty years old, and the tables and chairs were rusty and wobbly. A new paint job would refresh it. At least with the new *No Smoking* ordinance in the township, the air was noticeably cleaner, but Vito still smelled stale ashes in the place.

"What are you having?" April, the bartender called out to him. "The usual?" The *usual* was scotch on the rocks with a splash of soda.

"Not today. A cola will do. Thanks." He took off his coat and climbed on the tattered stool at the bar next to his co-worker, Brad Savory.

"Hey, man!" Vito said, shaking Brad's hand. "It's not Friday yet, and you're already on your second beer. Bad week? How about a soft drink instead?" He signaled with two fingers to April.

His friend chuckled and slapped his back. He was a big man. A few inches taller than Vito, Brad had played offensive lineman in college and still looked the part. A back injury blew his dream of playing professionally. He was a jolly guy, smiling, red-faced, with black unruly hair hanging over his eyes.

"Nah." Brad shrugged his shoulders. "And you. A pop? What's the deal?"

"I can't drink. I still have to go to Wakefield's Family Practice after this." Vito sighed. "It's only Tuesday, and it's already been a tough week. I have two hospitals not getting the prescriptions I ordered for them. One clinic doesn't want to sign me up because I don't want to give them any extra samples. All I'm trying to do is stay afloat. It's a mess, man."

"I know. I've had some oddball clinics giving me shit."

Vito hesitated, rubbing his eyes. "I also have troubles at home. I need a clear head."

"You and Antoinette?"

"Well—"

"You got to be *shitting* me?" Brad moved in closer.

Vito waved his arm at his friend. "You know what, forget it. I shouldn't have said anything."

His cell phone rang. He glanced at the caller ID; it was St. Elizabeth's Hospital. "I gotta take this. Order me a burger well-done and fries, will you?"

"Sure."

Walking out and into the foyer, he answered the phone. "MeritPlus, this is Vito Libero."

A woman's voice came through on the other line. "Hello, Vito, it's Cindy from St. Elizabeth."

"Hi, how are you?" He placed a finger in the other ear. The loud music in the background was making it hard to hear.

"Good. We need to put in an order for some medication."

"What? Run out of Fasomax so soon?"

"You can say that, and then some," she laughed.

Vito pulled his finger out of his ear and grabbed a tiny calendar from his back pocket. "Ah, I can come there day after tomorrow. Thursday mid-morning before noon. It's the earliest I can do."

"Okay, that will work. Thanks, Vito."

"You're welcome, Cindy. I'll see you then."

Vito clicked off and penciled in a ten o'clock appointment, studying the rest of his schedule for the week. It was full every day.

He strutted back into the bar area.

"Who was that?" Brad asked when he returned to his stool.

"I had to set up an appointment with Cindy at St. Elizabeth's hospital for later this week."

"You look like crap, man. I know you're not shy about your alcohol, but maybe *you* need to stay away from it for a while."

"Bullshit," Vito sneered. "I screwed up last night with Antoinette and said something I shouldn't have said in one of those 'in the heat of the moment' kind of things."

"Ah, can't be that bad. What did you say?"

Vito exhaled, running his hand through his hair. "I don't know…I guess I said…'if we can't have kids, then, I don't think we're meant to be together'."

"Wow, never expected to hear you say that. You guys are great together." His friend nodded. "I'm kind of having some problems with Amy. She's pressuring me to have kids, but I don't want any, for now."

"You're a fool if you could, and don't. I'd do anything to have a baby. Look what it's done to us?"

Brad shrugged. "I keep telling Amy we need to wait. The new marketing VP is a real asshole. He fired Collins for not moving enough products. I don't want to end up like him. We need to have a more stable income first."

"I get what you're saying, but kids are everything. Without kids, there's no family. It's just you and the wife. It gets kind of stale, if you know what I mean."

Their lunch arrived and Brad dived into his burger. After a couple of bites he said, "God knows if we had kids already, she'd expect me to spend more time with her and them. I don't need to tell you about the hours we have to put into this job to make it. We've both only been here five years."

Vito picked at his food. His ulcer was acting up. Fireballs danced within his stomach walls. "You know the more I think about what I said, the more I think it's true. I don't love Antoinette anymore." He took a big bite of his burger.

They ate in silence watching replays of the Super Bowl on the bar's big screen TV.

After a few more bites, Vito sighed, pushing his plate away. During his drive to see his clients in the morning, his mind had whirled about his tense marriage. He and Antoinette argued all the time. At thirty-eight years old, he wanted out of a failing relationship. This was not what he had envisioned his life had become. Why stay, if it wasn't going to get any better? What was the point if there weren't any children?

He stared at what remained of his half-eaten burger. He had nothing left to give. He was burnt out. Maybe, it was time to move on. He took a deep breath. *Move on. That's what I'm going to do.*

A weight lifted from his shoulders. He needed to tell Antoinette he wanted a divorce.

Vito lifted his head and called for April, "Give me a shot of whiskey, will ya?" Then he nudged Brad. "You gonna do one with me?"

CHAPTER 3

Sixth period already? Her lunch hour. Slowly, Antoinette entered the teachers' lounge hoping to sit alone and eat without interruption.

Built four years earlier, Griffen High School was a large monumental structure just a few miles from the Libero home on Acres Lane. State of the art technology and biology labs as well as an outstanding baseball and football field, made up the successful institution. Over six hundred kids attended. It was rated in the top twenty for schools in the state of Illinois. One of eleven teachers for the sophomore class, Antoinette taught English Lit four times a day.

Her mind had been in a fog all morning and not on classwork. She replayed the incident over and over from the night before. It had been a mistake to see Father O'Malley. By doing so, she knew she had made things worse between her and Vito.

She yawned for what felt like the hundredth time that day. The night before her husband had slept on the couch in the den, and she hadn't been able to sleep without him next to her. She was exhausted, and the tension was beginning to take its toll on her overall well-being.

As soon as she was through the lounge doors, she spotted Lindsey Keller. "Crazy Keller" as the kids called her because she ran her science classes like a military boot camp. Eccentric at times, but a nice woman, Lindsey was very much respected among her peers.

Antoinette grimaced and gave the woman a short wave, who motioned her to the table.

She threaded through the jumble of tables and chairs, stopping at one of the vending machines to get a soda, and to the refrigerator to grab her brown paper lunch bag. She then weaved her way to Lindsey's table, took a seat opposite her, and faced the parking lot.

"Hi."

"Hya. I was beginning to wonder where everyone was." Lindsey took a bite of what looked to be a chicken salad sandwich.

She forced a smile. "Everyone ate already during fifth period."

"Of course," her colleague tapped her head. "I don't like to eat this late myself, but the kids are in lab today. I have a young teacher assistant sitting in."

From the window, Antoinette could see more snow flurries beginning to fall. They had several inches overnight and still the side streets weren't plowed. Regardless of the close distance from school to home, it was going to be a slow going commute after work. She sighed.

"So, how are you?"

"Tired. These kids are wearing me down. Maybe I'm getting old," she snickered. "How about you?"

"Kids wearing you down, huh?" Lindsey groaned. "My day never ends with kids. I go home after this and get bombarded with helping them do their homework, not to mention the extracurricular activities they're involved in. From piano, to dance, to basketball, the list never ends."

Pulling out her plastic container and opening the lid, Antoinette sank a fork into a bed of mixed greens. She studied Lindsey's lunch and decided her sandwich was much more appetizing than her own salad. Unfortunately, she had to start somewhere—eating healthy. She had gained weight over the Christmas holiday and was just realizing how snug her slacks were fitting.

Lindsey took another bite of her sandwich. "Sometimes I wonder why I had four kids to begin with. Paul was never one for birth control," she snorted.

Antoinette nodded. Feeling irritated, she shoved another fork-full of red leaf lettuce into her mouth.

While her colleague went into a discussion about birth control and religion, her mind recalled what her husband had said at the church in front of Father Robert. 'I don't love you anymore. I can't stay in a relationship without children. We're not meant to be together.'

She thought tough times made a marriage stronger. Antoinette believed when a commitment was made before God in Holy Matrimony, it meant the good should be taken with the bad. It was her Catholic upbringing. She couldn't give up on Vito, or their marriage. Somehow their relationship had to be saved. *How are we supposed to get through this and back to the way we were? What would I do if things didn't work out between us? I'd be all alone.* Anxiety surrounded her heart at that thought.

She interrupted Lindsey, "What's your secret to your marriage? You have four kids, how do you make it work between you and your husband?"

"Compromise, honey. I've been married twenty years, and you're constantly letting something go in exchange for something else at another time."

Antoinette poked at her salad. "Does it work? Compromising? Shouldn't it be collaborating—like working together?"

"Collaboration is for the birds," Lindsey smirked. "You collaborate in an office, not in a marriage. Sacrifice is what I honestly say. *Your* sacrifice. Remember, everyone else comes before you do."

The woman pushed her chair back, inched her way out from under the table, and stood up. "I have to run to the ladies room and freshen up before my next class."

"Sure." A wave of nausea came over her and she grabbed her stomach.

"Are you all right? You're looking kind of yellow."

"I'm fine."

Lindsey bowed toward her; a spicy perfume wafted Antoinette's nostrils. Another wave of nausea came over her, and she tasted bile in her mouth.

"I don't mean to pry, but I'd be feeling queasy myself if I only had a salad. Get something else from the vending machine."

She nodded, turned suddenly in her chair, and vomited on the floor.

"Oh my!" Lindsey cried.

Antoinette grabbed a napkin and put it to her mouth. She shivered; a cold sweat came over her.

"I'm fine, I'm fine." She pushed back in her chair and dabbed her forehead.

"Ah, no you're not," the woman fussed.

"I'm so embarrassed. I'm sorry."

"Girl, forget it. Drink some soda. Here." She handed Antoinette her can. "Kids. They're always carrying around all sorts of germs in schools. I'll let Leroy know to come and mop up. You better go to the school nurse and get checked out. Do you hear me?"

"Yeah," Antoinette murmured still holding her stomach. Was it all the anxiety and stress making her feel ill? This was not what she needed now.

CHAPTER 4

At almost six-thirty, Vito pulled into the driveway. Another couple of inches had accumulated from the afternoon. Lake effect snow, the weather channel reported on the radio. His neck hurt and he wondered if it had to do with the weather or stress. He rubbed it with his hand to release some of the tension.

This morning before he had left for work, he had shoveled the driveway. Now he was going to have to do it all over again less than twelve hours later.

Vito shook his head. He was tired. He had quite an afternoon, first with Brad and then delayed at Wakefield's Family Practice. He hadn't even called Antoinette to let her know he'd be coming home late. He'd been too busy with returning calls, and, he'd rather take the drive home to rehearse what he was going to tell her. For him, their marriage was over. His heart was void of any affection and love for his wife. He blamed it on the roller coaster of hope and hopelessness of being without a child. It's what had mattered most in the years of trying to have kids; his wife had not delivered on her end.

When he entered through the side door, he noticed Antoinette sitting at the kitchen table eating. She sat with her black heels off, resting her nylon-covered feet on the opposite chair. She still had on her work clothes; a pair of black slacks and a white blouse. Her hair was pulled back into a ponytail; her make-up faded from her face.

She turned around. "Hi."

Vito took off his jacket and put it on the back of one of the kitchen chairs. He saw his plate wrapped in foil paper on the stove, and washed his hands in the sink. "Work was very busy today," he paused trying to sound casual, "and traffic was a real bitch."

"Hmm…" Antoinette continued eating.

Vito took his dish and sat opposite her. "We need to talk."

"Yes, we do need to talk," she said, not making eye contact with him.

He uncovered his dish. She had made stuffed manicotti, his favorite. He felt a burning sensation in his stomach—his ulcer acting up again. He couldn't eat; he was full of anxiety. He needed to tell her how he felt. He needed to tell her at this moment. It was now or never. He poured himself a glass of wine to relax his nerves, but found he couldn't drink it and put the glass down.

Get it over with, you idiot.

"Antoinette."

She raised her head in his direction.

"I...I meant what I said last night. This journey, experience, whatever you're calling what we've gone through these last few years has drained me. I'm not happy...not happy with myself and not happy with—"

"I'm pregnant."

A boulder could have hit Vito and he wouldn't have moved with the shock of the news. He swallowed. "What did you say?"

"I'm pregnant," she repeated, still staring at him.

"How?" He grabbed the glass of wine and downed it.

"How else, you goof."

"But we haven't—"

"Had sex in a while? Yes, that's true. But I counted back—that night in January, remember? It was the first week of the New Year and you were out at Stadiums, drinking with Brad."

"I don't remember."

"Of course you don't remember. You were drunk off your ass when you came home."

"I was not."

His wife rose and placed her dish in the sink.

Suspicion was nagging at his heart. Was this another set-up like the meeting with Father Robert? *What the—? This isn't going to ruin my plan to get out.* "I don't believe you."

She wheeled around and glared at him. "You're an ass." Grabbing her purse off the counter she flung the pregnancy stick at him.

Vito caught it with his hand.

"You see two lines. Two lines mean I'm pregnant. Is this enough proof for you?"

He turned the stick in his hands to study the results. He still hadn't touched his food. *I can't believe this.* He pushed his plate away, his appetite gone. "These aren't one hundred percent accurate." He dangled the stick.

"Yes, I know. I thought of that, so I made an appointment tomorrow with Dr. Langford. You want to come and see for yourself? You obviously don't believe me." Antoinette snatched the pregnancy stick back. "Why would I lie about something like this?"

"Now you're noticing the signs? How far along are you?" He got up, disgusted. How could she do this to him when he didn't have feelings for her?

He slogged past his wife. At the kitchen sink, he turned on the faucet, and washed his hands again.

"For your information, I've been under a lot of stress lately, with work and, and...us. I hadn't noticed my period was late until today—when I was at school," she said behind his back.

He whirled and faced her. "But you regularly monitor it. You're like clockwork. Why is this time any different?"

Antoinette put her hands on her hips. "I don't know. I haven't had my period in six weeks this time."

Vito moved away from her, angry. She must have known and didn't tell him. *This is not happening. Not with my decision already made. I'll make sure it doesn't.* "Yes, I'd love to come to the doctor…see for myself. What time? I'll meet you there?"

"Four o'clock."

"Fine. I'll put it in my calendar." He grabbed his jacket, his patience gone, and stormed out the door.

CHAPTER 5

The next day, Antoinette and her husband sat side by side in the sterile white and gray waiting area of Dr. Reynold Langford Obstetrics and Gynecology offices. Her hands were cold and clammy. She turned her wedding band on her finger over and over. She wanted so much to be pregnant.

She watched her husband out of the corner of her eye as he thumbed through his day planner. She still loved him. But something had definitely evaporated from their togetherness. He was distancing himself from her, and the reality of the situation plagued her. *This might very well be the end of our marriage.*

But Antoinette still had a flicker of hope. Hope she was pregnant, and hope this would bring them back together—the way they used to be before all the treatments. She hated using the lack of having a child as her excuse for their difficulties, but miracles did happen for a reason.

Moments later, she was called in to take a urine test. The nurses checked her weight at the same time. The truth was on the scale; she had gained nine pounds since her last visit a year ago.

After the physical, Vito joined her in the examination room and they waited for the doctor. Sitting in the pale-yellow room, she fumbled with a torn strip on the seat cushion as her husband stared at the wall. He hadn't said more than two words in the waiting room. A knock on the door broke the awkward silence.

Dr. Reynold Langford had been Antoinette's gynecologist for several years. He entered wearing a white lab coat under a starched white shirt with blue pants.

Taking a seat opposite them, he pulled out thick rectangular-rimmed glasses. "Thanks for waiting."

"No problem. So, Dr. Langford...Am I really pregnant?" Antoinette blurted. She couldn't hold it in any longer.

"Yes, you're definitely pregnant!" The doctor confirmed, smiling. Looking genuinely pleased to be sharing the news.

Her heart jumped in her chest. *It's true.*

The doctor brushed away greasy dark brown hair from eyes. "I can understand your shock, considering what you both have gone through, but these things do happen."

Speechless, Antoinette noticed Vito's face had lost its color.

"We'll need to start you on prenatal vitamins," he advised, handing her a slip of paper. "I am very happy for you both. So, start eating healthy."

Her hand shook as she grabbed the paper from him.

"Now the serious part," Dr. Langford paused, patting her leg.

With her other hand she touched her face. It felt hot. *I'm pregnant! I'm pregnant!*

"You're thirty-eight now. I want to see you every month to monitor your progress. There are different types of testing and overall health monitoring of expectant mothers that can be done. I don't want to take any chances with your history of miscarriages. Here's a packet of useful information about high-risk pregnancies," he said, handing her a folder. "As far as testing goes, I recommend you look through the possible tests carefully. We'll talk more on your next visit. This shouldn't be new information—just more updated technologies. Beverly is getting a referral ready for you to do a series of blood tests—Hepatitis, AIDS, Cystic Fibrosis, the usual."

The doctor paged through her chart. "I'm scheduling you for an initial ultrasound, so we can see early on how the baby is doing."

With all this information being thrown at her at the same time *and* the shock of being pregnant, Antoinette suddenly couldn't concentrate. Looking at the doctor, she tried registering what else he said. His mouth moved as if in slow motion, and she couldn't make out the words. It was like being in a train tunnel, and then…

She dropped the folder on the floor. Papers scattered. She picked them up.

"Get the blood test referral from Beverly, and she'll schedule you for your next visit." He closed the chart. "Do you have any questions?"

Arms crossed, Vito asked, "When is she due?"

"Let's see, this is the third week of February, and based on your last date of menses, I'd say," he took out a tri-fold brochure, "November seventh." He coughed. "Anything else?"

Still unable to believe the news, Antoinette shook her head.

"Good. I'll see you soon. Take care of yourself. Congrats." Dr. Langford shook Vito's hand and then hers, and departed from the room.

After a minute or so, she stood and stared at her husband. "Well? Are you convinced now?"

"This still doesn't change how I feel."

"How can you say that, Vito? I thought you'd be happy. We're pregnant!" Antoinette ran her hands through her hair. "Can we talk about this at least?"

He abruptly stood up. There was sadness in his demeanor. "I have to go. I'll meet you at home."

"Honey? This is great news, isn't it?"

"Please. I can't—" He turned away from her, took his jacket and left.

***

Driving home, Antoinette felt numb and confused. She couldn't understand why this was happening to her. From the beginning she and Vito both wanted children. Antoinette felt a void in her life in terms of siblings. She had a brother, Salvatore, but he was twelve years older, and he had left home for good when she was just fifteen after being away for weeks on end for his job. With such an age gap between her and Salvatore, she might as well have been an only child. Her deepest desire had always been to have a home filled with children close in age. Vito understood her dilemma. He was an *only* child.

She stopped by their neighborhood park, Sumner Sills. She sat in the car staring at the frozen man-made pond. No one was around at the moment, not even ice skaters graced the nature-made rink.

I'm pregnant and my husband wants out of our marriage. It was sinking in, and Antoinette was frightened.

What if? Her stomach gurgled like a shaken up soda bottle. Bubbles burned her insides, and her hands shook uncontrollably. Tears overflowed from her eyes until she couldn't see. Every muscle trembled. She heard Dr. Langford's voice in her head, "Considering what you both have gone through..." The memories filled her mind as quickly as the tears rolled down her face. She swiped them away, but it didn't matter. The tears just continued to flow.

Beautiful, tiny, with fine yellow hair, her son, her only son, Devon came out in the world, blue and limp. She couldn't shake the image of her son's lifeless body for the longest time. And still now, she shivered, remembering—remembering *him*. Remembering all of it...the physical loss, the financial loss, and the greatest—the emotional loss.

The In Vitro-Fertilization (IVF) shots were the worst. The needles were thick, and Antoinette had bruise marks on her abdomen, buttocks, and the back of her thighs. They couldn't plan for much during the treatments because the shots had to be administered on a set time schedule every day. Her stomach was bloated; she had gained weight, and felt uncomfortable all the time. Had she known then all the suffering they'd gone through to still leave them *empty-handed*, Antoinette would never have done the treatments.

During the challenges of IVF and the painful experience of a miscarriage at three months and then losing Devon when she was eight months pregnant, her marriage was on constant edge. Thousands and thousands of dollars spent on IVF treatments. Antoinette had only her mother to turn to for consolation.

Her mom, Martha, encouraged her to be strong, finally confessing that she had two miscarriages herself before getting pregnant with Salvatore and then her. The doctors told Martha she couldn't have any kids. It was devastating to her and her husband. Her parents and in-laws were quite upset. But Martha said she and Frank made a pact to live life to the fullest, and pledged not to worry about what other people said.

And then, a miracle happened, and she conceived Salvatore. Martha said he was the best blessing in the world. Then she and Dad tried a few more times because they didn't want her brother to be alone. After twelve years, miraculously and without any expectation, Antoinette came along. She often told her daughter not to lose heart and promised blessings would come her way some day. Antoinette had to be patient. "Remember," her mother consoled. "God's time is not your time. You have to trust His timing."

The advice her mom gave was inspiring, but she still desperately wanted a baby. She wanted it to fill her "sibling void," and help Vito carry on his lineage. It didn't matter how much more money they'd spend, she wanted a *baby*.

Her desire for children was an obsession. It consumed her like an ache, constantly throbbing. She longed for Vito to feel the same way. Four months after delivering their stillborn child, Antoinette considered adoption. Dropping hints of adoption and leaving flyers lying around the house; a *Chicago Tribune* article about adoption in America, adoption packets from various agencies, and scribbled notes from three women's experiences, which she had gotten from the agencies.

One night after dinner while clearing the dishes in the kitchen, she decided to broach the subject again. Vito sat on the couch in the den watching a baseball game on TV.

"Vito, we need to talk."

"About what?"

"You know what."

No answer.

"Vito?"

Looking away from the TV, he said, "It's about the adoption thing, isn't it?"

Wiping her hands on the dishcloth, Antoinette stepped cautiously over to him. "You make it sound like it's a bad word, or something. Why won't you consider it?"

He turned and stared at her. "I don't *want* to consider it. It wouldn't be my bloodline; I couldn't love it like my own. You know how I feel about adoption. I don't want to do it."

"That's one of our best options to be parents," she managed to say without choking.

"I've told you, I'm done, I'm done!" he said, raising his voice. "Can't you understand what I'm saying? It's over for me. Please stop collecting these stupid articles. It's not going to change my mind. There is no hope of us having a baby, anymore. It's done."

Her heart sank. She had found it difficult to breathe and trudged out of the room.

He followed her. Grabbing her from behind and facing her, he said, "I can't. Give *us* some time, Antoinette. You and I have been through a lot lately. Not to mention the money. We spent a lot. You had agreed this was expensive, and for what? We've got nothing to show for all of it. I need a break. I want to forget about it for a while. You should, too."

She hesitated a moment before speaking, "Maybe time is what we need, and what I need."

But as the words left her mouth, she sensed failure. Mixed emotions wrestled within her heart. She hated and loved him at the same time. Maybe jumping too fast, filling a void probably wasn't the best solution. She needed time, time to heal. *Time*. But time told her their "family" plans would be delayed. How long could she wait? Her biological clock was ticking. Adoption could take years. If they let *time* take over, it might not ever happen. She was conflicted.

It had been the most stressful four years of their married lives. All the focus on baby-producing had caused insurmountable pain and anguish between them. They became like two strangers lying in bed next to one another.

He became depressed and angry. Antoinette blamed herself. It was hard to swallow. She'd become a "barren woman". An image of an old maid with the letters BARREN written across her chest like a scarlet letter swirled in her mind over and over. She carried the burden in her heart like an anchor hitting the sea floor. It was unfair. Though neither was diagnosed with a problem, she couldn't help feeling responsible. Antoinette would never be able to carry a baby in her womb, she was convinced of it.

She became conscious of her husband's decreasing affection toward her. They weren't the same young, joyous couple with hopes and dreams anymore. They had been polluted. Vito was moody and short-tempered with her all the time. She was frustrated with him.

The emptiness of knowing she'd never be a mother to her own child was a painful reality. They had 'closed the book' on babies and dove into their careers, doing their best to erase their infertility. Things hadn't changed another three years later. The hurt was still there.

Now, Dr. Langford was telling her she was pregnant. Antoinette didn't know what to make of it. This unbelievable pregnancy was a real curve ball.

What now? Where do we go from here?

Wiping her eyes and blowing her nose for the third time, she heard her cell phone ring. It was Vito.

She exhaled and answered, "Hello."

"Antoinette?"

"Yeah," she said, trying to sound chipper.

"Where are you?"

"At the park."

"What are you doing there?"

"Sitting in the car—"

"When are you coming home?"

"I'm on my way."

"Okay. I'll meet you there."

After hanging up, a few more minutes went by, and Antoinette found she couldn't move. Slowly pulling down the visor, she stared at her face in the mirror. A bundle of twisted nerves, her mascara had run down her cheeks from all the tears she had cried, and her nose was bigger than a plum tomato. She resembled the raccoon version of Rudolph the Red-Nosed Reindeer. She wiped her face, put on some lip gloss, and started the car.

She was dreading their encounter. Vito had bolted out of the doctor's office as if she had contracted a disease instead of this newfound knowledge of being pregnant. Frankly, she was scared. Scared about what was going to happen.

Is there a remedy for us?

The Red Sea had parted. Antoinette was taking her first lone steps into it. She wasn't sure whether the waters would drown, or cleanse them. But she had to try…

CHAPTER 6

Pulling into the driveway of their burgundy-brick bungalow, Antoinette slowed her car alongside the house and pressed her foot on the break. She took a deep breath and gathered her thoughts as she watched the setting sun reflecting off the snow-covered lawn and onto their front windows.

She thought about the structure that she and Vito called home. So many joys and pains—mostly pains, of the last few years had happened within those walls, and when things were tense and falling apart between them their home still remained intact. Unfortunately, the foundation of their marriage had cracked. Her husband had said he was done.

Holding herself together, Antoinette studied her favorite faded blue rocking chair covered with snow on the front porch. In the summer and fall months Antoinette enjoyed sitting on the rocking chair—reading and reflecting on life, watching the cars go by on their street, Trevor Lane. Peaceful moments were far and few between now.

Memories flooded back, and tears threatened. They had found and bought the house seven years earlier. It was the home on Ridge Drive, the next street over, they were supposed to check out, but Vito turned too soon and ended up on Trevor Lane. The previous owners were moving into a retirement community and had put the house on the market that same day. It was love at first sight.

The front porch, then painted white, was the biggest selling point for Antoinette. She saw herself growing old here with Vito, and *their* family. It was big enough to grow into, but not too large for two people to handle the upkeep. Her husband, on the other hand, liked the property because it sat on a half an acre of land. He desired space, while she yearned for comfort.

Three bedrooms, two and a-half baths, a small family room/den, a modest dining room, and an unfinished basement they could finish as time and money permitted. One of the bedrooms had been converted into an office, and the other room held her old twin bed. A bedroom she had presumed to be occupied by a child rather than a crash pad for one of her husband's friends who couldn't drive home after a night of card playing and drinking.

Releasing the break, she eased into the two-car garage, brought the car to a halt, and got out. Walking carefully down the slick drive to the mailbox; she enjoyed the cold air on her skin, and thought back to the day they moved in.

Hand-in-hand, they wandered through the rooms. Antoinette saw Vito beam with pride, finally being able to afford this house they'd call home. In the den, he let go of her hand and pulled out a bottle of Champagne from a paper bag. Handing her two plastic cups, he opened the bottle. He poured the liquid into the cups, and held his own in a toast.

"To us and a brand new life."

"To us, my love," Antoinette said with an English accent.

"Ah yes. May this den be relaxing after a long day from work," Vito said, smiling, and following along with the goofy accent.

Giggling, they raised their cups and drank.

Vito led Antoinette to the kitchen, and then nodded to her. It was her turn to make a toast.

She cleared her throat, "Um... May I always prepare us well-nourished meals," she giggled again.

They toasted, and then entered the dining room.

"May this room be filled with family and friends," Vito said.

"I'll toast to that."

Together, they climbed the stairs to the bedrooms. Entering the Master bedroom, he pulled her close to him. "This is our private place. This is where we'll rest and make love. May it always be filled with joy."

"Amen."

When they entered the second bedroom, he lifted up his cup. "May this room be host to a beautiful bambino."

She laughed, "What about a bambina?"

Her husband joined in on the laughter. "Whatever. You know what I mean. As long as we have many bambinos, you can have your one bambina."

Antoinette playfully jabbed Vito, "If that happens, you better buy me a bigger house."

Her husband took her in his arms. They kissed, consummating their dreams and desires for their future.

Thinking back to that perfect time in their lives, a rivulet slipped down her cheek as she opened the mail box and grabbed the envelopes inside. They had invested a lot of time, money and work into the house, and redesigned it to raise a family. The first year they lived there, they knocked down the old, detached one-car garage and rebuilt it to fit two cars. The second year, Vito tore away at the front porch and put in a cedar wood porch while Antoinette painted the then white rocking chair, left by the previous owners, blue.

The home had carpeting in the upstairs bedrooms, linoleum in the kitchen, and cheap wood flooring everywhere else. So, the third year, they hired a contractor who tore out all the carpeting and flooring and put in new hard wood floors throughout. Taking a couple of years break, Vito was now in the process of fixing up the basement himself to include a wet bar and theater room, something of a dream project, and it was slowly coming along.

She entered from the side door, removing her wet shoes, setting down her purse, the mail, and taking off her coat. It was quiet and dark.

She flipped the lights on in the kitchen, and reluctantly climbed the stairs to their bedroom. She passed a standing mirror in the corner, and caught sight of her reflection. Today's news of the pregnancy had added new *worry* lines to her face. *What if Vito wanted to go through with a separation or divorce, despite the pregnancy?*

She couldn't think of the "what if" now, not before talking to him. Maybe he'd change his mind; want to work things out.

She put on black sweats and a white hoody and headed into the kitchen to see what she could whip up for dinner, her mind now on food.

Hearing a sound outside, Antoinette turned her attention to the door. Vito was home. She walked over to the fridge, opened it and grabbed a beer. *Should I be drinking? Probably not, but he would appreciate it.*

She watched him as he shook the snow off his loafers and strutted in, looking handsome with windblown hair and cherry-cheeked in his charcoal gray suit. Her stomach doing a flip upon seeing him. She remembered back to the day she had met Vito at her friend, Sheryl, who was hosting a summer bash. They had started talking immediately while he made drinks behind a white plastic picnic table that served as a make-shift bar, stacked with liquor bottles and cups. She had liked him right away.

"What can I fix for you?" he had asked her, pushing up his sunglasses over spikey blonde hair, revealing light hazel eyes.

"A margarita," she replied, eyeing him. Sheryl, hadn't told her about this one. He was a friend of a friend, and good-looking.

"Sure."

"Are you the bartender for this party?"

"Only for the pretty ladies," he grinned, showcasing a crooked dimple on his left cheek. "I'm Vito, by the way."

She extended her hand. "Antoinette."

He shook her hand, then pulled a bottle of Margarita mix from under the table and began filling her glass.

"Wait. Stop. Are you using that?" she pointed.

"I was going to. Why, what's wrong? Isn't that what you're drinking?" he gazed at her.

"No, mine's naturally made," Antoinette answered. He obviously didn't see, or know about, the lime juice and triple sec she'd brought to the party.

"Naturally made, huh? What are you talking about?"

"Here, I'll show you. Move over."

Going behind the table, she incorporated her ingredients and blended two authentic margaritas.

Vito had been impressed by her drink-making skills because he asked her out that evening and soon they began dating. Three years later, both at the age of twenty-nine, Antoinette and Vito walked down the aisle together.

She shook off her memories, twisting the cap off the beer bottle, and handing it to him, "Beer?"

"Yes, thanks." He grabbed it from her and chugged it as she reached for a bottle of water.

Closing the fridge door and leaning against it, she looked into his eyes. "Vito, talk to me. What's on your mind?"

His Adam's apple bobbed up and down. "I don't have anything to say."

"I need to know where we stand on all of this. What you said to me at church you can't take back—you said so yourself. So where do we go from here? Obviously you're not thrilled I'm pregnant."

He played with the empty beer bottle in his hand, not saying anything.

"Look at us," Antoinette continued, her voice hoarse from crying earlier. "I want our marriage to work. I love you. I need a commitment from you."

He breathed out heavily. "I don't know." He turned away from her. "I know I've been an ass, and I'm sorry."

Antoinette crossed her arms, still not convinced.

Vito turned to look back at her. "I'm confused. I'm tired. I've had a grueling day, and frankly, I want a change in my life."

"Isn't this change enough? To be having a baby—*our* baby. Isn't this what you wanted?"

"Yes, but…can you handle carrying *another* baby? What if you lose it like the others? I can't go through another loss."

"You think I can?" Antoinette noted the insincerity in his voice. It wasn't her fault she lost the baby.

Vito opened the fridge and grabbed another beer. "It's true, isn't it? You're the one who lost the other two."

"That's not fair." She pushed him. "You contributed to the pregnancies, too. They weren't immaculate conceptions."

"Antoinette, I don't want to be hurt again. Let's leave it alone."

"No, I won't leave it alone. So, tell me what you want me to do? Get an abortion, continue with the pregnancy, *what?* Just because your little ego has been bruised doesn't mean you can slip out of responsibility whenever you want."

"No, I'm not telling you to get an abortion. Are you nuts? You're pregnant. Okay. See what happens. And frankly," Vito glared at her, "my ego isn't bruised. I'm more of a man than you think."

Antoinette hesitated. "What does that mean 'see what happens'? Where does that leave us?"

"I don't have an answer." He downed his second beer, and threw the bottle in the trash.

This was it, wasn't it? What would happen to her and the baby? What would she do if her husband wanted a divorce? Antoinette was scared. She knew some women who were single moms but she couldn't do this alone. She needed Vito.

Hands on his hips, he wore a blank stare across his face as if nothing was the matter.

She pushed him again. "Go away, Vito!" Tears welled in her eyes. She couldn't help but be hurt. *What was wrong with him?* Trying to control her emotions was difficult. Like another burst of a shaken-up pop bottle, she began to sob. She couldn't hold it back any longer.

He reached for her. "Stop that, Antoinette. Stop crying, okay?"

"I...can't..." She started to walk out of the kitchen.

Vito's hands grabbed her shoulders and spun her around. Before she could get away or fight him, he seized her in his arms and they sank to the floor together. He held her as the tears flowed nonstop, and for a moment, she thought she heard him sniffling, too.

CHAPTER 7

Vito held his wife for a time in the kitchen before helping her upstairs to their bedroom. On the bed she continued to cry, and he stayed with her until she fell into a deep sleep.

Now he needed a breather, away from Antoinette and all her emotion. He changed into a gray sweat suit, went downstairs, grabbed another beer and headed for the garage. He had a stash of cigarettes in his car's glove compartment just for times like this, when days were a little rough. A smoke would calm his nerves.

"Chicken shit," Vito muttered as he took a long drag while standing inside the garage next to his car. Why did he do what he did? One minute he's celebrating with Brad, planning how he's going to start anew. Next, he's collapsed on the floor holding his wife, and crying with her. What a puss, he hated it when Antoinette cried. He sure wasn't *Harry Callahan*—aka Clint Eastwood, his "unemotional" idol in the *Dirty Harry* films.

Growing up, Vito loved watching crime and police thrillers on TV with his father, Leonard, on Saturday afternoons. It was the one thing both he and his father shared in common. Their favorite Clint Eastwood movies included *Dirty Harry, Magnum Force, The Enforcer,* and *Sudden Impact. The Good, the Bad, and the Ugly* also made the list of favorites. How he wished to go back and relive those childhood days, and rekindle the father and son relationship he had had with him. It was a different time now. He had no one to turn to for advice, not even his dad because of their distant relationship.

What should I do? How could I leave now with her in this condition? He wouldn't be much of a man if he upped and left. Besides, his mother would kill him.

He kicked the tire on his car. "Damn it."

The cold air inside the garage penetrated his skin. Without a jacket on, Vito shuddered and pulled at his sweatshirt. He opened the garage door and leaned on the door frame watching the ringlets of smoke come out of his mouth.

Antoinette had become such a nag; he felt like a robot, and they lost their steam. And now... Was this the miracle they needed? With all they had endured in the last few years, he didn't think there was hope for their marriage. But Antoinette had conceived. Would their relationship change as a result of this baby? Could he love her as he had before?

He thought of his mother; a tiny, round, tough Italian woman with a hot temper of her own, and married over forty years to his father. Their marriage could have ended years ago when she found out he was having an affair with another woman. Yet, she forgave him, and took him back for his mistake. *Stupid of her.*

Vito still hadn't forgiven his father after all these years. It was no wonder he was more protective of his mother. But, the question was, would he ever be able to forgive his wife for the loss of his son?

He threw the butt of the cigarette on the side of the garage and buried it in the snow with the heel of his shoe. *Maybe I should try to work things out with her.* Then he thought better of it. He couldn't. He just couldn't make this marriage work any longer.

He gazed at the half-moon all alone in a starless sky. *I don't have to love her, do I? If she goes to term—with her track record, it might not even happen—but if she does, she'll just be the mother of my child. At least it will have my genes and I don't have to adopt.*

He took a last swig of his beer, tossed it into the garbage can and pressed the remote to close the garage door.

Yeah, he nodded. He'd ride it out. They were through, but he could be there if a baby *was* born.

CHAPTER 8

The following Saturday, after spending the morning reviewing his volume and sales numbers, Vito reclined on the sofa in the den to take a nap. It was early afternoon, but he was spent.

On the verge of going into a deep, restful sleep, he felt a nudge on his arm. Opening his eyes, he stared directly into Antoinette's dark-brown almond shaped eyes.

"Hmm…what is it?"

"It's after one. Aren't you going to get ready?"

"Ready? For what?" he mumbled.

"Michael's first birthday? We're invited to Sally and Tim's. Did you forget? We RSVP'd a couple of weeks ago."

Vito sat up, rubbing his eyes. A sharp pain blasted on the side of his head. Now he had a headache. He knew a party at Tim's no matter what the occasion, led to a hangover the next day. "Shit. I don't feel like going."

His wife crossed her arms. "I don't think so. We're going. I bought Michael a gift. Besides, Tim is your friend."

Antoinette then turned on her heels as Vito shook off the drowsiness. He wasn't in a sociable mood.

***

"Vito, about time you made it," Tim bellowed from the hallway as they entered the red-brick bungalow. Tall, with thinning brown hair and stylish Burberry glasses, Tim could easily pass for an Ivy-Leaguer.

Tim kissed Antoinette. "Lovely to see you, babe." He then added, "I'm jealous."

"Of what?" Vito asked.

"You guys look like two newlyweds. All sparkly. Sally, come over here and look at these lovebirds, don't they look great?"

"Tim, you're so sweet," Antoinette said.

Sally strolled in showcasing her busty hour-glass figure and manicured fingernails. "Glad you could come. Woo-hoo, they do look great."

Vito forced a nod and shoved his hands in his pockets. Tim and Sally were great friends, but they could also be overbearing with their *too perfect* family outlook. Everything was so squeaky clean and spotless with them. It repulsed him. Vito scanned the corridor; their basement door was open to the sounds of children laughing and screaming below.

"The men are in the den. I have some great stogies and libations. Sally, my dear, can take your lovely bride and escort her to the 'tea room'." He laughed out loud.

Sally playfully punched her husband. "Tea room, my ass. What are we in London? It's the kitchen for God's sake." She nudged Antoinette. "Don't worry; I'll take care of you."

Tim wrapped an arm around Vito and the two of them entered the den. Sitting on a black leather couch were Brad, his colleague, and Rich, a lawyer and high school classmate. Standing in the corner near a marble fireplace was Bill, the local mechanic, and another gentleman by the name of Steve who Vito never met before.

"Hey," they greeted.

"Hi," Vito responded as he took a seat opposite Brad. A dark wood coffee table between them; he smelled whiskey on his friend.

"Are you going to drink with us?" Brad asked.

Vito laughed. "Do I have a choice?"

"Not today. We have an afternoon of some serious drinking, right Tim?" Rich chimed in.

Tim prepared a scotch and water and handed it to Vito. "Yes, sir. The women are in the kitchen. Our nanny is watching the rug rats in the basement, and we, gentlemen, are here, relaxing and shooting the breeze."

All the men laughed, except Vito. He tried to get into the spirit of things, but his mind was somewhere else.

"So," Bill crouched down, rubbing his large oil-stained hands together. "Who's getting laid tonight?"

Tim slapped his back. "Surely not you, big buck. Your wife's looking like she's going to pop out with a little Bill soon. When is she due? Today?"

Deep chuckles went all around.

"That woman can still take care of me," Bill said defensively.

Rich, with his starched black shirt, gray slacks, and shiny penny-loafers, spoke up. "This your first? You're lucky if she's willing to give you any. Wait until you have more kids like me. I have to get me 'some' somewhere else."

"Somewhere else?" Steve asked. His flushed face spoke volumes about his comfort level with the current topic.

"Like internet porn," snorted Rich, motioning with his hand.

"Give me a break," Brad slurred between sips of his drink.

"Lisa knows I do it. She doesn't mind, either. It's not like I'm cheating on her, or anything. I'm just releasing a little pent up energy."

Vito shrugged his shoulders. *Is this the discussion were having today?* He was in no mood to banter or compare sexual notes. He'd rather be by himself.

He sipped his drink.

The men laughed. Vito kept thinking of Antoinette and their new pregnancy. It had taken him by surprise. He recalled what he had said to her in previous conversations.

"Maybe...we're not meant...to be together...I'm confused. Tired. I want a change in my life...I don't know if I have the same feelings as before. I'm burnt."

Other thoughts crept in his mind as he downed his drink. He observed his friends, his married friends with children. Suddenly, they appeared fake and classless to him. He didn't belong here with them. He wanted out from them as much as he wanted out from his wife. *We shouldn't have come.*

His thoughts were interrupted by Tim pointing out that he and Brad were the "baby" bachelors of the group.

Brad shook his head. "No baby for me. It sucks, though. Amy's been nagging me about making babies."

"Oooh..." whistled the men.

"Don't do it," Rich remarked, smiling. "You'll end up like me and my computer."

Brad snickered. "I don't need a computer. I have connections."

The men roared in response.

Tim stretched out his arms. "Huh. The lucky stud is Mr. Vito there, and his hot wife. Huh...I bet you get it a lot? Vito? Vito, are you listening?"

What the—? Vito jumped up at Tim and grabbed him by his sweater; right arm raised back, hand in a fist. His face hot. He didn't appreciate other people teasing him about his personal business with his spouse, even though nothing was "going on" anymore.

"Relax," Bill bear-hugged Vito.

"Whoa, buddy. What the hell?" Tim stumbled back, his face ashen. "I was kidding, bro."

Steve and Rich circled around Vito and Tim, unsure what to do.

Still sitting on the couch, Brad hollered. "Looky at Mr. Vito, causing a fight. Woo-hoo."

Embarrassed, Vito shook his head and lowered his arm. "I'm sorry, man." He didn't mean it though, as he still wanted to pop Tim in the nose and belt him in his stomach. *What the hell was he blabbing about?* The guy knew about what they'd gone through and their losses. Tim had everything he wanted. And, it all came easy. Unfortunately, it was not the case for him and Antoinette.

Vito then studied Tim's red face. His friend was intoxicated.

Exhausted, he dropped back down on the couch, "Give me another drink, will ya."

"That a boy," remarked Tim as he took his empty glass and refilled it.

CHAPTER 9

High fives, laughter and obnoxious male-bonding could be heard from the den. Antoinette uncapped her bottled water and took a drink wondering what the men were discussing. She sat with the ladies in the kitchen, snacking on chips and spinach puffs.

Sally must have read her mind, rolling her eyes, "Wonder what the boys are hooting and hollering about?"

"Sex. What else?" said Carol, Bill's wife, a short stocky brunette with a very protruding stomach. "I can't move for shit with this big belly." She stuffed a few potato chips in her mouth.

Lisa giggled. She was tall, red-haired and slender. "You be careful, girl. We don't want to deliver a baby here in Sally's kitchen."

"Men? Is that all they think about is sex?" Maria, Steve's wife squeaked.

"Yep," retorted Carol. She burped heavily. "Ever since I got pregnant, Bill has wanted to have sex more often. Look at me! I'm bigger than a barn. I can't see my feet, let alone my vagina."

Sally laughed, wiggling her busty-bod. "It's there, believe me." She pointed her finger downward. "Men always find a way to get to it."

Carol shook her head. "No, you don't understand. I'd like to, but my libido is dormant right now. Poor Bill, he has no choice but to wait."

Antoinette grabbed another spinach puff, staying quiet. She remembered a time when she and Vito used to make love with a passion and desire for one another. The touching, the kissing, the cuddling. She missed their intimacy.

When she was thirty-one; they began trying to get pregnant. Both she and her husband thought it would be easy, and a lot of fun at first. Every other night was "baby-making night". They had sex all the time. They were young and healthy; what problems could there be?

But that was a long time ago—before infertility had taken over their lives; sex became a chore, and two conception losses. At thirty-five, they gave up. She gave up, devastated and heartbroken.

What did intimacy even feel like anymore? Prior to their January "conception," she couldn't remember when they had last kissed or even had sex. Hearing about libido and pregnancy from the ladies made her feel uncomfortable.

"Not my Rich," Lisa said, running a hand through her red curly locks. "If I don't feel like it, he has other options to keep himself busy."

"Busy? What do you mean?" Amy, Brad's wife, jumped in, sitting in one of the chairs at the table and nervously twisting at her flaxen hair with one hand, while nursing a red-colored drink in the other.

"I'm embarrassed to say," Lisa said. But then she smiled and winked. "I'll let you girls in on the secret. Rich has found some porn site and when he's feeling frisky I send him to the office."

Sally shook her head, "I don't believe in all that. How satisfying can it be?"

Lisa popped a strawberry in her mouth. "I'm a busy woman and it makes him happy. It works for me when I'm not in the mood. But," she added, her voice softer, "when I am in the mood, it's awesome."

Carol's eyes lit up. "You're going to have to give me that information so Bill can feel better instead of being crabby all the time."

Lisa nodded. "No problem."

Antoinette rolled her eyes. Vito would never think of doing something like that. She strolled to the sliding door while the ladies continued talking. Her mind still on how she and Vito used to be. The emotional intimacy they reached last night was good. But, the words they exchanged prior, still stung. She pushed the thoughts away. They were going to make it. They had to. She rubbed her stomach softly. This baby was going to bring them back together and make them a family.

She stepped to the fridge and grabbed another bottle of water.

"Look at miss skinny, drinking water. What's going on there?" Sally remarked.

Antoinette froze.

Not sure what to do, she averted her eyes from her friends. *Oh crap, what should I tell them?* She took a deep breath. "I've gained some weight lately. I'm trying to cut down on the calories."

The women nodded in unison. "Ah, huh."

"I want to try…to have a baby," Amy announced, putting her drink on the table, and then smoothing down her oversized Chicago Bears sweatshirt.

Antoinette was relieved the attention was taken off of her.

"Wow. How's it going for you?" Carol asked.

Amy slumped lower in her chair. "Not good. Brad says he's not ready. He wants to wait a little longer. I want to try now though; it's depressing me."

"Oh, no. What are you going to do?" Sally remarked, moving closer to Amy and putting her arm around her.

"I wish I knew. I want to have kids before I get too old. My biological clock is ticking, you know?"

Antoinette observed Amy. She knew very well the feeling; the desperate desire to have a child.

Most of the ladies responded, "We know. We've been there."

Lisa chimed in. "I'll give you the porn site, honey, and you can lure your man to you very quickly. He'll think it's just for fun. When you get pregnant, he can't turn back."

"Ah... That's blackmail!" Carol responded, popping another handful of chips in her mouth.

"I have four kids out of Rich. Girl's got to do what a girl's got to do, right Sally?"

Sally coughed. "No, no, no. I didn't exactly do that with my three kids. Though, Michael was the surprise child. And, Tim didn't mind the kids. All I can say is this ladies, love your man. God knows they aren't perfect. It's hard. Marriage is hard with kids. Keeping it going and all. If you give in and be nice to them, they'll come around."

Then Antoinette remembered what Lindsey had told her and spoke up. "Kind of like compromising?"

"It is, but it's not. It's like what the male animal species do to attract and lure the female. It's kind of like a compromise. More like collaboration if you think of it from a man's perspective," Lisa replied.

Sally nodded her head in agreement.

Hmm... Antoinette thought. To her it still sounded like compromise. *You're always letting something go, in exchange for something else at another time.*

Could I live with Vito not loving me, in exchange for being pregnant, going to term, and bearing us a child?

As she pondered on that question further, Antoinette found she wasn't sure. She dreamed this miracle to help them become a family, but there was so much unfinished business between her and Vito. She was uncertain they would be able to patch things up—baby or no baby.

A child was crying; the women's attention turned to the sound.

"It's probably one of mine," remarked Sally as she rushed out of the kitchen.

"No, it sounds like one of mine," Lisa answered, following Sally.

All who remained in the kitchen were Carol, who was rubbing her belly, Amy, who had finished her drink and was already making another one, and Antoinette who was standing there, a half-empty water bottle in her hand.

They stared at one another not speaking. Each pondering on what was currently distracting their minds. They could still hear the men in the other room, raunchy and loud.

Antoinette wanted to leave. Fidgeting with her water bottle, she placed it on the counter. She had made up her mind. *Where was Vito?*

"We need to get going. Can you guys tell Sally we had to leave?"

The other two women gave her a surprised look and nodded. "Sure."

"Sorry... Thank you, and good luck ladies. I hope it all works out."

Taking her purse, Antoinette bolted out of the kitchen grabbing her coat from the closet in the hallway. She was about to go into the den when she saw her husband coming out.

She stopped in mid-step, and so did he. They eyed one another. *Was he thinking what I was thinking?*

He nodded. Got his coat as well, and they headed out the door.

CHAPTER 10

April

It was now Antoinette's tenth week of pregnancy. Vito was driving her to the doctor's office on a Friday morning, around ten. They hardly spoke to one another. He focused on the road ahead, while she looked out the window. "Keep the faith" by Bon Jovi played on the radio. He thought it ironic that the song playing was about holding onto faith when things didn't go one's way. Where had God been when they had their two losses? He scratched his head contemplating the results of the upcoming ultrasound.

Vito hoped Antoinette would be able to go to term. Nine months was a long time. Despite feeling distant from her of late, they were on this ride together, and now, he had to go through with it. He was still thinking when she interrupted his train of thought.

"I'm nervous about the ultrasound. I know it's a normal procedure, but..." she paused before she took a couple large gulps of water from a bottle. "What are you thinking about?"

Vito shrugged, lying. "Nothing. Why?"

"You're so quiet."

He sighed. "Why is it I have to say something all the time?"

"Because I never know what you're thinking."

Vito made a left turn onto another main road ignoring her remark. "How about you? Do you have something you want to talk about?"

"Well, I'm nervous."

"You said that already." He responded with another sigh. He'd agreed to go with her because he wanted to make sure the baby was okay. Vito shuddered, remembering how excited he had been when Antoinette was carrying Devon. The ultrasound images during the last three months showed a growing baby, alive, and then, how he came out. Perfect, but dead. That's what he knew, that's what had been engrained in his brain, and it's what he was fearful of.

"Well?" He repeated.

Antoinette breathed loudly.

Here it comes, he thought.

"I feel like a yoyo. I'm teetering between feelings of elation and sadness. I'm scared and happy at the same time. I can't believe *we're* pregnant again."

Vito glanced at her, "Those are normal feelings, I guess. It's what the doctor said, and what you already—"

"Experienced. And, it's what *we've* experienced before." She finished his sentence.

"Right. Thanks." He wanted to get this over with. Hear things were going well, make sure she was taking care of herself, and move on.

"I'm nervous, Vito," she stressed.

"You said that twice already. I got it. Everything will work out. Are you eating healthy? Taking your prenatal vitamins?"

"What do you think?" Her response was defensive.

"I'm just asking. Take it easy."

Antoinette seemed to settle down a bit as she drank more water, and Vito pursed his lips thankful for her silence.

He pulled up into the Greenwood Memorial Hospital parking lot next to the professional building where her doctor's office was located. He circled the outside jammed parking lot twice before seeing a car pull out. The hospital was on a corner of two very busy streets, directly across was the local community college.

The air was mild and smelled like blooming flowers. There were many tall trees lining the walkway. He and his wife weaved between patients and visitors as they entered the main entrance of the hospital through a large revolving door.

Greenwood—a well-established Catholic hospital in the southwest suburbs of Chicago, had been around since the early 1940s. Rectangular in shape with brown brick, the hospital had made several changes over the years; including a new maternity wing, revamping all of the parking lots, and the addition of a new multi-level parking lot where one could walk through an enclosed hallway into the hospital.

"Vito, I have to pee—badly."

"You shouldn't have drank all that water."

She glared at him. "The nurse told me to do so."

He gritted his teeth. *I should keep my mouth shut.* He knew she was trying to follow all of the doctor's suggestions on how she should be taking care of herself.

Looking at the kiosk for directions to the radiology department, Vito observed the beautiful renovations. One wall contained stained glassed designs of the Stations of the Cross. In front of another wall was a sculpture of Jesus with outstretched arms. There were vases of plants—lots of plants which dressed the hallways. Doctors, nurses, and patrons bustled about.

After getting directions from the front desk, he and Antoinette roamed down two corridors until they found the radiology department.

Two women, in their early fifties, sat at a narrow, cream-colored desk with a glass partition. The ladies greeted them eagerly. Antoinette checked in. One of the women, wiry with short-cropped copper hair led Vito and Antoinette through a hallway to a brightly-lit examination room. The woman placed a paper sheet on the exam table, and closed the door behind her. Vito sat on the chair near the wall as Antoinette sat down on the table holding the sheet across her legs.

"Why couldn't we do this up at the doctor's office?" Vito asked.

"One of the nurses called earlier this morning, she said something about the machines being down."

He shook his head, "Whatever."

The room was small. Bright circular lights overhead. A dark beige paint coated the walls. The large ultrasound machine took up most of the space; its fan producing a buzzing, humming sound. The air was cold and smelled of antiseptic.

"Are we going to get the results afterwards?"

"Yes, as far as I know. Why?"

"Well," Vito said, looking at his watch, "I have several calls to make this morning." He was feeling anxious. He wanted this to be done and over, and go about his day. He was still having trouble believing Antoinette was pregnant. Maybe he'd meet up with Brad at Stadiums and have a drink later. It would help take the edge off.

"You could make the calls while we wait up in the waiting room for Dr. Langford to review the ultrasound."

He nodded. "Yeah, maybe."

An ultrasound technician entered the room and introduced herself as Hayes. She was an older woman with medium-length black hair graying at the roots. Her face, smooth without a hint of makeup smiled at them. She told Antoinette to lie back on the table and get comfortable.

"I really need to use the restroom."

"I know. It's one of the discomforts of getting an ultrasound. We need you to have a full bladder in order for it to be successful. We'll be done with this part soon," Hayes responded.

She began working on the computer, not saying much more. She entered information on the keyboard, the black monitor blinking and beeping as she typed.

Curious, Vito pulled his chair closer to the table so he could see what the technician was doing.

Hayes raised Antoinette's shirt, folded the sheet below Antoinette's stomach, and over her pants. She explained, "I'm going to put some gel on your abdomen, it might feel cold, and then move this instrument over your stomach," she said waving a wand-like instrument.

"Okay," Antoinette squeaked.

Vito watched his wife; her jaw was tight. Without realizing it, he grabbed her hand. He was feeling a little nervous himself.

Hayes moved the wand back and forth, stopping at intervals to capture snapshots, the monitor responding with its accepting bleeps.

Vito squinted at the monitor trying to make out the dark spots on the screen. "Wow. Look at that."

"Do you know what you are looking at?" Antoinette joked.

He tried recalling the previous pregnancies, but found his mind drew a blank. "I'm not sure, but it looks good."

When Hayes finished, she pressed a button, and the remaining ultrasounds printed. She took them and placed them in a folder on top of a counter alongside the wall.

Handing over a tissue, she said, "You can go through those doors, the bathroom is to your left. I am going to step out and come back. Please remove your pants and underpants for the next procedure."

Antoinette nodded, wiping the gel from her stomach. She then lowered her top, zipped her pants, and ran out to the bathroom.

Vito sat in the chair shaking his leg waiting for his wife to return. His ulcer was acting up. He couldn't make out the images. The uncertainty of the pregnancy process was testing his patience.

When his wife returned, a big relief had spread across her face. "Much better. You have no idea."

He smiled, "I can imagine. Women have better bladder control than guys do."

Antoinette pulled off her pants and covered herself with the sheet.

Hayes knocked on the door and entered. "Ready for the trans-vaginal part?"

She nodded. Vito pulled the chair up to the exam table again. Round two, he thought.

Hayes dimmed the lights and began with the procedure. Soon, a bean-like image appeared on the screen. He studied Antoinette. Her eyes unblinking and focused.

He took a deep breath, and peeked at his watch. They'd been there a half-hour already.

Hayes printed more pictures and put them in another yellow envelope. She got up abruptly. She flipped a switch on the wall nearby and a strong-white light flooded the room. Vito blinked his eyes, rising from his chair.

"So, how does everything look?"

"You'll need to talk to the doctor when you go up to the office," Hayes said, leaving.

"Wow, she wasn't very nice," Antoinette commented after Hayes closed the door behind her.

"Yeah, what a bitch. Hey, I think I saw a bean."

"Stop being silly. You can't see anything during this stage. I couldn't make anything out; it looked like a blob." Antoinette removed the sheet and started to pull on her pants. "This was nerve-racking. Shouldn't this be a joyous moment doing the first ultrasound? We've done this twice before; it shouldn't have been any big deal. Somehow I feel this time is different."

He tried to smile at her, but it came out more like a grimace. "But it *is* different this time." Everything's different, he thought. *You and me. Our marriage. This pregnancy.* "Let's go."

His wife gave him a dirty look. "Wow, you weren't kidding when you said you wanted out of here."

The route they had taken into radiology was suddenly blocked off due to cleaning, so they had to go all the way around through another narrow corridor to get to the main entrance of the hospital, and then go outside to get to the professional building to Dr. Langford's office. The hallways were crowded with patients, attendants, and visitors. Each wing they passed was painted and decorated with pastel colors but had different artwork dressing the walls.

Agitated, Vito said, "This is bullshit, walking through an entire freaking building because of *one* blocked corridor."

Antoinette shook her head. She didn't seem bothered.

Once in the doctor's office, they sat in the waiting area. A soap opera was on the TV screen in the corner of the room. He checked his phone; he had six messages. "I'll be back."

"Okay."

He left to make several calls out in the hallway, mostly leaving messages. He solved a few issues, but there was paperwork and contracts he needed to pick up from home before he could get back on the road.

When he returned, he saw Antoinette still sitting in the chair. "You mean we haven't been called yet?"

"No, not yet. I know. Everything all right?"

He cracked his knuckles, a little frustrated on how his morning was going with so much follow up to do. "Paperwork. I'll have to stop at home, collect my things and go."

A few more minutes passed before a nurse called their name, and they were led into the doctor's office.

The office was a nice change from the usual patient rooms with faded green-colored leather chairs and sterile exam tables. Here it was comfortable and warm, with mahogany furniture; large bookshelves filled with medical textbooks covering three walls. Dr. Langford's chair backed up to a window. Vito made out the morning traffic on Cermak Road below.

Dr. Langford entered the office. "Hi, Antoinette. How have you been feeling?" He extended his hand to her.

She shook his hand. "Good overall, thanks."

"Hello, Vito," the doctor said to him, putting out his hand.

"Hi, Dr. Langford," he answered, nodding in his direction, and returning the handshake. The doctor then made his way around the desk. File folders and loose papers lay in neat piles.

He took a manila folder from under his arm, opened it up, and sat down in his black-colored leather chair. "I'm not going to sugar coat this. I've been your doctor for several years, and I have some concerns," he said gravely.

"Like what? What do you mean?" Antoinette whispered.

Swallowing, a sharp pain pierced through Vito's stomach. *No, don't say that...*

"From the ultrasound, it looks as if the fetus isn't growing at the rate it should be for almost being three months along. Have you both read the packet I gave you about testing?"

"Yes we have, why?"

Vito fidgeted in his chair. *No.* She had read through it, but not him. She had asked him to look at the packet several times but he had told her he had too much work to do. She lied, lied for him. He should have read the information. *Damnit! I feel so stupid.*

"Dr. Langford, could you be more specific about these concerns?" Vito asked.

"Here is what I'm seeing from the ultrasound printouts," the doctor remarked as he put on his glasses, and pulled out the prints. They both leaned forward in their chairs and put their elbows onto the mahogany desk. Using his pen, he continued, "I'm concerned about the development of the fetus. Have you heard of Neural Tube Defect, or NTD?"

He shook his head. He had heard of NTD, but didn't know a whole lot about it. A black and white kind of guy that he was, he had opted out of reading anything related to diagnoses and diseases involving children. It was a sore spot. However, he was sure Antoinette had studied up on it when she was pregnant with Devon.

Dr. Langford continued, "NTD is a birth defect that occurs when the spine, the brain, or the bone and skin that protect them do not develop properly. The most common type of neural tube defect is Spina Bifida, in which the bones of the spine, the vertebrae, do not form properly around the spinal cord. It can occur anywhere along the spine. Anencephaly is the second most common type of neural tube defect. And, it's almost always fatal."

Stunned, Vito collapsed in the chair. "Are you saying our baby has this neural tube defect?"

"No. I don't want to alarm you. Rather, we don't know, not without further testing." Now it was Dr. Langford's turn to fidget in his chair. "One such test is an alpha-fetoprotein or AFP blood test. It checks the level of AFP in a pregnant woman's blood. AFP is a substance made in the liver of an unborn fetus. The amount of AFP in the blood of a pregnant woman can help see whether the baby may have such problems as spina bifida and anencephaly. An AFP test can also be done as part of a screening test to find other chromosomal problems, such as Down Syndrome or Edward Syndrome. An AFP test can find an omphalocele, a congenital problem in which some of the baby's intestines stick out through the belly wall. It's usually done between the sixteenth and eighteenth week—six weeks away for you, Antoinette. It's an extra precaution, and by then we will have solid conclusions."

Antoinette let out a breath. It was more like a squeal, than anything else.

Vito abruptly stood up, stalked away from the desk, and slammed his hand on one of the bookshelves. "Damnit!" *Shit, shit, shit. Why was this happening? Why?*

"Please stop. What's wrong?"

"Why does this happen to us? Huh? Why?" he shouted. Then realizing what he was doing, he caught himself, "Ah…I'm sorry, Dr. Langford."

The doctor nodded and waived his hand.

"What if we don't do any testing?" his wife asked.

He glared at her. *What are you talking about?*

Dr. Langford crinkled his brow. "Why wouldn't you want to know? To prepare yourselves. Of course, it is up to you."

"What are you nuts?" Vito let it slip before he knew it was out.

"Dr. Langford, can you excuse us for a few minutes?"

"Antoinette—" Vito started.

She held up her hand. "Wait a minute."

The doctor pursed his lips. "Sure. I'll give you two a few minutes alone." He closed the manila folder, stood up and took it with him as he walked out the door.

When the door closed, Vito stomped over to where she was sitting. "What the hell is this all about?"

"Do you remember when I was carrying Devon, and we did the amniocentesis, as a precaution because we had miscarried already with the previous baby?"

"What about it?"

"You told me you were uncomfortable with going through the test. You were sure everything would be fine, and we still went ahead and did it. What happened then?"

He nodded, remembering. "We lost our boy. But, what does it have to do with the amnio?"

His wife stood up and faced him. "Don't you see? You told me your gut said not to do it and we still did it. Then, we had a stillborn baby. Now, Dr. Langford mentions these tests to see if our child has spinal deformities and *my* gut is saying no. I can't explain it, Vito. I don't want to do this test. Or, any testing for that matter."

"You're crazy. Not do any testing at all? You're older now, Antoinette. We need to make sure of what we are getting ourselves into."

"Has it occurred to you I'm the one carrying the baby? I don't want to be poked like all the other times. I'd rather not put myself through it. I'm sorry."

Vito's belly was burning with indigestion and he was sweating. *What a bitch.* How could she make the decision for both of them? "This is my baby, too. I do have some say."

"Yes," she hissed. "Some. But it's ultimately my choice."

"You're a bitch."

"I could say, you're an asshole."

"Hmm..." *Am I getting outdone?* "But what if there is something seriously wrong and we need to make a decision, then what?"

"I reviewed the packet of information. I'm aware of the tests they do, and I don't want to do them, period."

"But—"

Antoinette waved her hands at him. "I'm scared to do anything. I'd rather let it be. Besides, women have been having babies for thousands of years without testing, or monitoring, for that matter. They get pregnant, and nine months later, boom, they have a baby." Sitting down again, she pointed to herself. "Why can't I do the same? We will take whatever we're given. I can't go through this like before. I don't want to know. I'm sorry. I can't. This is a miracle we're pregnant. Okay, so there is a possibility of something wrong. Fine, we know that now."

Vito sat next to her. "I want to be—" He couldn't finish. Disappointment ran through his body.

Antoinette touched his arm. "Didn't you tell me the other day, to go with it? That's what I'm doing. And besides, why do you care? You're probably not going to stick around with us."

A fiery pain continued churning in his stomach. She was definitely pushing his buttons. "I don't want *out* of *my* baby. You're being selfish here."

"No, I'm not. I'm going on my intuition. It doesn't feel right, okay?"

There was a knock at the door before Vito could respond. Dr. Langford walked in. He sat back in his chair, folding his hands on his lap. "Why don't you two take some time, read up on the tests and think —"

"We're not going to do anything. No additional testing, just the heartbeat check and stomach measuring, or, whatever the technical term you use."

The doctor's eyes widened. "This is very risky; you've already had a miscarriage and a stillbirth. You're both sure about this?"

"Yes—" Antoinette replied.

"No—" Vito blurted.

Dr. Langford's eyes darted from Vito to Antoinette. "If further testing is not what you want to do, I don't agree. Medical issues are at stake here, and I want to prepare you with what's to come. I definitely don't want to cause any false expectations for you."

He watched his wife. *I want to know the disappointment and what I'm getting into before I get my hopes up.* She didn't budge. Her face was rigid. He saw a strong woman sitting next to him, a confident woman. His gut was telling him to do the additional testing. He needed reassurance; it was part of who he was; knowing what was to come. But now…

"We understand, doctor," Antoinette responded quietly.

Still shaking his head, the doctor said. "Though I don't agree, I respect your decision. You're both fearless. But…" his voice trailed.

"Stupid if you ask me," muttered Vito, still shaking his head on the decision his wife had made.

Dr. Langford forced a smiled. "Is this really what you want to do?"

His wife straightened in her chair. "Yes."

He clenched his fists. The stomach acid was burning in the pit of his belly and he swallowed hard.

The doctor nodded. "Okay. We will still continue with the monthly visits. Of course, if you notice anything out of the ordinary, anything at all, please contact me immediately."

"I will. Thank you," Antoinette replied.

"Do you have any questions?"

"No," Vito answered.

"You have a few weeks, but if you change your—"

"We won't, doctor," she interjected.

They said goodbye and left the office. Vito brushed past his wife, as they went through the glass entrance doors. Stomping ahead into the parking lot, a spring breeze encircled them.

His heart raced. He couldn't believe what they agreed to do, or actually not to do. There were no guarantees on the outcome of this decision. He was beyond furious with his wife.

"Vito?" Antoinette called as they neared the car.

He turned around and faced her. "What are we doing? No, let me rephrase, what the hell are *you* doing?"

"Letting nature take its course. Going with my gut," she answered flatly.

"Give me a break. That's not smart."

"You're not always smart about things yourself." Antoinette strutted around to the passenger side of the car and got in.

Vito's hands shook as he fumbled with his keys. He marched to his side of the car, got in, and slammed the door shut.

If she wasn't pregnant, he'd have left her already, gotten out of Chicago.

There wouldn't have been anything to keep him here. Now she was pregnant, carrying his lineage. The child probably wouldn't be normal or not even be born alive? Out of all the crap they had gone through before, it came down to this? This was too much to take in.

He started the engine and peeled out of the parking lot leaving a trail of smoke, as he headed toward their home.

CHAPTER 11

May

It was the fourteenth week of her pregnancy. Overall, Antoinette was feeling the same except her belly was beginning to grow. She hadn't experienced a lot of morning sickness like other women she knew, but she did get tired during the late afternoons. It was a good thing she was a teacher; it afforded her the luxury to rest when she came home from school, before dinner.

She and Vito had been more distant than usual since the results of the ultrasound a few weeks earlier. She could tell he was not happy about the decision she made to avoid the additional testing. They hadn't talked about it much, either. They were both consumed with their own thoughts.

The truth was Antoinette had been frightened about her decision. At the moment, it felt like the appropriate thing to do. Though it wasn't too late to start doing the tests Dr. Langford had recommended, she had to go with her gut.

Now that she had spoken up to Vito, some days she pondered the situation they put themselves in. It was believed that the baby's health was at risk, but how would they handle a challenged child in this world? Did she make the right decision to carry a child who would not be normal? Could she even make it full term? What about her and Vito? Where would they end up with their marriage? It was already on the rocks.

So many thoughts churned in her mind every day, but she tried to remain positive. Antoinette knew in her heart she couldn't go through any kind of testing. But rather, lay it all on the line and surrender to the gift God had given them.

Today though, she decided to put aside all her questions, anxiety, and thoughts as she prepared for a Sunday dinner for her parents and in-laws. Antoinette talked with Vito and told him they needed to let their parents know the good news. She had to tell someone. A secret this good had to be shared. She knew that family would be very happy for them. He, on the other hand, had been opposed to inviting them, but after a couple of days had eventually given in, telling her he wasn't quite comfortable announcing the pregnancy. She tried to remain positive; after all she had a baby growing in her womb. That was exciting enough.

Of course, what better way than to share it over food. Italians loved good news as much as great food. So, Antoinette carefully prepared her menu: first course, the antipasto platter—which consisted of Genoa Salami, Parma Prosciutto, San Danielle Mortadella, and assorted cheeses; second course, penne pasta with meatballs; to help with digestion, mixed green salad with glazed pears, and for dessert, a Tiramisu cake. It would be perfect.

***

As she turned the pasta in the boiling water, her husband trekked into the kitchen.

"Your mom's asking if we have any club soda."

"Yeah, we do, there's a bottle in the garage."

"In the garage?"

Antoinette gawked at Vito, "The basement is a mess with all the two-by-fours and other tools you have down there while you're fixing it. So, I put a little cooler out in the garage with beer and soda. Why are you making such a big deal about seltzer water?"

"Who says I'm making a big deal about it. I just commented on it, that's all," Vito huffed.

"Your attitude says it all, honey."

"Whatever."

He grabbed his windbreaker off the chair and went outside through the side door.

"Here," he said when he came back inside.

"Can you please pour it into a glass with ice and take it to my mom for me? You can see I'm trying to finish things here."

Without saying another word, Vito got ice from the freezer and poured the soda in a glass.

Antoinette checked the pasta. It was almost done. "How are they doing in the den?"

"Fine."

"Can you call them in because the pasta is ready?"

"Sure. Anything else?" he said, leaving the kitchen.

Antoinette remembered. "Yes. Are you still uncomfortable about making the announcement?"

Vito stood adjacent to the door, frowning. "I'd rather we not say anything at all. You want them to know, you can tell them."

"Tell them what?" Martha, Antoinette's mom, asked as she roamed into the kitchen. "Ah, here's my soda." She grabbed it out of Vito's hand. "What's going on?"

He shrugged his shoulders. "I'm going to round up the others, Antoinette says everything is ready."

"Yes, Mom. I need some help preparing the dishes."

Soon everyone was seated at the table in the dining room. Antoinette was a little frustrated by her husband's attitude and response to her regarding the announcement. She shot him an expectant look. *He should be the one to announce it. He wanted to be the man of the house; well he certainly better act like one.*

Vito shook his head disapprovingly, but then reluctantly pushed his chair back, and stood up.

"Where are you going?" Rosa, Vito's mother, asked.

"I'd like to make an announcement, everyone. A very important one, please." He picked up his wine glass.

"You better hurry, son. My pasta's getting cold," Leonard, Vito's father kidded.

Everyone laughed except her husband.

"What's so funny, huh? This is serious, Dad," he shot back.

Antoinette sensed the tension between father and son. They hadn't been close in years, but it appeared his father was trying to keep things light this evening.

"Figlio Mio, *My Son*," Rosa said, extending her arm to her son.

"Not now, Ma."

"Vito. Go on," she consoled, giving her husband an encouraging smile.

"Antoinette and I are expecting a baby," he said flatly.

Martha dropped her fork on the floor and Rosa screamed. Antoinette's dad, Frank, beamed, and Leonard smiled, taking a bite of his pasta.

Everything around Antoinette moved in slow motion as the parents jumped up and hugged her and Vito.

The pasta got cold on the plates as their parents asked all sorts of questions about the new miracle baby, and how far along they were. Things had been so tense between them; it was exciting to get some attention, good attention. But Vito, she noticed, didn't say another word dinner. She didn't press him. They had their own issues to resolve.

Afterwards, while the ladies washed the dishes, the men retreated to the den for after dinner drinks. Antoinette found herself alone with her mother for a few minutes while Rosa went to the bathroom.

As her mother wiped the dishes, she asked. "Is Vito all right? He was awfully quiet during dinner."

Her heart jumped in her chest. *No. No, he's not all right.* How she longed to tell her Vito wanted out of the marriage and had given up on them. She wanted to tell her how it was so exhausting trying to keep their relationship intact. She wanted to tell her the baby may not be normal, it may have a deformity or disease. She wanted to release all the truths of her life to her mother. But as she stared at her aging face, her smiling face, Antoinette knew she couldn't burden her mom with any of her problems.

She and her father were older, they needed to monitor their health, and take better care of themselves. Martha had a loss of her own. Her firstborn son, Salvatore, Antoinette's older brother, was estranged from the family, living in Portland, Oregon somewhere. It was an emptiness that still hurt her parents, but she knew they hoped their son would come back to them one day.

During her teens, Antoinette had regularly felt like an only child. She didn't know her brother that well; he had kept to himself growing up, and then there was the age gap. The family never understood why he left—they rarely discussed it. But, they felt the loneliness. Touching her stomach, she felt secure this baby could help fill her void.

She forced a smile to her mother, a fake smile, one she hoped she'd get across without breaking down. "He's very tired. Work's been rough for him lately. All the pressure of sales, you know."

Martha responded, "I bet. But, if *you* ever want to talk about anything, let me know."

"Talk about what?" Rosa asked as she entered the kitchen. "What did I miss? Anything good?" She laughed loudly. A short and stocky woman, she could belt out a chuckle. Rosa was a complete opposite of Martha, who was thin and fragile.

Martha turned to Rosa. "I was telling your daughter-in-law here, if she ever needs anything to let us know."

Rosa nodded, and rubbed Antoinette's belly. "Why yes, we're here for you."

The rest of the evening was pleasant as they ate dessert in the dining room, basking in the good news. Later, when their parents left, Antoinette went back into the den where Vito still watched TV.

"Thanks for doing the announcement tonight."

"Sure," he answered without turning.

She decided to take a gamble with her next question. "Are you going to stay mad at me forever?"

Vito whirled around, raising his voice. "Who says I'm mad?"

Bloodshot eyes stared back at her.

"Aren't you? We haven't talked much since the doctor's appointment. Obviously, you aren't happy with the decision I made."

Vito rubbed his eyes, "It's late. The news is out, we're pregnant. Yippee! The decision has been made. Now, if you don't mind, I'd like to watch this basketball game, please."

Antoinette winced at her husband's remark. Emotionally, it was all she could muster, and now physically with this growing baby, she didn't have the strength to argue with him further. Shaking her head, she realized it was becoming evident this might be the reality of their relationship.

"Yeah, I'll let you be." Yawning, she headed up to bed.

CHAPTER 12

When she could, Antoinette made it a point to attend mass. Our Lady Catholic Community was a small church of about four hundred families, and was built on ten acres of land behind a large farm. The circular beige-brick church was surrounded by tall grasses, often referred to as the "prairie" by the pastor and deacon.

Vito was not in favor of attending mass. This Sunday, Antoinette awakened early and dressed, preparing to go. She was craving encouraging scriptures with divine intervention.

Grabbing her keys from the desk drawer in the kitchen, she sauntered around Vito without a word.

"Where are you going?" He stared after her.

"Church. Why?"

"Oh," he shrugged.

She reached the door and stopped. *Why was he looking at me like that?* She turned around and saw Vito still watching her. On a whim, knowing Vito didn't like going to church, she thought maybe, maybe he might—? "What? Do you want to come, too?"

He put his hands in his pockets. "I don't have anything to do, if it's okay with you?"

Antoinette was shocked. He whined and complained every time she asked him to go to church, practically begging and dragging him out of the house.

She smiled. "Yes, I'd love for you to join me."

He grinned. "Okay. Let me get my jacket and wallet and we can go."

It was an easy ten to fifteen minute ride of mostly residential back roads to the church when weather wasn't a factor. When they arrived, the parking lot was already full. Easing into one of the spaces, they hurried through the cars to the service. They slid in, second to last pew in the back.

***

During Mass, Father Robert O'Malley gave a particularly poignant homily. Standing on his tippy-toes balancing his round frame, he bowed into a microphone at the lectern, encouraging everyone in their pews to a relationship with Jesus.

"Look at your loved ones sitting next to you, and ask yourself, 'What kind of relationship do I have with them?'" he spoke to the congregation. "Open your heart to Jesus and love one another like He loved all of his disciples. Make God your centerpiece to your life. His love was and still *is* unconditional. He is waiting for you to turn away from sin and turn to Him."

Antoinette listened intently to Father Robert. She watched her husband for a reaction, but he sat straight with his eyes looking ahead. *What was he thinking*? She prayed he would change his attitude one day and become part of their marriage again.

After mass, she and Vito made their way through the open foyer, heading out the door. The recently remodeled church had a number of skylights in the foyer. It was warm, the rays of sunlight flooding the space around them.

Before they reached the door, Father Robert stopped them. His white beard glistened with perspiration.

"Hello," his voice echoed. "How are you?"

"Hi. Fine," Vito said.

Turning his attention to Antoinette, Father Robert cocked his head and asked, "And you my dear… Oh, are you feeling all right?"

At the sound of his voice, her knees gave way. Everything went black.

***

When Antoinette came to, she was lying on a cream-colored leather couch in an office. A young man in a blue uniform checked her pulse.

"Who are you?" Antoinette said with an effort.

He smiled, showcasing a set of beautiful white teeth. "I'm John."

Lifting her head up, she saw her husband talking to talking the priest in the doorway. She waved with little strength and he rushed over.

"What happened?"

"You fainted. We called the paramedics."

"Where are we?"

"In Father Robert's office. He's making some tea for you."

The paramedic looked to her husband. "Her blood pressure was very low. Have her call her doctor if she has another fainting spell."

"Thanks." Vito turned back to her, "How are you doing?"

She shook her head. "As best as I can be. Maybe I need to eat something? Why did you call the paramedics?"

Vito, still wearing shock on his handsome features, answered, "Because you're pregnant, and I didn't want to take any chances with the baby."

John, the nice-looking paramedic, cleared his throat.

Her husband turned his attention toward him. "We're good here, thanks. What do I need to sign?"

As Vito finalized the paperwork, Father Robert came in with a tray holding three Styrofoam cups filled with brown steaming liquid and a paper plate filled with sugar cookies.

"How's our Antoinette doing?" he asked, setting the tray on the coffee table.

"Better now. My stomach is growling," she answered still feeling wobbly, and trying to extract herself from the sinking leather couch.

"Here," he said, helping her sit up and handing her a cup and one to Vito. "Drink this. Eat a cookie."

"Thank you," she and her husband answered in unison.

Reaching for the sweet, she took a bite. The sugar in her mouth made her feel better. Antoinette knew she should have eaten more breakfast earlier, but she got distracted and excited with Vito's sudden desire to join her at mass; she had forgotten to take a snack along.

"Is there something you two want to talk about?" Father Robert asked.

Sitting next to her, Vito answered, "We're pregnant. Or rather, she's pregnant," he pointed to his wife.

"That's great news," the priest said clasping his hands together. "I figured as much. You see, I grew up with five sisters. You know the kind, a nice Irish Catholic family," he smirked. "Well, every time one of my sisters was pregnant, they turned this pea-green complexion, kind of like the way you did."

She coughed, "I'll take that as a compliment, Father. Thanks. But there's more to our story."

"More? What do you mean?" Father Robert stroked his beard.

Antoinette straightened up. Within a few minutes, she revealed their whole story—about the potential complications with the pregnancy and the decision to forgo additional testing—while, she noted, Vito sat with his arms crossed.

Father Robert stood up. Wearing regular clothes now; a button down white shirt and dark green khakis, he wrung his hands in front of him, "I see. So, how about Wednesday nights, around seven-thirty?"

"Wednesday night what?" she said, baffled. Was he suggesting that they restart the meetings? They had tried the one and only meeting before, and that didn't go over very well with Vito's explosive reaction.

"Come here for Bible study and prayer time—the three of us. Better yet, the four of us—the baby included," he said pointing to her stomach.

Antoinette noticed her husband's frown.

"No, Father Robert. I'm not doing this."

The priest waved his hand. "It's no trouble at all. Please come. I'd like to share some scriptures with you. We'll meet in the rectory as before."

Vito stood up and started to walk away. "We tried this before, remember?"

He laughed. "Yes, yes, I remember. But see? Antoinette's pregnant!" He paused. "Give it a try. If you find it's not for you, then you can refuse. No questions asked. How about it?"

Her husband folded his arms again and shook his head.

"One more try?" she whispered.

He groaned. "What's the use? You know about our 'agreement'."

Antoinette nodded reluctantly. Yes, she knew the agreement they had. Vito had been clear about it. It was a constant reminder every day that their relationship wasn't what it once had been even though they shared the same bed. She missed those days of their tender love. But at the same time, she held onto the hope of their marriage renewal with this child inside her womb because it was all she had to bet on.

"Yes," she managed.

"Father. I know you mean well, but I'm sticking around for the kid, now. This is what we agreed upon."

The priest smiled, "I see. We will pray together for the child, then."

Antoinette brightened. "Yes, that's a great idea."

Father Robert cocked his head at her. The priest could tell something was still amiss with them. He was trying to help her.

"Fine," Vito said.

Her heart leapt for joy. *Yes.*

The priest put his hands together. "Good. I can't see you this Wednesday, but let's make a date for the following Wednesday."

After answering a few more questions about how she was feeling, Antoinette finished her tea, and slowly stood up. She believed things happened for a reason. *Was this one of those times for us, this pregnancy?*

It was strange; she had never had a fainting spell before. She was glad it was over, but thankful it happened at the church because after their intense first meeting with Father Robert, they were going to see him again.

It was a little past twelve-thirty when they finally slipped out of the priest's office. The second mass had started at noon and was still going on when they left the church. They could hear Deacon Barry's homily over the intercom:

"Let God become the focal point of your relationship...Keep your eyes on Him...He will help you with your afflictions and conflicts...Trust in Him..."

Together, Antoinette and her husband plodded silently through the parking lot back to her car.

CHAPTER 13

A week and a half later, on Wednesday, Antoinette and Vito arrived for their appointment with Father Robert. They sat in the car for a few minutes before going into the pastoral center. The large farm area surrounding the church presented a restful scene, unlike the tension in the car.

"What are we supposed to talk about?" he groaned. "I'm not sure why we agreed to come. We could be doing other things. *I* could be doing other things."

"We made a commitment and need to stick to it. What do we have to lose? We're praying for the baby."

"Yeah. The baby."

"It's not like we're paying him. Wait, do we have to pay him? We didn't get charged before."

He huffed. "I'm not paying him anything. He's the one who offered his services. Besides, the church makes enough money."

"Stop already. It's time." Antoinette climbed out of the car.

They stepped up to the rectory—a short building, dark and ominous-looking with ivy growing on the black and gray-speckled brick. Three steps led up to the entrance. She and Vito moved to the door slowly, taking in the surroundings. There were flower pots on each side of the doorway with unusual-looking colorful plants unfamiliar to Antoinette. Coming to this little house made her uncomfortable, as she remembered the night a few months back when her husband told her their marriage was over. *What was to come out of all this from tonight's meeting?*

She rang the doorbell.

Father Robert opened the door wearing a black short sleeve T-shirt, cargo shorts and sandals. "Hi there. Come in, come in."

She smiled, taking in his casual attire. It was a sharp contrast to Vito's business suit, which he still had on from the day's work. She fortunately had changed to a pair of maternity jeans, low heels, and an oversized blue top.

The priest led them through a corridor. They made small talk about the weather and the drive to the church, their shoes echoing on the hardwood floor. At the end of the hall they turned right and entered the kitchen area.

Antoinette wrinkled her nose at what smelled like boiled cabbage, though she didn't see any. On the kitchen's center island, she only saw a brewing coffee pot. But she couldn't smell the coffee, only cabbage.

Vito nudged her, rubbing his nose. Father Robert asked them to make themselves comfortable in the dining area. They sat down at the same large cherry-wood dining table as they had before. She squirmed, trying to get herself comfortable on the cold, hard chair but nothing helped.

The priest came back with the coffee pot and paused, ready to pour coffee in her cup.

She put her hand on top of the cup. "None for me, Father."

"Don't worry, dear; it's decaf, organically grown. It won't hurt the baby."

She smiled and moved her hand away as he filled her cup. He did the same for Vito and himself. From the table, he passed them a cup with cream and a small bowl with sugar cubes.

Father Robert settled in a chair across from them, hugging his mug of coffee. "Before I had my calling and became a priest thirty-five years ago, I was a civilian like you, Vito," he said. "I was in love with a woman named Beatrice. We were going to marry. Engaged less than three months, I realized she was more consumed with acquiring my family's money than with me." He paused and took a sip of coffee. "You see, being the only son in a family with five sisters, I was to inherit my father's milk distribution business in Ireland. It would be my responsibility to keep what my father had built, prospering. I thought me and my girl were in love. When my fiancée, Beatrice, learned about the money inheritance, she became consumed with what I call the 'third ring'.

"In a marriage, you have two rings that become entwined together. She wanted the third part—the money." He rubbed his hands together. "I broke off the engagement once I realized the truth. Then, strangely enough, soon after, I received my calling for the priesthood."

"How did your calling happen, Father Robert?" Antoinette asked.

The priest chuckled. "It wasn't glamorous like you see in the movies where the angel of the Lord descends upon you while you're praying on some mountain top," he laughed. "I was riding my bike when the front wheel twisted in a muddy ditch. I fell, scraped my knee, and as I was grabbing my leg because of the pain, that's when I knew I had to be a priest. Like I said, it wasn't anything spectacular. I had gotten a pretty good gash on my leg too. I still have the scar," he pointed to his left knee cap.

"Interesting," she said, taking a sip of coffee.

"What about the family business?" Vito asked, draining his cup.

"The milk distribution. A lucrative one to say the least. After I told my parents about my decision to enter a seminary, my father turned the business over to my eldest sister's husband. My brother-in-law was more involved in the business than I was at the time. The business is still thriving; my nephew runs things now."

"How did your father take the news?" Antoinette had never heard the priest's story before. She finished her coffee, putting the cup down, wanting to hear more.

The priest poured himself another cup. "Like any father who knows the family name would not be carried on. He was disappointed, but he soon understood my mission and was supportive. It took him awhile, but afterwards, he often bragged to his friends he had an 'in' into Heaven with his son being a priest." Father Robert grinned. "I do my best. And I don't regret a minute of my chosen life. It's what I was meant to do. I've traveled the world trying to help others find faith, and came to the states about nineteen years ago. I came to Chicago about six years back and then landed here at Our Lady Catholic Community Church. It's been an easy road to get here, but I like the church and the parishioners."

Vito asked, "You never wanted to try to get married?"

The priest shook his head. "No. I found my love with God."

"Wow. Not my thing."

Father Robert chuckled. "It's a different lifestyle."

"I bet," he murmured, shaking his head.

Antoinette reached for the pot to refresh her cup. When she offered it to her husband, he declined. "Tell me, Father," she said, "what are we going to be talking about?"

"Yeah," Vito said.

Father Robert reclined back in his chair, his large frame making the chair creak. "So many questions, I'm sure you are wondering, no doubt. We'll take it one day at time, eh? First an important question: how are you feeling by the way?"

She shrugged. "I'm doing well. I'm in my twentieth week. Half-way there according to those 'official' pregnancy books." Rubbing her belly, she continued. "I'm starting to feel little jerky movements in my tummy from the baby hiccupping."

"That is wonderful to hear. I'm curious though, have you chosen any names for your baby?"

"Umm, no we haven't, Father. First, we don't know the sex of the baby. Nor, do we want to know. We're waiting…" her voice grew quiet. Unsure what the priest was getting at.

"For what?"

"For the birth, you know," she hesitated looking at her husband who was staring blankly at her. "Make sure the baby is—"she couldn't finish the rest, so she took another sip of coffee.

"I see. Antoinette, what do you feel as far as names?"

"I…I don't have any." She hadn't wanted to think so far ahead, though, she was beginning to like Jonah, for a boy, and Naomi for a girl. Antoinette didn't dare let Vito know just yet.

Father Robert asked, pointing to Vito. "What about you?"

"I don't care. A healthy baby is what matters. At least I hope it's healthy."

"A healthy baby, huh? We live in such a self-centered world. People have everything pre-determined. What kind of person they want to marry, where they will live, how much money they like to make, how many kids they want to have, the list goes on. They take health and life itself for granted. We all do. Then, when something bad happens, we desperately search for the latest fix and solution."

Antoinette was trying to comprehend what her priest was getting at.

"So, why am I telling you this?" Father Robert said as if reading her mind. "Be careful not to let this child consume *all* of your happiness. Don't lose sight of yourselves and your commitment to one another. Remember, there shouldn't be a 'third ring'."

She nodded, now understanding why he had told them about the third ring. *That's it! They* had put all their energy in baby-making because of the individual voids in their lives that they lost their relationship. She peered at her husband who quickly averted his eyes.

Suddenly Vito popped up from the chair, face flushed. "Wait a minute! What do you mean? Are you saying we shouldn't appreciate this child? We went through *hell,* excuse my language, to get this far. We're still not out of the woods... We... We don't know what's to come out of this."

"Yes, but now your complete focus is on the baby, is it not? Even with this baby being born with a possible birth defect, it still consuming your thoughts."

Antoinette stiffened.

"Is it bad to think about the health of your child? Sure I worry. I worry all the time about the *crazy* decision my wife here has made for us not to do any additional testing. I don't even know how this baby is going to turn out?" Vito said, pointing to her.

Then, sticking his finger in the priest's face, he said, "Didn't *you* say we were going to pray for the baby in this meeting. What's up with this crap?"

Antoinette was so embarrassed. She wished she could get swallowed up by her uncomfortable chair. *How could he lose his temper like this?*

Father Robert held up his hand. "Sit down. Give me a minute to explain. What I don't want you to do is lose your focus on what you both vowed to each other when you were married. A child needs two strong, loving parents—and one union to raise him or her."

She jumped in, feeling the need to take the conversation to a safer level. "Okay. I'm getting it, Father, but can you please clarify for my husband?"

"Please," Vito chimed in, taking a seat.

Ignoring the question, Father asked, "Your vows, did you write them yourselves, or did you use what the church provided?"

"We wrote them ourselves," Antoinette replied.

"Good. Here's your homework, then. Dig up your vows. Review them. Think about the type of parents you want to be." The priest rose from his chair. "Let's meet next Wednesday."

Vito sighed.

Disappointed, she asked, "Wait. How come you're stopping?"

"In time, both of you will know. For now, we will take little steps like I said. So, let's say a prayer for our little growing baby Libero, shall we?"

Antoinette and Vito reluctantly nodded.

Father Robert then bowed down his head. "Dear Lord, we've come to you this evening with uncertain hearts and pained emotions. You have given Antoinette a joyous gift growing in her womb. We ask you, Lord, to help the baby grow healthy and strong. Thank you for your mercy, your love, your joy. In Jesus name we pray. Amen."

The priest motioned with his hands for them to get up from the table. "Now go," he shooed. "Thank you for coming."

Realizing she wasn't going to get any further with the priest, she took Vito's arm and they exited out the door. Silently, they trudged back to the car.

Once inside, Vito spoke, "This was weird. This third ring thing he's talking about is bullshit. It's a waste of time. Mine and yours. This is why I never wanted to come in the first place."

She remained quiet, not wanting to upset her husband further. Father Robert was asking them to think about the vows they took, things impacting them and their baby. Maybe they *did* need to be here and listen to him. Maybe this was the journey they needed to take to come back together for the baby.

She looked back at her husband, "Hmm... There's something here we're not seeing. Let's dig up our vows and go from there. Can you at least help me?"

"No," he pointed to her. "You can dig them up yourself. This is your *big* idea."

She shook her head in frustration.

CHAPTER 14

For three days, Vito watched Antoinette search for their vows. He could care less; it didn't matter to him.

In the kitchen on Saturday while making a turkey, ham, and tomato Panini for lunch, he heard his wife call from the basement. "I found them, come down."

He took a bite of his sandwich, grabbed a beer from the refrigerator, and sat down at the kitchen table.

"Are you coming?"

"In a minute," he grumbled. He shook his head. *Damn woman.* He took another bite, and opened his beer.

A moment later, she appeared in the kitchen and plopped a large white plastic bin on the table. The bottle of beer shook, spilling some of its contents all over the tablecloth. Vito eyeballed her.

"What are you doing? You spilled my beer." He grabbed a napkin and dabbed at the tablecloth.

"You could have said you were eating. Don't you think we should look at them together?" she said, out of breath.

He took a gulp of beer of what was left in the bottle, scanning the contents of the bin filled to the top. There were receipts, notes, and left-over wedding invitations. The container looked heavy too, at least for his wife.

"Why didn't you...?"

"Wait for you? Get off yourself," she said, sitting down on one of the kitchen chairs.

Hesitantly, Vito watched his wife. He had been playing along all these weeks with her, making sure she was okay with the baby—his only goal. Now, he was starting to regret it. He believed he wasn't in love with her anymore. She had suckered him into meeting with Father Robert. *Now this.* He didn't want to rekindle their marriage. He could see her hopefulness, her wanting to make their relationship work. He had to be firm. He had to—

"Are you going to stop staring at me, and help me go through this bin?"

"No," he said, shaking his head and taking another bite of his sandwich.

With a sigh, Antoinette pulled off the bin cover and began flipping through random photos, reminiscing about their wedding blunders. "Remember when the cake almost didn't make it to the hall because they had the wrong address?

Or, how about the lead singer, who sang with his zipper open the whole time. Here's a good one...Uncle Lou's Elvis impression on the dance floor. Ah, bless his soul."

Vito remembered and chuckled along with her. He hadn't thought about their wedding day. So much had happened these last few years. Their holy sacrament hadn't defined their lives like he wished.

Antoinette pulled out a sheet of paper with their vows. "Here they are." She began to read them aloud:

***Antoinette and Vito**: I have come here willingly to commit myself to you... To be true to you in good times and in bad... I will accept that we will experience joyous moments and trying times in our lives together... Upon the highest mountain to the lowest of valleys, our love will always be true... We will honor and love each other, all the days of our lives...*

***Vito**: You are the princess who I will always protect...*

***Antoinette**: You are my knight who I will cherish and honor as the head of our home...*

"Wow," he replied, wiping his mouth. "Pretty heavy stuff we wrote here. Funny, I don't remember writing those vows." Nine years wasn't too long ago. But then he knew why he couldn't remember, he no longer believed in them.

"Yeah," she agreed. "It was a while ago, I can't remember, either. Oh wait... I do remember. We were at the park near my old house. What's it called?"

Vito closed his eyes. "Lake Apache Park."

"Yep. I made us sit at different picnic tables and then we came together to see what we had written."

"What a pain. I hated doing that." He drained the beer bottle.

Antoinette nudged him on the elbow. "But look at how beautiful the words are, even though they were a pain to write." She paused. "This pregnancy has been a trying time for us."

He shrugged his shoulders, "Don't I know it." Then he got up and put his plate in the sink and threw the bottle in the trash.

"Why are you so negative all the time," she said, turning around. "Despite our challenges, we've had some great moments."

He raised his hands in the air, "I'm just stating the facts."

"Aren't these wonderful vows?" she said, holding the sheet in front of him.

Vito took the paper from her hands and reread it. "I guess. But we can't go back. What's done is done. We aren't the same couple anymore."

"We can still be those two people again."

He stepped away from her. He was abandoning her of all hope. But he didn't have hope for them anymore. "What do you want from me?"

She reached for him and put her arms around him. "Your willingness to try.

For us."

He pulled away. He was still apprehensive. "I told you already. For the baby, I'll try. But for us, I can't promise you anything."

He saw her lips quiver.

Without another word, Antoinette left the kitchen.

Vito knew he had burst her bubble, but he couldn't help it. He had told her and she still wasn't getting it. He didn't feel anything for his wife anymore. He was disgusted at everything. At her. At his life. Didn't she understand him? How would he know if the baby was going to turn out normal? Or, if she was going to have another stillbirth?

He heard the shower running upstairs. Grabbing another beer, he headed for the den to watch TV. Anything to get his mind off the reality he was living in.

CHAPTER 15

It had been a tough week between Vito and his wife. Since finding the vows, he avoided her at all costs; working longer than usual, eating out on his own, and staying up later so she'd go to sleep before him.

The day came though, of their next appointment with Father Robert. It finally dawned on him as to why the priest wanted them to review their vows—it was his way of bringing them closer together, and Vito was not having any part of it. He felt cornered into attending another meeting, but at the same time didn't want to be the *bad* guy in front of the holy man; a commitment was a commitment as his wife said.

They sat at the table in the dining room. Coffee brewed, but there was no cooked cabbage odor this time. What a relief.

After sitting for only a moment, Father Robert stood up and paced. "There are three phases to a marriage. First, there is the 'bliss' period. The relationship is prospering; you are totally in love with one another. It's a sensual euphoria of loving and being loved, and you are floating on cloud nine." He gestured with outstretched arms up to the ceiling. "Have you both been there?"

Vito nodded and Antoinette followed. He remembered their honeymoon in St. Martin. They had a stretch of beach all to themselves, soft white cotton robes, stocked mini-bar, and late night Jacuzzis. He smiled; he had a strong bond with her then.

Still standing, Father Robert placed his hands on the back of a chair for support and continued, "Then, a circumstance happens, which I call the 'cross.' We all go through them, those troubling times. It can last a day, a week, a month, or years. Who knows why a cross was given to us or how long we will need to endure it, hence your pregnancy losses—your son, Devon."

The priest took a deep breath, rubbed his white bearded chin. "And finally, the 'resurrection;' coming up for air, breathing again, and standing on top of a mountain. The calm *after* the storm, so to speak." He stopped and then asked. "Have you both resurrected and accepted your infertility experiences and your losses?"

It was a question Vito hadn't wanted to think about. He noticed Antoinette. She seemed worn over by the subject. When she didn't say anything, he stayed silent.

"Hmm..." Father Robert replied. "See the problem? If you can't let go, then you can't let be, and move forward."

"I disagree," Vito said. "What we went through will plague us for the rest of our lives. I can't forget it. How does one 'move forward'?"

"Tell me more."

"We lost a child. That's a huge cross to bear." He turned toward his wife. She diverted her eyes from him.

"I'm not asking you two to forget it, I'm asking you to accept it and move on with your lives. It's okay to remember what happened. But, it's unhealthy to punish yourselves for something beyond your control."

Vito pondered the priest's words for a moment. It was true. They had never moved on from their experiences. At least he hadn't. How could he? He had pressure from his parents because he was an only child—the only son. He had to carry on the duty of the family lineage. He was "the man". The infertility did affect him. *Greatly.* And it embarrassed him, too. But instead of confronting the issues, he threw himself into his job. Antoinette was now pregnant—a high-risk pregnancy—and Father Robert was certain they'd never let go of their past pains.

He nodded his head, slowly.

The priest came over to them and patted their shoulders. "Sometimes in life there are things you can and cannot control. It's best to walk by *faith,* and not by sight."

"It's easy for you to say, Father," Vito said, facing him.

"No, it's not. Tell me, why is it easier for me than for you?"

His heart ached of all the memories. He turned back around, staring down at the table. "Because...because you never had to go through this."

"Really? Show some respect," Antoinette jumped in.

He'd been carrying the whole conversation. A conversation he didn't care much to be involved in. Vito frowned at his wife. "Huh. Nice of you to join in."

She fumbled with her hands. "I'm sorry. This is hard for me to take in."

"And, not me?" he shot back.

The priest shook his head. "I am still a man. I have family, too. If I had married Beatrice, we might have gone through similar issues."

"But you didn't," he raised his voice. How could this priest compare his life to what he and Antoinette had gone through?

His wife touched his hand, and he pulled away.

"You're correct, I didn't." Father Robert said quietly, and meandered around the table and sat down across from them. "This is a cross you are bearing now. Resurrect from it, breathe again. Help each other through it. No two pains are the same."

"How?"

"Work through it and talk *to* each other, not *at* each other. Listen to one another. Don't be spiteful. Work as a team and learn to compromise. Try falling in love again."

Vito glared at Antoinette. "This is unfair, putting me on the spot like this. Am I supposed to change because you forced me to come here and attend these stupid meetings?"

"Please don't call these meetings, 'stupid,'" cut in Father Robert. "We're making progress. *You're* making progress."

"Yes, we are," Antoinette chimed in.

He stood up and pointed at his wife. "I don't want to fall back in love with her."

She stood. "We can stop whenever you want. And, for your information, I'm not forcing you to do anything. I would like us—you and me—to be a couple as we had been, but, you're too afraid to work this out."

"Me? Afraid? *Bullshit. You* made the decision not to do additional testing, and now *you* want *me* to sit here and play happy husband when I'm not happy. I don't think so."

Antoinette turned away. "I didn't know you kept score. At least I still love you."

Whoa, Vito thought. *She still loves me?* That's not what he wanted to hear. What should he say? He remained quiet, digesting his wife's words.

Father Robert answered instead. "No one's trying to do anything to you. Why don't you and Antoinette try talking to one another?"

He nodded out of courtesy. "Whatever."

"Good. Let's end this session here. See you next time."

The priest rose. Vito rose. But, Antoinette stayed seated.

"Get up, we're leaving."

His wife slowly nodded and then followed him out.

Silently the Liberos trudged out the door. He ahead of her. Just before he put the car in drive, he noticed his wife gazing down at her hands.

How many times do I have to tell her? It's over! I'm here only for the baby. They aren't getting the best of me. Her, or that old priest. It was them versus him. They were trying to break him down. He wasn't giving in.

CHAPTER 16

August

"What kind of dumb asses have they hired at these doctor's offices?" Vito lamented, as he got undressed in their bedroom.

He had arrived home from work frustrated and in a mood to vent about his day. Traffic had been a bear, a couple of clinics complained to him about the medication they had received, and he'd spilt coffee on his pants at lunch.

It was Wednesday night, and he and his wife had another appointment with Father Robert so he wasn't even able to stay home and relax. They had been going to these sessions sporadically with the priest for over two months. At first it was every week, but then things had gotten busy with him at work and now they were going twice a month. More often than he wanted, as he still felt obligated to go.

Not much had changed between him and Antoinette. He was standing firm on his position, even though he felt that the priest had cast a guilty conscious over him—a spell he couldn't undo or break.

"What happened?" Antoinette asked, trying to sit up on the bed.

He paced between the bathroom and the bedroom, taking off his shirt. "I had two shipments of Lipitor and Fasomax delivered last Thursday to the Willow Medical Clinic. When I arrived there today, their receptionist tells me they never received it. Okay, no problem. So, I called the delivery service and they said the package was signed by a Miller, the same last name of this receptionist. So, when I questioned her, she denied the whole thing. Now, I've lost money on the delivery and medication. I know the woman was lying, but I have no way to prove she was the *one* who signed for it." He put on a brown-striped buttoned shirt.

"Why do I care?" He added. "It's so frustrating. To top it off, they're one of my top pharmaceutical customers, and now they're sticking it to me."

"You're kidding. How horrible. What are you going to do?"

"They're done according to my book. No more free stuff for them." Sweating, Vito sensed his blood pressure rising. "And, the other thing pissing me off today is that I found out they are buying from one of our competitors. I need to update Nick and let him know what's going on. We could start losing clients if we don't find a way to be more competitive."

"You'll have to call him after we get back from our meeting with Father Robert," she said, still trying to sit up on the bed.

"You know, I don't feel like going tonight," Vito said, zipping up his jeans. All he wanted to do was watch a baseball game and forget his troubles.

"We made a commitment."

That's what he should have expected out of his wife. She never budged once a decision was made. Couldn't she try to understand where he was coming from every once in a while?

"This is *your* commitment, not mine; I'm going along for the ride. How many sessions have we gone to now? I don't want to do this anymore."

"Fine. We won't go."

He stood in front of her. "And what are you going to tell Father Robert next? I'm some asshole or something worse?" *Shit.* Why did he care about what the priest thought of him? Here was his chance to skip out, but guilt was overtaking him. *I'm getting soft.* He could feel it.

Vito watched his wife slowly slide off the bed. She was a lot bigger now. Her stomach resembled a large round basketball. Her face was fuller, and there was constant pink coloring to her cheeks. She was glowing. Of course, he also knew she had trouble sleeping at night because she awoke several times to toss and turn, and pee. Every time he asked her how she was doing, she said she was fine. She wasn't being a burden on him at all.

He sighed to calm his nerves. "Let's go."

"You look tired. Why don't we skip out on this one? I'll go call Father Robert."

"Forget it." He started toward the bedroom door.

"Okay, but hold on. I can only hobble so fast," Antoinette said catching up to him at the foot of the stairs.

A pain stirred in his gut as he watched his wife approach him. He was restless and frustrated. She was calm and composed. He turned away from her and sprinted down the stairs. She followed, taking the steps slowly.

They drove in silence to the rectory. Once inside, Father Robert got down to business.

"We're going to do something a little different tonight," he said as he opened a large, black Bible.

Vito cracked his knuckles. *Great, just great. I should have taken her up on not going. I'm such an idiot.*

"Vito, I want you to read a couple of passages from the book: *The Song of Solomon.* Start at chapter seven, verse one through nine. This particular book has been called the most passionate book of the Bible." He handed Vito the Bible open to the page.

He whistled, not trying to hide his displeasure. *Terrific, this is exactly what I need. What next?*

The priest continued, "This particular book praises marriage and the passionate love God intended for married couples."

"It sounds beautiful, Father," Antoinette replied.

Vito stood up with the *Bible* in hand; extending it to the priest. "I know what you're trying to do here between me and her," he pointed at his wife. "But I'm not interested."

Father Robert stood up as well, "Humor me, then, son."

He sat down again crossing his arms in front of him.

"So, where was I?" the priest said, tapping his mouth. "Oh yes. As you read the passages, I'd like your bride to take notes on the emotional aspects of the scriptures."

Vito didn't like reading anything out loud, let alone the *Bible*. "What's the purpose of this exercise?"

"If I told you, you wouldn't do it, would you?" Father replied, raising an eyebrow.

Annoyed and squirming in discomfort, he noticed a smile plastered across his wife's face.

"Vito. In a marriage, don't you have to trust your spouse?"

"I guess."

"As you read the passages, your job is to read the words so Antoinette can capture the emotions. I call this 'dependent transfer.' During your marriage, you and your spouse are both responsible for creating a loving environment. The key here is to develop selfless attitudes to make this happen. Do you understand?"

"Maybe."

"Are you willing to try?"

"What the—sure."

"How about you, Antoinette?" he said, handing her a couple sheets of lined paper and a pen.

"Yes, I'm ready," she replied, grabbing the sheets and pen.

"Good. Let's begin. Vito, go ahead and start reading."

Vito located the particular passage. He began reading, stumbling over some of the words. His voice sounded flat to his ears, and his chest was constricted.

"How beautiful are your feet in sandals,
O prince's daughter!
The curves of your thighs are like jewels,
The work of the hands of a skillful workman.
Your navel is a rounded goblet;
It lacks no blended beverage.
Your waist is a heap of wheat
Set about with lilies.

Your breasts are like two fawns,
Twins of a gazelle."

"Ahem," he coughed. *From the Bible? This is embarrassing. What the hell am I'm reading?* "This sounds a little—"

"Keep reading."

Antoinette giggled.

What was the point of this? He wasn't getting the meaning of the words. He hated poems. It didn't make any sense. He struggled on.

"Your neck is like an ivory tower,
Your eyes like the pools in Heshbon
By the gate of Bath Rabbim.
Your nose is like the tower of Lebanon
Which looks toward Damascus."

Vito paused, "'your nose is like the tower of Lebanon'? Give me a break." He sighed. "Father?" But the priest sat with his eyes closed and didn't respond.

He reluctantly continued.

"Your head crowns you like Mount Carmel,
And the hair of your head is like purple;
A king is held captive by your tresses."

Then, something started to change. Where there had been tightness in his chest, it was now replaced by a sense of relaxation. It was like he was actually there, and he pictured a beautiful woman.

"How fair and how pleasant you are,
O love, with your delights!
This stature of yours is like a palm tree,
And your breasts like its clusters."
His heart began to thump faster...
"I said, 'I will go up to the palm tree,
I will take hold of its branches.'
Let now your breasts be like clusters of the vine,
The fragrance of your breath like apples,
And the roof of your mouth like the best wine."

As he finished, a warm sensation came over him. He looked at the Father who opened his eyes and smiled at him.

"Well done, lad," the priest exclaimed, patting Vito's hand from across the table. "How did that feel?"

"Weird, but fine, I guess. It's pretty graphic there."

Father Robert shook his head. "This, my son, is God's wish for married couples. To have a love that's pure and genuine. You need to let those words sink in."

He considered the priest.

"Yes," murmured Antoinette.

The priest then turned to his wife. "Any comments you'd like to offer?"

"Why yes." She faced Vito. "In the beginning it was a little rushed, but then as you slowed down, I saw a gorgeous woman, and a man who so loved her. It was sexy. I wished I was her. You allowed the emotion to speak through your words to me."

He straightened up in his seat and leaned over the table to his wife. "You understood all that?" Something stirred inside him, and he wasn't sure how to express it.

"I did."

"Wow, I didn't know my voice had such an impact."

Father Robert appeared delighted. "Didn't you feel it, Vito?"

"I did a little, I think." He gazed at the him, desiring his approval.

"A little is fine. When you read with surrender, you took Antoinette, your listener, on a journey about a beautiful woman. Remember, you are both on this journey—together. Lean on one another. Love one another. Share that passion for each other as the author did with this woman, whom he so treasured. And kids, whatever the outcome, embrace it."

All of a sudden, Vito felt happy. The day's pressure was off, and he was focusing on something totally different. What had he been putting up a wall for? Pride? Machoism? He didn't know exactly. Would this change him? Would this change his feelings for Antoinette?

He wasn't going there at the moment, but rather he chose to enjoy the good feeling inside instead. Vito then took careful notice of his wife, realizing how beautiful she looked carrying their unborn child. His heart took a leap. He shook it off, embarrassed. "So, are we done here? And, you're not going to give another homework assignment, are you?"

"First question, yes. Second question, no. Not this time," Father Robert raised a brow. "Now, off you two go. This little lady," he pointed to his wife, "needs to go home and rest. See you next time."

CHAPTER 17

September

It was Saturday morning at eleven o'clock, and Antoinette had just finished making a pitcher of lemonade. She poured herself a glass, and strolled towards the front window. Lately, she'd been craving anything with lemons. Like lemon meringue pie, lemon drops, lemon ice, lemon squares, and lemonade.

Vito had gone grocery shopping. Normally, she was the one who did all the shopping. Her husband didn't like going to stores, whether it was retail or grocery. He complained of being claustrophobic in large closed areas. The last couple of days though, she'd been feeling very tired and had made a list for him, as they had ran out of all dry goods, meats, and vegetables.

She approached her husband with caution when she asked him earlier. He huffed a bit, but when he checked the cabinets and the refrigerator and saw they were all empty, he agreed. She was very grateful for his gesture.

Outside, it was balmy; the city was experiencing an Indian summer in early fall. Settling into the old blue rocker on the front porch, Antoinette placed her glass of lemonade on the table next to her. She relaxed back in the chair, rocking; her thoughts a continuous whirlwind. She'd been haunted for some time now by what Father Robert had spoken to them about their infertility experiences, and how it still affected them.

As they moved forward in the pregnancy, she continued to have fears, like an aching insecurity Vito wouldn't be there. He still hung around though, for the baby, as he stressed. The real question was, would he be around once their child was born and he saw the baby and its imperfection? Regardless of what the future held, she was very lonely for his love.

Her stomach growled. *Again!* She had finished eating an hour ago. Antoinette touched her belly. A warm glow spread through her. She was so happy to be pregnant with this child.

Taking another sip of her drink, she closed her eyes. In her thirty-fifth week, things had progressed. Rapidly. Baby "X" wasn't moving around much; she assumed it was because of the cramped space. Her brown hair had grown out a lot, and was now past her shoulders. The little wave in her hair she once had was now gone. Her feet were swollen and sleeping was out of the question, with this awkward body. She shifted again in her rocker.

Prayer and reflection had become part of her nightly rituals. Antoinette was also doing deep breathing exercises to help with her anxiety. She wondered often what her child was going to look like. Would it look like Vito? Or her? Was there a miraculous chance of the baby being normal? Father Robert was right; she couldn't help but not be consumed with this baby. All kinds of thoughts tested her faith and patience every day.

At that moment, her husband pulled into the drive. A few minutes later, he came up the front porch stairs, carrying two bags.

"Hi. What are you doing?"

"I'm resting. Need some help carrying in the groceries?"

"No, I've got it. There are three more bags left in the car. Could you open the door for me? I got everything on the list. What do you think about barbecuing meat this evening for dinner? I bought two Filet Mignons, they were fresh."

"Sure." She got up to open the door and followed him into the kitchen. "That sounds delicious. I could boil some potatoes and make potato salad."

"Great." He put the bags on the counter. "Did you notice the moving truck in the drive of the Ryland's house across the street? Looks like a new family is moving in."

"No. Gee, shows how observant I've been."

Antoinette strutted through the den and peeked out their large bay window at a small ranch with white siding. A moving truck was parked in the drive. The Ryland family had lived there before. They hadn't known them well, except they were a retired couple with two adult children living in Florida. Maybe the couple had moved to be closer to their children? *Who bought their home?*

Walking back into the kitchen she began taking the food out of the bags.

Vito came back, and helped her unload the remaining products. "I wonder what they're like? All the neighbors around here are old. Some days, I feel like we live in a retirement community."

"I know what you mean."

"What do we have here, lemonade?" Vito asked, placing some of the items in the fridge.

"Yup. I made a pitcher."

"Perfect day for it. What do you want me to do with the lemons I just bought?"

"Leave them on the counter by the sink, I'm thinking of making lemon bars later."

Vito laughed. "Okay. You and your lemons," he finished putting the perishable products in the fridge. "I'm going to go change. Need anything else?" he said, before climbing up the stairs.

Antoinette shook her head, stopping to watch after him. She and Vito continued to be courteous to one another, even though she longed to touch him like she used to: massaging his temples and shoulders after a tiring day at work, and being intimate with him. But most of the time he was far away and cold. She was surprised he had found the lemon bars she planned to make funny. Regardless, she tried to keep her spirits positive. At least he was being cooperative and going with her to see Father Robert and the doctor visits.

As she tinkered in the kitchen she was reminded of how Dr. Langford had told her to stay away from salt and sugar as much as possible. He had also been very supportive of their progress, giving her a lot of information about children with spina bifida, other neural tube defects, as well as children with Downs Syndrome, just in case.

Antoinette rubbed her belly. She talked to "Baby X" every chance she got.

"What do you think of lemon bars?"

Grabbing the meat, she placed them on a dish and marinated them. "How about steak tonight? Don't want you turning into a vegan on me."

Vito waltzed in. "Who are you talking to?"

She smirked. "Your child, silly."

He grinned. "Huh. I'll be in the garage." He headed out the door.

She tidied up in the kitchen, tired again, and went back outside to her rocker, watching a few cars speed by. *Slow down! What jerks. Someday someone is going to get hurt by their speeding.*

After surviving a hot summer in Chicago where Antoinette spent the majority of her vacation in the air conditioned library reading the required books for her English Lit classes, which consisted of...William Faulkner, *Light in August*, John Steinbeck, *The Grapes of Wrath*, Nathaniel Hawthorne, *The Scarlet Letter*, and F. Scott Fitzgerald, *The Great Gatsby*; it was suddenly two weeks into the new school year.

This year she had freshman students in her classes. A diverse group of kids—high-tech and self-absorbed. She missed the days when kids didn't have as many distractions and could focus on their studies, but this was the world they were living in.

Antoinette had a few more weeks left before she went on maternity leave. Her goal was to get through Halloween and take off the first week of November and start her leave, as she wasn't due until November seventh.

Dr. Banor, the Principal, had informed her that a substitute teacher was lined up for her maternity leave. Time had flown by. Her due date was coming around the corner.

Taking a drink of her lemonade, Antoinette did a mental checklist in her mind of the baby's needs. The room had been painted a few weeks ago, a nice light green—Sea Foam Green as it was called. Vito had done it a couple of weeks ago, only taking a half-a-day. It was cozy and smelled like freshly washed linen dried outside on a line. A yellow and green patterned bassinet her parents bought sat in one corner, while a matching oak crib and dresser, in which Vito's parents had given, lined another wall. The room was complete, and the wait almost over.

Next weekend was her baby shower. Her mom was hosting the event at the Blue Fountain banquet hall. About a hundred family members and friends were to be in attendance, including Vito. He outright refused when she asked him, admitting he'd rather watch a football game on a Sunday afternoon than sit with a bunch of women dining on chicken breast, roasted potatoes, and drinking non-alcoholic fruit punch. When his mother, Rosa, got wind of his refusal, she gently coaxed him into changing his mind, or rather threatened him with a wooden spoon. Antoinette was thrilled he was coming.

Though Antoinette was excited for her upcoming shower, the feelings were a little bittersweet as well. She couldn't help but recall the last time she was preparing for a baby shower. She had been pregnant with Devon, and she and her mother were planning all the extravagant details when she suddenly had gone into labor a month early and delivered Devon, whom was stillborn. All the time spent on invitations and favors, picking expensive items at the baby stores, gone in one swoop. This time, she hadn't gone overboard with the invitations and party favors.

Thinking about it now still made her nervous. She knew she carried a baby, a live baby inside of her. Antoinette felt the kicks and movement. Her biggest concern was its health. Shivering, she removed the thought from her mind. *Everything will be fine. I need to take it one day at a time and rely on you, God. It's all I've have.*

Taking another sip of lemonade, she squinted, this time catching sight of a woman just before she disappeared behind a moving truck. She was pregnant, too. *How far along was she?*

CHAPTER 18

October

The trees displayed beautiful colors of yellow, red, and orange as Antoinette drove through her neighborhood on a crisp Saturday afternoon. All the homes were decorated with pumpkins, gourds, and scarecrows. Trevor Lane was ready for the Halloween trick-or-treaters on Monday. She had come home from the grocery store with just two bags and finished putting the milk, deli, fruits and vegetables in the refrigerator. Her stomach was bigger than a sack of large potatoes; getting around was a challenge, especially climbing the stairs to their bedroom, but today she felt energized.

Opening the other bag, which contained candy to distribute for the trick-or-treaters, Antoinette had an unusual urge for a candy bar. She ripped through the plastic, grabbing a bite-sized chocolate covered peanut-and-caramel and popping it in her mouth. When she finished chewing, something wet ran down her left pant-leg.

Stunned, she realized her water broke. *This couldn't be!* She wasn't due for another two weeks. Leaving the rest of the groceries on the table, she grabbed a kitchen towel and slowly hobbled to the side door. She cried out to Vito who was in the garage.

Upon seeing her terrified face he rushed inside. "Are you okay?"

"We need to go. Now."

He nodded, and grabbed her packed maternity suitcase from upstairs.

As he threw the rest of the groceries in the refrigerator, and locked up, Antoinette called the doctor. He'd meet them there, the nurse told her.

They got into their car, and Vito pulled out of the driveway. The ride to Greenwood Memorial Hospital, twenty-five minutes away, felt like a roller-coaster.

"How are you doing?" He asked, racing down their street.

"Terrible." Antoinette moaned, trying to rub the pain out of her stomach. "I have painful cramping. It's like this squeezing and throbbing in my lower abdomen. It's hard to breathe."

"Shit!" he exclaimed, wiping away beads of sweat from his forehead.

"Stop speeding!"

"I'm not! Relax!"

Her heart beat rapidly and she tried doing some breathing exercises, the ones she had learned from the Lamaze classes she took with Vito when she was pregnant with Devon. Breathing in and holding for ten seconds, and then exhaling slowly for another ten seconds. Anxiety set in.

"Breathe with me."

"Not now. I have to drive." His eyes glued to the road ahead.

She managed to smile despite her pain.

Vito regarded her; his faced registered confusion. "What? Are you okay?"

"I'm thinking..." Breathe in, one, two, and three, breathe out... "It's happening. We made it till the end. I made it to the end."

"Yeah... And, you're almost a week and half early. How can you be rational at a time like this? I have no idea how to deliver a baby. I hope we make it to the hospital in time."

Antoinette groaned. A sharp pain like a dagger slicing inside her made her bend over, clutching her stomach.

"Hang on. Almost there. Almost there."

They arrived at the hospital emergency entrance. Vito grabbed a wheelchair and a nurse wheeled Antoinette in. Through the emergency area they rolled by curtained rooms and medical staff. She was put on an elevator to the fourth floor. Her husband held onto her hand as she was brought to a labor and delivery room. Then, he left to sign in at the front desk and notify the parents that they were at the hospital, as they prepped her for the delivery.

Suddenly, she was frightened. The reality of this baby not being normal hit her hard. *Oh Lord, protect us. Don't let the baby be stillborn. I won't be able to handle it.*

Four people were constantly surrounding Antoinette, three nurses and an intern. She was getting dizzy deciphering who was who. The contractions came in stabbing waves. It was all she could do not to cry.

Back in the room, Vito held her hand. Palms sweaty, she dug her fingernails into his fingers. The pains felt like knives jabbing her abdomen. She cried uncontrollably now, not caring who saw her tears. An anesthesiologist came and offered an epidural.

"No, I don't want it," she insisted. If her mother could do it without any pain killers, so could she.

"Don't be stupid," Vito exclaimed. "You're going to need all your strength to push."

Still, she declined. Until... Until the contractions increased, and the pain too much to bear, Antoinette screamed for someone to get an epidural.

As she lay on the bed feeling a little less pressure, she observed her husband. All the color had drained from his face. Wearing light blue scrubs and sweating profusely under his arms and on his forehead; he paced back and forth, staring helplessly at her.

Closing her eyes, she tried to relax. Antoinette touched her head and hair, wet from perspiration. She tried to sleep, but the nurse wanted her to stay awake.

By the time she dilated to ten centimeters, it was almost fourteen hours later. While she huffed and puffed, it was time for the final push. Then she heard a beautiful sound. A sing-song cry vibrated through the air, as Dr. Langford announced the birth at 4:23 a.m.

Before their eyes, Antoinette and Vito witnessed the emergence of a beautiful, pink-faced, bald-headed baby girl out of her body. With the guide from two veteran nurses, her husband cut the umbilical cord, and the shorter of the two women cleaned up the baby and weighed her at six pounds two ounces. The woman wrapped the baby in a green hospital colored blanket, and handed her over. She held her little girl for the very first time, overwhelmed with joy.

In an instant, a name came to her. It wasn't Naomi, the name she was thinking, or Sophia, another name she was beginning to like. It was a name that meant beautiful.

"What about Isabella?" she whispered, weak from the exertion.

Antoinette wasn't sure where the name had come from, but it fit. Isabella was beautiful, and alive. During her pregnancy, she and Vito never discussed names. It was an unspoken agreement that whatever came out of this, they'd have to accept. This wasn't their doing, but God's, and they were obliged to follow it through.

Through a flood of tears flowing from his eyes, he kissed her forehead, and said, "Perfect. Isabella. I like it."

Antoinette then tried sitting up. "Do you like Audrey for a middle name?"

He smiled. "Yes, yes. Now lay back down. Isabella Audrey Libero. I like it."

"Thank you, hon."

It was Sunday early morning, October 30th, and after ten years of marriage, the Liberos welcomed their new born daughter. Antoinette couldn't be happier.

Beautiful as the baby was though, she wasn't *whole*, as a normal child would have been. Little Isabella was missing part of her right leg below the knee, the nurse said. She had a whole left leg, both arms and hands, and ten fingers; she just didn't have the remaining right leg and foot.

Antoinette let her fingers run across the child's glowing pink face. Her heart momentarily darkened as she held her. They had known the risks and took a chance. Fortunately, she made it to term. *Could we handle this? How will the world view my child?* She looked from Vito to the baby. Her husband's tears continued to trickle down from his eyes. She couldn't tell his emotional state.

Isabella then began moving her head from side to side, crinkling her nose, and crying. Antoinette sobbed and laughed at the same time. Despite missing the physical attributes, this child *was* their gift—their flesh and blood. *She's here, she's here!* She was convinced they were now going to be a real family. To her, her daughter was perfect. *This is okay. I can do this.*

Exhausted, she lay back on the bed. In all the miracles of this world, she knew they were blessed enough to conceive a child. She was finally a mom.

PART 2: REALITY

"Truth and reality go hand in hand. One is painful at first; the other grounds you into acceptance."

—From Antoinette Libero's Sticky Notes

CHAPTER 19

The nurses made sure Antoinette and the baby were comfortable before moving them to a recovery room. Meanwhile, Vito left the delivery room, exhausted, and emotionally drained. His cell phone buzzing in his pocket.

Drenched with sweat and wobbly, he trudged the halls of the maternity ward. His child was handicapped. He repeated the words in his mind over and over. But she was cute, too, resembling him when he was a baby. His heart melted when he touched her little fingers, but reality had struck—she *was* handicapped. She'd be like that all her life. Kids would tease her. W*ho'd want a woman who was missing part of her leg?*

He stopped and clung to the cold wall of the hallway, and let the tears streak down his cheeks. He slammed his hand against the wall, hoping he'd break its bones to relieve him of the pain and unhappiness churning within his gut. All it did was make his hand hurt.

A resident doctor stopped and asked if he was okay. Embarrassed, Vito nodded and hurried to the men's locker room where he'd be able to shower and change back into his own clothes.

Once under the scalding stream of water, he cried like a child. He couldn't stop the flood of rivulets spilling from his eyes. Why had he let Antoinette continue the pregnancy when they knew about possible complications? *Why?*

Shutting off the shower and grabbing a towel, Vito dressed quickly. He studied himself in the mirror. His father's voice rang loud in his ears, haunting him now, as it had when he played soccer in high school. "Whatever you do, you have to take full responsibility for your actions. You stick to your decisions, and never waver. You hear me, son."

Ironically, his father had wavered when he cheated on his mother, but Vito had to hand it to him, he took responsibility for his actions, making up for his mistake ever since to his mother.

My daughter has a deformity.

His cell phone buzzed again. He checked the Caller ID. He had three missed calls from his parents, and two missed calls from his in-laws. *They were in for a shock.*

The thought kept intruding upon his happiness. Isabella was missing her tibia bone, fibula bone, ankle, and foot. This was the condition referred to as Congenital Limb Deficiency, one of the things Antoinette had refused to be tested for. He felt cheated. The only child they could ever possibly have was not normal. But what *was* normal?

Suck it up for God's sake. His wife had made it to term and the baby was born alive. *I have to give her that credit.* He knew he had to be a good father to his challenged daughter. Somehow he'd find a way to help her live a normal life. *But how do I do that? I don't know the first thing about limb deficiencies. What about Antoinette? What do I do about my relationship...my marriage...with her?*

Dizzy from many of the other questions spinning in his mind, Vito left the men's locker room and headed toward the elevators to the cafeteria for some coffee, a bite to eat, and to call the parents.

CHAPTER 20

Forty-eight hours later, after visits from a social worker, Dr. Langford, Father Robert O'Malley, the resident pediatrician, a pediatric and orthopedic surgeon, and a lactation consultant, Antoinette and baby Isabella were released from the hospital.

During those first two days, Antoinette coped with ongoing stinging sensations and spasms shooting up from her pelvic area. The nurses informed her that her body would slowly be retracting back to its normal state. This could take up to three months. The consolation didn't help as she wasn't feeling very attractive, and struggling with Isabella refusal to latch onto her breast at the same time.

Antoinette felt rejected. She had wanted to breast feed. A lactation nurse encouraged her that even with bottle feeding, mom and baby could bond together. So, reluctantly, she gave little Isabella the formula.

The baby took it easily, and she was happy to eat. Vito helped with some of the feedings, too, even though he was nervous handling a small child. He was trying, and Antoinette was grateful of his gesture.

The big surprise came when both sets of grandparents arrived to visit in the hospital room after the birth and had seen their granddaughter's leg. She prayed they'd be more understanding considering what they went through, but, the look on their faces shone nothing but shock and disappointment. Vito let her know he prepped the family of what to expect, but in their excitement of the birth, had ignored his warnings.

Martha cried, "How is this child going to walk? Didn't the doctor tell you something was wrong when you were pregnant? Why didn't you tell us about the baby? What are *we* going to do?"

Rosa and Leonard responded the same way. "She is not going to be normal. What are kids going to say when they see her at school?"

Their inquiries were thoughts Antoinette had questioned herself, their doubts as real as hers. And it went on and on for days, even after they went home and adjusted to their new life. Vito was silent during their parental emotional outbursts, but it ruffled her nerves. She tried desperately to ignore their negative remarks. Even if their comments weren't intentional, they still stung.

Each time, Antoinette remained calm, responding "She'll be okay. She's strong like her daddy. See how she looks like him." But the looks she got in return were still disheartening.

***

One evening, Antoinette lay on the couch in the den trying to relax her cramp-like spasms in her stomach, while Isabella slept next to her in the bassinet. Vito sat in his favorite chair nearby, drinking a beer and watching a football game.

Quietly, so as not to disturb the baby, she asked him, "Why don't you tell your parents to leave us be? It's not as if we planned to have a baby without one of her legs."

"What about your parents? They're bitching, too," he said, rubbing his eyes.

She exhaled. "I know. I told Mom and Dad to stop already. I hope they understood. It's a shock to all of us, not just them. I'm just tired of hearing all the questions."

"What did you expect? They'll all quit soon enough. Now, can you leave me be?"

"Vito, what's the matter with you? You're so grouchy today. Help me out here."

"What is it you want me to do? Yell at them? This sucks, okay. I didn't want a baby with only one leg. I can't blame them for their reaction. I feel the same."

She adjusted herself on the couch as another jolt of pain shot down her back. "Really! I'll tell you this, if they continue on their ranting, I'm going to let them have it."

Vito laughed, taking a gulp of beer. "Sure."

Antoinette had struggled for months with the decision of not telling the parents about the high-risk pregnancy. She made a pact with herself not to tell them she had put the pregnancy in God's hands. She didn't think they'd comprehend their decision to keep the baby, *her* decision really. And now her angel was out in the world, and they still didn't understand. She did her part in taking care of herself; the rest was His doing. Frankly, she had expected worse.

"You watch. I will. We have a newborn. A new life. I need your help. I *need* you. We have her handicap to cope with I know, as well as getting used to all the feedings around the clock."

"I'll do my best, but don't forget I'm the only one working here."

"Yes, I know. You keep reminding me of that," she whispered, too tired to speak anymore.

She had eleven more weeks of family medical leave left, and was getting paid for six weeks which included vacation and sick time. The rest would be unpaid. A guilty feeling momentarily crossed her heart. She closed her eyes, while Vito continued to watch his game ignoring her. They'd have to figure something out when her time was up, now that Isabella had this deficiency.

She thought things would be different since the birth was over with—and that *they* would become a family. Instead, nothing had changed. Her husband was still as crabby as he had been while she was pregnant. *Where were his fatherly instincts?*

***

The day came though, when Antoinette had heard enough of the family complaints. She was in the kitchen preparing lunch. The grandmothers had stopped by to visit, and were sitting in the den watching Isabella sleep in the bassinet. Vito had run out to the store to get more diapers.

"Look at the baby, she's so cute. Round face, big eyes; like my son. And then, without the leg. Eh, Dio Mio, *My God*, what did You do?" Rosa complained, making the sign of the cross.

Martha hovered over the bassinet and put her arm around the other woman. "I know," she sniffled. "It is what it is. She's still beautiful. Look, she has my daughter's chin."

They continued whispering and regurgitating the same issues. After several minutes, Antoinette, patience worn over, had heard enough and screamed, "Damnit!" getting both of their attentions.

She was sick and tired of their tirade, and threw the bowl of salad to the floor. The bowl broke into several pieces; romaine lettuce, sliced tomatoes, cucumbers, and dried cranberries dropped everywhere.

"Stop it. Both of you!" she yelled, wiping her hands on a dish towel, stomping into the den.

A hushed silence followed, as both mothers stared at her in disbelief. Isabella stirred in her bassinet and made a sound but continued sleeping.

"For God's sake, she's healthy," Antoinette said, regaining her composure. "What's the big deal? So she's missing part of a leg, huh? I don't care if she had no limbs at all. She is our baby—our miracle. After all we've been through, can't you at least have the decency to say *THANK GOD* she's here? If you don't like her, don't come over anymore!"

A startled Isabella let out a loud cry.

Something inside of Antoinette had released. Her shoulders relaxed, and she breathed easier for the first time in weeks. Blame it on hormones. Blame it on little to no sleep. Or blame it on her disgruntled husband who hadn't been much of a father lately. She had had it.

Martha and Rosa nodded, and came toward her.

"You're right, honey," Martha said quietly.

"Especially you, Mom," she was standing in the doorway and pointed at her mother. "With what you went through to have children. Where's your support?"

Martha hung her head low, "I'm sorry."

Rosa wiped a tear from her eye. "Yes, yes, we are, you know, very sorry."

Walking around her, both women began picking up the vegetables from the kitchen floor while Antoinette attended to her daughter.

Leaving the grandmothers to their chores, she took the baby in her arms and went up to her bedroom to get away from everyone. She sat quietly on a tan rocking chair in Isabella's room. Rocking back and forth, she stared at her daughter; her fingers caressing the child's head and cheeks.

Smiling, she thought Isabella was definitely her husband's daughter. The resemblance was amazing. Her baby cooed softly at her. Her chest warmed for the love she had for the tiny infant. She knew her mother and mother-in-law would be fine in time. They'd learn to love Isabella for who she was, and not what she was supposed to be. She'd go down and check on them once she laid Isabella in her crib.

Nobody's perfect, and neither are they. Sometimes the joys of life come in unusual shapes and sizes, and some are just imperfect.

CHAPTER 21

During the next few weeks Vito wrestled with the reality of his daughter's condition. He hated everything about her missing limb, and he needed the truth. He wanted to know why and how this had happened to his baby girl.

As he and Antoinette did research on the Internet regarding limb deficiencies, clarity slowly began to seep in. They learned an estimated one in ten thousand babies were born each year with all or part of a limb missing, from missing part of a finger to the absence of both arms and legs. In Isabella's case, she had all her limbs except the lower part of her right leg.

He learned the first trimester was the crucial time for the limb formation, specifically the first four to eight weeks of gestation. Dr. Langford had been correct when he told them he found evidence based on the ultrasound for potential birth defects.

He and Antoinette met with Dr. Drew, Isabella's new pediatrician, referred to them by Dr. Langford. He suggested they get in contact with a pediatric orthopedic surgeon, by the name of Dr. Sidney Maxwell. He was renowned for his expertise and knowledge in children born with Congenital Limb Deficiencies (CLD) and he wasn't that far away, considering he was at Holy Name Hospitals for Children located in downtown Chicago.

They were told Holy Name Hospitals for Children was part of a network of pediatric specialty hospitals founded by Holy Messengers, a religious order, where children under the age of eighteen received medical care free of charge. These hospitals served as major referral centers for children with complex orthopedic, cancer, or burn problems.

Taking an additional few days off here and there, after his two week paternity leave, to help out with the baby, Vito researched and contacted the hospital about steps for Isabella to become accepted for treatment. They required an application form. He downloaded the form from their website, and together he and his wife completed it and sent it back to the hospital, as the process would take several weeks for review and evaluation.

***

Five weeks later, a call came in from Dr. Maxwell himself. He had spoken with Dr. Drew, Isabella's doctor, about her case, and looked forward to the opportunity to treat her.

In addition to getting all the medical details confirmed, both Vito and Antoinette still had to deal with the emotional reality of their "challenged" child. He sensed his wife was probably doing better than he was; she was a motherly-type by nature. As for himself, he wasn't so sure.

Isabella was like any normal month-and-a-half old baby. She cried when she was hungry and tired, had normal bowel movements, and slept all the time. The only physical disability was her leg. She was a happy baby, unworried about her limb. It was an adjustment for him to accept, but he knew he had to do it—for Isabella. This was their life now.

But his feelings about his wife hadn't changed. He still didn't feel in love with her as he once had been, and he was getting comfortable with their "roommate" arrangement. His focus was on the baby, but every so often he'd stare at his wife and admire her almond-shaped brown eyes, or the way she pulled her hair behind her ear.

***

Two weeks after their call from Dr. Maxwell, the Libero family sat in the doctor's office. Standing taller than Vito, with white curly hair and dark bushy eyebrows, Dr. Sidney Maxwell explained, "So, you see, Isabella's right leg has all the same muscle structure as her left leg up to her knee cap or her patella, but is missing," he pointed to a chart on the wall of the patient room, "the tibia (the largest bone below the knee cap, often referred to as the shinbone), the fibula bone (the small, skinny bone on the outside of the leg below the knee), ankle, and foot; often referred to as a *below the knee transverse* deficiency."

"How does that happen?" Vito asked.

Shifting from one foot to another, Dr. Maxwell continued, "Mr. and Mrs. Libero, Isabella's limb developed normally to a particular level—the knee bone, but beyond that there is no skeletal elements that exist. However, there may be digital buds later as she grows."

"Did you say digital buds? What are those?" Vito shook his head. *This sounds like computer jargon.*

"Yes, digital buds. In some cases, there is actual formation of a hand, fingers, or toes onto the residual limb."

"Oh." He nodded slowly. *Thank God, my baby doesn't have these digital buds.*

"May I?" The doctor asked, reaching for Isabella who was cradled in Antoinette's arms.

"Sure," Antoinette responded.

Pulling off the baby's pants, he pointed, "This amelia or absence of limb Isabella has is like a 'clean cut' per se. See, no digital buds. Her thigh and muscle structure developed as normally as it could during your pregnancy.

But for some reason it stopped. I've seen a lot of cases where the residual limb is much more deformed."

"Quite amazing," Antoinette said, standing up and rocking the baby.

The doctor continued. "Sometimes genetic issues from one or both sides of the parents might be the contributing factor for the limb deficiencies. In other cases, there are no reasons. Recurrence risk is low. Bizarre as it may sound; it is something the medical field continues to study regarding congenital deformities." The doctor grinned. "Just when you think you have all the answers, new information comes out. I'd say, keep an eye on her leg growth and monitor it for any bruising, discolorations, or swelling at the base of her residual limb," he said touching Isabella's leg.

The baby started crying.

"What about walking?" Vito asked, wringing his hands. This was his little girl. Would she even walk like other children?

"A child will begin to lift themselves up anytime from seven to nine months. It could take Isabella longer. We don't know yet. But one thing is for certain—when she is ready to lift herself up, she will. When that happens, we can look at getting her fitted for a prosthesis. The limb deficiency has nothing to do with her intellectual development, but every child is different."

"Are children accepting of a prosthetic limb?" he questioned. "What problems can we expect if Isabella doesn't want her prosthesis?"

The baby's cries became wails.

"It's okay, sweetie...shh...shh..." Antoinette whispered.

Shifting, Dr. Maxwell said, "I've had children who were not very welcoming of foreign limbs, but it's been more often the case with upper limb deficiencies. Remember, children don't know what they're missing and could get by with what they have. They are very resourceful. However, in Isabella's case, and her need to learn to walk, I don't believe there should be much resistance or problems."

"Will Isabella need surgery?" Antoinette asked, pulling up the child's pants. "There, I bet you were cold."

"It's too early to tell. In some cases, we've had to do some constructive surgery to allow the proper prosthetic fitting. I don't want to make any assumptions yet, but so far things look normal. She'll also need occupational therapy to strengthen her leg and get used to wearing a prosthesis. I can refer you to a great clinic specializing in the type of therapy Isabella will need when the time comes."

Dr. Maxwell continued. "She's a healthy baby. Unless you make it a handicap for your daughter, it won't become one. She doesn't know the difference, and you want to encourage that as she gets older." He smiled. "Isabella should be fine, with two loving parents supporting her; she won't have too many difficulties."

More questions stirred in Vito's mind, as they gathered paperwork the doctor had given them and Isabella's things. "Doctor, one more thing. What will be the process going forward?"

"Well, when Isabella begins to lift herself up, or around her nine or ten-month visit, whichever comes first, you'll see Dr. Drew. He'll make the appropriate assessment and send it over to me. Then you'll be sent to a prosthetic center, and my Certified Prosthetist will determine the best prosthesis for your daughter."

Vito, relieved having a little more information, said, "Yes, thanks."

Later, while exiting the doctor's office with Antoinette, an uncertainty came over him. Stopping outside the doors, balancing the car seat in his arms with a sleeping Isabella, Vito asked, "Do you think this doctor knows what he's doing?"

His wife rocked on the ball of her feet. "I think he's great. He's highly recommended and he has experience. We have to trust that," she touched his arm.

He nodded nervously. He liked the doctor, but at the same time, he was feeling overly protective of the new baby. *So, is this what it feels like to be a dad? This lion's protectiveness over his cubs. This is all new to me.*

Isabella cooed, and Vito fixed her blanket so it wouldn't cover her face. "Okay, let's get moving, it's cold out here."

"I agree. I'll need to feed her as soon as we get home."

Vito got to the car and opened the back door and placed Isabella's car seat in securely. *Things could be worse*, he thought. He should feel lucky but found it difficult to do so. Whatever issues were at hand, he was stuck with the situation. He had to make it work. He wasn't abandoning his child.

CHAPTER 22

After a busy couple of months, Isabella turned eight-weeks old. It was hard for Antoinette to believe how fast time was flying. Adjusting to parenthood had been challenging, especially taking care of someone else other than herself but she wasn't complaining. She loved having Isabella. Still on maternity leave for another four weeks, she found herself slowly easing into a motherly groove.

She had set a routine with the baby. A nap in the morning, a nap in the afternoon, in bed by nine, and one to two feedings at night. Isabella was starting to show a very spirited side of her personality for a little baby. Making faces, blowing bubbles, and wrinkling her brow when she was staring at her mother's mouth as she talked. Even with her limb deficiency, no one would be able to notice anything, unless she was undressed.

Antoinette had her *own* eight week follow up visit with Dr. Langford. Everything was looking good and her uterus was healing. She was still expected to feel some spasms in her back and stomach from time to time for about another month. This was due to her belly still shrinking and the exertion of pushing during labor. She was getting her body back and was feeling less conscious about the little protruding pouch she still carried.

In addition, the doctor had recommended she and Vito go see a medical geneticist by the name of Dr. Hedi Lu. She was highly trained in diagnostic and therapeutic procedures for patients with genetically-linked diseases, and specialized in genetic counseling. Dr. Langford wanted them to be tested for genetic diseases which might have contributed to Isabella's condition, since they had decided not to do any preventative testing during her pregnancy.

When Antoinette told her husband that evening after her doctor visit about Dr. Langford's request, he wasn't thrilled.

"This is bullshit. Why do we have to go?" he protested, as he took a swig of beer and a bite of pepperoni pizza. They were having dinner, while Isabella napped peacefully in her bassinet in the den.

"Will you stop it and relax." Her patience waning, as she picked greasy cheese off her slice.

"Still, I don't like it."

"That's obvious, Vito. Do you think I like it?"

"How could I forget? You didn't want to do any testing at all when you were pregnant and now, we should both get tested for genetic diseases. Give me a break, Antoinette. You're so wishy-washy."

He had a point. She had been adamant in her decision to not do any testing; she hadn't thought through what the consequences might be. She put her faith in God and let Him decide how Isabella would arrive in this world. Luckily, her limb deficiency was the only issue. Regardless she was a perfect little baby. But this was for their daughter. She might want to have a child of her own someday and want to know about her family genetic history.

"Fine, you win," she said. "But this is diff—"

"How?"

"Let me finish, please. For one, this is not only about us and why we couldn't get pregnant, or hold the pregnancy, but rather about our future genetic offspring. Yes, I didn't want to do any testing to affect the health of the baby, or the process of pregnancy. We were blessed, considering." She sighed. "And frankly, Isabella might need to know some day. So, I want to do it."

"What are they going to tell us? It's not like we're going to have more kids. And if we did, who knows how they'd turn out to be? They might be worse off than Isabella."

Antoinette gasped, but managed to hold back her tears. "You're such a jerk." She got up from the table, running out of the room leaving her husband alone in his misery.

She ran upstairs to their master bathroom and locked the door behind her and stared at the reflection in the mirror. *Why did he have to spoil the joy in our life?* They had a child, a miracle in itself—a beautiful child who was changing her. A blessing God had bestowed upon them. Her husband had a negative response to everything. She had to be patient for him…

***

They went to a genetics office a couple of weeks later, while Martha babysat Isabella. Dr. Lu was a petite, Asian woman, looking to be in her mid-forties. She greeted them in her office, a modern and sterile-looking work space with a small glass desk that held a thin laptop, surrounded by three brass-coated chairs, against off-white colored walls.

Taking a seat in front of the desk, the Liberos waited while Dr. Lu proceeded to go over their file. When she finished, she put down the papers and spoke. Her voice was soft and rich with a hint of a foreign accent.

"Do you plan on having more children?"

The question resonated in Antoinette's mind. Could she *have* more children? Doing it all over again after all she'd gone through, even if she'd love for Isabella to have a sibling, was little frightening.

"This pregnancy was a surprise to us, and unplanned for the most part. I'll be forty next year, Dr. Lu. I prefer to take it one step at a time." This was her truth.

"I understand, Mrs. Libero. Does your family have a history of any genetic disorders?"

"No. Not that I know of," Antoinette said.

"What about you, Mr. Libero?"

Vito tapped his finger on the chair, looking every bit as bored. "No."

"Mrs. Libero, do you smoke?"

"No."

"How about you, Mr. Libero?"

He smiled. "No."

Antoinette glared at her husband and kicked his leg. She knew he kept a stash of cigarettes in his car, even if he wouldn't admit it to her.

Vito winced. "Okay… Occasionally. It's not consistent."

"A social smoker." The doctor jotted down notes on a document. Looking up at Vito and Antoinette again, she asked, "Have either of you been exposed to any type of radiation?"

"No," they replied in unison.

"Any treatments with radioactive dyes?"

Antoinette said, "No."

"Dental x-rays?"

"Yes, regularly per our insurance coverage. You can check with our dentist," Vito responded.

"I will." Dr. Lu made some more notes. "Because your child was born with CLD, with your permission, I'd like to get some blood work done, and see what we can uncover. Dr. Langford informed me of his concerns he had with your pregnancy."

Antoinette turned to Vito, who shrugged his shoulders, and then looked back to the doctor. "Yes. That would be fine. When do you want us to do the blood test?"

"As soon as you can. You can go to any blood diagnostic clinic close to your home. Here are some locations." Dr. Lu handed Antoinette a pamphlet she had on her desk.

"Any questions?" Dr. Lu asked, putting documents into a file.

"No, I don't think so. You'll let us know what you find?"

"Of course."

They were ushered out of the woman's office within ten minutes of being seated there.

"Wow, quick, huh? In and out," Vito said. "I thought she was going to ask a lot more personal questions."

"Me, too."

"So, we'll do this blood test and see what she says, huh?"

"Yeah. We'll keep the results for Isabella."

The following day, while Martha babysat Isabella again, she and Vito went to a nearby clinic to have their blood drawn.

Approximately ten days later, the results came in. A nurse from Dr. Lu's office called Antoinette in the evening and informed her that their blood work came back normal.

Her husband was bitter. "What a waste of time. I could have been working and making money instead of sitting in that chair and getting my arm poked." He stretched on the couch in the den. "It still doesn't answer the question of why our daughter is the way she is? How much is this going to cost me when the insurance bill comes in, stating what they didn't cover because it's *normal*."

"It might have been a waste for you, but not for me," Antoinette responded, putting the phone back on its cradle on the end table. Maybe there was a chance she could get pregnant again. Give Isabella a sister or brother.

She continued, "Weren't you the one who was so adamant to have all these tests done when I was pregnant. Now that *you* were told to get a little bit of 'blood' drawn, it's such a big deal. Just like you were all huffy, puffy about getting checked out when we were doing IVF." She shook her head in disappointment. "Sometimes, I don't understand you..."

"Boy, you don't let anything get by you, do you? Drop it." He stood up. "It's over and done with now." Then he stalked out of the room.

Antoinette bit her tongue. *What a jerk. Why am I still in love with him?* He had egged her on, typical Vito. She breathed a sigh of relief, though. During the last ten days of waiting for the results, she had been anxious and had a few sleepless nights. Taking another slow breath, she relaxed. It was a relief nothing was wrong with them physically. Still, Antoinette couldn't help but think as to why this pregnancy went the way it did, and how it happened now rather than earlier when they had been fervently trying. What kind of plan did God have for her? For them?

She stared down at Isabella sleeping quietly in her bassinet. *How are we so lucky to have something so incredible in our lives?* She was grateful for the blessing and optimistic that Vito would eventually come around. He had to...

CHAPTER 23

February, 2001.

Isabella, at four months old, was becoming a spunky, curious little person with a dimply smile and sensitive eyes. Amused and amazed with colors, she liked red-colored toys, such as cars, balloons, and keys. But, her favorite was the Miss Mary doll. Her eyes lit up and her arms flapped up and down whenever Vito or Antoinette gave her the doll.

She acted much older than her age, too, and was a good sleeper—six to seven hours a night straight. Despite her challenge, Vito adored her. He tried to ignore the way her leg looked—like a ball of skin at the end of her knee, but found he couldn't. Every time he had to fold the right pant leg and clip it when he dressed her, the reality stared at him directly in the face. The truth was he couldn't ignore his daughter's condition, no matter how hard he tried.

He and Antoinette, well, their relationship was routine and predictable. Two adults sharing a home with one thing in common—their daughter. They disagreed on a number of issues, but he was doing his best to hang in there for Isabella.

He had seen a change in his wife. She had flourished into motherhood. He liked the way she held his daughter in her arms and how she sang lullabies to her every night, her voice soft and calm.

Every so often, a fleeting thought would cross his mind of possibly mending his marriage to Antoinette, but that was as far as it went. His life was busy enough between work and the baby; he didn't have time to repair the relationship with his wife. As nice as she looked again, now that she lost all her baby weight, he still wanted out.

Vito wasn't drinking as much or frequenting Stadiums, either. He laughed to himself, and wondered if Brad was lonely. His friend had called a few times to join him, but with everything going on, he often declined.

He was feeling better without the booze in his belly, shedding a few pounds in the process. But one thing pressed heavily on his mind—Antoinette's desire to jump start the sessions with Father Robert. She was bringing it up again casually, asking him if he wanted to see the priest, just like the other night when she made him miss a half-hour of a documentary on Walter Payton. Vito refused each time. They had attended enough sessions already during her pregnancy. What was the point in going now? He knew though, she was still seeing him on occasion, on her own time during the day while he worked, and her mom watched little Isabella.

According to Father Robert, they had made *progress* then. He wouldn't admit it out loud to anyone; but he had eventually warmed up to the priest. The man wasn't so bad; he just gave him a weird vibe when he talked about religion and marriage in the same breath.

One afternoon, while heading downtown on the 90 Interstate, he received a call from his wife.

"Hi. What's up?"

"How's it going?"

"Fine. I should be home around six."

"Okay," she whispered.

He became concerned of her quiet voice. "Is Isabella doing all right?"

"She's fine. I had a conversation with Father Robert today."

Great. Here she goes again, asking to see him.

"What about?"

"If you were up for company, I invited him for dinner this evening. He wanted to see us and the baby."

He growled outwardly, not caring if Antoinette heard him. *So much for relaxing when I get home.* But then he sat up straighter in his car. Here was his opportunity to tell Father Robert face to face he wanted a break from counseling. If she didn't want to hear it, he'd make sure the priest did. *What a great idea.*

"Vito? Are you still there?"

Smiling he said, "Yes. I'm here. Sure, have him come over. I have to go now. Traffic is getting heavy. I'll see you later."

This time, *he* was going to tell the priest, and Antoinette wouldn't have a say.

Promptly at seven, Father O'Malley arrived wearing casual clothing. Vito led him inside to the kitchen.

"Hi, Father," she said, hugging him.

"Hello, my dear. Something smells delicious."

She chuckled, lighting up her whole face. "Hopefully it tastes as good as it smells."

Vito realized it had been some time since he heard her laugh. It was a nice sound.

Later, as they sat enjoying the remains of their dinner, Father Robert said, "What a great supper." The priest patted his large belly. "You can always call me when you make—what's this pasta called?"

Antoinette cleared the table, "You mean the rigatoni with meat sauce."

"Ah yes, rigatoni. It was so good." He rubbed his stomach again. "My belly is very happy."

Vito grinned. He held Isabella now, who had fallen asleep in his arms. "The pasta *is* addicting. But you know what they say… Too many carbs are not good for you."

The priest chuckled. "Forget the carbs. It's well worth every bite." He wiped his mouth with a napkin. "I have a proposition for you, Antoinette, regarding your cooking."

Vito watched Antoinette as she stood with dishes in her hand, wondering what the priest was up to.

"Yes?"

"Once a month at the church, about a dozen parishioners or so, cook free dinners for our displaced and homeless in the community. Would you be interested in volunteering? Your cooking is terrific."

A smile formed on her face. "Yes. I would love to. That sounds like fun."

Father Robert beamed. "Excellent! I will call you tomorrow with the details. I need to have the information in front of me, and don't have the schedule memorized."

"Oh, that's okay. But please, tell me a little about it now. You've got me all excited."

Isabella quietly snoozed.

Feeling a little out of the conversation as the two of them discussed foods, Vito rose from his chair. "Excuse me for a moment while I put this little one in her crib."

Walking up the stairs, he rehearsed in his mind what he was going to tell the man when he came back down. "Father, you've been a great help, but I think it's time Antoinette and I…took a rest from…counseling. No we don't need your sessions; now with the baby…things are so…hectic…."

Vito gently placed Isabella in her crib, turned on the monitor, pulled the door, leaving it slightly ajar, and hooked the receiver on his belt buckle. He skipped down the stairs, confident things would go smoothly.

Returning to the kitchen, he saw Antoinette and Father Robert still deep in conversation. *Were they still talking about food?* "What's going on?"

Father Robert leaned across the table. "I'm proud of you, Vito."

He sat and stared at the priest, "Me? For what?"

"For you and Antoinette, working as a team. Your daughter senses that. You need to keep it going, the three of you. But most importantly, you and Antoinette need to continue to enrich your marriage."

Vito thought for a moment. He *was* happier these days. He had his daughter to focus on, even though he worried about her leg, and didn't like her condition. For the time being, things were all right. "I'm doing what I can."

Father Robert cleared his throat. "If you'd like, we can resume our sessions together."

Perfect lead in. "Thanks, but I don't want to continue. With the baby and all, things are, you know, hectic."

His wife appeared stunned at his direct remark. He purposely hadn't included her in this decision. He'd made it for the both of them. *She had made the decision not to do testing; I'll make the decision not to do the sessions.*

"I like the sessions," Antoinette said rising from her chair.

Was she seriously going to do this in front of the priest? How could she be so naïve? Still looking at her, he said, "No. I can't. To be honest, I don't want to."

"I think they were productive."

"Not for me. They're—"

Father Robert nodded, "Understood, lad. Talk it out between the two of you. When you are both ready, together, you and Antoinette can come see me again. My door is always open." The man winked at his wife. "We can still meet on your own as we have been."

Antoinette nodded, lowering her head. "Sure."

Vito knew instantly she was disappointed. He could tell by the way her face reddened and her lips quivered. He should have been upfront with her and told her he was going to tell the priest his decision, instead of surprising her, but he didn't care anymore. She would have found a way to argue the point, he knew it. He was glad the man respected his decision. Easier done than he thought.

The rest of the night the subject was off limits. Father Robert left shortly after dessert and coffee, with a promise he'd call Antoinette the next day.

Afterwards, when the baby woke for her nighttime feeding, Antoinette fed Isabella her bottle, and then retired to bed. Lying next to her, a guilty wave came over him. *Should I apologize to her? What the hell?*

"Are you angry that I don't want to go to the sessions with the old priest? I saw the look you gave me."

His wife faced him, her eyes moist. "Yes, I am. I can't believe... But whatever, I guess."

"What does that mean?"

"Forget it."

"I'm sorry," he managed.

"Vito, stop saying 'I'm sorry' if you don't mean it." Antoinette rolled over, away from him.

"I do mean it," he said. *Don't I?* He turned her back to face him. "Fatherhood is a new role for me, okay? I want to use all my spare time to spend with Isabella. Give me a break."

"And motherhood is not."

Vito grunted.

"You should have talked to me about it first, instead of sabotaging me in front of him. Maybe I'd have agreed with you. Father Robert complimented us on working as a team, and you drop a bomb like that."

"Ha. Would you have agreed to stop?"

"I don't know."

"Now you know what I felt like when you decided you didn't want to do any more testing for the baby when you were pregnant."

"Is that what this is all about? Are you still harboring that grudge?"

Vito stiffened in the bed, "Of course not." *Yes...*

She slid away from him. "It's no use with you."

He sat up, "What is it with you?"

"You!" She pulled the covers over her face.

"What do you *want* from me, Antoinette?" Vito pointed to his chest. Wasn't it enough that he provided a home for her? She wasn't working even though she was getting maternity pay; but he was still the one carrying the financial burden.

"Nothing," she muffled through her pillow. "Nothing at all."

Then she raised her head and faced him, "Why do you stay, Vito? According to you, we have no marriage anymore."

He remained silent, staring back at his wife. This was his family. This is what he signed up for and vowed to stick it out. Antoinette hadn't done anything wrong. *It's me.*

He fell back down on the pillow, and put his arm around her. "I'm sorry." They gazed up at the ceiling. He heard her mutter.

"What?"

"I'm sorry too. You know, I liked bantering with you in the sessions," she said in a quiet voice.

"We could still banter here, at home," he grinned, mischievously.

"Yes, I guess we can."

Vito nuzzled closer to his wife; her hair smelled like vanilla. "You're a great mother."

"Thanks," Antoinette whispered. She then leaned in and kissed him on the mouth.

Taken back, something stirred within him; something Vito hadn't felt for his wife in a while...maybe years. It certainly had been over a year since they last had any sexual intimacy, and that had turned into conceiving Isabella.

Hesitantly, he kissed her back. She tasted minty.

What am I doing? But, this feels so good. His frustration quickly evaporated. "Do you think you want to?"

"Shh..." she whispered back, returning his kiss.

Vito carefully climbed over her and began kissing her neck, pulling at the straps of her night gown.

Then just as suddenly as they began, they heard Isabella's familiar cry.

He rolled over back on his side of the bed. "You're kidding?"

She giggled. "You have a problem of talking too much. So much precious time was wasted. You want to go, or should I?"

"No, no, I'll go. Don't move."

Antoinette laughed and stretched. "You'd better hurry. The store is only open for a few more minutes."

He jumped off the bed and bolted out of the room.

This was okay, wasn't it? It was just two people about to have sex. No attachment. No emotion. He smiled as he got to Isabella's room and comforted his daughter.

"Shh…shh…little pumpkin…shh…it's okay."

One down, one more to go.

CHAPTER 24

Late August

It was Tuesday afternoon on the day Isabella turned ten months old. Antoinette had been folding laundry on the sofa nearby in the den, while her daughter sat playing with her toys in the "pack-and-play" playpen.

Watching the baby, she felt a tickle in her nose and ran into the bathroom to grab a tissue. Upon her return, she noticed Isabella had lifted herself up and was holding onto the padded bars of the playpen. Three teeth peeked from her mouth, a huge smile plastered across her face.

Antoinette stopped and stared. *Oh my God!* Then she walked over to her daughter, who was slapping her hand on the bar.

"Isabella, look at you. Incredible! What a big girl you are."

Her daughter giggled. "Omma. Omma."

Antoinette remembered what Dr. Drew, Isabella's pediatrician, had said about what they should do once Isabella was able to lift herself up on her own. "…At that point we can look at getting her fitted for a prosthesis…"

She made a mental note to call the doctor soon. Wait until Vito sees this for himself, she thought with satisfaction.

Her girl spent the next hour plopping down in the playpen and lifting herself back up. Isabella repeated the process over and over. As Antoinette sang to her and watched her from the kitchen while preparing dinner, she couldn't help noticing her daughter's strength and tenacity. The little baby stepped over her strewn books, Elmo doll, and musical piano toy—using anything and everything to assist her with her climb. Her grunts and groans—a clear sign of determination running through her veins—each time she pulled the netting to reach and hold the bars. She didn't even look tired after going up and down so many times.

Antoinette phoned Vito to tell him of the news.

"No way?"

"It's the funniest thing. When she falls on her butt, her face gets red with frustration. You have to see this."

He laughed. "I'm so glad you're there to see it."

Instantly, Antoinette was reminded of how many things she was getting to enjoy every day, watching Isabella grow, while her husband worked. She was truly lucky to be home with her precious daughter.

A few months earlier, as her maternity came to an end; she and Vito sat down and reviewed their finances and home situation. They both agreed she should not work. It was the best decision they had made, and she was happier because they made it together. Though, now, she was feeling a little guilty about him not seeing the things she was taking for granted on a daily basis.

Quickly changing the subject, Antoinette asked, "So, what time are you coming home?"

He sighed through the phone. "Probably late. Remember I mentioned Nick, my regional manager, is in town. We're meeting for dinner to go over numbers."

"Tonight? I must have forgotten. Here I am making dinner."

"I know. It sucks. I have to see what he has to say."

"Hmm… Guess I'll eat alone," she replied, disappointed.

"I do remember telling you about this—"

"I know. I forgot. Sorry. I'm a little absent-minded these days. My fault, don't worry."

She heard his sigh through the phone again.

Antoinette hesitated, sensing something. "Is everything going okay with work?"

"Yes."

"So, where are you going to eat?"

"I believe Spencer's Steakhouse. He likes steak, and I've been there once before. The food's pretty decent."

"Sounds yummy. I'll let you go then. See you later. Love you." It came out so quickly. *Oh, crap! I let it slip. I've wanted to tell him that I still care for him; I'm just not sure how he's feeling.*

In fact, it had been quite a while since she and Vito had exchanged real "I love you's". And, she couldn't remember the last time he had said it to her first. They were getting along like roommates who had sex once in a while, but it was still awkward.

She felt foolish. Antoinette held her breath.

After a pause on the line, Vito said, "Yeah, me too. I'll see you later."

'Me too?' Did I hear correctly?

Giddy inside, she clicked off the phone.

Vito was taking small steps, and she'd wait on the sidelines for his love for her to return no matter how long it took. For now, she was enjoying her newfound love—her daughter.

Still staring at the receiver, she had a strange feeling her husband's response had been too fast in regards to his job. But she didn't have time to analyze it; Isabella was making all sorts of noise. Antoinette strolled over to see the baby clapping her hands as she bounced up and down in the playpen. Bending down and picking up her daughter, she kissed her on the forehead.

"Okay, kiddo. It's you and me tonight."

CHAPTER 25

Vito circled their street a couple of times before turning into the driveway. It was after ten but the lights were still on. He suspected Antoinette was awake, most likely ironing or straightening up.

He pulled the car into the garage and opened the rear door, taking out his briefcase. He was tempted to grab a cigarette from the glove compartment. He needed one this minute to release some stress. But instead, he closed the garage door with the remote and slogged into the house through the side door.

"Hi," Antoinette said, walking over to him and giving him a hug. She was sporting hot pink silk pajamas and matching robe. His body involuntarily stiffened under her embrace, and he pulled away.

"What's wrong?"

Taking off his suit jacket and putting it on the back of a kitchen chair, he said, "Nick had to put me on probation. I have a hundred and twenty days to increase my volume by thirty-three percent."

His wife shook her head in disbelief. "What?" She folded her arms. "I thought I had gotten a weird vibe from you over the phone."

He shook his head in agreement. "Things haven't been good for some time. I didn't want to worry you with the baby. Two other pharmaceutical companies have moved into my territory. They have the same products as we do, but slightly lower prices than our company. One of them offers an incentive to buy their meds over ours—'Reward Points' they call it. The hospitals and doctor's offices get to rack up points for things like gift cards or a lunch party. Then, when I go in and offer our products without any incentives, they tell me to take a hike. I can't believe it. Some of my best clients are selling out on me for a bunch of gifts."

He slumped in the chair, rubbing his hand on the back of his neck. There, it was off his chest.

He could tell Antoinette was worried by the way her hands fidgeting with her robe sash. But he had to tell her what was happening. It was eating away at his stomach lining.

Getting up and walking to the cabinet above the kitchen sink, he grabbed a bottle of scotch. He hadn't had a drink not since Isabella was born. If he couldn't smoke, then he'd drink.

He poured the liquid in a shot glass and gulped it down.

"Alcohol is not going to help, Vito," she said, standing behind him.

He shrugged and refilled the shot glass.

"So why are *you* on probation? How can this be your fault?"

"It's not that easy." Gulp. The shot glass clinked on the counter. He turned around, facing her. "Look, the fact is MeritPlus doesn't care about me—or anybody else. It's the bottom line they look at—the revenues from those sales." Vito ran his hands through his blond combed hair. Turning around, he poured himself another shot.

"Can they let you go if your territory doesn't improve?"

He downed it. This time his throat stung. Closing his eyes he knew this was the question he dreaded to answer, but his boss had said his job was in jeopardy if things didn't improve. Vito whirled around. "Possibly. Like I said, I have a hundred and twenty days to improve."

She stood, arms crossed, again. "What are you going to do? Are they going to increase your marketing budget?"

Another good question. This woman should have been a private investigator. "It's what Nick and I talked about. His hands are tied. Management is restructuring to be leaner. If I don't make an improvement, I could be out."

"How unrealistic. They're setting you up for failure. This will be impossible to accomplish."

"I know. But I'll figure out a way to do this."

"You've been there, what, six years now. Doesn't that count for anything?"

"Six years this past January." He placed the shot glass in the sink and put away the bottle of scotch. Then he faced her again. "You know, six years doesn't count for anything these days. In the end, we're all disposable." With that, he trudged out of the kitchen to the stairs. He'd had it, answering her questions, and his discussion with Nick hadn't been great, either. His head hurt. His stomach burned. And his dinner wasn't sitting well. He had to think of a plan.

She called after him, "What can I do?"

Vito paused at the foot of the stairs and said, "Pray for a miracle."

CHAPTER 26

A little before five the next morning, Antoinette awakened to the sound of their coffee maker. Stretching, she realized she was covered by a blanket and still sitting in the rocker in Isabella's room. In the middle of the night her daughter had been crying. After soothing her, she stayed, and had fallen asleep in the chair.

Getting up, she quietly peeked in the crib, the baby slept peacefully. Closing the door behind her, Antoinette tip-toed downstairs to the kitchen and noticed Vito working on his laptop.

"It smells good down here. Good morning."

"Morning."

"You're up early?"

"I couldn't sleep. I also wanted to get on the road and hit the south side of the city today."

His news had been weighing on her mind all night. She inhaled deeply. "I've been thinking, maybe I can help out by going back to work. School doesn't start for another two weeks or so. I could call my principal and see about a part-time teaching position. I know he wanted me to come back, and, I know we agreed for me to stay at home. But—"

"No!" her husband shouted, slamming his fist on the table.

"Wait," she said, putting her hands out before her. "My mom and dad could watch Isabella."

"I told you last night, I would work out a plan."

Goosebumps ran down her back. "Okay. Please, lower your voice. The baby's sleeping." She paused. "Why do you have to put on the macho tough guy attitude? We're on the same team."

"Don't jump to conclusions. Can you at least give me the support to figure stuff out first?" he replied, raising his voice again.

Antoinette grabbed a mug from a cabinet and filled it with coffee. "I'm trying to help."

"You're 'trying to help,' is not helping." Vito abruptly rose and headed to the den. His temper was flaring up again.

"Hey—"

"Put a plug in it. I don't want to hear it. This is my problem, not yours."

"It's *our* problem, honey."

She put the mug down on the counter and rubbed her eyes. *Did I go too far?* She walked out of the kitchen and climbed the stairs up to their bedroom not saying goodbye to her husband. When she lay down, her heart ached and she began to cry. *Why are there so many roadblocks to happiness in our marriage, Lord?*

Then she heard a voice inside her... *The calmness of light comes every day. Be the trunk that holds the branches. Let the wind shake the impurities from the leaves.*

The words were strange. What did they mean? Where did they come from? She began reflecting on the words echoing within her mind, and before she knew it, in her exhaustion, she drifted off to sleep.

***

Antoinette awoke in what felt like hours later. The alarm clock showed it was only seven-thirty. She heard Isabella cooing and stirring in her crib down the hall. She slipped out of the bed and peeked out their bedroom window. The garage door was open and Vito's car was gone. So much for Father Robert's wisdom of talking through things.

Walking over to her daughter's room, she picked up the baby, changed her diaper, and brought her downstairs for breakfast. Once they were finished eating, Antoinette put the baby down in the playpen with her toys while she washed the dishes. Around nine, she called Dr. Drew's office to make an appointment regarding Isabella's prosthesis fitting. An opening was available later in the week.

Later, feeling lonely for some adult conversation regarding her husband's work situation, she phoned her mom.

"Hello. How are you?" Martha's voice crackled through the line.

Antoinette sat on the floor next to Isabella's playpen, cradling the phone to her ear. "Hi, I'm here. You?"

Her mother coughed. "We're alive." She coughed again. "And you? Just 'here'? What's wrong? Baby okay?"

"Isabella is a dream, Ma. We're going to see a specialist this week about getting Isabella fitted for a prosthesis."

"Wonderful news! You think she's ready?"

"Of course. She's been lifting herself up for a few days. We are thrilled, but I admit I'm a little scared."

Her mother coughed.

She didn't like the sound of it. "Mom, what's this cough? Are you taking anything?"

Martha coughed again. "Yes. Your father got me cough syrup. It will pass—just a chest cold. So, tell me what's really bothering you, dear."

Antoinette smiled. Her mother always knew if something was up. Taking a deep breath, she said, "It's Vito's job. He's been put on probation. If he doesn't turn around his territory, he could lose his job. He's been a bear, Mom. I offered to help, but he screamed at me. I feel… I feel so helpless."

There was a pause and her mother spoke with a raspy voice, "Men are funny, dear. They need to control things and take care of their loved ones…You…Isabella. It's what men are wired to do. If he needs help, he'll ask for it."

Antoinette had picked up Isabella in her arms, snuggling her close to her chest. "I was thinking the same thing. Thank you for your confirmation, Mom. I needed it."

"Sweetheart, I'm glad you asked me."

Isabella was beginning to nod off in Antoinette's arms. "Ma, I'm going to have to let you go. Isabella is falling asleep. Please take the cough medicine. I'll call tomorrow to check on you guys. Thanks for listening."

Another cough. "My pleasure, honey. Bye, bye."

The rest of the day was filled with more laundry and play time with Isabella, who was unusually quiet as she focused on her toys. Vito hadn't called at all, and Antoinette wasn't sure whether she phone him. *Maybe he needed some time to himself.*

A little past four that afternoon, she heard him pull into the driveway. Isabella was napping. Cautiously, Antoinette greeted him at the door. "Hi. You look tired."

Vito's eyes were bloodshot. "I'm better."

"You hungry? I'll get dinner ready."

He nodded. "Yeah."

Taking off his jacket, he rummaged through the mail, while she busied herself in the kitchen. Putting down the mail on the counter, he said, "I'm going to go change. Where's the baby?"

"She's napping. We have some time to ourselves before she wakes up."

"Good."

As they ate leftovers—chicken vesuvio and a mixed-green salad, Antoinette tried making small talk with her husband. She played with the stem of her wine glass. "So, how was traffic on the highway?"

Vito chewed slowly. "The usual. Though, this afternoon was a little lighter."

"I'm glad." She put her glass down on the table just as her husband reached across and touched her hand. He smiled at her. She smiled back.

In that instant Antoinette decided to surrender, allowing him handle what needed to be done with his job. He wanted it that way. She needed to believe and trust in him, just as she had trusted God with their pregnancy.

Letting go of his hand, she heard her daughter's voice through the monitor. She rose to clear the table, but stopped. "Why don't you go and spend some time with Isabella? I'll take care of the dishes here."

"You're sure?"

"Yep."

For the next few hours, Antoinette watched Vito play with their daughter. She noticed how gently he picked her up and how patient he was as he tried to get Isabella to crawl. She let them enjoy their time together.

When it was time for bed, he helped Antoinette give Isabella a bath. He dried and dressed her, while she prepared the formula. When their daughter was back in her crib and asleep for the night, she strolled into the den and sat next to Vito on the couch.

"I called Dr. Drew this morning. He can see us Thursday afternoon at four-fifteen to look at Isabella's leg and determine if she's ready for a prosthesis. I'd like you to come with us. Can you rearrange your schedule to come home earlier?"

"Sure." Then grabbing her hand, he said, "I'm sorry about last night and this morning. I freaked out—this is big. I feel like such a failure. Sales is all I know how to do. But, it's so unstable sometimes. I'm literally going out every day, hustling to make sales."

"Vito, you're not a failure. We have to support each other." Squeezing his hand, she continued, "Talk to me. Please let me in."

He gazed away from her. "I saw the most beautiful thing this morning. I was at a stop light, and the sun was coming up along the horizon. As the rays peeked between the buildings, a flock of geese in a shape of a V crossed my path of vision, blocking the light from my eyes. When they passed, the warmth of the sun felt so good on my face. After that, I felt more relaxed. It was cool."

"Sounds wonderful."

"It put things in perspective. I'm going to do what I can with turning my territory around. If it doesn't work, I'll move onto something else. My resume is updated, and I have some contacts I'm calling just in case."

"Is Brad affected as well?"

"Possibly. His wife has a good job. So, he's not as worried. He also has a different territory than mine, and his volume goal is lower. When I talked to him this afternoon he wanted me to go to Stadiums for a drink, but I didn't want to go. I have to stay on track."

Putting her head on his shoulder, Antoinette sensed his vulnerability. She was proud of him for not giving in to drinking. Her man had to do what he had to do. If it involved her, she'd be there.

Snuggling into his chest, she said, "I'm right here, whenever you need me."

CHAPTER 27

On the following Thursday, Vito came home from work earlier than usual and went with Antoinette and Isabella to see Dr. Drew. He was a little nervous. Still grappling with the reality of his daughter's limb deficiency, he had another issue at hand. How was he going to handle his child wearing a prosthesis?

"Hello folks," Dr. Drew said as he waltzed into the patient room. "So, how is little Isabella doing?" He eyed the baby, who calmly sat on her mother's lap.

"Doing well. She keeps lifting herself up every time she's in the playpen," Antoinette said.

"Good. Looks like she's trying to make her upper body stronger and experiment with her left leg strength. Let's put her on the table. I'd like to examine her legs."

"Sure," his wife said, hoisting Isabella onto the table.

Vito watched as his wife removed Isabella's pants. Immediately, their daughter began crying.

"Everything will be okay, sweetheart. Dr. Drew is going to check your legs."

His daughter apparently convinced for the moment, studied Dr. Drew's balding head as he touched her right knee.

"It looks good. Her residual limb isn't showing any bruising." He flexed her knee. "Her joint is flexible and strong. I don't see any issues with fitting her with a prosthesis. However, I'd like to have Dr. Maxwell do a thorough exam. From there, they can make the proper determination as to specifically when she'll be able to be fitted for it."

A whole range of thoughts flooded Vito's head. Will there be any cost on their end? His job was unstable at the moment. He needed more information.

"What's next?" he asked, fighting to keep his anxiety in check.

"I'm going to write up my diagnosis and send it on to Dr. Maxwell," Dr. Drew said. "Someone from his office should call you within a week and schedule an appointment."

He'd have to check with his insurance company and see what was covered and what would be their out-of-pocket expenses.

The doctor pulled his stethoscope off his neck. "So, how about we proceed with Isabella's ten-month visit?"

"Sure," Antoinette responded.

"Let's get her weight and height." Dr. Drew picked up Isabella and carefully placed her on the scale. "Look what we have here…eighteen pounds—a good size for her age."

"She's a good eater," his wife replied confidently.

The doctor took the baby in his arms and laid her on the table, pulling out a measuring tape. "She's twenty-eight and a half inches long. Growing normally. Is she talking and saying any words?"

Picking up Isabella, Antoinette answered, "Yes, she can say momma and dada. I can tell she's trying other words too even if they sound garbled. She constantly watches my lips."

Dr. Drew nodded, and jotted down notes in a chart. "Is she crawling?"

"Yes."

"Is she moving her right hip when she's crawling, or does it appear like she's dragging her right leg?"

"I think so, as far as I can tell."

Vito jumped in, "Yes. Yes, I could tell. I've seen her crawl, myself."

Dr. Drew said, "Let's see if she'll crawl. Please put her back on the table."

Antoinette put Isabella face down on the table. "You can do it, kiddo. Let's show Dr. Drew what you can do."

His baby wiggled, but refused to move and began to cry.

Dr. Drew responded, scrawling on a pad of paper. "I'll take it as a yes. Let's not upset her."

Vito reached for Isabella, uncomfortable with his daughter's tears. "You betcha. Here, let me take her." He adjusted his daughter in a sitting position on the table. "It's okay baby girl. Daddy is here."

The doctor asked, "How's she sleeping?"

Antoinette answered, "Pretty good. She's in bed by eight now and up around six-thirty or so."

The doctor shook his head in approval. "Good to hear. So, no more middle of the night bottle feedings?"

"No."

"Great," Dr. Drew said. "Everything sounds normal. You're all set. We'll get this process started." He smiled. "Pretty soon Isabella will have a prosthetic leg. Any other questions I can answer for you?"

Vito folded his arms in front of his chest, "I didn't know to get a prosthesis, we had to come to you, then Dr. Maxwell, and then get the fitting."

"Yes, there are steps, every one of them needed, of course. This won't be the only prosthesis Isabella will have either."

His daughter then bent down, trying to suck her kneecap at the end of her right leg.

"Stop, Isabella," Vito said, pulling her back.

Dr. Drew squinted at the baby. "Don't worry about that. It's a normal occurrence. Children are often intrigued by their own limbs."

Taking her pants from his wife and pulling them up on his daughter, he asked, "I understand Holy Name Hospitals for Children pays for all the care of the children. This is a long shot, but would you happen to know a ball park range of costs?"

"There will be some preliminary cost on your end. A third-party company develops the prosthesis. We won't know what the design looks like until you visit with Dr. Maxwell and his team of experts. Unfortunately, that is all I can tell you at this time. Make sure to check with your insurance company."

"Thanks, Dr. Drew." *Great.* All this uncertainty and the unstable job situation he was in was creating all sorts of havoc in his stomach. *How am I going to pay for all this if my job goes bust?*

Once Isabella was dressed, he and Antoinette exchanged goodbyes with the doctor, and set up their next appointment. When the baby was safely tucked in the child safety seat of their car, he pulled out of the lot and started the drive toward their home.

"I like Dr. Drew," Antoinette commented. "He explains everything. I think our little angel will be fine."

Vito felt drained. This had taken a lot longer than expected. During the examination his cell phone buzzed, which meant several calls to return. He observed Isabella through the rearview mirror. She was beautiful. Her face was rosy, her eyes were light-colored, and she had a happy smile on her all the time. She was starting to get blond curls. He grinned, remembering his mother had recently given him a baby picture of himself around Isabella's age. Their features were identical.

He took a deep breath and focused back on the road. Fatherhood was tough. It was his job to protect her. He must be such a loser for thinking things were going to be easy especially with Isabella's condition.

He glanced at Antoinette. "I like the doctor too. It's, well... The steps to getting a prosthesis are complicated."

"What do you mean by 'complicated'?"

He squeezed the steering wheel tighter. "The cost, the process of fitting, rehab, etcetera. I'm overwhelmed. I've got to call the insurance and see what's up. Not to mention each time she grows, we have to get a new prosthesis."

"You want me to call the insurance company? I can do it."

"No. I'll do it," he huffed, making a left turn.

His wife touched his arm. "You don't expect her to stay the same, do you? We're going to need to either do adjustments or get a new prosthesis each time she grows. It's normal."

"I understand—"

"What do you want them to do, put any kind of prosthesis on her and off we go."

"No. Never mind, I can't explain," Vito said, watching the road and away from Antoinette's glare.

"Talk to me, honey."

He stared ahead. "It will never end. She'll always be missing part of her leg, no matter what device is put on her. She'll always have a deformity. I'm tired. I'm the only one working here."

"I said I could help—"

Damn it! I shouldn't have said anything about work. He knew Antoinette would be all over it. "I know you can. But let me be responsible for that, okay?"

"Then, why are you complaining?"

"I'm not."

"It's the way her life is going to be. Despite missing only a part of her leg, she's still whole. You have a little tiger sitting back there."

He glimpsed in the rearview mirror at his daughter again and then back to the road. "She'll be handicapped for the rest of her life, Antoinette. That's our reality," he said, feeling the stress.

"It never stopped other people who are handicapped. I want to give our daughter a happy and safe life. We can't shelter her."

"Sure," he nodded.

"I worry, too. Though I don't voice it, it's still there—the unknowing. We'll be fine, I know that. Remember what Father Robert said…to be strong, be role models for Isabella; be yoked together. She doesn't need the hoopla or babying. I want a fighter, and you probably want the same."

God, here she goes bringing in the Father Robert bull crap. Ignore it. "I hope you're right," Vito responded, unconvinced.

"Honey?"

"Antoinette, just forget it, will ya'."

His wife turned away. "I'm trying here."

He nodded. She was putting up with a lot of crap from him lately.

"I know. I'm sorry." And he was.

CHAPTER 28

It took about a month and a half to get the paperwork and consultation arranged between Dr. Drew and Dr. Maxwell, and his team at Holy Name Hospitals for Children. In the meantime, Vito was putting in a lot of late hours with MeritPlus getting his territory back in shape. He was missing a lot of Isabella's growing too and it pained his heart to feel that way, but there was nothing he could do to change his situation.

A couple of times after work, Vito and Antoinette met with Dr. Maxwell. Then, they were referred to Proven Prosthetics, an accredited orthotic and prosthetic center where Isabella would be prepped for her first prosthesis.

They met a prosthetist named Rob. He was in his early thirties with short-cropped blond hair and a constant five o'clock shadow. He informed them that it would take a couple of visits to build the prosthetic leg, which consisted of casting the residual limb, and measuring the check socket from the casting. Then, one to three visits if needed, to properly fit the prosthesis and help Isabella get used to her new attachment.

His daughter wasn't cooperative from the start. She had been exposed to enough doctors in the last year that she didn't take a liking to anyone with a white lab coat. It was so rough that as soon as they drove into the parking lot of the hospital, or her pediatrician's office, little Isabella was screaming at the top of her lungs. She had even learned the roads to the doctor's offices.

One Wednesday afternoon, Antoinette carried in a screaming Isabella in her arms into the offices of Proven Prosthetics. Once in the room, his daughter continued to howl. Vito was embarrassed not knowing what to do, so he stood in a corner staring at his child.

The room was large and square-sized. Painted a bright white, three of the walls had framed abstract artwork. In the center was a patient table, and on the other wall, a countertop with a sink, and above that, two large cabinets.

Talking over the baby's tantrum, Rob displayed a calm demeanor. "Okay, the first thing we are going to do is get a plaster mold of Isabella's residual limb. When the mold dries it will give us an impression of your daughter's limb and help us to build a socket to which the prosthetic leg will be attached."

His wife nodded and undressed Isabella; Vito nervously paced with his arms folded.

Rob wrapped Isabella's leg with a gel liner so that her leg wouldn't get wet from the molding. Then, he began soaking bandages in a plaster mixture, while Antoinette firmly held Isabella on the table. As soon as Rob started to put the wet bandages which looked to Vito like paper mache, on his daughter's residual limb, she started squirming in her mother's arms.

"Okay, sweetie," his wife coaxed.

His daughter continued wailing.

"Isabella, calm down. It's okay," Vito remarked.

More screaming.

Frustration set in, or was it impatience? Either way, he lost his cool. *You got to be kidding me!*

As Isabella cried with huge rivulets streaming down her face, he clenched his fists and stormed out of the room leaving his wife to attend to their daughter. "I'll be outside."

Following behind him was Rob. They sat side by side on a bench outside of the room listening to Isabella's high-pitched voice.

"Your wife's a saint," Rob said. "I deal with this type of reaction from children all the time. It's uncomfortable and scary for them. I can't blame her." Then he laughed. "Your daughter has got quite a set of lungs on her. Wow, what a little spitfire."

Vito smirked, "Stubborn just like her father."

After some time, Antoinette poked her head through the door. "All clear."

Vito and Rob filed back in.

He walked over to his daughter uncertain of her reaction. "Hi kiddo."

Isabella still sat on the table with her white onesie, clinging to her mother.

Antoinette responded, "She'll be fine. She's a little frightened. Let me do the talking."

He and Rob nodded in agreement.

Standing next to the table, she said in a quiet voice, "Isabella."

"No, omma," she fidgeted.

His wife pointed. "Mr. Rob is going to put some creamy stuff like lotion on your leg. Now, I know you like lotion. This is a little thicker and it may be cold, but I promise it's not going to hurt. Please."

Vito prayed in his mind. *Come on. You can do this.*

"No," Isabella whispered softly, lips upturned.

"We're going to keep it on for a little while until it dries, and then Mr. Rob will take it off. Please. Do it for Mommy?"

Vito remembered she had packed a doll in her purse before they left home. "Give her something," he whispered through gritted teeth.

"Oh, yeah. Look what I have for you, sweetie." Antoinette pulled the Miss Mary doll out from the diaper bag. Suddenly Isabella's eyes widened with excitement and she snatched it away from her mother, distracted.

Vito gave his wife a thumbs up. "Nice work."

"You're a good girl." His wife hugged and kissed their daughter. Then, looking at Rob, she said, "You have the time now. Hurry before she gets tired of the doll and causes another fit."

The prosthetist nodded and busied himself. The procedure took a half-hour. By then, Isabella and Rob had become old friends. He was good with her, Vito thought. Making funny faces and tickling her. He was also grateful for Antoinette's ability to calm and coax Isabella. He observed his wife, admiring her tenacity and patience.

Antoinette cocked her head over at him and whispered, "Patience. Something you need to work on."

"I know, I know. I shouldn't have blown my top like that."

***

A couple of days later, they went back to the prosthetic center where Isabella was fitted with a trial socket. This time Vito didn't lose his cool.

Rob explained, "From the mold of her residual limb, I will create a clear socket or 'check' socket. It's almost like a glass slipper that fits over the residual limb. This socket will tell me where Isabella's patella tendon or knee cap rests, and where her pressure points are, as well as where and how her weight will be positioned when we build her special prosthetic leg. So, I'll need to try it on her, and take additional measurements."

Vito shoved his hands in his pocket and nodded at his wife, hinting she should talk to their daughter. She was better at explaining than he was.

Antoinette shrugged and spoke to Isabella. "Quiet down, sweetheart. We have to undress you. You need to try this socket on that Mr. Rob built for you."

Rob waved to the baby who had her lips upturned in a frown.

Vito helped his wife undress their daughter.

Then, Rob took the socket and placed it over Isabella's leg, while Isabella sniffled with wide eyes.

He fidgeted with his hands. *I don't like this one bit.*

Antoinette reached for his hand and squeezed it. "It's okay."

Rob fussed with the socket. "Okay, I need to do a few adjustments here and there. You, know, the most common type of prosthesis for a 'below the knee' limb deficiency is called a *Patella Tendon Bearing* or_*PTB Socket*. The one Isabella will have is made of a high temperature plastic or lightweight composite material formed around a solid structural foam interior."

Vito began to breathe easy. His daughter was calm, but she was also clutching her Miss Mary doll tightly. Surprisingly, she was being very cooperative today. "You're doing great, Isabella."

Her eyes widened. "Dada…"

Antoinette smiled and nudged him. "See, I knew it."

He bit his lip.

Rob took a couple more measurements. Once the fitting was done, they dressed Isabella. Rob and his team would now be able to work on building Isabella's new prosthesis.

"We're done. Good job!" He then turned to Vito and Antoinette. "She's quite a trooper."

***

A week later, they returned for the fitting of her brand new prosthesis. Vito was nervous again. *This is it, isn't it?*

Rob showed them how to put Isabella's prosthesis on for the first time.

"What you want to do is follow these steps. First, here is a nylon sheath, kind of like a nylon stocking." He handed it to Vito who shook his head and pointed to his wife. *No way. I'm not putting some nylon on my little girl.*

"You go ahead. I'll watch. I'm not comfortable—"

She nodded, taking the nylon stocking. "Sure. I'll do it." His wife appeared giddy with excitement. *How can she be so excited at a time like this? Their daughter was going to be wearing a contraption in order to walk.*

Rob smiled. "Okay. Pull it all the way up to Isabella's thigh. Yes, there you go."

Antoinette followed Rob's instructions, while Vito watched over her shoulder. He asked his wife to fit his daughter because he was terrified to try out the new limb, and afraid he might hurt his little girl. A hot burning sensation rushed up his face. *My only daughter should not have to have this problem and wear a darn prosthesis.*

"Next, put this sock on over the sheath." Rob handed her a thin, child-sized white cotton sock that was round at the tip for the patella tendon. "This will help maintain the fit of the prosthesis."

Antoinette took the sock and pulled it over the sheath, and Vito smoothed it out. *Okay, it's not so bad.* Isabella watched, making babbling noises with her Miss Mary doll.

When his wife finished, they both gazed at their instructor for approval.

"There you go. Carefully insert the limb into the socket. It will automatically lock in place, so to speak."

Isabella let out a yelp. "Ouee…"

"It's okay, sweetheart. Mommy's here. There we go."

Isabella squirmed a bit, but then relaxed.

Vito noticed the prosthesis fit beautifully. It looked like an oversized Barbie doll leg. No bigger than the size of a mini baseball bat, the leg was a flesh-colored plastic material, and it slid right up into her knee cap.

During the fitting of the brand new prosthetic, Isabella had cooperated. No complaints or pouting, which was incredible for a baby not even a year old, and who had been fearful the first time she came in. He was amazed, but at the same time, a little shaken up. Though no surgical procedure was performed, he hated seeing his little angel handled by anyone else, besides him and Antoinette. He shook his head; Rob knew what to do.

Patting the man on the back he said, "Thank you."

Vito then helped his wife stand Isabella up on the table. She wobbled from side to side on her new limb. He let out a sigh. His wife saw his expression and nodded. Their daughter, on the other hand, seemed comfortable.

After receiving a referral for an occupational therapist, as well as information on how to sterilize the device, Vito and Antoinette took their daughter home. A new journey of understanding lay ahead for all three of them. He, more so than his baby. She seemed to have it all under control.

CHAPTER 29

October

Standing in the kitchen wearing a pink robe, while Isabella snuggled in her arms, Antoinette took a sip of coffee and stared out the window above the sink, looking out into her backyard. It was Saturday morning, October 16th, her and Vito's eleventh wedding anniversary. She had woken early wondering if her husband remembered their anniversary.

Things had improved in their relationship. They were communicating on a regular basis, and becoming more intimate with each other. She thought Isabella might be softening her husband, but still, she was cautious. Vito was unpredictable, and she didn't want to jeopardize the momentum between them. She smiled inside though, thinking how far they'd come—from almost getting divorced to conceiving a miracle child, and now raising their daughter *together*. Her main goal was still making her marriage whole again.

Vito came in from the side door. From behind his back, he whipped out a dozen roses and handed them to her. "Red roses for you," he said smiling.

She was speechless. He *had* remembered, and brought her flowers, too. "Wow, I wasn't expecting these. They're beautiful. Thank you," she said, eyeing the bouquet of red roses with baby's breath.

"I wanted to give you a little something for our anniversary."

Still in shock and a little embarrassed, she put the coffee mug down and embraced Vito with little Isabella still in her arms. He returned her affection with a squeeze back.

Antoinette's face felt hot. They stood awkwardly there for a moment staring at one another. Then, as if on cue, Isabella bounced about. "ed ouses…ed ouses."

She smiled. "You mean *red roses*."

Together, she and Vito laughed at their daughter's comments.

***

Halloween was a couple of weeks away. Pumpkins, taffy apples, and apple cider could be found at every neighborhood grocery store and farmer's market. With fall season upon them, Antoinette and her family took advantage of getting outside in the crisp weather.

One Saturday morning, the Liberos were outside enjoying the cloudless sky and fresh air. Isabella sported a pair of denim jeans, a white onesie, and a blue fleece jacket. Sipping hot apple cider with one hand, Antoinette and Vito held their daughter's hands with the other, steadily walking her up and down the driveway on her prosthesis. Isabella's whole face glowed, mumbling words like "omma, okay, and ed ouses."

"Good girl. Let's try again," Vito repeated. "Say it with me, *Ro-ses, Ma-mma, Oh-kay*."

Yes, their little star was walking slowly; unaware of what a miracle she was to them. Their daughter had been wearing the prosthesis for a couple of weeks now and had gone for physical therapy four times already. Today, a pink and white right-sized tennis shoe encased the foot attachment matching the other one on her left foot. Wobbling along, Isabella watched her feet with each step she made.

Antoinette felt content, and she anticipated in his quietness, Vito might be feeling the same.

After a time, Isabella let go of their hands and slithered down to the ground in a sitting position. "Sit, omma, me down."

Crouching down beside her, she asked, "What's the matter kiddo. You want to sit down? Are you tired, princess?"

Isabella nodded.

"Okay, Mommy is going to bring you inside. Let's have some milk."

Antoinette handed her mug of apple cider to her husband, and picked up Isabella in her arms.

"Are you doing okay?" she asked, taking a gamble on the question based on Vito's silence.

He nodded. "Yes. Why?"

Balancing her daughter in her arms, she replied, "You're quiet."

Her husband ran his fingers through his blond hair sprinkled with gray, and then tickled their daughter under her chin. Isabella giggled.

"Everything is fine, isn't it, baby?"

The child smiled up at him.

She nodded, not wanting to push the discussion further. She was learning more about her husband in the last year than ever before—when to probe further and when to stand back. Keeping the conversation light, she said, "Good. I'm going inside to get this little munchkin her milk. You coming in?"

He shrugged. "Nah, it's nice out here."

"Sure. We'll be inside."

Antoinette walked up the drive carefully balancing Isabella on a hip. At the door she turned and observed her husband with his hands in his jean pockets, staring up at the sky above. About to call after him, she stopped herself. *If he wants to talk, he'll approach me.*

She sat Isabella in her high chair, gave her the Miss Mary doll, and warmed up her milk. Taking another mug, she refilled it with some more apple cider, peering occasionally outside through the kitchen window watching her husband. He seemed deep in thought as he paced up and down the driveway, drinking his cider. *What could he be thinking about?*

Her thoughts were interrupted by Isabella dropping her doll on the floor. She turned and bent down to pick up the doll. "Isabella, be careful. You are going to hurt Miss Mary."

The baby clapped her hands, smiling.

Antoinette shook her head. Her mind now distracted from her husband, she finished getting her daughter's milk ready. *Let it go*, she consoled herself. *Let go. Everything will be fine.*

***

Two weeks later, on October 30th, Vito and Antoinette celebrated Isabella's first birthday. Both sets of grandparents came with arms loaded with more presents than a toy store could hold. Father O'Malley also stopped by to give a children's Bible, flash cards, and a few coloring books to Isabella. She often thought if Father Robert hadn't been a priest, he'd probably have several children.

Standing stronger and more confident more and more each day, Isabella stood on one of the dining room table chairs, wearing a light pink dress, cream-colored tights and black-patent leather shiny shoes. With the help of Antoinette, Isabella blew out her first candles. Digital video cameras captured every moment of Isabella plunging her hands in the frosting of a chocolate cream-filled cake. Everyone laughed at her innocent look as she licked her fingers. Antoinette rejoiced in her daughter's first year milestone, grateful for the love encircling their family.

While her mom helped her daughter in her high-chair, Antoinette dashed into the kitchen to get more paper plates. Suddenly, she was bear-hugged by Vito.

"Gotcha," he whispered in her ear.

"Hey!" She pushed him back as he tried snuggling into her neck.

"Let's make love tonight," he said with a heavy voice.

Laughing in his face, she said, "What's gotten into you?"

"You look so good," he said, and put his hand under her shirt, caressing the small of her back. Antoinette felt his desire. She was starting to get aroused, but a bunch of ooohs from their guests in the dining room ruined the moment.

"Stop it," she whispered, half serious. "Do you realize our parents are over?"

He nuzzled in her neck. "I don't care."

With a smile, she wiggled out of his grasp. "I do. Bad timing, honey, maybe later." Slapping his rear, she reached for the paper plates on the kitchen table. Still smiling, Antoinette strutted back into the dining room.

Later, she thought with a giggle. Later…

That night, with Isabella asleep and the dishwasher humming, Vito took Antoinette's hand and escorted her up the stairs to their room.

She gazed into his eyes as he lifted her shirt over her head. Then he unbuttoned her jeans and slid them down to her feet. He slid his hands over her shoulders, and then gently holding her face he kissed her mouth.

Removing his own shirt and jeans, Vito picked her up in his arms and laid her down on the bed. No words were needed. It was a tender moment between two people, who despite the challenges their relationship endured; there was still an underlying love for one another. They caressed and kissed, finding one another like two teenagers, first out of sync and then a knowing of each other's desires and needs.

Antoinette and her husband made love. Once their desires were fulfilled, they lay spent wrapped up in the cotton sheets.

"Nice," Vito whispered, trailing off and snuggling into her neck.

"Mmm…hmm," she responded sleepily. Was Vito falling back in love with her? This wasn't just sex. This was more.

She yawned, the day's activities catching up to her. Her daughter was a year old. She was not a baby anymore, but heading into toddlerhood. Now with her walking about, the thought of holding a baby… She looked at her husband. "Do you think we could try for another baby?"

"I don't know."

"I guess I'd love it if Isabella had someone to grow up with and not be alone."

"I've thought about it too. But, what if it doesn't happen? I mean, *you're* not—"

"Young anymore." Antoinette finished his sentence. She knew what Vito was driving at. She was getting older. They had trouble conceiving before, what were the chances of it happening twice? She wondered if she was heading into early menopause already, as her cycle was starting to change.

"I didn't mean that," Vito said, massaging his temples.

"No, you did."

"Look," he sat up in bed. "I'm sorry."

Antoinette sat up as well. "I know." She pulled the sheets up around her. "Lately you've been quiet; what's going on?"

"I'm fine." He touched her nose, being silly about it.

Suddenly, she laughed. "You're a goofball." *Screw it. Maybe I'm reading too much into it.*

Vito chuckled.

She'd like to have more children but…

Vito wrapped his arms around her. "No more talking," he said cajoling her. "Only sleeping." They fell into the soft pillows, snuggling together.

CHAPTER 30

The air was chilly and fresh. A great day for Halloween. Between dressing up Isabella and the nonstop traffic of trick-or-treaters at the door, Antoinette was spent. *Maybe I'm going through some tired phase.* Their neighborhood was flooded with children, all between the ages of one through eleven. She had bought six bags of candy thinking she'd have enough. By four-thirty, her supply was low. Every time she opened the door, goblins and goons holding open plastic bags, chanted, "trick-or-treat!"

As Antoinette looked out her front door, she noticed Trevor Lane was bustling with cars. She hoped drivers were using discretion as they drove through. She often thought the village should put a speed bump in the middle of their street to slow traffic down. At that moment, a blue minivan zoomed by. She shook her head.

Where was Vito? He'd said he'd be coming home soon. He promised to take Isabella trick-or-treating while she handed candy to the little spooks.

"Momma, momma."

She turned in time to see Isabella, hobbling through their foyer in a plush, orange-colored pumpkin suit and black-colored leotard.

She crouched down and waited for her daughter to walk to her. Her initial desire was to run and pick her up, but she remembered Dr. Drew had insisted they refrain from having their child depend on them. He said she had to get used to walking on her own with her prosthesis. So far, she was doing pretty well.

"What's the matter?"

"Up ommy," Isabella replied softly, lifting her arms up to Antoinette.

"Shit," she whispered under her breath. *Forget Dr. Drew's advice.*

Picking her up, she kissed her daughter tenderly on the cheek and forehead, and strolled toward the front door as Vito pulled into the driveway. "Look, there's Daddy."

Her daughter's eyes widened, bouncing with excitement in her arms.

"See," she pointed.

Walking over to the side door, they waited for her husband to come in. When he entered, a huge smile brightened his face.

"Hi. Hey, little pumpkin. Wow! You are a little pumpkin." Scooping Isabella in his arms, her husband whirled her around the kitchen.

"The costume is great. I love it. You look so pretty," he said to their daughter, who beamed.

Antoinette hovered over the kitchen table, watching the two of them. Vito looked handsome, wearing a tweed beige jacket over black slacks.

"Did you take any pictures of Isabella yet?"

Ding, dong.

"This morning, when your parents came to visit. I only took a couple of photos. I was going to do more but the doorbell—"

Ding, dong.

Turning and crossing the den, she replied back, "It's been ringing non-stop."

"Don't worry. I'll take some."

As she handed out candy, Antoinette heard the clicks of the camera, and Vito chuckling. She grinned, taking in the moment between father and daughter.

Once pictures had been taken, and he had changed into jeans and a t-shirt, she sent the two of them off on their Halloween adventure. She watched him for a while as he walked down the street, Isabella in his arms. Her heart was bursting with joy.

About an hour and half later, Antoinette completely out of candy from the trick-or-treaters, helped him inside with a sleeping Isabella in his arms.

"Boy, you guys were out later than I thought," she said, taking her daughter and nudging her softly, trying to wake her. "I was getting worried."

"Shh… Let her sleep," he whispered.

"I can't. She needs to have her milk. Isabella, wake up for Mommy."

"Sorry." Vito yanked off his navy blue hoody, opened the fridge, and grabbed a beer. "Isabella wanted to walk. Boy, this kid never gets tired. And then, I ran into the new neighbors, the Starkweathers—they have a little girl."

"What are their names?"

"Lee and Cheryl."

"How's the little girl?"

"She's a cute redhead. She was dressed as a peapod."

"Sweet. What are they like?"

"Nice. Friendly," Vito said, yawning.

"Here, hold her," Antoinette said, giving Isabella to her husband. "She feels cold. I'm going to heat some milk for her sippy cup."

He held Isabella, kissing her head.

"So, did the neighbors say anything?"

"Just asking about us all getting together some time."

Her daughter began crying and fidgeting. "Come on baby, don't cry for Daddy. Antoinette—"

"I'm coming, hold on," she replied, irritated. If they hadn't come back from trick-or-treating so late, Isabella wouldn't be so crabby. Antoinette poured the warmed milk into the sippy cup, screwed on the cap and tasted it to make sure it was okay. She nodded. "It's good."

Isabella's whining became louder.

"Mommy's here," she said, taking her back in her arms. "Here you go..." With a cup in her mouth, Isabella calmed down.

Antoinette sat at the table as Isabella drank her milk. With her free hand, she grabbed Vito's beer from across the table, and took a drink.

"So, you were saying... The Starkweathers want to get together?"

"Maybe. Before the holidays."

"Hmm, I should stop by next week and introduce myself to Cheryl."

"I agree." Vito suddenly got up from his chair. "It would be good for you."

"Where are you going?" She was taken aback by his abruptness.

"To the den. I need to look at some financial numbers."

"Now? But we haven't had dinner yet? You haven't talked to me about anything lately."

Vito leaned forward, kissing Antoinette on her forehead. "I got it covered. Don't worry, I'm not hungry, you go ahead and eat without me."

She stared after him as he left the kitchen. Meanwhile, about half-way through her sippy cup, Isabella suddenly pushed it away from her mouth.

"Don't you want any more?"

Her daughter shook her head from side to side, rubbing her eyes with her hands.

"A little more, honey, come on."

"No!" Isabella screamed.

"Hmm... Okay, my little crabby angel. Let's go upstairs and get you in bed then." Antoinette hoisted up her daughter and brought her upstairs.

Once bath and teeth brushing were done and Isabella was fast asleep, she closed the bedroom door and walked to the foot of the stairs. About to descend, she heard her husband on the phone.

"Awesome. So, Jack and Pete don't have...anymore...you sure? I can't believe it...I appreciate this, thank you...bye."

She heard a sigh from the den as the phone clicked off.

Walking into the room, she saw Vito stretched out on the beige leather couch with his eyes closed. A smile covered his face.

"Who was on the phone?"

Vito opened his eyes to look at her. "Nick."

"What's he doing calling you on Halloween?" Antoinette asked sitting next to him, worried. *Now what?*

"Nick redistributed the territories. Mine and Brad's weren't affected, but in addition, I'll have Jack's and Pete's accounts. They were both let go."

Reaching for his hands, she searched his hazel eyes. There was a new spark of life in them. "You're kidding. Awesome! I mean…for us, not them. Why are you so calm?"

"I can't believe it. No, I can believe it," he said looking into her face. "I've been trying to pray. Hard to admit it, but I don't want you to have to work. I want you to be home to raise our daughter—our beautiful daughter, so she can grow up to be just like her mom."

Tears welled up in Antoinette's eyes. His words were sincere and loving. She believed it was the right thing to do by not helping her husband, but rather support him, trust him, and wait for him to sort things out. It was what her mother had recommended.

"You're sweet." Wrapping her arms around her husband's neck and tenderly kissing him, she whispered, "Is this why you've been so quiet lately?"

"That, and then some." He kissed her back.

"So, what's next?"

"We switch everything over next month."

"I'm so proud of you."

"I'll be busier and have a few more late nights, but everything will work out."

She felt herself melting in his arms like she had done years ago. *Her* man, her strong man would take care of everything.

He spoke softly, stroking her hair. "Thanks for believing in me."

"My pleasure," Antoinette said, snuggling in his chest. *Thank you, God!*

Vito's breath caressed her hair. He was grinning. And so was she.

CHAPTER 31

One evening, while Isabella was at Antoinette's parent's for the night, Father Robert O'Malley came over for dinner. He loved her cooking. The week before she had brought three pans of lasagna for the church's homeless and displaced community members. It was a volunteer affair she helped with once a month. It gave her an opportunity to get out and be with adults. But more importantly, it fed her heart to provide for others in need.

When the priest tasted her lasagna, he couldn't stop raving over it. So, out of obligation, and enjoyment of his company, she and Vito invited him over for lamb chops, risotto, and roasted potatoes. It wasn't her traditional Italian meal, but she thought he would enjoy it. During dinner, her husband told him the news of his job. Surprised Vito had brought up work issues to the priest, Antoinette remained quiet, listening.

"No kidding. My son, what fabulous news," Father Robert remarked between bites. "Holdfast. God is there to help. The best part, you believed. You must have faith."

"I know, Father. I struggled with that for a long time."

"Faith is the key to all happiness. Even in the worst circumstances, trust in God's faith for you."

Antoinette set the coffee pot on the table and slid next to her husband.

Vito smiled at her and then his brow furrowed, "Why are you so flushed?"

"I am?" she asked, touching her cheeks. They *were* hot.

"I can't say you look pea-green, like when you were pregnant with Isabella," chimed the priest, smiling mischievously.

"Go and check for yourself," Vito replied. Antoinette sensed his concern.

"Maybe another little baby might be on the way, wouldn't that be great?" retorted Father, belting out a laugh. "It's all in God's plan."

"Hmm…" Vito responded.

She casually rose not making a big deal, and sprinted upstairs to their bedroom. Her heart thumped rapidly. She was upset, but didn't know why. Hormones? She opened her husband's work calendar on the dresser, frantically counting the days.

Antoinette felt light-headed and dizzy. Was her cycle twenty-four days, twenty-six days, or twenty-seven days? She couldn't think straight, until she remembered the first day of her last cycle and began counting. "Twenty-eight, twenty-nine, thirty, thirty-one… I am a couple of days late. Could it be?"

While staring at her reflection in the mirror, Antoinette reached for the dresser to steady herself. She was afraid but excited. She wanted to have more children, but she didn't know if Vito did. He was so content with Isabella, and so was she.

"Is everything okay?" Vito called from downstairs.

I'll think about this later. "I'm coming," she said, smoothing her hair. Her face had cooled. She took one last look in the mirror, and plastered a big smile across her face.

***

A couple of days later, she got her period, except it lasted only a day and a half. *What's next?* This is a whole new experience she knew very little about. To be safe she wasn't coming down with something, she made an appointment with her doctor.

When she went to see Dr. Langford, he told her she had experienced a hot flash, a clear sign she was perimenopausal. He advised her to lay off the caffeine and begin drinking more soy milk. "Helps with the hot flashes."

She called her mom and told her about the appointment and found out early menopause was prevalent in her family. Could she possibly be starting it at forty already?

"Oh Mom, this is depressing. What do I do?"

"Nothing, sweetheart. I had it happen to me when I was forty-one. Your Aunt Lina, my sister, was thirty-nine. It's part of life."

Antoinette was still embarrassed, but she laughed. "I can't believe I had my first hot flash in front of Father Robert, of all people."

Martha chuckled through the phone line. "He probably knew already. After all, he had been able to determine your pregnancy with Isabella."

She shook her head. "Even worse. He thought I was pregnant."

"Better him than a stranger."

She grimaced, not wanting to broach the subject further, even while it stirred in her brain. "I guess having more children is out of the question."

Her mother sighed. "I know. You are *truly* blessed to have Isabella, at least."

Antoinette understood her dilemma. Still, she spent the next couple of nights privately giving herself the time to grieve over the knowledge she'd never be able to have more children. *If I was younger, maybe there would have been a chance. Now, forget it.*

She was beyond grateful though, for her daughter, who had speedily progressed walking confidently with her new prosthesis. They even stopped therapy based on how well she was doing. Isabella was truly a gift from God. Antoinette vowed to treasure this joy for as long as the Lord wanted her to.

She and Vito were also closer than they'd been. The love and attraction was coming back. Their relationship was not a hundred percent, but a huge improvement from a few months ago. Antoinette continued to pray for the full circle of love from her husband.

CHAPTER 32

December

The months passed and it was already the Christmas season. Antoinette and her husband, along with the help of little Isabella put up the tree early and placed a beautiful nativity display given to them from her in-laws on a mat under the tree. There were ten pieces in all. Each piece was hand-painted a cream color with an under-glazed porcelain finish. There was Mary, Joseph, the baby Jesus, the three wise men, and four animals. They all contained a very serene, holy look on the faces. On a few occasions when her daughter played on the den floor near the tree, she'd stop and stare at the figurines.

Antoinette pointed, "See, honey. This is the baby Jesus. This is the reason for Christmas. To celebrate his birthday."

Isabella repeated. "Bird day, momma."

She laughed. "I know. Now don't touch these figurines. They might break."

Her baby girl nodded like she understood. Over a year old, she was growing to be a very serious child. But there were a few times Antoinette tapped her little hand from grabbing the baby Jesus from its manger, occasionally testing her mother's boundaries.

***

Her husband was out of town on one of his business trips. Procrastinating since Halloween, Antoinette decided to go and introduce herself to the neighbors, the Starkweathers, who had moved in a year ago. She even had made a dessert for them, a yellow cake with chocolate frosting. Bundling up Isabella into her coat, the little girl immediately began fidgeting.

"Ot, Momma."

"I know, but wait until we go outside, you won't be so hot."

As her daughter stood stiffly in her pink coat, matching wool scarf, and gloves staring round-eyed at her mother, Antoinette slipped on a black coat with fury lining over a pale-green cashmere sweater and black jeans. Then, glancing in the little circular mirror on the wall near the front door, she touched up her lips with lip gloss, and chuckled. "I'm putting this on, and watch nobody will be home. Funny, I don't put lipstick on for Daddy anymore."

Isabella giggled. Her cheeks reddening under her scarf.

"Ready, my dear?" Antoinette grabbed the keys from the kitchen counter and dropped them into her coat pocket, put on her gloves and took Isabella's hand, exiting the front door.

The wind spiraled and encircled them. It howled against their screen door, slamming it shut behind them.

Her daughter's eyes watered. "Momma, cold."

"I told you, come on…" She reached down with one of her gloved hands grasping Isabella, and helped the child walk down the front porch steps. With her other hand she balanced the cake in a plastic cake holder.

They crossed the street quickly. It took a few minutes until they reached the Starkweathers, a few houses down. The ranch-style home had white siding. There were spruce trees, neatly trimmed in front of a bay window. White stones covered with a dusting of snow lined the walkway to the front door with little lamps to light the way. Antoinette saw a shed in the backyard next to a detached two-car garage. A green Jeep sat in the drive.

She rang the doorbell once and waited a few seconds. No one must be home. Then she rang it again. This time, the front door opened abruptly.

It startled her and Isabella. "Oh."

"Sorry, it's so windy," Mrs. Starkweather said. The woman who stood at the door could have been a model, she was so attractive.

Antoinette concluded she was younger by a good five years. Her pale skin was smooth like whipped cream, and she had large deep green eyes. Her curly, shoulder-length hair was the color of copper. She was roughly two inches taller than Antoinette too, about 5'9", and athletic-looking.

"Can I help you?" the woman asked, while fidgeting with her red San Francisco 49ers sweatshirt, standing halfway behind the oak door.

"Hi. I'm Antoinette Libero, Vito's wife, and this is our daughter Isabella. We're your neighbors across the street in the burgundy house with the blue rocking chair. My husband met you and your husband on Halloween. We've been meaning to come by and introduce ourselves. It's been overdue, and well I made you dessert—"

"Oh," Mrs. Starkweather answered, nodding her head. "Yes, Vito. I remember."

"Is this a bad time?" Antoinette stuttered, inhaling breaths of cold air, while Isabella clung to her pant leg.

"No, not at all." The woman gave a quick smile. "I'm Cheryl. Lizzy, my daughter, is napping. She'll be awake soon. Here," she said, motioning them in. "Come in, come in. It's freezing out here."

They kicked off their boots and shoes. She led them through a short hallway, passing a living room area on the right. It was sparsely furnished with a beige-leather couch and glass table where a decorative display of holiday candles sat. A tall white Christmas tree with gold balls and gold and silver garland took up a corner of the room.

Covering the entire hardwood floor in the hallway was a gorgeous patterned runner. Before entering the kitchen, they passed a guest bathroom, and closet.

The kitchen walls were painted a soft yellow; modern picture frames of spices, flowers, and Italian street scenes complimented the decor. Above the sliding doors was a silk spray flower. With its oak cabinets and comfortable seating design; the room was warm and inviting.

"Please, sit down. It's Antoinette, right?"

She nodded, setting the cake down on the table.

"Forgive me, I'm Cheryl," she said extending her hand. "Wait. I told you already."

"Yes." Antoinette took her hand; her grip was soft. "Nice to finally meet you." She removed Isabella's scarf and coat, and then took off her jacket as well, and placed it behind one of the kitchen chairs. Picking up Isabella, Antoinette sat down and adjusted her on her lap.

Grocery coupon clippings were tossed all over the table. A stack of newspapers sat piled on the floor next to one of the chairs.

"I apologize for the intrusion," she said feeling a little self-conscious.

"No, no, don't be silly. Please excuse the mess." Cheryl grabbed the clippings and set them on the counter.

A large white and orange cat slowly emerged from behind a silver garbage canister. Isabella saw it and began wiggling with excitement.

"Dog, og, og…"

Cheryl and Antoinette laughed in unison.

"No, sweetheart," Antoinette whispered in her ear. "It's a cat."

"At," Isabella said, happily clapping her hands.

Cheryl said, "Turner, our so called 'security dog'."

"It's—"

"A he."

"He's beautiful."

"He's harmless. But this one here," she bent down from her chair, touching Isabella's prosthesis— "is even more beaut—" Cheryl withdrew her hand immediately.

"It's a prosthetic leg," Antoinette said calmly.

"I see."

"It's not a big deal," she said, putting her daughter down on the floor. "Isabella was born with a limb deficiency. She doesn't have her right leg below her knee," she touched her own leg for emphasis.

"Wow. She walks quite normally." Cheryl stared at Isabella in amazement.

Antoinette grinned, proudly. "I know. She's only had the leg for a couple of months, but she has taken to it quite well. We're very blessed. She's doing great."

"I'm glad. Can I offer you some coffee to go with the nice looking cake you brought?"

"No, you don't have to—"

"I insist. Regular or decaf?"

"Regular is fine, or whatever you have."

Cheryl rose from the table and fussed with the coffeemaker.

There was an awkward silence between them. Luckily, Isabella provided some entertainment while she sat on the floor with Lizzy's Dr. Seuss book.

"Isabella, be careful. Don't rip the pages," Antoinette said.

"Don't worry about it. Lizzy has already ripped two books."

"How old is Lizzy?"

"She turned one September tenth."

"Isabella turned one October thirtieth. First baby?"

"Yeah."

"The same for me."

Then, they both started talking at the same time.

"So—" Antoinette said.

"What about—" Cheryl laughed and gestured toward her.

"No. You go first," she replied.

"No, okay. Are you a stay-at-home mom?" Cheryl asked sitting down.

"Yes. I was a high school teacher over at Griffen. But then, Vito and I had Isabella. We agreed it was best to have me home full-time. I might go back later on when she's in school. How about you?"

"I was in computer consulting back in San Francisco," Cheryl said, settling back in her chair. "My husband, Lee, received a great opportunity here with Shuster Jones. He's an accountant. So we upped and came to Chicago. Both our families are in California."

"That's hard."

"I want to work, but with Lizzy, I want to see her grow up. Kind of like the way my mom did for me. Having her has changed me. I used to be stressed out all the time and high-strung. Now, I'm easy going and clip coupons," Cheryl grinned, pointing to the stack behind her.

"Maybe after Lizzy starts school, you can go back."

"Maybe. We'll see."

The coffee maker beeped. Cheryl got up, her movements smooth and graceful. Antoinette could picture her in a business suit, negotiating with clients. Some people were polished that way.

"Do you take milk and sugar?"

"Black is perfect. Thank you."

With two filled mugs in her hand, the woman strolled over to the table, smiling. "That's the way I like my coffee, too."

As she sat back in the chair, the baby monitor on the countertop started. A little voice could be heard… "Ommy…Momma…"

From her sitting position, Isabella's eyes darted about.

"Who's that, Isabella?"

"Babeee," she said, enthusiastically.

"Wow. She's smart. Excuse me while I go get Lizzy."

Antoinette didn't have long to wait. When they returned, she and her daughter were greeted by a round-faced little red-head, her face—the spitting image of her mother. The child spotted Isabella and retreated behind her mom's leg.

"Lizzy, come and say hello to our neighbors," Cheryl said, crouching beside her daughter.

Isabella began to clap with glee. Then, she turned her head to get Antoinette's approval and slowly took a step toward them.

Lizzy saw Isabella come at her, and hid behind her mom. Her eyes, a light brown, were puffy from sleep. Her hair was as copper as her mom's, and it stood up straight everywhere.

Crouching still, Cheryl continued to comfort Lizzy. Then all at once she stepped tentatively toward Isabella. They bumped into each other like two soft pillows. Lizzy, the smaller of the two, took hold of Isabella's arm and the two of them started talking in a baby language only they could understand.

Antoinette watched as they plopped down on the floor together and grabbed for the Dr. Seuss book. Her neighbor quickly fetched a few more toys for the girls to share.

"There," said Cheryl, making her way back to the table. "Best friends already. Maybe they won't kill each other over the toys."

Antoinette smiled, "Yep." Visiting was a good idea. Vito would be happy to hear about her afternoon.

She and Cheryl spent the next hour talking about themselves while enjoying a piece of cake each. Cheryl was as down to earth as she was, and Antoinette enjoyed chatting with her.

Time passed quickly. When suddenly glancing at the time on the microwave clock, Antoinette realized they had been there for almost two hours. She hated to end the conversation, but she didn't want to be rude, either.

They concluded and agreed to meet the following week at the Libero's home this time. Their girls had become great playmates.

CHAPTER 33

Vito had been working a lot lately. He had flown back from Cincinnati after training new clients on a pharmaceutical tracking program. He was fatigued, but he couldn't tell his wife, or else she'd bring up the "working" thing again. He had a job more importantly and his territory was thriving.

The wind picked up and a freezing rain had begun after five on a Thursday. It was expected to shower all evening, with a slight possibility of it turning to snow overnight when the temperature was said to drop down into the twenties. For now, the roads were slick and traffic was bumper to bumper going west on the 90 Interstate heading home from O'Hare airport.

His cell phone rang. The caller ID showed it was Brad, his colleague.

"Yo, Brad, what's up?"

"Hey, Romeo."

"What's going on, buddy?"

"Nada, my friend."

From the receiver, Vito heard music in the background. "Where are you at? Sounds like you're at a bar."

"Come over to Stadiums for a drink with me."

"Tonight?" He quickly eyed at the clock on the dash, and then at the line of headlights ahead of him. He sighed. "I'm just coming back from Cincinnati. I haven't seen my little girl in two days."

"One drink, bud," he slurred.

"What's wrong? Are you drunk?"

"No, dude. Can you please come? Please…come."

Something was definitely wrong with Brad. "Okay. Let me call Antoinette, and let her know. See you soon."

He clicked off. He was now worried. It didn't sound like Brad's normal, cheerful self. This traffic was no help, either. Car after car in front of him. They were going only five miles an hour at the moment. He slammed his hands on the steering wheel. *Damn.* He could use a shot of whiskey after the day he had. But, he was trying not to drink.

He phoned his wife. "It's me. Brad called."

"He's at Stadiums, isn't he?" she said flatly on the other end.

Vito rolled his eyes. "Yes. And don't worry, I won't drink. I can't."

"What about Isabella? She's been waiting for you all day."

"I know, I'm sorry. Something's up. It sounds serious."

"What about dinner? I've already started cooking."

"Go ahead and eat with Isabella. I'll grab a burger there. I'll eat whatever you prepared for lunch tomorrow."

"Fine," Antoinette said. She sounded irritated.

"I'm sorry. I'm just worried about him."

"Okay. Be careful. See you later."

As Vito drove, he wondered what the problem could be. Brad was a cool guy, always upbeat. Over the phone, though, he hadn't sounded so jolly. Life had been so busy for him lately with work, Isabella, and everything else, that Vito hadn't kept in contact with Brad outside of work; only the biweekly conference calls with their boss, Nick.

Forty-five minutes later, he pulled into Stadiums' lot. It was strange being there. A chill ran down his spine and he shivered. He recalled the night he was last there with Brad. It was *that* night, when he was going to tell Antoinette they were through. It was also when he found out she was pregnant. What a difference a year had made. Instead, he had committed to sticking around.

He walked in and saw Brad slumped over the bar, head in his hands. Three empty beer bottles and a full shot glass was next to him.

The bartender, April, saw him, waved, and nodded toward Brad.

Oh shit, this is serious.

"Hey buddy," Vito said, as he slid on the stool next to Brad.

"Romeo, you're here," Brad slurred and hugged him.

"I'm here. Whoa, someone's had too much to drink." He pushed him away.

"Have a shot with me."

"Can't."

"Why not? I'm celebrating."

"Celebrating? What's the occasion?" Vito observed Brad. He wore a five-o'clock shadow, and his nose and cheeks were plum-red colored.

"Amy's pregnant. April, give me another—"

Vito waved his arm, "No, make it coffee, black. Get us a burger and fries each—well done, please."

"I don't need coffee; I need a shot of whiskey, like I told you."

"Brad, Amy's pregnant," he slapped his friend on his back. "Congratulations!"

"Awesome for you, not me," Brad breathed heavily. "I don't want kids."

"Were you trying?"

"She got off the pill—that sneaky woman. She tricked me."

Vito debated over his next words. He'd been in Brad's shoes, and had wanted out of his failing marriage. But his friend's situation was different. At least he and Antoinette had both desired kids, but all they got were complications. Then, his wife pushed him to see their priest, thinking she was being deceptive. Only later did he realize her intention was not to hurt him but help their marriage. He needed to talk sense into Brad.

The coffee and burgers came. "Eat and hear me out."

"Why? I want out," Brad railed. "You did, too. Didn't you? Let's be bachelors, you and me. Leave town. Who needs our wives?"

Vito shook Brad. "Stop talking stupid. Face your responsibility. You're not seventeen anymore. You're a forty year old man with a wife who's now pregnant."

"*You're* some saint," Brad chided between bites.

"No, I'm not. Nor will I ever be. Antoinette and I aren't perfect, but *I'm* trying. For my *only* child." He took a sip of hot coffee.

His friend put his burger down. "I'm...scared, Vito. I had shitty parents. I don't want to become like them."

"You don't have to be like them." He thought of his mother and father. His mom took back his unfaithful father.

"What if it happens? What if I become like my dad?"

"Then change it. Don't let it happen from the get-go. My dad wasn't perfect either, but my mother forgave him."

"What about you, have you forgiven him?"

Vito hesitated, unsure about his feelings for his dad. But that was another situation altogether. "This isn't about me. It's about *you.*"

"And you. Are you happy?"

He folded his arms on the bar. "For the most part I am. It's not easy with Isabella's condition. I hate it, I hate the damn prosthesis she's wearing, but I'm working on it. Antoinette and I are doing all right. I'm pretty lucky to have her. Our focus is on Isabella."

Brad finished his coffee. "I yelled at Amy earlier, said some nasty things to her."

He nodded, remembering his arguments with Antoinette. "It happens." He put his arm around his friend's big shoulders. "Let's finish these burgers. I'll take you home. Leave your car here; we'll get it in the morning. Sober up. You have to talk to your wife. Tell her you're sorry. You have a baby on the way. Don't screw it up."

Brad's eyes moistened as he nodded. "Okay, bro. I'll do it."

After dropping Brad off, Vito drove home in silence. He prayed he had helped his friend. Brad would realize one day the impact of a child on his life just like Isabella had done for him. He and his wife were making strides and that was just as important.

It was after nine. He speed-dialed home. "Hi, it's me. I'm on my way."

"I'm glad," Antoinette said, and they hung up.

When Vito arrived home, he found his wife thumbing through a magazine at the kitchen table and sipping tea. She had on her pajamas, her brown hair pulled back in a ponytail, and her face clean without any makeup. She was so beautiful to him, just like that.

He took off his jacket, kissed his wife and sat down in the chair next to her.

"Isabella sleeping?"

"We've had an active-filled day. She was tired. "

"You look tired."

"I am," she sighed.

"How was your day, besides tiring?" He smiled at her.

Her face flushed with excitement. "We went and visited the Starkweathers."

He leaned back, "You did? Wasn't it cold out?"

"Yes."

"Tell me about it. I want to hear about your day." He reached in, taking a sip of her tea.

"It was great." She then recounted the conversation she had with Cheryl and how they planned to get together more often now that the girls took a liking to one another.

He smiled; glad his wife had listened to him.

Antoinette paused. "And you and Brad, how did things go with him?"

Vito knew she had never liked Brad. The guy was rambunctious and loud, and tended to drink a lot. His spouse, Amy, was a good woman, but somehow Brad in his selfish state, never saw what an amazing person he had married.

He was going to be cautious about talking about Brad to Antoinette, not for his wife's sake, but for his friend. He wished at this very moment the man was apologizing to his wife and patching things up between them. After all, a child's life was now involved.

He took a deep breath. "The guy is having some work issues, you know, and I kind of helped him."

"Work issues?" She raised an eyebrow.

"Yeah," he smiled.

"Hmm. You know, Amy wants kids. Was your discussion about babies?"

He laughed, "How did you know?"

"She was pretty distraught over the situation at Sally and Tim's a while back."

He rose from his chair and got a glass of water, unable to keep the truth from her. "She's pregnant."

"Fantastic!" His wife clapped her hands together.

Vito finished his water and put the glass in the sink. "Not for Brad. So, I guess it's why we met. He's unhappy. I tried talking sense in him. Then, sent him home to talk to his wife. I have faith it will work out for them."

He sat back down beside his wife and exhaled. He was exhausted. Putting his head on the table, he closed his eyes. A moment later, he felt Antoinette rubbing his neck.

He was tense, but his wife's hands were soft and warm. It felt good to be touched. He breathed deeply feeling the relaxing tingling in his neck.

"I'm proud of you," she bent down whispering in his ear. "It takes a strong man to realize what he has in front of him and appreciate it. Thanks for sharing with me."

Vito raised his head and stared at a loving woman before him willing to stand next to him whatever the adversities. Taking her hand, he said, "Thank you for listening."

His wife smiled and tugged at his arm. "Let's go to bed."

He nodded, rose from the chair, and followed her up the stairs.

CHAPTER 34

Right after Vito's birthday in December, Antoinette noticed some blue and purple bruising at the base of her daughter's knee cap. Isabella wasn't complaining about it, but it was beginning to worry her.

This was a prosthesis issue, so she phoned Dr. Maxwell's office and explained the situation that her daughter preferred to be free of the prosthetic leg when she crawled around. The nurse assured her it took a while for the prosthesis to fit properly. "The sleeve is expandable, and after some time it will become snug and fit the way it should fit. Isabella needs to wear the prosthesis more often. However, if the redness persists, call us back and bring your daughter in."

Antoinette decided to wait another week. If the child wasn't experiencing any pain, then it was fine. But why the bruises? Isabella had only been wearing the prosthesis since October—over two months.

Her biggest challenge was getting Isabella to wear her prosthesis all the time. She and Vito tried for two days to get their daughter to cooperate. First, Antoinette took her out to the grocery stores without placing her in the carts, but Isabella refused to walk. Then, Vito brought her down to the basement to run around with him, but she'd plopped herself on the floor not wanting to get up.

"No...no yeg," Isabella stammered.

"Isabella, the doctor says you need to wear your leg. Let's put it on," Antoinette begged.

"No," she pouted.

On the third day, Antoinette tried a tag team approach where they took turns individually talking to Isabella and encouraging her to wear her prosthesis, but that didn't work.

"You know, you're responsible for this," Vito said taking a seat in the den.

"I'm responsible?"

"You don't always put her leg on. Every time I come home from work, I see her playing with her toys in the playpen with her leg off." Vito's voice got louder with each word. "You can't do that."

"Shh...can you lower your voice?" she nodded. "Yes I know. I should have tried harder with her. But, I don't believe it's the reason for the bruising. She was walking fine with it. I don't understand what happened."

"Isabella has to wear her prosthesis, or she'll never get used it."

That night, frustrated, Antoinette wrestled with where she had gone wrong. She tossed and turned in bed not knowing what had caused her daughter's bruises.

On the fourth evening, after finishing up the dinner dishes in the kitchen, she and Vito were sitting at the table when an idea popped in mind. "Maybe we can show her the consequences of not wearing a prosthesis."

"Like what kind of consequences?"

"How difficult it is to walk with only one leg?"

"How are you going to pull it off?"

She jumped up and rummaged through the drawers. "Where's the roll of string you put in here?"

"What string?"

She pulled out a roll. "This string."

"What are you going to do with it?"

"Lift your right leg," she said walking over to Vito.

"What for?"

"We need to show Isabella if she doesn't wear the prosthesis, she won't be able to walk. Hence our consequence."

"What does this have to do with me?"

"We are going to use you as a prop and pretend you can't walk," she replied, peeking into the den where Isabella was playing in her playpen.

"She's not going to go for this."

"Yes she will. You have to limp and play the part of a—"

"One-legged man. Really?" he shook his head.

With string and scissors in hand, Antoinette said, "It's the only chance we have. Okay, turn around and lift your right leg."

Reluctantly, her husband turned around, bent his knee, holding his leg with his right hand. With his left hand, he gripped the back of one of the chairs for balance. Antoinette began wrapping the string around his thigh.

"It's not going to hold, my leg is too heavy."

"Shh...I'm concentrating."

At about the twentieth loop around, she pulled the string hard to tighten the grip.

"Ouch, that hurts."

"Let go of your hand from your leg."

When he did, his leg was somewhat secured.

"This is not going to stay."

"I know. So, we need to move fast."

She placed the string and scissors back in the drawer while Vito waited by the chair.

"It's going to rip soon—" a look of concern on his face.

She put her hand over his mouth. "No time for that. Here's the plan. We walk in together and you hobble next to me, holding my arm."

"What's that going to do?"

"Show your dependence upon me, which we don't want her to do. Are you ready?"

"Do you think it's going to work?"

"Do you have a better idea?"

Her husband stood there for a moment trying to balance. "No."

"Let's go, then."

Together, they carefully walked into the den. Vito was having a hard time hopping on one leg and was leaning on her left arm. He was heavy. With some persistence though, they managed. When they entered the den, Isabella smiled at them from her playpen. Then, her expression changed.

She cocked her head to one side. "Dada?"

"Isabella, what are you doing?" Antoinette asked.

Looking at Vito and touching her right thigh, she replied, "Dada…booboo…"

"Oh my. See!" Antoinette reacted.

Her husband nodded and he ripped his leg loose from the string and ran to his daughter, scooping her up in his arms, while Antoinette bolted to the kitchen to call the doctor's office.

She asked the receptionist to be connected to Dr. Maxwell's nurses' station. Antoinette was on hold for a few minutes. Vito joined her with Isabella in the kitchen.

Worry hung in her throat. "I knew something was wrong. My gut told me so." She caressed her daughter's face. "We're going to get this taken care of for you."

"Okay, okay." Vito replied touching her arm.

Antoinette shook her head. She continued looking at her daughter. *Poor child. No wonder she'd put up such a fuss with the prosthesis.*

A nurse came on the line. "Dr. Maxwell's office, this is Jackie."

"Hi Jackie. This is Antoinette Libero. I don't know if I spoke to you last week regarding my daughter, Isabella. She's the one who has been showing some bruising on her knee cap."

"I believe I remember."

"My daughter pointed to her knee and said she has a booboo. She's also been refusing to wear her prosthesis. We'd like to come in and see the doctor."

"Okay. I will make a note of the issues in her chart and patch you back to the receptionist to make an appointment."

"Thank you."

***

At ten-thirty in the morning two days later, Vito, Antoinette, and Isabella sat in Dr. Maxwell's office.

"Yes. It looks as if the sleeve is too tight for Isabella, and therefore causing the bruising," The doctor stated plainly, examining Isabella's prosthetic leg, scrutinizing its structure. "We'll have to do some adjustments to resize the socket."

"What are we looking at here, in regards to time?" she asked.

"A couple of hours at the most. I'll have Rob make the adjustments." He started for the door. "We'll see if we can squeeze you in this afternoon. I'll be back, let me check their schedule."

Proven Prosthetics had an opening in the afternoon for two-thirty. The Liberos went to the clinic and had the sleeve of the prosthesis loosened. It had been an easy adjustment and Isabella would not get bruised by it.

By the end of January, Isabella's bruises had disappeared. Isabella didn't fuss anymore, and wore it when she played in the playpen. Their child had gotten used to the limb after all, and was walking without any issues. Both Antoinette and Vito were relieved and happy with the progress.

In the meantime, Antoinette and Isabella began having play dates with their new friends across the street, Cheryl and Lizzy. Once a week the foursome would get together, alternating houses. It was the best thing Antoinette could ever have asked for. She had a "grown up" to share parenting tips, and her daughter had a friend who was oblivious to her prosthetic leg.

PART 3: COMFORT ZONE

"Enclosing yourself in a bubble won't protect you from the elements."

—From Antoinette Libero's Sticky Notes

CHAPTER 35

September, 2005. Four years later.

Antoinette had tossed and turned in bed most of the night. When the alarm rang at six Monday morning, she fought to make herself get up.

Her mother had gotten the flu, and so she had spent most of Saturday and part of Sunday taking care of her as well as getting Isabella, ready for her first day of preschool. She would have been going to Kindergarten, but missed the September first cutoff date that had been indoctrinated in all the elementary schools.

When Antoinette rolled over in bed; Vito lay still, sleeping peacefully.

"Honey," she whispered.

He looked at her with sleepy eyes. "What?"

"Get up," she nudged him. "You got to go to work and Isabella starts preschool."

"Five more minutes," he groaned and turned over.

She laid in bed for another couple of minutes with her eyes closed to the sunlight streaming in through the window, and then opened her eyes, observing her husband. Gray strands blended in with his blondish hair. His face was older, more mature. Still with MeritPlus Pharmaceuticals, Vito had been promoted to Manager, two years earlier, replacing his old boss, Nick, who had also been promoted to Vice President.

Her husband traveled twice a month to Cincinnati and Cleveland, and Indiana and Michigan, as the company had expanded. He had seven sales representatives under him, including his good friend, Brad, who had taken over Vito's old territory, and kept it growing, considering his busy home life.

Brad and his wife, Amy, had two children, two boys, four and two, and a baby girl on the way. It was amazing to see what having a family had done for her husband's friend who just a few years back wanted nothing to do with children.

This was Vito's off week from traveling out of town, but it meant he'd be on countless conference calls, and making his rounds on the road to several clinics and hospitals here in Chicago with Brad. She was happy it had worked out that he'd be home at night to be with their daughter during her first week of preschool.

Rising from the bed, Antoinette stumbled into the bathroom and turned on the faucet to wash her face. She was excited for Isabella but nervous for herself. *Did I miss anything, getting Isabella ready for this first day?* She had contacted the school principal, teacher, and assistant teachers in preparation. She had had extensive conversations with her daughter about her first day and what to expect. The reality of it all hit hard this morning; she'd slowly lose her child to the world. This *world.*

She wasn't alone in this feeling. Cheryl Starkweather, her neighbor, had been feeling the same way about her own daughter. Since meeting them three years earlier, Antoinette and Cheryl had become fast friends, and had weekly play dates with their girls.

The Starkweathers added a new addition to their family, a son named Connor who was now a year old. He was a darling little boy with dark blond hair and red freckles. She remembered when she found out Cheryl was expecting. Happy about the news for her friend, Antoinette had been a little saddened about her predicament. Her biological clock had clearly stopped ticking.

In the past couple of weeks, the two women consoled each other in preparation for the big day. Buying school supplies requested by the teachers, backpacks, and of course, new clothes and shoes for the girls.

The previous night Vito felt positive this day would be a great day for Isabella, especially being with other children. She agreed with him for the most part, but another part of her still wanted to protect her child from the ignorant, the bullies, and the ones who would be afraid of Isabella because she wore a prosthesis.

Looking herself in the mirror, Antoinette repeated, "You need to be strong. You have to do this."

Hearing her husband stir, she stepped into the shower.

At seven-fifty, Antoinette was in the kitchen making her daughter toast. "Isabella, come down. I have breakfast for you."

Vito strolled in from the den with papers under his arm.

"What's going on with Isabella? She's not answering."

He put his empty coffee mug in the sink. Shrugging his shoulders, he said, "A while ago I was upstairs and gave her a pep talk. She seemed fine with me."

"Hmm... Isa...bell...la?"

No answer.

Her husband grabbed his briefcase and kissed her on the mouth. "Okay, I have to go. I have a number of stops to make. Good luck today."

Antoinette smiled. *I hope so.*

"Bye, Isabella. I'll see you later, kiddo. Have a great day!" Vito yelled as he made his way out the door.

The toast popped up. *Where was that kid?*

She took the toast and placed it on a plate. Wiping her hands, she headed up the stairs to her bedroom. When she entered, Isabella was on her bed sitting in her underwear, holding her prosthesis.

Standing in the doorway of her daughter's bedroom, Antoinette asked, "Isabella, why aren't you answering when I call you?"

She didn't look up.

She plodded up to her. Bent down and lifted her chin. Her eyes were moist.

"I don't want to go to school," she cried.

"Why not?"

"Because."

"Because, why?" Vito had told her she was fine. What was *this* about?

"I'm scared, Mommy."

Antoinette caressed her face, brushing the golden locks from her eyes. A rivulet rolled down her daughter's cheek. "Everyone's scared the first day of school."

"What if...what if...they laugh at me?"

"Laugh at what?" She had a suspicion her daughter was referring to her prosthetic limb, but she wanted to hear her say it aloud for confirmation. They already had this conversation several times before.

"My leg."

"What about your leg?" *Keep calm. Make it light. Don't make it a big deal.*

"They're going to laugh at my leg," Isabella whispered.

Antoinette took a deep breath. "You laugh back at them, you hear." She handed her the prosthesis. "Remember, you can put this on and take it off whenever you want to. None of the other kids can do that." She pointed to herself. "I surely can't do it."

Her daughter sniffled, and then began giggling.

"See... What did I tell you?"

"Yeah."

She kissed her forehead. "It's a little warm out. Do you want to wear a skirt or shorts?"

"Pants."

"Isabella, they are going to see your leg, sooner or later." She got up. "Your choice. You're a big girl. You decide what to wear."

Antoinette stepped out of the room and fell against the wall in the hallway. She fought back her tears as she went downstairs. This was hard, so hard, but she knew she had to be strong for her daughter, no matter how difficult it was to get her through the first day jitters.

A few minutes later Isabella wandered into the kitchen, just as Antoinette finished buttering the toast and setting it on the table with a glass of orange juice. She wore the blue-plaid skirt with a white-collared blouse they had laid out together the night before.

She walked over and fixed her collar. "You look beautiful, pumpkin. How about some breakfast?"

The little girl nodded.

At eight-thirty, Cheryl and Lizzy Starkweather arrived. The girls were going to start school together. Over the weekend Connor had gotten a high fever. This morning, Cheryl called Antoinette to tell her she and Lee were going to take him to the doctor, and asked if she could drive both girls.

Cheryl hugged her daughter, "You have a great day today, sweetheart. I'll be here when you get back."

Antoinette touched her friend's arm.

She sighed. "Thanks for doing this. I owe you one."

"No problem. Go and take care of Connor. You don't want to mess around with fevers. My mom's been sick with the flu all weekend."

A look of concern crossed Cheryl's face. "I heard. Vito mentioned it to Lee. I hope she gets better."

"Thanks. That makes two of us."

Antoinette and the girls climbed into the car. She strapped Isabella first in her big girl chair—her booster seat, and then had Lizzy climb in her own booster seat, borrowed from the Starkweather's car. Both girls waved to Cheryl.

A few minutes later, she pulled into the parking lot at McKinnley Elementary School. McKinnley was not as big as the other elementary schools; it only had about two-hundred kids from kindergarten to sixth grade. But in the last five years, McKinnley had added a new preschool wing.

Isabella, Lizzy and Antoinette trekked up to the preschool playground. At least eleven other children waited with their moms and dads. Some kids played hop scotch, others swung on the swings. *This is a big day for these little ones. I wish Vito could have been here.* A milestone for his daughter; he was so nonchalant about it. Sometimes he could be so involved and loving with Isabella, and other times, he was totally hands off and more worried about work.

A tall, twenty-some year old woman with light brown hair, dressed in a white cotton blouse and khaki pants appeared. The children gathered around her. She introduced herself as Ms. Stevens, their teacher. There were two other young women with her, assistant preschool teachers. She explained how much fun they were going to have. Isabella stood shyly outside the crowd of kids. She turned and gazed at her mother. Antoinette gave her a thumbs up.

It was nine o'clock. The bell rang and she waved goodbye, standing around to watch her daughter and Lizzy go in. One little boy clung to his father until one of the assistants gave him a sticker. Antoinette then lumbered back to the car alone.

Driving the few blocks home, she blasted rock music from the radio. Once she pulled in the drive, she stopped the car before the garage and a thousand tears flooded her cheeks like a waterfall. *Jesus… And this is only preschool.*

Walking into the house, she poured herself a cup of coffee and sat down in Vito's favorite chair in the den. *Why do I feel like I'm losing Isabella? She's growing up so fast. What is it going to feel like when my daughter goes off to college?* She dialed Vito's cell number.

"Hey," his calming voice flowed through the receiver.

"I'm a mess, Vito."

"There's nothing to be upset about. It's just preschool."

"I know," she said quietly, wiping the tears from her face. "It's—"

"What?"

"She's so vulnerable, and maybe the kids will make fun of her."

"Aren't you the one telling me to let her spread her wings and not to make it a big deal," Vito answered sternly.

"You should have been here."

"I couldn't, okay?"

"I know. I'm sorry."

"I have to go. Can we talk about this later?"

"Sure." Antoinette hung up. Vito was sympathetic, but cool. His usual self. Isabella would be all right; she was the one crumbling.

She put the phone on its cradle and stretched her back. It was so easy for her husband. Women were usually the primary caregivers. Add all the maternal emotions, and it was no wonder why she was stressing. Antoinette wished she could turn it off sometimes, like a radio dial.

Next, she called her mom to check up on her and get some motherly advice.

"Hello," came a scratchy voice over the phone.

"Mom, it's me. How are you feeling?"

"I've been better. Did my little pooky-girl go to school?"

Antoinette smiled at her mother's words of endearment. "Yes, she did. It's me who's a basket case."

A cough came through the receiver. "I remember when I brought Salvatore to his first day of day care. I cried all the way home."

She nodded. *Yes. Someone who can relate to my fears.* "What did you do, Mom?"

"It was easier with you. Salvatore was a whole other story. I guess you need to let it be. She's going to grow up, dear. You and your brother did. I wish I could go back, but I can't. I miss those days. So—" Cough and a sneeze. "Excuse me, wow. When will this be over? I had pneumonia a few months ago, and now this."

Antoinette swallowed. She worried about her mother. This year she had been getting sick a lot. "I won't keep you on the phone. Go get some rest and drink plenty of liquids. Is Dad helping out?"

"Ha. He doesn't do anything without me. This is *his* vacation."

"You better tell him to help out. I'll call you later."

"Thank you. Give a big hug to my baby when she gets home. And remember, breathe, and don't take things so seriously, okay? Love you."

"Thanks, Mom. Love you, too."

***

By noon she was relatively composed, and returned to the parking lot to pick up her daughter and Lizzy.

She waited in anticipation, wondering what kind of morning Isabella had experienced. *You ready, Antoinette?* She heard her mother's words in her head. *Don't take things so seriously.*

With their teacher and assistant teachers holding the doors, the preschoolers ran out. Antoinette spotted Isabella and Lizzy right away, who at first glance seemed a little distant from one another.

"Hi, girls," she waved, as they came closer. "How was it?"

"It was great. I met a lot of kids," Lizzy said, as they climbed in the car and into their seats.

"Great, Lizzy. How about you, Isabella?"

"It was okay."

"Isabella doesn't play with the other girls," chimed in Lizzy.

"No," Isabella answered back. "Not true. I want to play with you. You don't play with me."

Antoinette strapped the girls in and got in the driver's side. Something was wrong. She peeked in the rearview mirror; the girls weren't looking at one another.

Lizzy faced Isabella. "I play with you, and I want to play with other kids, too," she said crossing her arms.

"You're my best friend," her daughter said, sniffling.

Maybe I should cut in and play referee.

"My mom says it's okay to play with other kids."

Forget it. Let them work it out.

"I don't want to," Isabella huffed.

"Girls. Let's stop arguing. We need to be nice to each other. Isabella, did you talk to anyone else besides Lizzy today?"

"I talked to Marty."

"Who's Marty?"

"A funny boy," Lizzy whispered.

"He's nice," responded Isabella, grinning.

"See," Antoinette said looking back at them. "It's nice to talk and play with other kids, like Lizzy's mom said."

"Hmm…" Isabella gruffed.

Antoinette took a breath. She knew it would take time.

She pulled into the driveway and parked the car. Cheryl was already waiting on the front steps.

Once unstrapped, Lizzy ran toward her mother, talking up a storm about her first day. Isabella and Antoinette took their time, joining the others on the front lawn.

Antoinette asked her how Connor was. His fever broke. Her friend was relieved. They bid their goodbyes and departed; Cheryl grabbing the booster chair out of the car on the way down the drive.

Once inside, Antoinette made Isabella a peanut butter and jelly sandwich, watching as she ate it quietly. When finished, her daughter asked to be excused and jumped out of her chair, heading to the den to watch cartoons. She nodded, letting her go.

CHAPTER 36

Upon entering the house that evening, Vito was bombarded by his wife with what had transpired at school between Isabella and Lizzy. Antoinette seemed frazzled. He listened quietly until she finished.

"I wish you could have been there. This was such an important day."

"I understand, I've been busy with work, but I'm here now." *Would she ever stop nagging me?* He took a couple of deep breaths. "Stop jumping to conclusions, will ya?"

"Sorry I brought it up."

"I'll see what's going on with Isabella." He volunteered to give her a bath and get her ready for bed, so he could get away from his wife for a bit.

With returning e-mails from the day and preparing for the next day, Vito occasionally gave his daughter a bath when he didn't travel. Bath time was something he enjoyed, as it was a fun time between father and daughter. But he knew it would change in the near future, once Isabella realized she was too old to be bathed by her parents, let alone her dad. He put her favorite squeaky ducks in the water, and they giggled together at the sounds they made. Listening to his daughter's squeals tonight, it was obvious how happy he had made her by taking part of the nightly ritual.

Vito helped his baby girl into her polka-dot pajamas, and watched her brush her teeth. Then he picked her up, twirling her around in her room, as she giggled in his arms, and carried her to bed.

"Okay, little super girl. It's bedtime." He pulled the covers over her and cuddled with his daughter. "So, how was school today?"

Isabella lowered her eyes. "It was okay."

"Hmm…just okay? Are you sure? Mom said you were kind of upset."

With a trembling lip, she answered, "Lizzy wants other friends."

Vito shifted on the bed beside her. "How do you know that?"

"I heard her say that to Mary and Katelyn."

"Is this why you're upset?"

"Yeah. She's my best friend, but she wants more friends."

He stroked her hair. "You can have more than one best friend."

Her eyes grew wide, "I can?"

"Yep. You and Lizzy can play here together. At school, you can have other best friends to play with."

"Can best friends be a boy?"

Vito thought for a moment. *Starting early already?* He sure was going to have his hands full with this one. "Does this boy want to be your friend or kiss you?" he tickled her.

Isabella giggled. But then she grew serious. "Lizzy says he's her friend."

"Does he want to be your friend?"

"I don't know."

"Honey, you can't claim someone as 'your friend,' unless they want to be your friend, too. You have to get to know them first, you may not like them. Just because Lizzy claimed him as her friend doesn't mean you have to. What's his name?"

"Marty."

"Marty, huh?" he sighed. "Lizzy may have bad taste in friends. You need to find your own friends at school. You understand?"

Isabella nodded.

"You are your own person, Isabella Audrey Libero. Choose your friends wisely. But that person also must want to be friends with you. Take your time. It's only the first day."

She moaned. "Lizzy makes friends fast."

"Are you jealous of Lizzy?"

She nodded, shrugging her shoulders shyly.

"There's nothing you should be jealous of. Lizzy's a nice girl and all, but you do what makes *you* happy, understand?"

Isabella smiled. "Yes, Daddy."

"Off to sleep. I love you, kiddo." He kissed her forehead and tucked her in.

When he entered the den, he grinned from ear to ear. He was proud of himself. He had been patient, and helped resolve Isabella's problem. He was glad it wasn't about her leg after all.

Sitting next to Antoinette, he cleared his throat. "There are two things being played out here. The first is she's jealous of Lizzy."

"Jealous? Of what?"

"Wait…let me finish. The second is our daughter has a crush on this Marty boy."

"How come I didn't get that?"

"He tickled her. "It's what fathers are for."

Antoinette rolled her eyes. "Whatever. Before we let this ego trip go to your head, let's get back to this jealousy thing with Lizzy."

"Yeah." He closed his eyes, remembering his thoughts. "Isabella apparently overheard Lizzy telling the other girls in her class they are her best friends."

"On the first day?"

Vito laughed. "So, she's hurt. She doesn't want to confront Lizzy. She's jealous she doesn't have more than one best friend."

"So, what did you tell her?"

"I asked if there were other kids in her class she'd like to play with. She said yes. Marty is one of them, but she only talked to him a little bit. She automatically assumed he's nice because Lizzy talked to him." He took a deep breath. "I then encouraged her to make new friends but also have Lizzy as her best friend. I told her there is no limit to how many friends she can have, just choose them wisely." He paused. "The bottom line, she thought you could only have *one* best friend."

"What about Marty?"

"I told her to be friends with Marty and not to look at another boy or else I'd lock her in her room forever," he said mischievously.

"You did not!" Antoinette said, slapping his arm.

"No, I didn't. Seriously. I told her friends will come and go. Have fun and to be herself."

"She believed all you said?"

"Yep," he smiled proudly. "It's a father's influence that wins a daughter's heart every time."

"Great," his wife said, a bit sarcastically. "When she starts dating, you can insert your 'fatherly influence.' We'll see where that takes you."

"She won't be dating until she's forty. I'll make sure of it."

"Mmm…we'll see."

They both laughed together. Vito liked this parenting thing. He had made some headway with his daughter tonight.

"But what about her leg?" Antoinette asked. "Did any of the kids make fun of her?"

He shook his head, "She didn't mention anything to me about it. I assume there's no problem."

"Let's hope so," she sighed.

Growing serious, he then asked, "How about you? Are you okay with Isabella in preschool? I know we talked earlier about it."

"I'm okay now," she nodded. "I was being overly protective. It hurt seeing her go off, not needing her mommy anymore. I'll get over it."

"Mother's instincts, I'll never understand them," he said putting his arm around her and kissing her cheek.

"I guess I'm a little bit nervous with her going off into the big, bad world. I'm sorry if I'm coming off as insensitive to all you do. Your influence on her was remarkable tonight."

"Influence. Nice word. How about some husbandly influence?" Vito grabbed his wife in his arms and kissed her.

"Pervert," Antoinette giggled, as he led her upstairs.

***

It had been a successful first week of preschool for Isabella. By Friday, she made friends with most of the children in her class, including Marty. In addition, his daughter had adjusted well with the new schedule of going to school every morning.

The children learned about Isabella's condition during a show and tell about what makes each of them unique. Isabella had taken it upon herself to show her classmates she was special because she could take her prosthesis off whenever she wanted. Vito was so proud of his little girl for being courageous in front of her peers.

CHAPTER 37

December

On a cold Tuesday morning, Antoinette headed to Finley-Smith Hospital on the north side of the city. Her dad had phoned the night before. Her mother had been admitted to the hospital; her pneumonia had come back for the third time this year. Antoinette called Cheryl at the last minute to cover preschool driving duty for the girls.

Vito had voiced his concern several times. He thought her mom had never healed properly because she didn't give herself time to rest. Antoinette agreed with him on this issue.

First thing in the morning, she met a young doctor by the name of Dr. Glazer outside her mother's room. "Besides the pneumonia, my mother has had the flu a couple of times too. This is crazy, doctor."

He gripped his round glasses as he studied Martha's chart.

"Her immune system has been weakened, and so body has become susceptible to illnesses. She's on antibiotics now, and we are giving her oxygen as well. We'll need to keep her a couple of days and run some tests."

"More tests?"

"A chest x-ray to look at her lungs. Your mom's been coughing a lot. I want to do a CT scan to see if there is any fluid in her lungs."

Apprehensive, Antoinette stood in the sterile hallway. "She's done all those before. Have you reviewed her previous test results?"

"I have. But, I want to be thorough and recheck everything."

She studied him. His skin was smooth and youthful; he didn't have one gray hair in his black buzz cut.

Dr. Glazer continued, "I'll be doing a sputum test later today to see what kind of secretions are coming out when she coughs." The doctor touched her arm. "Don't worry; we'll get to the bottom of this. Your mother will be up and running around soon."

"I hope so. Mostly, that's what I'm afraid of. She's constantly running around."

"She's in good hands," he grinned and strolled away.

"Thanks," she murmured to his receding back.

Taking a deep breath, she hesitated, before entering her mom's room.

Having her mother sick so much this year was worrying her. *Lord, if you're there, please help my mom. Help her to get well.*

Martha lay on the hospital bed, flipping through the TV channels. "What channel is the Danny Davis show on?"

"Channel seven," Antoinette said, pulling up a chair beside the bed next to her father, giving him a hug first and then her mother. Antoinette observed her mother. Her silver hair was an unpleasant contrast to her yellowed features. She had aged so much in a short amount of time.

"There it is," Martha said with satisfaction.

Her father looked at her. "What did the kid tell you out there?"

She laughed. "He's not a kid, Dad. He just looks young."

"I don't trust him. I like Dr. Richards better," Mom said between raspy coughs.

"He's going to do some tests, chest x-ray, cat scan, and some sputum thing."

"I've done all those tests," Martha sputtered, irritated.

"Yeah," Frank agreed.

"He has to go through protocol. This is the third time you've gotten pneumonia this year, Ma."

"Protocol, *my ass*," retorted Martha, her arms folded across her chest.

Frank asked, "How long in this pit?"

"A couple of days. So, you both need to relax. You need anything?"

"A bullet in my ass."

"Settle down, Dad," Antoinette laughed, patting him on the arm.

"*What?* I hate hospitals."

"Frank, shut up." Martha turned to her husband. "You think I like it here? I'm the one on the bed, not you. You get to go home tonight."

Frank raised his arms above his head. "God help me with this woman."

Antoinette grinned. Her parents loved to put on a show, and had this comfortable and honest banter between them. They could say anything to each other without fear of crossing the line. She wished she and Vito had a more comfortable relationship, one with kind words and more intimacy. They were on their way. She could sense it.

"Your father and I are going to Florida next month."

"Great. You guys should go."

"Hopefully, I'm out of here by then," her mother coughed again.

"You will be. Come on, Ma, be positive." Antoinette grabbed her things, and turned to her father. "You staying here?"

"I'll leave in a little while. They're going to serve chicken noodle soup for lunch. Don't want to miss that," he said grinning.

Antoinette smiled, looking at her parents. "You two behave, and no hanky-panky, either. I'm going to check when they are going to do those tests."

Martha coughed loudly, "Okay." With outstretched arms, she said, "Come here, will ya'? Give me another hug."

Her eyes got moist. "Sure." She embraced her mother holding her tightly.

Martha released her first and laughed. "What? Why the gloomy face?"

Antoinette tried to smile, staying strong for her. "I want you to be well."

Her mother waved her arm. "Ah...don't worry about me. I'll be okay."

Frank grinned, chiming in. "Now go on. We'll be fine here."

She nodded and headed for the door.

"Give a big kiss to Isabella for me. Tell her I love her."

"Will do, Mom. I love you."

"I love you, too."

Antoinette left the hospital with a feeling of dread on her shoulders.

***

In an intimate ceremony, eighty-one year old Martha Anna DeSalvo was laid to rest on Wednesday, December 10th; barely a week after she was admitted to the hospital.

A telegram expressing his sympathy arrived from Salvatore, Antoinette's older brother, who was in Africa on a safari. Her father was beyond upset. His first born couldn't even come home to bury his mother.

"*Bastard*. Not even to come home and bury his mother. How I can call him my son, my *only* son," Frank muttered between tears during the service at Constantine Funeral Parlor.

It made Antoinette angry as well, but Salvatore had been detached from the family for so many years she often thought of herself as an only child.

Her mother's death, though, was a devastating blow. *Did I expect Mom to live forever?* Martha had been admitted into the hospital for pneumonia on December first, and died peacefully while watching the Danny Davis show several days later on December eighth. The doctor had told the family her heart had become so overstressed from the reoccurring bouts of pneumonia that it gave out.

Her poor heartbroken father was extremely saddened by the reality; his life partner was no longer around. He told Antoinette he'd now be biding his time until he was reunited with his wife. This was his "death row."

Emotionally worn, and completely grief stricken after the funeral, Antoinette spent the rest of the day in bed at home sobbing. She thought about her mother, and the life she had led. She and 'her Frank' had come to the United States sixty years earlier from Italy. It was a tough decision, but trades like dressmaking and tailoring were scarce, so she and her father followed one of his aunts and came to the states to make money. Their plan was to work a few years and go back home, but their jobs got busy, and when Salvatore came, they decided to stay. Her father prospered as a tailor and Martha was content sewing dresses for her growing clientele. Children didn't come easy after Salvatore, but twelve years later, Antoinette had been born.

Her mother could be described as a quiet soul. But, if you got on her bad side, she'd let you know. Honest and generous, Martha had been a content woman. Her only wish was that her son, Salvatore, would have come back home.

Her mother was *her rock*, and had been there for Antoinette, supporting her decisions, and guiding her to succeed through school, boyfriends, work, friendships, and everything else. Most importantly, she helped her with the infertility issues and treatments during those four tough years when she couldn't get pregnant but wanted to.

She remembered the time her mother said, upon the news of their engagement. "You're going to marry an Italian boy, huh? You're sure about that? Those boys have tempers." They had a good laugh. Antoinette reminded her mother that she, also, came from a line of Italians who had *hot* blood inside their veins.

As she sat in her room reliving memories of her mom, Isabella came in and visited her several times.

"Daddy sent me up to see if you need some more tissues," she said on one occasion.

Another time she came and brought a cup of tea. "Daddy said it will make you feel better."

She hugged her daughter both times for her thoughtfulness. It felt good to be taken care of. Antoinette didn't like the situation, but none-the-less, she was grateful. She imagined Vito coaching Isabella and the two of them conspiring on what to do to help her. By late afternoon, she was sitting up in bed staring out the window, when Isabella knocked on the door.

"Come in."

She came empty-handed.

"What, no goodies?"

Isabella climbed in bed with her and they cuddled. "I'm going to miss Grandma Martha."

"So will I."

"She was funny, Mommy."

"She was a little wacky, wasn't she?" Antoinette said, a smile almost appearing on her face.

"Is she in Heaven?"

"Yes, probably having a ball with God."

"Mom," Isabella asked, looking up at her mother. "Are you afraid to die?"

"A little, I guess."

"Father Robert says Jesus died and then came back again. Will Grandma come back?"

"No, honey," she said touching her daughter's chin. "This is different. Jesus was God's Son and was sent here to earth to save us from sin. Grandma is in Heaven. We'll see her again someday."

"Soon?"

"No. Not for a long, long time. You're not going to die."

"But if I did, Mommy, I wouldn't be afraid."

"Huh? Where did you get that from?"

"Get what?"

"What you just said."

Isabella shrugged. "I said I love you, Mommy."

Antoinette, about to press further, thought better of it. "I...love you, sweetheart."

A soft rapping came from the door.

"May I come in?" Vito asked, opening the door a small width.

Antoinette poked Isabella, "Hmm... Should we let Daddy join us?"

Her daughter smiled shyly, clasping her hands together. "Yeah."

Vito walked in and climbed into their bed, Isabella between them. Together they lay until dark.

***

Three nights later, Antoinette awoke drenched in sweat from a terrible dream about Devon, her stillborn son she lost at eight months pregnant when she was thirty-five years old.

In the dream he was older, maybe ten years old. He played in the backyard with Isabella. He had light brown hair and Vito's hazel eyes. Smiling, he and Isabella ran around rolling in the grass while Antoinette watched from the deck. A peace came over her, watching her children play. Devon and Isabella waved at her—brother and sister together.

Antoinette was so shaken up by the dream she couldn't sleep the rest of the night.

Maybe I should tell Isabella about her brother?

CHAPTER 38

A few nights later, Vito retreated to the den to do some work while his wife and daughter cleaned up the dinner dishes in the kitchen. The mood in the home had been somber coming off of his mother-in-law's passing. He was glad to have some work to keep him focused.

A half-hour later, Antoinette burst into the den. "Can I talk to you?"

Vito was startled from her abrupt entrance. She stood fidgeting in the doorway.

He scowled. He hated being interrupted when he was reviewing reports and studying next month's projections. "What's going on?"

"Umm…Never mind, you're busy." She turned around.

"Antoinette, stop." He watched as she dragged herself up to him. "Your face is pale. What's the matter? You hardly talked during dinner." Putting down his papers, he moved and made room on the couch for her to join him. *It must be about her mom. They were so close and shared so much.*

She slid next to him. "You're not going to believe this, but I've been dreaming about Devon."

Devon? Not her mom? He shook his head. "What was it about?"

"In the dream, Devon was older. He was so cute, Vito—I can't explain it. He was playing in the yard with Isabella. Could it be because of Mom's death? Old Italians often say sometimes during the loss of a family member, other deceased members of the family may come into their thoughts. Maybe it's nothing but it felt so real. Strange, huh?"

"Very."

"Do you ever think about him? What he'd look like or, how he'd be?"

"I used to. Honestly, I don't want to remember. It hurt too much to lose him, so I've tried to forget."

His wife glared at him. "How could you forget your *own* son?"

"Antoinette, we didn't know him. They say it's not good to remember those things. It was shocking and painful for me. Why would I think of him?"

"He was *your* child."

"Yeah?"

"Well?"

"What do you want me to say? I was never able to hold him, feed him, or do any of the things we've done with Isabella. Why are we talking about this?"

Vito fumbled with his papers, now thoroughly upset she'd brought this up.

Antoinette exhaled deeply. "I think I want to tell Isabella about him."

"*What?* Why?" This was getting ridiculous.

"Because Vito, it's important she knows about her older brother."

"She's not going to understand. She's a child."

His wife stood up and walked around the couch. "She will understand. I think she should know."

He stood, his papers discarded on the couch. "At her age? Be realistic. She just turned five. Maybe when she's twelve or thirteen. Your mother passed less than a week ago, for God's sake." What was she thinking?

"No. It has nothing to do with my mother's passing. I believe she needs to know. Now! I feel strongly about this. That's my gut feeling."

"It's always about 'feelings' with you. You're still grieving. Give it some time."

"I can't. I thought maybe you'd be on board and we could tell her together."

He waved his hands in front of him. "No. No, I'm not 'on board' with this. Nor, am I comfortable with it. I'm sorry, but it's not good to tell a small child this. It could be traumatic."

Antoinette stood with her hands on her hips. "Fine. If you don't want to tell her, I'm going to do it myself."

Vito raised up his hands. He'd had it. Every time they argued, she had to have the last word. "I can't win with you. Ever. If there's trouble with Isabella after she finds out, it's your problem. Do what you want."

"Support me on this. Please. At least I came and talked to you."

He shook his head. "No. This is a bad decision. Besides, it sounds like you already made up your mind. Why did you bother telling me at all?"

"I wanted you to know."

"Great. Thanks for the heads up." *So I can deal with it when she's confused.* "So, how are you going to tell her?" He crossed his arms, waiting.

"I'm not sure."

"You'll figure it out. I'm not getting involved. I don't agree with you on this. You're on your own."

Antoinette called after him. "Honey—"

Vito didn't stay to hear the rest of her response. He took his papers, grabbed his jacket from the hall closet, and burst out to the garage.

Once outside, he felt better. What would Isabella understand about this? It could screw things up with her. He was so angry with Antoinette. *Why did she have to bring up Devon?* He wanted that memory to be buried—the memory of seeing the birth of his lifeless child.

Vito opened his car door and grabbed a cigarette from the glove compartment and lit it. *She better not come to me with problems.*

CHAPTER 39

The next day, Antoinette picked up Isabella alone from preschool, telling Cheryl they had errands to run. When her daughter was strapped in her seat, she informed her they were going to visit Grandma Martha at the Lincoln Memorial Cemetery. From there, she planned on taking Isabella to Devon's tiny grave.

As they drove, she pondered on whether or not to tell Isabella about her brother. Last night's argument with Vito hadn't gone well—he was very upset with her for bringing it up in the first place. But something inside was urging her to tell her daughter; she needed a release from her heart.

Would all her past pains ever go away? Father Robert had told her and Vito when she was pregnant to 'let go and let be,' especially the past. What if her husband was right that by telling Isabella, this could spark other issues? She shook her head, unsure.

Against the winter cold, they both clutched their buttoned coats and scarves over their mouths. Antoinette carried two roses. They stood on lightly fallen snow next to Martha's grave surrounded by gray clouds. Antoinette laid one of the roses on the headstone.

Hi Mom. Isabella is with me. I had a dream about Devon, and I feel it's time to tell Isabella about her brother. Vito is very upset about the idea, but something is telling me to do so. Why else would I have this dream, now, after all this time? Is it you, urging me to do this? I wish you were still around so I could hear your voice. You would know best how to deal with this situation.

Isabella nudged her leg, "Mommy, what are you doing?"

"Talking to Grandma."

"But I didn't hear you."

"I talked quietly, sweetheart."

"I love her."

"Me too, kiddo."

"Mommy, you forgot to put the other rose by Grandma."

She stared at her gloved hand holding the other rose. "Yes. I do have another rose. But it's not for Grandma."

"Who is it for, Mommy?" Isabella asked, rosy cheeks peeking beneath her hood and scarf.

She grabbed Isabella's hand. "I'll show you."

They tread over the covered snow. "Remember how you asked me if you could have a brother or sister? What did I tell you?"

Isabella giggled. "You said God gave only me to you and Daddy."

"Yes. You are our special gift. But sweetie, Daddy and I had another gift before you were born. We couldn't keep it."

Isabella's eyes grew wide with curiosity. "Why, Mommy?"

Antoinette inhaled the cold air as they approached Devon's grave. She closed her eyes, remembering when they had pulled baby Devon from her. The devastation couldn't be expressed without tears. She was about to open a buried wound. *Could I do this?*

Looking over at her daughter, she began, "Isabella, you might not understand this, but you had a big brother. He couldn't stay with us; God needed him back in Heaven."

"A brother? He went away like Grandma?"

Antoinette's eyes welled up. "Yes, honey. He's with Grandma, and we buried him here in this cemetery, just like Grandma." She then pointed to his grave, near a young willow tree. On a simple concrete tombstone was etched Devon's name and date of death.

Antoinette recalled Vito had been so devastated by the loss of his son, he hadn't wanted to do anything, and had suggested cremation instead. However, she wouldn't allow it; she wanted to place her son in a cemetery. A place where she'd be able to physically visit him and place flowers at his grave from time to time. Lost in her thoughts, she wondered what Devon would have looked like. He would have been eight years old.

Isabella gazed at the grave, still holding her mother's hand. "It's nice here, Mommy. It's pretty."

Tears fell down Antoinette's face, and she wiped her eyes with the other hand. "It is pretty, yes. Your brother Devon is in Heaven with Grandma and God."

"Mommy, I hope I get to go to Heaven someday."

She bent down and pulled Isabella close to her. "Sure, kiddo." She gave the rose to Isabella, and had her lay it on her brother's grave.

They hung around a while before walking back to the car, both quiet and thoughtful.

Later, after they returned home, Isabella was her usual self. She watched her. *She probably didn't understand, like Vito had said.*

That night after dinner Isabella sat in the den coloring. Antoinette hadn't had a chance to tell Vito the day's happenings. He looked to be in an angry mood and she did her best to avoid him when he was like this. *He must be still mad at me.*

Isabella walked into the kitchen. "Mommy, Daddy, look! I drew a picture of us."

Antoinette was wiping dishes. She took the picture in her hand. "You did? Let me see."

The picture showed four stick figures. She covered her mouth, showing it to Vito, who was still sitting at the table looking over the mail.

"There's you, Mommy, and you, Daddy, brother Devon, and me," Isabella beamed, pointing out the four crayon-drawn stick figures.

Vito blinked twice, staring at Antoinette who couldn't believe it herself that Isabella had drawn a family picture of all of them.

"Very nice. What a pretty picture. Thank you," Antoinette said, her heart pounding.

"Good job, princess," Vito said slowly. "Why don't you go and draw us another picture."

"Sure, Daddy." Their daughter then exited the kitchen.

She leaned on the counter waiting for Vito to say something.

With Isabella out of earshot, he didn't waste time. "What happened today?"

She smiled. "I thought you didn't care. Now, you want to know?"

"It's kind of weird, don't you think?"

She shrugged her shoulders. "No. Our child is definitely gifted. She drew *our* family."

Vito stood up, hands on his hips. "Are you happy you told her? Got it off your chest? Let it be someone else's burden? What happens after this?"

She shook her head. "Isabella knows about her brother. She may forget tomorrow, but tonight she knows. Devon's tribute—he deserved it, Vito." Antoinette was ready to move on. One day, when the time was right, she'd tell her daughter the full story about her own miraculous birth.

"You're unbelievable," he pointed at her.

She glared at her husband. "I feel good about this. I'm going to leave things be now."

"But what did you accomplish?"

Antoinette feeling a sense of pride, said, "I can let Devon rest."

"He *has* been resting for God's sake."

"Chill out, will you. I'll take full responsibility of any issues that arise. You don't have to worry about it." But something told her Isabella could handle this.

"Perfect. I want no part of this ridiculous plan of yours." Vito stomped out of the kitchen.

"There is no plan," she called after him.

Antoinette picked up the picture again. What Isabella drew struck her heart. She grinned. Her husband should be glad their daughter was mature enough to handle something like this. Unfortunately, he was acting like a baby himself.

Come around, Vito, and see. Our child is truly something special.

CHAPTER 40

Vito climbed into his car and pulled out of the drive. He turned off of Trevor Lane and made a couple of right turns before he got on the main road—Route 64. He decided to head to the local hardware store for two 40-watt light bulbs.

He drove in silence, not even bothering to turn on sports radio. Shocked at his daughter's new understanding of their family, he wasn't sure how to handle it.

Turning into the parking lot of Sam's Hardware, he slid his car right in front of the entrance. He slipped out of the car and pushed through the glass door. Walking to the light bulb section, he perused the shelves for the correct watt size. Picking up two from the middle shelf, he turned then abruptly stopped.

Coming up the aisle, a father and son strolled together. They were laughing and pushing each other around. The boy, fair with red hair resembled his lanky father.

Vito moved out of the way as they passed. He stared after them. It could have been him and his boy if he hadn't died—a son to carry on his Libero name.

Memories of the day when Antoinette lost the baby flooded his mind. She had been in a lot of pain; her contractions had started a month earlier. Dr. Langford had recommended they go to the hospital and she cried all the way there.

When they pulled the baby out, he was already dead. He had light blondish, thick hair and a small perfect body. All his limbs intact.

Seeing the father and son made Vito's stomach churn. Why did she have to resurrect what could have been with Devon?

He shook his head and began walking to the cash registers. Then, thinking of Isabella's handicap only spurred on the acid in his stomach. She was his *only* family. *That damn prosthetic leg too. Forget it, Vito.* He felt ashamed for having those thoughts about his child.

He reached the cashier, paid for his light bulbs and lumbered out. *I'm not going to think about this anymore.* He prayed Isabella forgot about the picture she drew so he wouldn't be reminded of his previous loss.

CHAPTER 41

The trees were bare, the air was cold, and the land was in a dormant state. This year the Liberos put on their best face and attempted to celebrate Christmas with both sides of the family, especially with Frank, who was still struggling with his wife's sudden death.

The decorations were a little scarce when compared to the previous years, but they made do, for Isabella. As much as Antoinette tried to avoid talking about her mom in front of her dad, she found it difficult. The holidays always revolved around Martha. The Italian pastries she made, the twelve course fish dinner she prepared on Christmas Eve, and the little gift bags she gave each of them. Everything about Christmas was made beautiful by her mother. The realization of their loss sunk in more deeply.

Antoinette knew Isabella also missed her Grandma Martha. Her daughter had looked forward to receiving a surprise gift from her grandmother every Christmas, but since her death, Isabella told her mother she didn't care about presents anymore. Her new focus was the porcelain nativity-set figurines her other grandparents, Rosa and Leonard, had given her when she was a toddler. She had become so transfixed on the figurines and how it related to the Christmas season that one day while Antoinette was putting away the groceries, Isabella caught her mother by surprise with a request.

"Mommy? Can I—"

"Hold on. Let me finish," Antoinette replied, organizing her vegetables in the drawer of the refrigerator. She stood up. "Okay. What's up?"

Her daughter was holding the figurines in her arms. "Can I move these nativity figurines to my room?"

Antoinette crouched down, grabbing the figurines from her hands. "Isabella! These are porcelain and could break. Do you know how much they cost? No." She stood up extending the figurines back to her daughter. "Can you please put them back under the tree where they belong?"

Her daughter shook her head, arms folded across her chest.

"Why not?"

The little girl began to sniffle. "Because I want them in my room. I love them, Mommy."

Antoinette sighed. She felt badly for raising her voice at her child. "I'm sorry, honey. I didn't know how much you liked them." She put the figurines on the counter. “I’ll tell you what. There’s a small round table down in the basement. I’ll go get it. Then, we’ll go upstairs and place the nativity set figurines on it. Sound good?”

Her daughter’s face lit up and she smiled. “Thank you, Mommy.”

From that day on, Isabella began spending a lot of time in her room with the figurines.

***

When Christmas Eve arrived, Antoinette did her best to have a festive dinner, but her heart was dark and sad like the rest of the family. So, rather than platters of raw fish, she served cocktail shrimp she picked up at the local grocer; and instead of surf and turf, she made baked chicken breasts with green beans. For dessert, she served homemade cupcakes courtesy of Cheryl and Lizzy. Her re-creation of her mother’s holiday cooking could never measure up, but her dad, husband, and daughter appreciated her efforts.

On Christmas Day, the Liberos went to Vito’s parents, who for the first time in years decided not to go to North Carolina but rather spend the day with their son and family. Vito was glad, and had been relaxing more around his father. Antoinette observed they made more than small talk at the table now, talking about sports and his work. At one point after dinner, she noticed they had disappeared together. When she questioned her mother-in-law, she winked and said she saw them go out to the garage.

When father and son returned from outside, Antoinette noticed a smiling Vito. She smiled back, comforted that her husband had mended their estranged relationship. Maybe, she thought, her husband had finally forgiven his father.

CHAPTER 42

January, 2006.

It was a brand new year. A year of new things for Antoinette's father. He was getting lonely in his house all by himself. She wondered if he was ready to sell it and move into a retirement community. Her father could have friends to keep him company and he wouldn't have to worry about the upkeep of a home—the house she grew up in, and that her parents had shared for forty-five years. Vito thought it was a good idea.

When Antoinette mentioned to Frank about a retirement community, he said very little. Her father was not much of a talker, but he couldn't hide the physical toll the sadness and depression of losing his wife was taking on him. Only 5'10," Frank was getting bony; hardly eating and sleeping a lot.

They had to do something. So, she and Vito began researching independent living communities. After much searching, they found one in Naperville called Spring Meadow Community and made an appointment.

On the drive over one morning to pick up her grandpa, Isabella asked, "Mommy, can Grandpa stay with us?"

"How generous and loving of you, sweetie, but I think Grandpa wants his own place," Antoinette replied, looking over her shoulder at her daughter who was sitting on her booster in the back seat.

"Are we going to move from here?"

"Do you want to move?"

"No."

Vito glimpsed in the rearview mirror, "Then, why are you asking?"

"I like where we live."

"I do too. But maybe one day we might move and get a bigger house." She answered, looking over at Vito.

"You and Daddy have to live there forever," Isabella stated firmly.

She laughed, "I hope not."

Vito nudged her, "I'll buy you a mansion, Isabella. You want a mansion?"

"No. Our house is where I want to be. Always."

"Okay, if you say so," Antoinette laughed.

After picking up Frank, they arrived at the Spring Meadow Community business office and were greeted by Paul Cisco, director of recruitment for active adults. A thin, wiry-looking man wearing a tight-fitting maroon-colored suit.

They were standing in the sales center entryway—an exquisitely decorated building. Five glass offices lay ahead of them with fully furnished mahogany desks. Antoinette made out a couple of sales people or "home agents".

"Good morning," Mr. Cisco announced skipping to Antoinette and Vito. Then, extending his hand to Frank, he said, "You must be Mr. DeSalvo."

"Good morning, Mr. Cisco," they said in unison.

"Please, call me Paul," he corrected.

Then, kneeling down, he greeted Isabella, "Who is this pretty little girl? What's your name?"

"Isabella."

"Oh my, Isabella, what a beautiful name," the man grinned at her. "Will you be moving in with your granddaddy and keeping him company?"

Frank muttered, "I don't know if I like the place and you're already convinced I'm moving in."

"Dad," Antoinette said, eyeing him.

"Why, no, sir," Paul said, standing up. "Let's check it out, Mr. DeSalvo, so you can see for yourself."

Her father nodded.

They exited the office into the chilly air. Turning right onto the walkway, they noticed how carefully the sidewalk had been shoveled and salted. The walkway led to a condo building, which was marked number one.

Paul stopped before the front door and said, "This is the first unit, it was completed this past November. There are four floors, each with ten condos per floor."

Rectangular in shape, the exterior was all brick; a dark red color. From the outside, they could see each second, third, and fourth-floor condos had their own balconies, while the first-floor condos had concrete patios.

"How many of these condo units are you planning to build?" Vito asked, as they moved forward and made their way into the building.

"There will be four units in all, or four buildings: one-hundred and sixty condos," Paul said. Then, pointing to a mass of excavated land outside, he continued, "There, we are going to have a community center in the middle of this development. The four buildings will encircle the community center. We'll have a cafeteria serving buffet-style breakfast and lunch. There will also be a recreation room with a built-in theater, a workout room, and an indoor swimming pool." Then, pointing to the left of the community center, Paul finished, "There will be an outdoor pool over there."

They entered the building. The foyer had French design written all over it. From the ornate gold last name directory, to the flowery patterned sofas.

"Will all the units have the same foyer design," Antoinette asked, taking in the rich decorations.

Paul stood proudly. "Why yes. We believe in consistency."

Antoinette shook her head. "Oh, okay." *This is ugly.* She observed her father and husband whispering in what looked like disapproval, as they circled the area.

"Paul, are all these units sold in this building?" Vito asked.

"Yes, they are. We are currently in the second phase of development, which is the second unit. The condos all come with a kitchenette, two bedrooms, combined living and dining area, and one-and-a-half baths." He walked up to the elevator and pushed the third floor button. "Let me show you our model."

As the elevator ascended, Isabella counted, "1…2…3."

"Good girl," Antoinette said, smoothing down her blond curls.

The elevator bell beeped and they exited. "We have stairs on either side of the floor for those inclined to walking up and down," Paul said, winking at Frank.

They wandered down the corridor and stopped at room 309. Paul pulled out a master key ring and inserted a key into the keyhole. One-by-one, they filed in.

The room smelled like freshly applied paint. A short corridor carpeted with a light beige rug greeted them. They passed a half-bath to the right. Then, to the left, the kitchen. A silver refrigerator and oak cabinets complimented the area. Next to the stainless-steel sink was a silver and black stove. Across from the kitchen, separated by a countertop, was a dining/living area.

As they meandered around in the kitchen and moved into the living area, Paul said, "All appliances are included. As you can see, we've included stools so you can use the countertops as part of your dining area."

"Hmm…" her Dad replied.

Straight across the area, a sliding door opened up to the balcony. Isabella ran and peeked through the window. "Mommy, Grandpa, come and look."

Frank removed a three-foot bar from the crevice of the screen and turned the knob to unlock the door. Sliding open the door, he peered out onto the balcony. Ice and snow covered the concrete. "Looks nice," he said to Paul.

The man strutted up behind Frank. "All the balconies have concrete flooring, like the patios. We have an inner facing and outer facing view. This side of the building is the inner side. It will face the community center when it's finished. The other side, or the outer facing view condos, faces a garden. It's the same for all the units. I do need to mention there is a cost difference between the inner and outer sides."

"Of course," her father grunted.

They walked into a spacious nine-foot ceiling master bedroom with a sitting area. It was across from the dining/living area. Vito came up next to Antoinette, "I like this condo." A bathroom connected to the second bedroom, but it was much smaller than the master bedroom.

Isabella pulled on Antoinette's leg. "I can sleep here with Grandpa when I visit."

Antoinette laughed, "Only if Grandpa will have you."

Frank blew a kiss at his granddaughter. "Sure you can, princess. I'd love to have you over."

Isabella twirled in delight.

They circled the condo a couple more times. Antoinette watched her dad. A sadness surrounded him; an apprehension of a new life he'd be entering, one without her mother. When he caught Antoinette staring from across the room, he gave her a half smile.

"How many condos are left in the second unit?" Frank asked.

"About ten, and they're going fast."

They exited the building and strolled back to the sales center where Paul gave her father additional brochures to look over.

"Thanks, we'll let you know."

On the drive back, Antoinette's dad was quiet. In the backseat, Isabella chatted to him about panda bears, Barbie dolls, and everything else. Suddenly out of the blue she said, "Grandpa, move there. Grandma likes it."

Antoinette turned in time to see Frank's eyes well up, startled by Isabella's comment. He touched Isabella's hand, lightly, sounding choked up, he responded, "You think Grandma would like this?"

"Yes," Isabella said.

"Hmm... It's a done deal then," Frank remarked. "Antoinette, Vito, did you hear me? I'm going to get myself a new home."

Surprised, Antoinette couldn't believe her father's quick decision. She spun around at her husband, who wore a shocked expression.

"Okay, Dad, we'll take care of the details for you," Vito said.

After dropping Frank off, they returned home, and Isabella excused herself to go up to her room.

She and Vito stood in the kitchen, staring at the coffee maker as it was brewing.

"Do you think Isabella has special powers?" she asked breaking the silence.

Vito laughed, "What do you mean by 'special powers'?"

"Can't you see?"

"What are you talking about?"

"I'm not sure. The day of Mom's funeral she said she wasn't afraid of dying, and how I shouldn't be either. She liked the cemetery when we visited it, saying it was nice there. You don't find it weird, coming from a five year old? Who likes cemeteries? Now she's convinced my dad to move to the retirement community because Grandma 'likes it'. As if she's talked to her. He's never made such hasty decisions before. I don't get it."

"I think you're overreacting. The condo is great for your dad. You heard the guy, they're going fast."

Antoinette nodded. The coffee maker beeped. Grabbing the pot, she poured coffee into two mugs. Handing one to her husband, she said, "Something's off."

"You're weird," he said with a smile.

She took a sip of her coffee listening for a sound. Then, she put her mug down on the counter. "I'm going to go and see what she's doing up there. It's way too quiet."

"Suit yourself," Vito shrugged.

Climbing the stairs, Antoinette heard Isabella giggling behind her closed bedroom door.

She rapped softly, gently opening the door, "Isabella.

Isabella stood in front of her nativity set rearranging the figurines.

"Who were you talking to?" she asked, walking in.

Her daughter turned. "Baby Jesus."

"Baby Jesus?"

"See?" Isabella said, pulling out the baby figurine from his manger.

"Oh," Antoinette hesitated before asking her next question. "What are you talking about?"

"That Grandpa will be happy in his new home."

She crouched down beside Isabella, checking her forehead. "Are you sick?"

"No, Mommy," she said, putting her arms around her neck.

She pulled away, holding her daughter at arm's length. "Are you sure you're all right."

Isabella nodded. "Hmm...mmm."

Antoinette looked closely at her child, who just admitted to talking to a baby Jesus figurine. "You know, honey, it's okay to talk to the figurines as well as pretend they talk back. Just as long as you know it's pretend."

Isabella smiled. "Okay. Can I play now?"

She rose, not feeling confident her daughter understood what she had said to her. "Sure, you can play."

But as she watched Isabella go back to playing with the figurines, her gut was telling her this wasn't pretend at all.

CHAPTER 43

May

It was Wednesday afternoon, after preschool. Antoinette sprinted down the drive to get the mail. Today, the air was warm. Spring was here with a promise of summer not far ahead.

Sporting a pink V-neck t-shirt and jean capris, she walked into the house, put all the mail on the kitchen table, and pulled out the telephone bill.

Isabella shuffled through the other letters. "Mommy, Mommy, look. Is this from Dr. Maxwell?"

Antoinette squinted and grabbed the envelope. "How do you know it's from Dr. Maxwell's office?"

Isabella pointed. "It has a funny picture on the envelope, same as on their door."

The 'funny picture' was the doctor's emblem—a circle with two stick figures holding hands. "Wow, you're a pretty observant girl." She put down the telephone bill. "Let me see what it says."

Isabella jumped up and down at her side. "What does it say, Mommy? Tell me."

"Hold on a minute. Let me open it first."

In the envelope was an invitation from Holy Name Hospitals for Children to attend a picnic for kids with limb deficiencies: congenital and amputee. It was signed by the medical staff.

Antoinette was conflicted. It sounded like a great idea to have these children mingle and get to know one another. But, wasn't the hospital also isolating the kids by having a picnic for them only?

"Mommy, what does it say?" her daughter insisted, pulling at her mother's shirt.

Antoinette snapped out of her daze. "Ah, it's nothing," she quickly slipping the invitation back into the envelope.

"No it's not," Isabella protested. "You're lying, Mommy."

"Sweetheart…"

"Tell me," Isabella huffed, turning away.

Maybe she was overreacting. When they went to get her prosthetic fitted, or for follow up visits, they had seen many kids with missing limbs. Why was this any different? Antoinette shook her head. She picked up Isabella and sat her up on the table.

"It's an invitation to a picnic at the hospital."

"A picnic!" Her daughter clapped her hands. "I like picnics."

"I know you do," Antoinette replied, rubbing her shoulders. "But, this is a different kind of picnic."

"Why?"

"Well," she said, taking a deep breath. "The families who are invited are ones whose children don't have all of their limbs, like arms, and legs. Like you." She then waited, holding her breath for Isabella's reaction.

"It's okay, Mommy. God loves every boy and girl. That's what Father Robert says."

Antoinette grinned, embarrassed. *She got me there.*

"When is it?"

"Not for another three weeks."

"Can we go?"

"Let's ask—why not?" she said, throwing up her arms in the air. A light feeling washed over her. *What do we have to lose?* Smiling at Isabella, she said, "We'll tell Daddy we have a picnic to go to when he gets home from work."

Throwing her arms around her mother's neck, Isabella gave Antoinette a warm hug. "I love you, Mommy."

"I love you even more."

CHAPTER 44

June

It was a breezy Sunday afternoon with a cloudless sky. Perfect for a picnic. Antoinette only hoped the day would be perfect for her daughter.

Normally a forty-minute ride to Holy Name Hospitals for Children, it took her and Vito extra time as traffic on the highway was surprisingly heavy.

"Are we there yet?" Isabella whined, fidgeting underneath her seat belt in the backseat.

"Pretty soon," Vito said. "Gosh, I forgot there was a Cubs game this afternoon. We should have left earlier."

Antoinette scanned the invitation. "It says here, noon to four, but it doesn't necessarily mean we have to be there right at noon."

"I like to be on time," her husband replied, eyes focused ahead.

"Me, too," chimed their daughter.

"Not me," Antoinette said.

"We know," Vito smirked. "Queen of lateness."

The Liberos pulled into the driveway of the hospital parking lot, and found a spot in the back. The property was surrounded by a black iron fence—both the entrance and exit had gates which locked after a certain time.

Balloons were posted at various areas of the lot. A large banner hung across the front of the building: *Welcome to the First Annual HEART Event.* HEART was an acronym for *Hope*, *Encouragement*, *Aim*, *Resource and Training* for limb-deficient children.

Antoinette and Vito strolled hand-in-hand with Isabella through the main entrance of the hospital. A security guard directed them to the stairs leading through the indoor playground out to the picnic area. Then, staff members greeted them as they signed in and received name tags.

"Isabella! Isabella!" someone shouted.

The Liberos turned and saw Cindy Blake, one of the nurses who had taken care of Isabella weaving through the crowd. Cindy had been with Holy Name Hospitals for Children for nineteen years. Her son, Jacob, also born with a congenital limb deficiency, was missing his entire left arm. At thirteen, Jacob pitched for one of the local elementary school baseball teams. It was an amazing feat, but their nurse admitted that with the care received from the hospital and the experience she gained from working there, her son had excelled in many activities otherwise impossible.

Her daughter turned at the sound of her name. She screeched in recognition of her nurse, and ran to Cindy who scooped up Isabella, twirling her around.

"How's my angel?" Cindy said, planting a big kiss on her cheek.

Isabella squealed with delight and snuggled in Cindy's arms. "Good."

"How are you? Antoinette, Vito? Glad you could make it."

"We're doing great, Cindy," Antoinette said. "Thanks for having us."

"Sure. It's our pleasure."

"Is Dr. Maxwell around today?" Antoinette asked.

Cindy sighed. "No. Unfortunately, he was called in to do an emergency operation this morning. He won't be making it. Sorry."

Vito said, "That's too bad. We wanted to see him without his white coat and stethoscope."

"Yeah," Isabella said, showing her disappointment.

Turning to the little girl, Cindy caressed her chin, "I know. It would have been nice, but Dr. Maxwell is doing a great thing helping another child."

Isabella nodded.

"In the meantime, we have a lot of fun things for you!" She started counting on her hand. "We have a drawing table, a T-shirt tie-dye table, a clown show, a hoola-hoop contest, raffles and, of course, hotdogs and hamburgers, over there." She pointed to the right side of the building.

Vito rubbed his hands together. "Mmm…that's where I'm going."

"Excellent," exclaimed Cindy, putting Isabella down. "There's plenty to do and eat, and, there are tons of kids to meet. Enjoy."

"Great, thanks Cindy," Antoinette said. "See ya' later."

They all waved as Cindy hurried away to her next duty.

"What do you guys want to do?"

"Eat!" Vito responded.

"Play!" Isabella said.

Antoinette laughed. "Here's the plan. Vito, you find us a table and eat. We'll catch up in a little bit. Isabella and I are going to do some drawings, tie-dye our shirts, and then we'll get something to eat. Sounds like a plan, baby girl?"

"Yes," her daughter jumped up and down.

As Antoinette moved through the tables with Isabella, she took special notice of the children. There were children missing one or both of their arms, or had partial growth. Children with missing fingers, or who only had a few fingers on each hand. Still, others in wheelchairs because they didn't have both their legs. Many kids, like Isabella, were wearing prosthetic limbs—arms or legs. Despite missing parts of their flesh and bones, these little angels were full of laughter and spirit.

She and Isabella took seats at the drawing table and received two large cardboard sheets. The volunteers explained they could draw whatever came to mind. Thinking for a moment, Antoinette decided to draw a simple house with a garden. When finished, she sat back and watched her child carefully and methodically color her picture.

"What are you drawing?"

"Heaven," Isabella answered proudly.

"Wow, honey. Heaven looks very pretty. Are those clouds and an ocean?"

"Yes."

"Why are there so many clouds by the ocean?"

"Because God likes to float on clouds and go swimming in the water."

"Very interesting, sweetheart."

"You like it, Mommy?"

"I do."

They signed their names on the cardboard sheets and handed them in, then moved to the tie-dye shirt area where Antoinette and Isabella created brightly-colored masterpieces.

Once they had finished, they grabbed lunch and met up with Vito who was sitting with a tall man sporting a thick black mustache twisted up at the ends.

"He's funny looking," Isabella whispered as they made their way toward them.

Beside the man sat a little boy about Isabella's age with both arms only extending to his elbows. On his left arm, he had a full-size hand grown onto the residual limb of his elbow. He was eating a hotdog with that one hand.

"Hi there," her husband greeted them. Turning to the man, Vito said, "Tom, this is my wife, Antoinette, and our daughter, Isabella."

Tom nodded at them. In a deep, radio-like voice, he said, "Good afternoon. This is Tommy Jr., my son."

Isabella quietly sat down and stared at Tommy. He had dark black hair and light brown eyes. His face was flushed.

Antoinette nudged Isabella, gently giving her the "that's rude" look.

As the adults made small talk, Antoinette kept her eye on the kids as they ate.

Pointing, Isabella asked, "Does your hand hurt there?"

"No," Tommy responded. He then pointed with his other elbow toward her prosthesis. "Does your leg hurt being in that thing?"

"No. Sometimes it gets too tight and we have to make it bigger."

"Do you have any friends?"

"Lots of them," Isabella happily said. "Do you go to school?"

"Yes. But I don't have a lot of friends. Some moms don't let their kids play with me."

"Why?"

"Because of my arms."

Antoinette, upon hearing this, wasn't sure how Isabella was going to respond. She decided to keep quiet and watch to see what happened.

"I'll be your friend."

Good girl.

"You want to be *my* friend?"

"Sure, why not? My dad said I can choose whoever I want to be my friends."

"Okay."

"You want to draw? I drew a picture of Heaven."

"Yeah."

Turning to her mother, Isabella asked, "Mommy, can we go to the drawing table?"

"Only if his father..." Antoinette pointed to Tommy, Sr., "will allow it."

Tommy Sr. picked at his moustache for a moment. "That's fine, but stay in our view."

"Thanks, Daddy!" Tommy exclaimed, climbing down from his chair.

The children ran to the drawing table, and Antoinette watched them as they played. Isabella guided Tommy as he placed his hand on the paper and she traced his fingers. They were fast friends.

As the day progressed, she and Vito met other parents and exchanged stories about their children. So many incredible experiences shared; from one mother's agonizing decision to amputate her one year old daughter's congenitally deformed leg, to a couple whose family disowned them because their son was born handless. Heart-tugging tales that families with normal children couldn't possibly understand. From Isabella's perspective, God loved all children. Antoinette wished everyone could see things that way.

She and her husband each grabbed a Popsicle, sat down in the grass, and watched their daughter hoola-hoop with Tommy.

"I'm glad we came," Antoinette announced.

"Me too," Vito said.

"I must confess, at first, I thought this wasn't a good idea because it was isolating children who have limb deficiencies. And I know we've been trying to raise her as 'normally' as we can. I realize now how good this is for Isabella and us."

"Yeah. There is a sense of community here."

"Our little miracle is truly beautiful, inside and out. I wouldn't know what to do if something ever happened to her," Antoinette said, as her eyes watered. A sense of uncertainty coming over her.

Vito touched her arm. "What's with the negative comment?"

She ran a hand over her forehead. "Sometimes I get the sense we've been too lucky."

"Stop. Don't jinx us. And for your information, we've haven't been so lucky. We've had our share of pains, too, remember?"

"I'm sorry. I can't help it. It's overwhelming, seeing all these children. I must be getting sentimental at my age." Antoinette continued watching her daughter play with the other kids. *My baby looks so happy.*

Isabella wanted to stay the entire time, and so they did. As they were leaving, their little girl noticed a garden area besides the doorway. Dozens of beautiful red roses covered a patch of dirt. Her eyes sparkled with curiosity as they walked to them.

"Mommy, these flowers are so pretty," Isabella said, bending down to touch them.

"Isabella, don't touch the stems," Antoinette cautioned. "There are thorns on them, and they could prick your fingers."

Her daughter jolted upright and stared at the roses. Antoinette and Vito bent down on either side of her.

"I like them, Mommy."

"They're roses, Isabella," Vito said.

"Can we have a garden, Daddy?"

"You want a garden now?"

"Yes, Daddy. A rose garden. Jesus likes roses. Please, please, Daddy?" she pleaded.

Her husband scratched his head. "Hmm, I'm sure He does. He made everything. But I don't know where to start. I don't even know how to build a rose garden. We'll have to do some research. Can you help me?"

"Yes, Daddy," Isabella screeched.

Antoinette stood up. "You're so easy."

Vito gave her a told-you-so look. "Something about a pretty little girl I can't resist."

CHAPTER 45

September. First day of Kindergarten.

Antoinette felt herself being shaken by little hands.

"Mommy, Mommy, get up."

"Huh?" Awaking out of a deep sleep, she adjusted her eyes to the light in the bedroom.

"Get up. We're going to be late for school!"

"School? My God!" Antoinette abruptly sat up in bed. "Why didn't anyone wake me sooner?"

"Daddy said you'd get up."

Antoinette rubbed her eyes. "Where *is* Daddy?"

"He said he had to leave early."

"Sh—" Antoinette covered her mouth.

Isabella giggled. "Mommy, don't say a bad word."

She laughed. "I know. Move over. I have to get dressed."

As she scooted Isabella off the bed, and pulled herself onto the carpeted floor, Antoinette glanced at her daughter's outfit. She looked pretty in her red-and-brown pleated skirt and matching cardigan. On her way to the bathroom, she checked the clock: 8:15.

Oh no! Isabella needed to be at school by eight-forty-five. "Did you eat yet?"

"Yeah," she responded, lying back on the bed. "Dad made me toast and a bowl of Cheerios."

"You had all this time and you guys didn't wake me up?"

"You needed your rest, Mommy. Jesus said you would need it."

Antoinette smiled at Isabella's thoughtfulness, unsure what to make about her Jesus comment. In the meantime, she hurried between the closet and bathroom with two outfits in hand—a gray pant suit, and the other a navy pant suit.

She had gotten a part-time job as a teacher's assistant at McKinnley Elementary School for Mrs. Pam Johnson, a second grade teacher, three days a week. The time had come when she was itching to go back into the classroom. She had approached Vito on the "working" subject regarding the opportunity. He hadn't been on board when she offered during the time he was struggling with his job and had been put on probation. But five years had passed, his job was stable and thriving, and to her pleasant amazement, he supported her decision. He knew teaching was in her blood, and agreed it would be great for her to get out of the house. Since Isabella was going to be in Kindergarten at the same school, Antoinette could meet her when she got out at two-forty-five, and they wouldn't have to rely on babysitters for afterschool care either because of her hours.

Teaching high school as she had done before was her first love, but for the moment, she was ready to try a new challenge—grade school children. Mrs. Johnson assured her that they were no different than older kids; their attention spans were just a lot shorter.

Holding both outfits, she asked her daughter, "So, which one should *I* wear for my first day on the job?"

"Um…that one," Isabella said, pointing to the gray suit.

"Hmm… The gray it is."

"Dad and I ate on the deck."

"You did? Is it nice out?"

"Yes, Mommy."

In the bathroom Antoinette washed her face, threw on day cream, and started applying eyeliner and mascara. Isabella followed her in.

"So, why wasn't I invited?"

Her daughter shrugged. "You were sleeping, Mommy."

"Thanks. But, I would have liked to have had breakfast with you two." She tousled her hair.

A twinge of jealousy ran down her spine. This was Isabella's first day in kindergarten, and *her* first day back at school. They could have spent family time together. She shook off the thought as she put on her camisole and pulled up her pants. When Antoinette rechecked herself in the mirror, she noticed her eyes were puffy. *How did I oversleep?* Good thing she had showered last night. Her hair was still decent.

Back in the bedroom she finished dressing. She put on her wedding band, "Are you ready?"

Isabella jumped off the bed. "Mommy, aren't you going to eat?"

Hooking in gold hoop earrings and slipping on a pair of flats, Antoinette said, "I'm okay. We don't have time."

She felt unprepared, and was angry with herself for over-sleeping.

"No, Mommy. It's seven—two—nine—see?" Her daughter pointed to the alarm clock.

Antoinette did a double-take. It was 7:29, not 8:29. She slumped on the bed. How did she not notice the real time? She ran a hand down her face. Was she losing her eye sight?

"Why didn't you say anything?"

Isabella whispered, "You were mad."

She pulled her close, double-checking her prosthesis. "No, honey. I'm not mad, just in a hurry."

"Oh."

Shaking her head, Antoinette said, "I think my eyes played a funny trick on me. I really thought it was later." She touched her daughter's nose. "I probably should have some breakfast. What do you think?"

Isabella giggled.

In the kitchen, Antoinette made a cup of coffee and a bowl of cereal for herself, while Isabella had another glass of juice.

The anxiety about the day ahead remained in her mind. How will these kids be? *I need to make sure to provide the best assistance to Mrs. Johnson. Gosh, I feel so out of sync. It's been years since I've been in a classroom. I sure hope Isabella has a good day.*

Antoinette's mind was still in flutter-mode as she drove all the way to school. She was able to walk Isabella to her classroom and then head down the hall to her own class, where she heard a lot of loud voices coming from inside. *Here goes...*

***

As Antoinette expected, the day proved to be hectic with twenty second-graders in the class. Pam Johnson, the woman she assisted, handled all of them like a pro. In her sixties, Pam still had the spunk of a thirty year old. The kids adored her. Thin with short dark hair, the teacher had a funny quirk of pacing back-and-forth in front of the room while talking.

During recess, Antoinette asked her why she paced.

Pam laughed. "Two reasons. First, I can keep an eye on them from both sides of the room, and secondly, when you're dealing with second-graders who have *no* attention span; you better move around and be entertaining."

Antoinette completely understood. She remembered when she was teaching high school sophomores; she had to step up her so-called "classroom performance" because she could tell from the front of the room her kids' attention spans were waning. These days, kids had so many distractions, and second-graders were no exception.

By the time the bell rang for dismissal, Antoinette's brain was like jelly. Teenagers were nothing compared to this bunch. It would take some getting used to teaching younger children. There was a raw innocence to them that older children grew away from, but she was hopeful. Here was her chance to mold and shape a child with education. She left feeling encouraged, looking forward to her next day at school.

Meeting up with Isabella outside her Kindergarten classroom, she noticed her daughter was in a great mood as well, beaming from ear to ear.

"Hi, kiddo," Antoinette said hugging her. "How was it today?"

Isabella couldn't hold her excitement, she was bursting with stories. "Mom, it was great. Lizzy is in my class and I have so many friends. I love it."

She smiled. "Good. I'm so happy for you. Nice job."

Hand in hand, mother and daughter paraded out of the school. Isabella raved about her experience, and she, reveling in the joy of motherhood. Considering how the day had started, it was nice to know it all worked out.

CHAPTER 46

"I hate it, Vito. The best day was the *first* day," Antoinette said, rinsing romaine lettuce in the sink.

"Give it a chance. It's the first week," Vito consoled between reading the paper and listening to her. "You've also been out of the classroom for some time." *Maybe*, he wondered, *she shouldn't have returned to teaching so soon; she's pretty flustered over a bunch of kids.*

"They're maniacs! They put glue on my chair; they made farting noises as I walked by. It's humiliating."

He belted out a laugh, and handed her a glass of wine. "What did you expect from a bunch of eight year old second graders; college graduates?"

"No. For starters, better manners would be nice," she said, taking a sip. "Don't their parents teach them anything?" Antoinette lowered her voice, "I would never allow that kind of lack of manners from Isabella. Never."

Vito leaned up over the counter, staring intently at his wife. Her hair was flat and her skin looked ashen under the kitchen fluorescent lighting. "Yes, but, we can't compare anyone to Isabella; she's a twenty-five year old in our almost six year old body. Relax, will ya'?"

Antoinette handed him the salad bowl. "I don't know. I'll see what happens next week." Putting the wine bottle on the table, she yelled out, "Isabella, come down for dinner."

Vito turned his wife toward him. She needed some further support. "If you don't like it, then stop. But, I know how you've wanted to get out and do something. Whatever you do, you have my blessing, okay?"

She kissed him lightly on the cheek. "Thank you. It means the world to me. I'll see how it goes. I don't want to give up. Pam is a sweet lady. I'd hate to leave her without anyone, either."

He smiled at her. "It will get better. I know you're not a quitter."

Just then, Isabella came down from her room and sat down at the table. Vito noticed her eyes red and swollen.

"Honey, what's the matter?"

"I had a fight."

"With who?"

"Jesus."

Vito sat back and shot a glance at Antoinette as she passed a plate of pasta to him.

"Isabella, you have to stop this imaginary friend thing you've been doing," she said.

"Jesus is real, Mommy," Isabella shouted. "He's real! You've even said so."

"I'm sorry, I know He's real. It is why we go to church to worship Him."

"He made me mad," Isabella said, pounding her fist on the table.

Vito put down his fork and gawked at her. He'd never seen this reaction from his daughter. *What was going on?* On several occasions, his wife mentioned odd behavior from their daughter from the time she moved the nativity figurines to her room. One such oddity was overhearing her talk to the baby Jesus figurine as if she were talking to a person. He had shrugged it off as her being a kid with a creative imagination. This sounded different. She was serious.

"Hey, we don't slam fists on the table. Do you understand?" he scolded.

Isabella put her head down. "Yes, Daddy. I'm sorry."

He recalled other things Antoinette told him. He knew his wife was concerned. This Jesus talking started after his mother-in-law passed away almost a year ago. Isabella had been acting weird and saying all sorts of strange things regarding Jesus, death, and Heaven.

"Isabella," Antoinette said, touching her hand across the table. "What happened?"

Sinking lower in her chair and looking from one parent to the other, Isabella asked, "Why do I only have one leg?"

"Isabella, you don't have one leg," Vito said calmly. "You're missing a part of one of your legs. There is nothing wrong with you."

Deep down inside, he had this inkling Isabella might bring this up again. First, preschool with his wife, and now Kindergarten. He stared at his wife, not sure what to do.

"Jesus told me there's a reason for me being like this."

"You spoke with Jesus? He actually talked to you?" Antoinette asked.

"Yes, Mommy. Why don't you ever believe me?"

"It's not like I don't—"

Vito interjected, putting his hand up to Antoinette, and then looking at his daughter, "Did He tell you why?"

"No."

He continued, "Isabella, did someone pick on you at school today? Tell me the truth, now."

"No."

Agitated, Vito said, "Then what is the matter? I don't understand."

His wife touched his shoulder as if to tell him to take it easy.

"I'm not like everyone else, am I?"

Antoinette jumped in, "You are special. Special to me and your father."

"That's what Jesus told me. But I don't want to be special," she stammered. "I want to be like everyone else."

"How boring, Isabella," Vito raised his voice. "Go ahead and be like everyone else and never do anything different. Being the same will never get you anywhere."

His daughter seemed confused.

"Isabella," Antoinette said. "You didn't do anything wrong to be born this way. It just happened." Pointing to her leg, she continued, "You know the mole I have on my left foot? The one you say looks like a chocolate chip? This is the way I was born. So, it looks like I have a speck of dirt on my foot all the time. Big deal. It is something special about me. The leg of yours is unique and special about you. Don't forget that."

Yes. Vito agreed. "If someone has a problem with you about that," he said, slapping his chest, "then they can take it up with me."

"Jesus said I was special," his daughter repeated. "When I asked if I could have my other leg whole, he told me it's not what God wanted for me."

Frightful of the answer, Vito asked, "Do you believe Him?"

"Yes."

He grabbed the salad bowl from the other side of the table. "Sweetheart, how about some salad?"

He gave his wife a "we'll talk later" look. He now believed what Antoinette had been telling him all along.

CHAPTER 47

Somehow drastic measures had to be taken. Their daughter was saintly, or extremely intuitive. Vito wasn't comfortable about either option. Antoinette had suggested sharing the situation with Father Robert O'Malley.

At first, he resisted, reluctant they'd have to attend a session with the pastor. But who else could they talk to? Maybe some divine intervention *was* needed. So, Vito had volunteered to call the parish. Antoinette had a lot on her plate with school these days, and his job was settling into a nice manageable routine.

When he called the parish, the church secretary, Renee, informed him Father Robert was in Rome at a conference. She kidded him, being a parishioner, about not reading the parish bulletin regarding the priest's absence. Vito laughed it off over the phone with the secretary, but he was feeling guilty. He and Antoinette were slipping back into their old habit of not attending church. They had frequented it for a time, he going more than he ever had before. However, lately, it was a different story, as things had gotten hectic at home. Sunday was the only day to do family things, so they had stopped attending services altogether. Most of their Sundays were now filled with visiting Frank at the retirement community, who had moved in a few months ago, or getting together with his parents. It was no excuse, but after an exhausting week at work, the last thing he wanted to do was go to church and disrupt their family time. He knew church was very important in creating a spiritual foundation for Isabella, but some days it felt like a chore.

Family time. Vito surprised himself thinking about it that way. He enjoyed spending time with his daughter and Antoinette. His marriage was in a comfortable state. He and his wife had reconnected and were working through things, even spending more intimate times together as well. He had fallen back in love with her. She was a good woman and he knew she cared deeply for him.

With Isabella acting strange lately, he wanted a resolution. Before he hung up with Renee, she confirmed to leave a message for Father Robert to contact them.

***

Three weeks later, Father Robert arrived for a visit at their home. Over coffee and apple pie, they chatted about his trip to Rome and seeing the Pope. Father Robert excitedly announced that the Vatican was making new plans to recruit priests because there was a shortage across the United States.

He chuckled. "How about you, Vito? Want to join the priesthood? We could use a few good men like yourself. You could be a Deacon. They're married."

Vito laughed. "I don't think so."

"The benefits are great."

Antoinette joined in on the discussion. "Oooh, good health benefits, huh?"

When Isabella left to go to her room and play, Vito and Antoinette recounted the events to the priest, who raised his eyebrows with each new development. They also told him, since the incident at dinner when Isabella announced she'd spoken with Jesus, she hadn't talked about the leg issue, but rather informed them how Jesus instructed her to get down on her knees when she prayed; saying grace before each meal; and loving her friends without judgment.

The priest breathed deep. "Surely, these comments are not ordinary. She might have heard them through you both, or at church."

Vito nodded, brightening. "Yes. Yes, that could be so. Even though we haven't gone in a while."

Antoinette shook her head. "But, I overhear her talking to the baby Jesus all the time, like it's a real person."

Father wiped his mouth with a napkin. "I think it's time to see little Isabella."

During the priest's absence, Vito paced the den.

Antoinette sat on the couch. "Did you notice Father Robert's buttoned shirt fit a little more snug than usual? He must have gained some weight."

Vito shrugged, not noting the little details his wife picked up. Instead, after a few moments he said, "What do you think is going on up there?"

"I don't know, but your pacing is making me nervous."

He sat next to his wife. "You don't think she's possessed, do you?"

Antoinette folded her hands on her lap. "No. Let's wait and see what he has to say."

Forty minutes later, the priest reappeared in the den.

Vito stared expectantly at Father Robert, whose face was flushed and had beads of sweat across his brow.

The priest lowered himself slowly on the couch across from them. He cleared his throat. "I found nothing wrong with Isabella."

Vito crossed his arms, not believing him. *Then why are you sweating?*

"I don't understand," Antoinette said. "Like we said, she talks to those nativity figurines like she talks to us."

"She's an only child," Father Robert said, wiping away sweat from his forehead. "She has a creative imagination. Most *only* children do."

Vito stood up. "Do you think we need an exorcist in here? What if she's possessed by a demon?"

"Calm down, Vito. Don't go there," Father Robert said as he waved his hands. "Whew, is it hot in here, or is it me?"

He scrutinized the priest. His face was the color of a ripe tomato. "Are you okay? Here," he filled a glass of water from the pitcher sitting on the coffee table, and handed it to him.

"Father, I must confess, I feel so exposed with her. It's like she knows what I'm thinking all the time," Antoinette said.

"She's a very sensitive girl," Father Robert said. He drained the water in one gulp. "And, she does appear to have the Holy Spirit within her. It could very well be a gift from God."

"Did you find out anything more specific? About the kids at school? Are they saying things to her?" Vito asked. *There's got to be more than this "Holy Spirit" thing.*

"No," the priest said calmly.

"I don't know about this," Vito stumbled.

Father Robert wiped his forehead. "She's okay."

"How?" Antoinette asked.

"She convinced me," Father Robert replied.

"So what do we do now? If it continues, are we to ignore it?" Vito asked.

The priest stood up, fanning himself. "I probably should be going. I must be having a hot flash." He laughed. "Seriously, Vito, I've traveled the world and have met many remarkable people. Consider this an extraordinary blessing. Who knows where it could lead?"

"I hope not to the convent," he murmured under his breath.

Father Robert cracked his knuckles. "Got an early morning mass."

After a hurried goodbye, Vito escorted the priest out the front door. He walked back into the den where Antoinette still sat on the couch. "I think there *is* something remarkable about our child."

He sat down next to his wife. "You noticed how fidgety and sweaty Father was?"

"Yeah."

He hugged her close. "What do we do?"

"I don't know. Take it for what it is."

"You don't think I was harsh on the priest? I mean, am I overreacting, or did I sense something weird about him? Maybe Isabella put a spell on him."

His wife nuzzled into him. "No. I'm as dumbfounded as you are, but I can't stress over the situation. We need a plan."

"Like what kind of plan."

She cocked her head. "Like a confirmation. Cover all our bases. I could talk to Mrs. Kendall, her teacher. See if she's noticed some odd behavior in Isabella at school."

Vito brightened. "Good idea. I could call Tim; see if he and Sally have ever experienced any of this with their kids."

Antoinette nodded. "Yes. I like it. I could also talk to Cheryl. Maybe Lizzy or Connor are doing some of this 'imaginary' thing."

He held her tighter. "Our child is different. I just hope other kids in her class aren't making fun of her leg and she's having these issues because of it."

His wife nodded.

Vito pulled away and stood, feeling the urge to see his daughter. "I'm going to go and check on my little princess."

He turned and headed for the stairs.

CHAPTER 48

October

From the kitchen sliding door leading to the backyard stood a 16' by 20' rectangular cedar deck. Straight ahead, four steps led to a patio. From there, almost a quarter acre of lawn covered the Libero property. A rose garden—Isabella's rose garden now occupied part of the yard.

The desired rose garden took some time to come together, a few months actually. Since the picnic at Holy Name Hospitals for Children back in June, Antoinette had been doing research at their local library on how to plant roses. She found they preferably should be planted in the spring, but could also be planted in the fall.

She and Vito had to determine where to plant the roses and whether to buy bare root plants or potted roses. Neither she, nor her husband, possessed a green thumb between them, so they decided potted roses would be easier for them—more expensive, but less work.

Next, it was all about location. Vito suggested they plant the roses by the garage or near the walkway, while Antoinette wanted the garden around the patio. A trip to the garden nursery solved that problem. She drew up plans and her husband bought special soil, consisting of peat moss and compost. The roses had to be planted along a wall permitting at least six hours of sunlight. It left no option but to excavate the grassy area by the fence to the left of their property. So, one Saturday morning, with shovels in hands, Antoinette, Vito, and Isabella cleared a section.

Following the directions on planting roses from a web site, Vito and Isabella dug approximately 15-18 inch deep holes, roughly every three to four feet, while Antoinette pruned any damaged, dead, or broken roots and stems. The last task was left to her husband who planted the four potted rose bushes in a row.

It was dusk by the time they finished. She, Vito and Isabella sat wrapped in a large blanket on a brand-new wicker bench with cups of hot chocolate, enjoying their "bare" rose garden.

"Cheers," Vito said, clinking the cups. "To the roses in my life. May their beauty mirror the lovely ladies in my home."

Isabella giggled.

Antoinette sat back, taking in his words. "Wow, I never knew I was married to a poet."

Pointing to his back pocket he said with a smile, "For your information, I do still have a few hidden tricks that haven't been exposed yet."

Antoinette grinned, picking up on his sexual remark. "Oh. When will they be 'exposed'?"

He kissed her. "Soon."

She kissed him back. "I can't wait."

Isabella jumped from her seat, "Yuck. You guys are yucky." She then stepped over to her rose garden. She bent down and one-by-one touched each of the stems with her little hands.

Antoinette watched her, nudging Vito. "Look at her. What is she doing?"

"I don't know."

When Isabella returned, she slid between them and grabbed her mug.

"What were you doing?" Antoinette asked.

Isabella took a short sip of her drink, "I said a prayer for each rose stem to grow."

"Okay," remarked Antoinette not sure what else to say.

Her husband's brow creased.

Their daughter never ceased to amaze them—like she didn't belong to this earthly world, and could say the most profound things. Despite her daughter's physical challenge, which wasn't a challenge at all; she ran, biked, skated, and jumped like any other child her age.

For some peace of mind regarding Isabella's odd behavior of late, Antoinette had followed up with Mrs. Kendall at school to see if anything was out of the ordinary. The teacher could find none. In fact, the teacher praised Isabella's ability to grasp the learnings. She also mentioned how well-behaved her daughter was in class. She then talked to Cheryl, and learned only Connor talked to himself occasionally, but it wasn't out of the ordinary, either. She'd heard of other kids exhibiting the behavior, too.

In the meantime, Vito called Tim and told him about Isabella's behavior. When he heard about his daughter's saintly ability, he told his wife, Sally, and they were ecstatic for them—being very religious themselves. He said, "Buddy, this is fantastic. Rejoice in her ability to speak to Jesus and God."

Later, when she and her husband regrouped with their findings, they didn't know what to make of this new behavior from their daughter.

"So, what's our next step? Should we see a therapist?" Vito asked, wringing his hands together.

Antoinette shrugged, "I don't know. At least not right now. I'd hate to put our daughter through that kind of screening. Maybe we should surrender to the wonders of our gifted daughter."

She noticed her husband's confused look on his face. Their daughter was different physically and behaviorally. In time, they would learn more. For now, it was best to leave things as is.

She smiled. “God has a funny way of working. I trust him. You need to do the same.”

CHAPTER 49

April, 2007. Six months later.

After a blistery winter, spring and Easter had arrived hand-in-hand a bit later than usual. It was a Wednesday afternoon, and Antoinette and Isabella were home for Spring break. The grass had poked out to the urging sun's rays, and the air carried a hint of flowery fragrance blooming from the earth.

Exhausted from her morning chores, Antoinette sat in a chair drinking ice tea and watching her daughter through the kitchen sliding door playing in the backyard on her swing set. Isabella suddenly hobbled off and hurried up the back deck steps with a big grin on her face.

She opened the sliding door, "What are you so smiley about?"

"Mommy, you have to come and see," her daughter exclaimed, grabbing her hand and pulling her through the door.

"See what?"

"The rose garden!"

"Yes. I saw it the other day; your father had removed the plastic covering from the rose bushes. They're slowly beginning to bud—" Antoinette stopped in mid-step and stared at the four planted bushes. Every single shoot held a beautiful partially-opened rose.

"See!" Isabella said, pulling her closer.

"I was out here the other day. I can't believe how they've opened up. They've bloomed so early. I don't understand."

"I just talked to them, Mommy, and they opened up for me."

She blinked. "Now? What did you say?"

She shrugged. "I can't remember."

"What do you mean 'you can't remember'?"

Isabella jumped up and down. "They're so pretty. They're so pretty, Mommy! I love them."

Stunned, she stared incredulously at her daughter as she galloped around the patio.

Later that afternoon while Isabella laid down claiming she wanted to nap, Antoinette unable to get out of her head what she witnessed with the roses, called Vito on his cell.

"MeritPlus, this is— What's going on?"

She was standing next to the rose garden. She made the call outside because she didn't want Isabella to overhear the conversation.

"Hi. How's your day going?"

"Fine. What's up?"

She could hear his impatience through the phone. *I should have waited until he got home.* She couldn't. Her mind was reeling over the miraculous budding of the roses.

Antoinette ran her hand through her hair, not sure how to begin. "The roses are blooming."

She heard hesitation through the line. "So?"

Now it was her turn to be impatient. "Vito! You don't understand. I'm talking *full bloom*. Isabella said she prayed for them and they opened. Just opened. Today!"

Silence.

"Vito? Are you there?"

Quietly, his voice came through the line. "Yes."

She whispered, "What do we do? Father Robert claims it's a phase. Our friends and teacher say it's all normal behavior. I don't know what to—"

He cut her off. "I've got another call I need to take. Let's talk to her tonight… Together."

Antoinette nodded, staring at the beautiful roses. "Okay." Then the phone went dead.

She crouched down near the garden and touched each rose. They were fragrant and alive. It was impossible for them to bloom so suddenly. She was worried and nervous at the same time. Isabella obviously wasn't a normal child. As she rose to her feet, she turned toward the sliding door. There stood her daughter staring back at her.

That night when Vito returned from work and they had finished dinner, she and her husband asked to speak to Isabella in the den. They sat on the couch, their daughter between them. The Liberos questioned her about the miraculous blooming of the roses, her fascination with the holy figurines from the Nativity set, and her wondrous ability to talk to Jesus.

As Antoinette and Vito waited expectantly for answers, Isabella smiled and just said, "You're the best Mommy and Daddy I can ever ask for. It makes me happy to see you happy together again."

Goosebumps ran down her arms. *Yes, how far we've come. You have definitely played a role in our relationship, kiddo.*

Vito was speechless. His eyes moist.

Isabella suddenly hugged them. "I love you. Can I be excused?"

Antoinette shook her head. "Sure, sweetheart."

With their daughter out of the room, she and Vito sat dumbfounded staring at one another. After the "interrogation," they agreed if things became more peculiar, they would seek professional help—specialists who dealt with spiritually gifted children.

They were still boggled with their daughter's intuitive gift. But for now, they had to surrender themselves to their amazing daughter. She had made a rose bloom! Several, in fact. What child or human could do that? That was a miracle in itself and they needed to embrace Isabella for who she was.

PART 4: MOVEMENT

"Dark becomes light, night becomes day, and a frown becomes a smile."

—From Antoinette Libero's Sticky Notes

CHAPTER 50

July, 2008. A year and a half later.

It was Friday afternoon around three-thirty. Alone, Antoinette perused coupons at the kitchen table—a frugal habit she had picked up from their neighbor, Cheryl Starkweather.

The doorbell rang and she went to see who it was. Opening the front door, she was greeted by Cheryl, Lizzy, Connor and Isabella.

"Hi, guys. How was your day?"

All four of them marched inside chatting about their afternoon at Sumner Sills Park.

Isabella leaped forward and hugged her mother. "Mommy, can I join swimming? Please, please!"

"Swimming?"

Her friend raised her eyebrows as the girls danced around chanting 'swimming'.

"Okay, girls. Let me talk to Isabella's mother. You guys go play. Lizzy, take your little brother with you."

Lizzy untangled herself from Isabella. "But I don't want to."

"You have to."

Connor, four, trudged over to his pouting older sister. She reluctantly took his hand, and the three of them walked to the den.

"Thank you," Cheryl replied to their backs.

Antoinette and her friend went into the kitchen where she prepared two ice-cold drinks. "What's this about swimming?"

"Lee and I talked the other night about getting Lizzy involved in swimming at the park district. We get the park program every quarter. You get the program too."

"We do. I haven't looked at it recently."

"You should. They have a lot of great kid programs. Every time we visit Lee's cousin in Arlington Heights, Lizzy swims in their pool. We thought it be a good idea if we put her in swimming this summer for a few weeks, kind of like camp before they go back to school." Cheryl exhaled loudly. "You know as well as I do, that child can be a handful. She needs to put her energy in a physical activity to wear her out. Then, I could spend some quality time with Connor."

Sitting down at the table, Antoinette handed Cheryl a glass of ice tea. They heard the girls and Connor giggling and squealing in the other room.

"You guys play nice." She turned to her friend, "I'm going to call Dr. Maxwell's office and ask about the prosthesis. I know Isabella likes the water a lot, but she doesn't have a clue how to swim yet."

Cheryl crouched forward. "They're at a good age. They're both almost eight. They can learn how to swim, and have so much fun doing it."

"Let me check with Vito and the doctor."

"Sure. If you decide to do it, we could go shopping while the girls are in class."

"What about Connor?"

Cheryl laughed. "Oops. I forgot about him."

Later in the afternoon, after the Starkweathers left, Antoinette called the park district and gathered some information about the lessons. She then telephoned Dr. Maxwell's office and spoke with Jane, the head nurse, about Isabella taking swimming lessons. Jane told her it was okay; her daughter didn't need her prosthesis in the water, and that swimming would actually strengthen her hips and leg muscles.

She thought more and more about it. They had brought her many times to the pool and even to the Montrose and Oak Street beaches downtown. Isabella really enjoyed splashing in the water.

***

Over dinner that night, while Antoinette asked Vito about his day, Isabella blurted.

"Daddy, guess what?"

"Honey, please wait until your father and I are finished speaking before interrupting, understand?"

"But—"

"It's fine," he said to her. "We can talk later." Vito then gazed at Isabella. "What is it, sweetheart?"

"I'm going to learn how to swim! We're going to sign up at the park and Lizzy is going, too. We'll have so much fun. I can't wait."

"*Whoa*. This is news to me," her husband said a bit bewildered.

She jumped in, looking sternly at her daughter. "Your father and I haven't discussed this, or said you could join swimming, now did we?"

Isabella shook her head, but continued rambling.

Antoinette knew Vito never liked being the last to find out things. After some time, she could tell the idea wasn't sitting well with him. He put his fork down and gawked at his wife. She smiled mischievously at him between bites of pasta. After a while, Isabella began giggling in her chair.

"Is anyone going to tell me more about this? Besides how excited you are?" He pointed to her.

"Isabella, should we tell him more?" Antoinette teased.

Her daughter continued giggling.

Vito began laughing. "Tell me, please."

Antoinette took a deep breath. "Cheryl came over this afternoon, and we talked about putting Lizzy and Isabella in swimming classes. I called the park district; Isabella would start with the beginners. Lizzy knows how to swim and would be in a different group. It's only three days a week for two hours during the next few weeks. I talked with Dr. Maxwell's nurse and they said it's okay. I'm actually warming up to the idea. It might be good for her." She winked at her daughter.

"What about the leg?"

"Covered. She doesn't need to wear her prosthesis while swimming." Antoinette knew her husband worried as much as she, if not more, about their daughter's prosthesis.

"I'm not so sure about this."

"Please, Daddy," Isabella begged.

"Are you positive you're okay with this?" Vito said. "You'll be learning how to swim *without* your leg. *You're* going to have to take it off before you go in the water and then put it back on to walk around the pool area." He moved closer to his daughter. "Mommy and I won't be in your class during your lessons; we can only watch you."

"Don't worry, Daddy. I'll be fine. I've played in the water before without my leg."

"I know sweetheart, but now you'll be learning how to actually swim." A look of concern across Vito's face.

"Yes. Jesus will be there to help me," she replied positively.

At her daughter's response, Antoinette silently prayed. *Lord, if this is a sign of our daughter's faith and trust in You, then I accept it. She is your perfect servant. You have given us the best gift we can ever ask for. We'll continue to honor and trust in You with the life plans you have in store for our extraordinary child. And, I thank you, Lord, for my husband and his growing patience.* Then, she nodded at her husband.

"What?"

"I'm admiring my overprotective husband."

In an instant, she remembered another time when Vito had been overprotective with their daughter. It was when Isabella had first started walking with her prosthesis that he put a gate at the foot of the stairs. He spent all afternoon carefully testing it and making sure it locked appropriately. Only to have Isabella walk over and push it open with her foot. It was the funniest scene because the gate wasn't childproof, but adult proof. She felt secure knowing he was cautious and concerned about their daughter's well-being.

"I'm not overprotective," Vito protested. "I know we've been to the pool before, but I want to do a thorough check again to make sure it's safe for the lessons, as well, as talk to the instructor. Even if," he paused and gazed at his daughter, "Jesus is there to keep you safe. I also need my peace of mind."

Isabella nodded. "Okay, Daddy."

Antoinette agreed. "Great idea."

"So, you want to learn how to swim, huh?"

"Yes, Daddy, very much."

"Hmm... Okay sweetheart?" He reached over and squeezed his daughter's arm.

Antoinette laughed. Her husband liked covering all the bases.

***

The next afternoon, Saturday, the Liberos climbed in the car and took a ride to Sumner Sills Park. They passed the pond, now filled with geese and ducks swimming about, then parked in front of the park district building which had a workout area, indoor track, indoor pool, and outdoor pool.

They made their way to the front desk to gather additional information about the swimming classes. Isabella skipped around her parents; she was excited about the opportunity.

An employee, a pimply young seventeen year old male introduced them to Mrs. Bailey, one of the instructors for the swimming lessons. She was tall, thin, and blond-haired probably in her early thirties. She showed them the outdoor pool area, explaining where the lessons would take place.

There were two whirl pools in one corner, a twelve foot section with a diving board, a six foot section, a three-to-five foot section, and a toddler area with slides. No classes were in session, only open swim. But, there were a dozen people in all in various areas of the pool area. It was surprisingly quiet for a Saturday afternoon, considering the temperature was around eighty degrees.

Mrs. Bailey explained all children between six and ten learned in the three-to-five foot section. They strolled to the indoor pool area; the air smelled like chlorine. It was the same setup as outdoors, except there weren't any whirlpools, or the twelve foot section.

The woman continued, "If it rains or we have storms, we move indoors and continue with the class inside. The kids then don't have to miss their lessons."

"Good thinking," Antoinette responded.

She observed Vito as he asked many questions on what a typical lesson entailed, how many children per class, and what type of safety precautions did she uphold during classes. Isabella held onto her father's hand the whole time.

"I don't know if you've noticed," he pointed to Isabella's leg, "but my daughter wears a prosthesis."

Mrs. Bailey nodded. "Yes, in fact I did."

"My biggest concern is she'll need to remove it for swimming and then put it back on to walk around the area. I need to know if *you* or someone else will be able to help her with that."

"Certainly," the teacher nodded her head. "I usually have two other assistants with me; high school students who help with the children. It is no problem. We will take good care of your daughter, and provide her the assistance she needs."

"Thank you. That makes me feel a little better."

Antoinette took her daughter's hand and squeezed it. Whispering, she said, "Daddy is great, isn't he?"

Isabella grinned.

After her husband's interview with Mrs. Bailey, they walked back to the outdoor pool area. Their daughter couldn't hold it another minute.

"Okay, Daddy, can I? Can I?"

Vito was silent. He turned to Antoinette and pointed. "I don't like these whirlpools. Especially outside, near the locker rooms. These kids can walk over here and slip in."

She nodded in agreement. In order for the kids to get to the three foot section, they had to pass the whirlpool area and six and five foot sections.

All the while, their daughter hung on to her father's arm, begging for him to concede. "Daddy, please. I'll be safe. Don't worry."

Vito sighed. "Okay. On two conditions, though. First, you are to be careful. Don't run but walk when going to your section. And secondly, when you take off your prosthesis, you put it down carefully where it is safe and won't get damaged. Your prosthetic limbs cost a lot of money for Mommy and Daddy."

Isabella danced and jumped around. "Yes, Daddy. Yes. I promise I will."

He picked her up and kissed her. Antoinette grinned. Her heart bursting with love for the two most important people in her life. *God, I'm so lucky. Thank you for my family.*

They left holding each other's hands.

***

It had been a fruitful summer. Antoinette had read half-dozen books, relaxed, and watched her baby girl learn how to swim at the park. Isabella was in a beginner's class with nine children; five boys and four girls, ages five through seven.

She was a natural swimmer. Isabella was one of the fastest learners, not needing a nose plug or ear plugs. She learned how to hold her breath underwater, and how to doggy-paddle quickly, even jumping off the diving board into twelve feet of water. Her coach was amazed at their daughter's tenacity. The other children adored her, not one of them making a big deal of her missing limb, and naming her captain of the class.

Then, at the end of August, all the kids from each of the swimming lesson groups put on a water show. Working on a team, Isabella and three other kids choreographed the moves. There were bathing suit costumes made, and all the moms baked treats for the end of the season show. Participating families helped in making the night an extravaganza. Isabella's beginner's group shined with their acrobatic ability, winning second prize.

Mrs. Bailey suggested to Antoinette and Vito about putting their daughter in Level Two with the nine year olds the following summer because she had excelled so quickly beyond her age group.

Their daughter had been right. She took responsibility of taking care of her leg as promised, and she triumphed in swimming; all the while reassuring them Jesus had been there to protect her and keep her safe. Antoinette and Vito were so proud! Their little girl was growing up.

CHAPTER 51

October

Every fall, Vito raked up all the leaves on the grass which had accumulated from the two oak trees in their backyard. One Saturday morning, he and Isabella began removing the dirt from the flower pots while Antoinette cleaned up inside. Upon finishing, she joined her husband and daughter on the lawn. A little past two-thirty, Lizzy stopped over.

"Mommy, can I go and play at Lizzy's house?"

Antoinette moved a bag of leaves, contemplating whether to let her daughter go and play, while Vito continued raking.

"We're almost done here, and I'll be starting dinner soon. Only for a while okay? Then, Daddy will come and get you."

"That's right," her husband nodded to his daughter. "I'm starving."

Both girls squealed in excitement.

"Isabella, don't forget to wash your hands first, though."

"Okay, Mommy."

She watched the girls walk together. Isabella then disappeared inside, while Lizzy skipped ahead down the drive to her house across the street.

Antoinette turned around and held open the bag, as Vito tossed in more leaves.

A few minutes later, a door slammed.

"I'm going."

"Okay, have fun," Antoinette shouted back.

Suddenly, a horrible thought crossed her mind about the cars zooming down their block. In the last few years, ever since Liberty Lane, the street one block over, closed and was made into a cul-de-sac, they'd had many more cars cutting through Trevor Lane. Antoinette's mind raced. She'd forgotten to tell Isabella to be careful crossing the street. She stood completely motionless.

Vito stared at her, with leaves in his arms, "What's gotten into you?"

There was a loud screech from tires scraping the pavement; then, a thud. In a flash, she tore off the work gloves and sprinted down the driveway.

"Isabella! Isabella! Isabella!" Antoinette screamed, running into the street. She saw a woman stumbling out of a green van, and wailing hysterically.

In front of the van, Isabella lay on the ground. Shaking and jerking.

Antoinette threw herself to the pavement, and unzipped her daughter's jacket. Her light blue turtle-neck was stained. The prosthesis was shattered in pieces a few feet away.

She gently picked up her child and cradled her hands behind her head. Within seconds, her fingers were wet.

Looking up, Antoinette cried. "Vito! Vito! Help me!"

Tears streaked her cheeks as she clutched her baby close, rocking back and forth, "Oh my God! Oh my God! It's going to be okay, honey. Mommy's here."

Isabella's lips were blue and her eyes watery.

"Momm…mee. I'mmmm…ssss…orr…"

"Shhh…don't worry. Oh dear Lord… We're going to get you to the hospital. Hang in there, baby girl," Antoinette said, gently holding her daughter, fighting all emotions in order to stay calm.

She watched her daughter's eyes move up to the sky. "No… No…Isabella! Stay with Mommy… You're okay…"

"I…babe…Jessus…" A soft breath escaped her lips, and then her body went limp in her arms.

Antoinette screamed uncontrollably. "No!"

Hugging her child's lifeless body, her head darted around for help. Her heart thudded rapidly in her chest, and her vision blurred.

A crowd had gathered around her and Isabella, encircling them. She saw Lizzy push through the neighbors, falling at her daughter's feet, her face, stunned. Cheryl reached over, pulling Lizzy away, covering her eyes. The woman from the van stood off to the side weeping into a cell phone, as an ambulance, two police cars, and an unmarked blue car pulled up.

A young woman tried prying away Antoinette's blood-drenched hands from Isabella's body. She couldn't register what she was saying. A tag on her jacket glistened in the late afternoon sun; it said Angela Green.

Vito! Where was Vito?

Two strong hands cupped her shoulders, yanking Antoinette away from Isabella, shoving her aside. She watched the still body of her daughter lying on the ground. A man with dark slicked hair, wearing a black jacket, with lettering on the back that read *Medical Coroner* hovered over her child.

He rose and nodded to two other EMTs who carefully gathered Isabella's body and placed her on a stretcher. She was draped with a white, soft sheet, the color of snow.

Antoinette gasped and dropped to her knees just as a boot crossed the exact spot where Isabella's head had lain. Blood splattered onto her face, the taste of metal stung her tongue. She looked down at her wet, crimson-colored soaked hands. Something gripped her.

She pushed the heavy weight off her back, removed her jacket and threw it on the pool of blood. "There, there, no more spills. It's going to be fine, Isabella. Mommy's here."

"Ma'am, get up," pleaded the EMT named Angela, trying to pull Antoinette up from the ground. "Ma'am, please get up."

She squinted at the woman through blurred eyes, unable to speak. "What?"

"I'm so sorry. I'm so sorry. She's gone."

"No!" Antoinette cried, sinking to the ground.

Soon, another EMT, a short, dark-haired male was at her side. Together, he and Angela lifted her up, as Vito pulled her into his arms.

"My God! It can't be!" he screamed.

Together, she and her husband sobbed.

CHAPTER 52

A few hours later it was raining. The streets were slippery; the temperature hovered at forty degrees. For an October Saturday evening it was quite cold so early in the season.

Vito had paced all throughout the house wiping away tears. It was full of people; his parents, father-in-law, and the Starkweathers. The mood inside was one of grief and sadness with constant sobbing and wailing.

He couldn't take it anymore and quietly slipped out a little after nine-thirty. He had to get out and walk. He had on a black knit cap and wore a dark blue rain slicker with a hood. The air was frigid, but nothing could penetrate through the numbness and heartache he was feeling at this moment.

Grabbing his pack of smokes from the glove compartment of his car, Vito stepped out and smoked. Not sure where he was going, he must have walked six or eight blocks and smoked at least four cigarettes. His mouth tasted like ashes and he was soaking wet, but he didn't care.

Seeing a flashing sign with the name *The Paradise Bar* on the corner of Brentwood and Ridgeway, Vito headed to the flat square brick building. There were several cars in the parking lot and he weaved through them, past three smoking patrons outside, and opened the dark-stained glass door.

The establishment was small. Booths occupied the left side of the entrance, and straight ahead from the door was a wrap-around bar with stools which circled to the other side of the building. Across from the bar on the right were tables with tattered chairs, and a little dance floor in front of a stage. Dart boards and a couple of video games took up the corner area to the left of the stage.

Vito had been there once before a few years back, so he was familiar with the set up. He turned left and slid into a booth, not bothering to remove his cap or slicker. A woman in her early forties with straight, ebony colored hair pulled in a pony-tail and olive skin emerged from the back kitchen. She approached him.

"Hi, honey. What can I get you?" Her voice was deep and husky, carrying a tone of a long-time cigarette smoker.

"Scotch on the rocks."

"Okay."

He watched her walk away and around the bar. She wore a sleeveless Harley-Davidson black T-shirt showcasing her snake tattoo around her left arm and a crucifix tattoo at the nape of her neck. Tight blue jeans completed her ensemble.

She came back with his drink and set it on the table in front of him. "Should I start a tab?"

Vito nodded as he took a couple of sips of the drink. It burned his throat and his stomach. He couldn't rationalize what had happened to them—his family. One minute, Isabella was raking leaves with him, the next she was gone. *Gone.*

He downed the drink and motioned the bartender for another. The woman brought another drink. A few people had strolled in and sat at the bar. He mostly kept his head down, rubbing his fingers along the sides of his glass. But as he stared blankly at his ice cubes, something caught his attention out of the corner of his eye and he gazed toward the door.

A curvy woman with a red-colored windbreaker with "EMT" stitched neatly in white letters on her left breast pocket, lumbered in.

The bartender was taking care of another patron. She smiled at the woman as she slid onto a stool at the bar. Suddenly, her demeanor changed. A look of concern crossed her face.

"Angie, a cold one?"

"Yeah, but give me a little side kick to go with it, will you, Joni."

Vito stared at the woman, wondering where he'd seen her before, and then realized she was the EMT named Angela Green at the accident that afternoon. He was about twenty feet from her, pretty close in proximity and could overhear her conversation clearly. What were the odds of being in the same bar as the EMT who had witnessed his daughter's death?

She turned his way. They made eye contact but it was brief. He put his head down. *She didn't recognize me.* He looked up again and saw the bartender pull out a beer and a shot glass, and poured an amber-colored liquid into it.

Angela downed the shot. "Another, please."

Pulling out a hundred-dollar bill and slapping it on top of the bar, she repeated, "Another."

"Angie, take it easy," Joni cautioned.

He sipped his drink, listening.

"I said another, please!"

The regulars a few stools away stopped and gazed at Angela.

"Sure. But that's it for a little while," the bartender poured the shot and then disappeared.

Vito watched as Joni walked over to a large man with bulging forearms near the door. She murmured something. He hadn't noticed the man when he had come in.

She returned and hovered over the bar as Angela downed her shot and took a swig of her beer.

"What happened today?"

Angela took a deep breath. "A little girl was hit by a van today up on Trevor Lane and died. She sustained multiple head and bodily injuries."

Joni touched her hand. "I'm so sorry, Angie; how horrible."

"The hardest part—peeling the mother off of her little girl's dead body."

Vito gulped his drink, squeezing his eyes shut tight, unable to erase the image of his wife holding onto their precious daughter. A stinging tear fell down his cheek. *Holy shit!*

"Wow," said Joni.

"I just wanted to have a few drinks to kill the pain."

"How will you drive home? I don't want you getting hurt."

"I don't care. I'll call a cab if I need it. To witness this incident is too painful to digest."

"Angie—"

"Joni, please…" Putting her head down, she lowered her voice, "Years ago, I lost my seven year old sister, Bethany, to a car driving too fast down the street."

Vito leaned over the table, straining to hear.

She paused. "I was responsible for her. She died on my watch. She let go of my hand and ran into the street and was killed instantly. Today, it was like reliving that same moment when I saw that girl—her mother's anguish. I lost it."

Vito bit his lip. *What the hell!*

"I had no idea. I'm so sorry," Joni said, pulling the bottle from under the bar, and pouring another shot. "The drinks are on me tonight. When you're ready, Max can take you home."

Angie didn't respond.

Vito had heard enough. *My baby. My baby's dead!* Heart pounding, he was seconds away from lurching his guts out all over the floor. Instead he rose, wobbly from his chair. He pulled out a twenty-dollar bill and placed it on the table next to his half-empty drink.

He bumped into a man—Max on the way out, but not before looking over at Angela as she tilted her head back to down another shot.

It would be rough night. Not only for him, but, for the young woman who had seen his dead child. Isabella had died and he hadn't been there to protect her.

Once outside, the rain picked up. There were big droplets falling down now. He glared up at the sky and flipped his finger. "Thanks, God!"

He passed a trash can and threw the remaining pack of cigarettes in it. Antoinette would be worried about him. All he wanted to do was crawl into bed and cry himself to sleep.

He looked both ways before he crossed the street and sprinted all the way home as tears and rain slapped against his face.

CHAPTER 53

The next couple of days after the accident were a blur for Antoinette. Her eyes puffy from tears, she had no energy to get out of bed. She didn't want to eat or drink. And now she was feeling delirious. Vito had been the same. They held one another for hours and sobbed.

His parents and her father stayed over. As much as she appreciated their company, she would have preferred to be alone. She was hurting for her daughter; all she wanted was to have her back. She hadn't showered or washed her hair in days.

However, she knew preparations were required for their daughter's funeral. But before that, she and Vito needed closure as to how their daughter had died. Police had come over for their statement and to hear what the driver of the van, Rebecca Weidner, had told the officer on duty.

Rebecca and her family lived three blocks away on Raintree Grove. She had a fifteen month old son named Evan, and a nine year old daughter, Lauren. Evan had become feisty and didn't want to take his bottle at home, and Rebecca was running late to pick up her daughter from the park. Putting him in the car seat, she tried giving him the bottle once more while she scurried down Trevor Lane. Evan accidentally dropped the bottle out of his hands. When Rebecca turned, reaching for it, she hit Isabella. The speed limit sign on the street read twenty-five miles per hour. The woman was going approximately thirty-five. She swerved, but it was too late and she clipped the child.

The policemen speculated Isabella might have been bent down possibly trying to tie her shoe on the street. The impact of the van apparently hit her right side shoulder and head.

No matter how it was explained, it still didn't make sense to Antoinette. Isabella hadn't deserved to die that way. She was such a perfect little girl.

***

Three days later, the Liberos held a closed-casket wake at Constatine Funeral Parlor. The room was the smallest of the five rooms at the parlor, but it was filled with flower bouquets, all roses. Red roses. Sparsely furnished and dimly lit, it provided the perfect ambiance for the desolate mood surrounding the family. About forty guests, friends and extended family came to pay their respects. There were no words, only sobering pain...

The vision of Isabella's blood-soaked head haunted her. The whole day was surreal. Antoinette was emptied of all emotion. *Was this a dream?*

Frank and the in-laws cried constantly. Her mother-in-law wailed on how she and Vito were given such a horrible cross to bear. Everything was a blur.

Before the wake, Vito suggested they contact her brother, Salvatore, who lived in Portland now, and to whom she hadn't physically spoken to in more than thirty years. Her brother's idea of communication was a post card or email update every few months. And now, she was supposed to notify him of the news. *Their* daughter's death? At first, Antoinette refused; her brother hadn't known Isabella. *Why contact him?* He hadn't even come to her mother's funeral. *Why would he come here? Now, after all this time?*

However, her husband insisted. He persuaded her to try and save what was left of her family. She gave in, but she wasn't going to call him herself. "You call him, not me."

That night at the wake, when Antoinette saw her older brother for the first time in so many years, a flood of emotions took over. Vito had called Salvatore, and to everyone's surprise, he had dropped everything and flew out to Chicago to comfort his younger sister. Her knees gave way and she fell into his arms.

"Oh, Antoinette, I'm so sorry."

She just nodded and held onto him.

The next day at church, Father Robert presided over the funeral, giving a eulogy about Isabella.

"Good morning," the priest said, adjusting the microphone behind the lectern.

A murmur rippled through the pews. "Morning."

"Today is a day filled with deep, deep, sorrowful emotions and questions. Our little daughter, Isabella, God's daughter, has departed the human world to be with our Heavenly Father in his Kingdom.

"I remember the day when I first met Isabella. She was a tiny little thing, but she was strong, and willful. When Antoinette showed me her leg, I told both her and Vito this is only her shell; it's what's inside her heart God seeks. I constantly reminded Antoinette and Vito to be role models for their daughter. They succeeded, amazingly. Isabella resonated a Godly spirit within her each time I saw her in church and in her daily life.

"Some might say she was taken too soon, and question as to why this horrific tragedy happened. The reality of it is we're not the ones who can judge and predetermine our time—it's God's call. It's His will to decide when we are to depart and join Him."

Antoinette shuddered at the statement, still reeling and reliving the accident in her head. As she looked at her shaking hands, she could still see the stains of Isabella's blood on them. Isabella had suffered, died, and was to be buried today. A reality she couldn't grasp. Her heart was shattered.

"Isabella is with Jesus, her superhero, as Antoinette once told me, and I had the privilege of witnessing it myself. Most kids are fascinated by Hollywood stars or cartoon characters. Not our child. A few years ago, Isabella became fascinated with nativity figurines and loved the baby Jesus. She told her parents she saw Jesus once sitting at her desk in her room. We can feel comforted by her amazing love for Jesus, and when she passed, we know He was there to take her into His arms.

"Isabella was as pure as pure can be. She modeled true Christian faith in her everyday life. This isn't a time to grieve for Isabella; she is where she belongs. Home, with Jesus.

"We have been blessed by her divine life. May the Lord be with Antoinette and Vito as they transition to understanding and glorify God for giving them this gift.

"I'd like to leave you with this passage from Revelations 21:4. '*And God will wipe away every tear from their eyes; there shall be no more death, nor sorrow, nor crying. There shall be no more pain, for the former things have passed away.'"*

Silence followed Father Robert's words as he concluded and stepped away from the lectern. Antoinette looked to Vito, but he was bent forward with his hands over his head.

Her palms were damp. *My turn.* Antoinette felt compelled to speak about her remarkable daughter to family and friends. This was her eulogy to her little Isabella. With tightness in her chest, she waited for the priest to sit down. She slowly rose from the pew and walked to the lectern.

Struggling to take a deep breath, with sweaty and shaking hands, and without an ounce of preparation, she began. "They say the hardest thing a parent can ever experience is the death of their own child. I understand what this feeling is like…twice now. My son, Devon, and now my daughter, Isabella. As a parent, you are not supposed to outlive your children. Isabella came into the world missing part of her right leg, but you could never tell she had a handicap. When I learned about the pregnancy, I was so thankful for this blessing in our lives. The pregnancy wasn't smooth sailing, though. There were some complications…" She stopped, recalling it was *her* decision to forgo additional testing, and put her faith in God's hands. Then she sniffled, "I'm sorry…"

Antoinette swallowed, trying to regain her composure. "Our parents never knew about it because we never told them. Our faith prevailed, and we forged ahead with the pregnancy, ready for anything to come our way. When Isabella was born, she glowed as she announced herself to the world with a loud cry."

She then gasped, and swallowed hard again. She had to get through this and finish what she had to say. It was for her daughter. "Isabella was a curious child, intrigued by the holidays and their history. Her favorite time of the year was Christmas. It was her favorite because 'baby Jesus' was born into the world to save us. One year we let her place the porcelain nativity set her grandparents had given her, in her room. Isabella had it on a small table all-year-round. She loved having baby Jesus near her.

"Last Christmas she told me she awoke in the middle of the night and saw Jesus. He told her He would come soon. He did come. He came for her while she laid in my arms..."

Antoinette covered her mouth to calm her nerves. "A few days ago he took her away from me to her eternal home. I've learned so much from my little rose. She has taught me to laugh and be playful..." She peered at Vito, who hadn't raised his head but shook and cried silently, "...to love unconditionally, but most of all to let go and forgive. She might have been here a short time, but her life story will remain forever in my heart... Thank you."

***

Antoinette and Vito laid their baby, Isabella Audrey Libero, to rest on October 11th, five days before their eighteenth wedding anniversary, and almost three weeks before her eighth birthday.

A sunless sky clouded the day. A mild wind blew from the east. The air smelled sweet. It was silent at Lincoln Memorial Cemetery about a mile and half from their house.

The beauty of the day reminded Antoinette of the day Isabella was born. With the crunch of their shoes on the fallen leaves, family and friends treaded quietly toward the child's plot near an oak tree. Vito and Salvatore carried the small casket. Fifteen bouquets of red roses surrounded her grave.

After a short prayer, Antoinette and Vito laid three roses on top of the casket. They watched as it was lowered to the ground.

I love you, Isabella.

The rest of the day went in fast forward for Antoinette, as family and close friends came to their home after the funeral. There were trays upon trays of food sat on top of the kitchen table: miniature sandwiches, pizza rolls, egg rolls, and cheese and crackers. White and red wine bottles lined up neatly on the counter with plastic wine glasses, ready to be filled.

Two women bustled about in her kitchen named Maria and Lucinda. They wore identical white blouses, black slacks and white aprons. Cheryl had hired them to cater refreshments and food after the funeral.

Numb and sick to her stomach, Antoinette felt like a stranger in her own home. She sat at the kitchen table barely watching the action. She had never understood why people went to the deceased's home after a funeral; stuffed their faces and drank too much. *I didn't want this.*

She watched her husband through the doorway in the den, making small talk with their friends, Tim and Sally, and Brad and Amy. He noticed her, and forced a smile in her direction.

"Here, sis, have a glass of wine," Salvatore offered, handing Antoinette a plastic cup.

She took it without a word. After a few sips, she began feeling even more nauseous. "Thank you."

Salvatore was thicker and taller than Antoinette by several inches. Fifty-nine years old and twelve years her senior, white hair streaked through his dark brown curls, and a thick, wide moustache covered his weathered face. Antoinette's father was avoiding him at all costs. Her brother hadn't come for their mother's funeral, and here he was in her home for a niece he had never met.

"Thanks for coming," Antoinette managed. But inside she wanted to scream at him. What nerve! He acted like nothing was wrong.

He put his arms around her. "I'm glad I came. I know this is not the time or place, but I'm sorry I didn't keep in contact. It was a stupid thing to do. I wanted my freedom, I guess. I'm older now and desire to be around family more. Maybe we could…." His voice trailed off, and his eyes became moist.

"Sure," Antoinette nodded. Timing was everything. She was reconnecting with her brother at her daughter's funeral. Funny how these things happened. She only wished this reunion had happened when Isabella was alive. She knew her daughter would have loved to meet her uncle Salvatore.

She rose. "When are you leaving?"

"I can stay as long as you want me."

"Thanks. Let's continue this conversation later. I have to get some air."

"Sure, okay."

"Salvatore, you need to talk to Dad."

"I know."

"Take care of him first, and then we'll catch up." She left her brother and zigzagged about toward the front door. There were a lot of people over, all offering a kind word or two, and she had no desire to talk to anyone.

"Lovely home, Antoinette."

"The food is very tasty."

"We're here for you anytime."

Her legs were on autopilot, guiding her to the exit. Antoinette pushed the screen door open and stepped out on the front porch, allowing the cool air to hit her face. *Thank God, for air!*

Sitting in her old familiar rocking chair was Lizzy. With braided hair, she wore a navy dress with white tights. The little girl was staring across the street.

Antoinette sighed, walking over to her. She touched the girl's head, and then put her arms around her. "Hi. Do you want something to eat?"

Lizzy fell into her embrace. "No, thanks."

"Me, neither."

"I'm so sorry, Mrs. Libero. It's all my fault. I should have never asked her to come over. I can't believe she's gone! I should have waited," she stumbled, "for Isabella. And walked across the street with—"

"Lizzy?" Cheryl called from the screen door.

"She's out here," Antoinette said.

Cheryl came out the door and raced up to Lizzy. "Where have you been? I've been looking for you."

"I've been here the whole time."

"Let's get something to eat," Cheryl said, grabbing her arm.

"Leave me be, Mom. I'm not hungry."

"Lizzy, you need to eat something."

"Your mother's right," Antoinette managed a wink.

Lizzy slid from the rocker and barged past them, looking over her shoulder and back at Antoinette.

Cheryl put a hand on her shoulder. "Thanks."

She nodded.

Left alone standing on the porch, the wind suddenly picked up. Her hair gently blew in the fall breeze. Days earlier, Isabella had been alive. Now she was buried in a cemetery. How she'd miss her little girl. Her smile, the sunshine she brought with her when she entered a room… How was she going to go on without her?

Vito appeared at her side.

"Come on back in. People are wondering where you are," he said, putting an arm around her.

"I'm exhausted."

"I could say the same."

"I'm going to bed," she turned toward the door.

"We have guests, honey."

"Mrs. Libero?"

Tommy Jr., the little boy Isabella had played with at the hospital picnic a couple summers earlier, stood behind the screen door. Isabella and he had kept in touch via phone ever since.

Antoinette's heart jerked. She went over to him, opened the door and took him in her arms. He cried.

"Kiddo, thanks for coming."

"I'm so sorry, Mrs. Libero."

"You've come, and we are grateful."

Vito reached down and ruffled his hair. "Thanks, little buddy. It means a lot to us."

"She was my friend."

Tommy Sr. appeared. "There you are, son. Going off by yourself." He picked up Tommy in his arms. "We are deeply sorry."

"It means a lot you came, Tommy," Vito consoled.

"We're here for you. Me, and this little buckaroo."

She forced a smile. The heaviness of the day was quickly catching up to her. "If you will excuse me, boys, I have to go," and she headed toward the stairs.

"Antoinette," her husband called.

She stopped at the foot of the stairs. "I need to lie down."

He nodded and walked away.

She pulled herself on the railings, every step harder than the previous one to climb. Once upstairs, Antoinette shuffled past Isabella's room, to her own. She stopped at the foot of her bed and slipped off her pumps.

Turning around without another thought, she treaded back to Isabella's room. There, she opened the door and laid on her daughter's bed, hugging and squeezing her pillows as the tears rolled down her face as she tried to keep her precious daughter alive in her heart.

Isabella... My dear, dear, sweet child. I miss you so much. I miss you... The voices below becoming fainter and fainter, as Antoinette drifted off to sleep smelling her daughter's scent on the bed sheets.

CHAPTER 54

Everything in Vito's life stopped with Isabella's death. He had no strength to even breathe or the energy to do anything. Two weeks had passed since Isabella's funeral and all he did was walk around the house in a trance. Every room had a stinging memory of what he lost. A call from the VP of his region changed everything.

Coming out of the den, with his hands tightened into fists, he saw Antoinette. She wore polka-dot pajamas and a beige robe; the same ones she'd been wearing for days. The clothing hung on her body. Her face was ashen and wrinkly. Vito didn't recognize her anymore.

"Who called?"

"Nick."

"What did he want?"

His boss had asked him to fly out to Ohio for training on new products for children with Attention Deficit Disorder—also known as ADHD or ADD, as well as Bipolar medication. At first Vito was angry—he needed this time to grieve. Then he saw this as an opportunity. It would be a good thing to get out and concentrate on something else, instead of being cooped up, where every room, every chair, every strewn toy reminded him of his daughter.

Vito hesitated before answering, clenching his fits tighter. He wasn't sure how his wife would react. He wanted to be there for her, but he was also suffering himself. "I need to fly out to Ohio, tomorrow."

"For *what*?"

"A meeting on the new programs coming out."

"Couldn't this wait? You have to go now?"

"It can't wait. I'll only be away two days."

He looked past Antoinette. At the foot of the stairs was a pair of Isabella's gym shoes. A children's book sat on the coffee table in the den, and a Disney CD was still on top of the counter, near the mail in the kitchen.

His wife shrugged. "So be it. While you're at work, I'm going to organize."

"Antoinette," Vito said, grasping her arms. "There's nothing to organize. Why don't you come with me, instead?"

"To Ohio? To do what?"

"To get away."

"I can't," she said, pushing him away. "I have to clean up."

"Clean what?" he asked, following her into the kitchen.

"*Her* things, *her* room."

"Antoinette, leave it."

"Why Vito?"

He stumbled, not knowing what to say next. He knew they'd have to do it eventually. He couldn't at the moment. "Not now. We'll do it together."

She crossed her arms, her lips trembling. "No. It needs to be done now."

Vito sighed and bit his tongue, until he tasted blood in his mouth. He then took her in his arms, where she wept uncontrollably, holding her close to diffuse his own shaking.

"Please. Don't do it now. Give it some time. Rest and get your strength back. Everything will work out, I promise. Please."

She cried on his shoulder. "Promises are overrated."

"I know. I know." He tightened his grip on his wife, not knowing what more to say.

CHAPTER 55

The next day Antoinette sat alone in the kitchen. Vito had already left. She slowly sipped her morning coffee looking out through the sliding door at nothing in particular. Two child losses she had endured. First Devon and now Isabella. She slammed her fist on the table.

"Damn you, Lord! Damn You!"

She rose and refilled her cup, hanging over the kitchen sink. She wanted to vomit, scream, tear her heart out, and beat someone to a pulp. But she couldn't and wouldn't. She wasn't the violent type and would never hurt anyone, not even the little mosquito making its way into the sink drain.

Antoinette missed her mother. She needed love, advice, and consolation as to what to do. She felt so alone. Looking out toward the rose garden, she shouted, "Jesus, what the Hell is this supposed to teach me? First I can't have children, then I do, then I lose them. What's up with all this?"

She threw the mug in the sink. Coffee spilled and the cup shattered. "Am I not good enough for You?" she screamed at the ceiling. Falling into the chair, she buried her head in her hands, sobbing.

"I hate you, God!" she screamed. "I hate You."

Kicking the chair next to her to the floor, she continued to weep. "What do I *do* now?"

Antoinette then stared at her hands. The days were dragging by. Today was just the same as yesterday. Her heart depleted; grief surrounded her, and Vito was on his way to Ohio on a business trip. *How am I ever going to overcome this tragedy in my life?*

The phone rang startling her.

She ignored the first and second ring.

On the third ring, she forced herself to answer, "Yes?"

"Mrs. Libero?"

"Yes?"

"It's Father Robert."

"Father," Antoinette said, looking at the clock. It was nine-thirty-five.

"Antoinette, my dear. I was calling to see if you and Vito would want to help out with the Thanksgiving delivery this coming weekend? We are a little short on volunteers, and I know last year we were successful in getting everything done, thanks to your help. So, if you're up to it..." His voice trailed off on the other end.

"I'm not sure. Vito's out of town for the next few days. Can I get back to you?" Her eyes rolled. How could she possibly volunteer for anything at this point, when she'd suffered such a huge loss in her life? How inconsiderate of Father Robert she thought, feeling a little angry at him.

"Sure. Let me know as soon as you can. We'd love to have you." Father Robert paused. "How are you and Vito holding up? Why don't you and Vito come to the rectory some time? To talk."

Antoinette stiffened, and began playing with her hair. *What timing?* "We're getting there, Father." It was all she could muster.

"You know I am here for you both."

"Yes, we know. Thank you," she replied impatiently.

Holding her breath, it was all she could do not to cry on the phone. She wanted desperately to be hugged, and tell Father Robert how hurt she was feeling. Instead she was silent.

"I'll talk to you soon."

"Sure. Goodbye, Father."

Antoinette clicked off on the receiver, rose, and began clearing up the mess in the sink. *I have to get boxes. I have to clean up her room.*

Once showered and dressed, she headed out the door. Two hours later, she returned and unloaded seven empty boxes and brought them up to Isabella's room.

***

Antoinette sat on Isabella's bed and took in the details of the room that had comforted her child's short life. Her room was painted Marsh Fern—the name of the color on the can when Isabella chose it. To her, the color reminded her of green olives. Both she and Vito had wanted Isabella's room to be light blue or soft mauve, but their daughter wouldn't have it. She wanted this ugly green, and was adamant about it. As soon as she turned six years old, she claimed she could make big, life decisions, including painting her room the color she chose, so they went from Sea Foam green to this icky color. When it was painted, she and her husband made one thing clear; once the color was on, she had to live with it. Isabella accepted her responsibility and never changed her mind about it.

Her bed sat up against the wall, facing north. To the west, two windows were on either side of a six-foot wall. Antoinette had dressed up the olive color by adding maroon-colored sheer drapes which hung over a valance on each window and draped to the floor. It had a dramatic effect; a little mature for Isabella, but it was something Antoinette had thought she could grow into. Her comforter had swirls of red, brown, and green. It was festive and accented the walls and drapes beautifully.

Near the door on the east side of the room stood an oak dresser with a mirror. Next to the dresser stood a medium-sized book shelf with five levels. Vito bought it a year ago because he was tired of seeing Isabella's books strewn around the light beige colored carpet.

Isabella, an avid reader, had enjoyed many books. Antoinette perused her collection: *Charlotte's Web*, *Stuart Little*, *Green Eggs and Ham*, *Cat in the Hat*, and *The Giving Tree*. She planned to begin reading the *Nancy Drew* series any day. They lay untouched.

At the foot of the bed rested a wooden chest. Antoinette carefully opened it. There lay Isabella's first prosthesis and a slew of Barbie dolls and coloring books. She picked up two of the dolls, the Miss Mary doll and Elmo doll still preserved after being played with so much over the years.

Underneath the dolls, she uncovered a red folder. Opening it, she pulled out a drawing. A picture of the Libero family, including Devon. It was the picture she had drawn when Antoinette had brought her to the cemetery to visit Grandma Martha and told her about her big brother. Tears fell down Antoinette's cheeks. She couldn't believe Isabella had kept the picture. She was now with Devon in Heaven, and with her grandmother. She put the picture away in the folder and placed it back into the wooden chest.

Over at the south side wall in front of the bed and chest, there stood her desk. The desk was a build-it yourself project. It had taken Vito three hours to put it all together. A black-and-white notebook sat on the desk. Alongside the desk chair rested a pink-and-black backpack with Isabella's school supplies. It also sat undisturbed.

Perhaps the most treasured piece of furniture in the room was a simple round table-top to the right of the desk, below the first window. It was one of those tables over which you could throw an ornate table covering. Antoinette wanted to keep the coloring theme of her room, but Isabella insisted she didn't want anything on top of it except the porcelain nativity set with the figurines from Vito's parents. Every year, Antoinette had put it under the Christmas tree until the year her mother passed away when Isabella took it into her room.

Isabella used to tell her mother and father she talked to Jesus often. She loved going to church and was very fond of Father O'Malley.

Antoinette did believe Isabella was chosen by the Lord to be their child. She stared at the religious figurines now and suddenly recalled a conversation with her daughter.

"Mommy, Jesus tells me He loves me."
"That's great, honey. Jesus loves all children."
"I know, but he tells me He really loves me."
"And what do you tell Him?"

"I love him. And He should love you and Daddy."
"You're sweet, thank you."

Antoinette wished she'd paid more attention to Isabella's connection with the Lord. She had been such a beautiful child who'd given them so much joy. She wondered if Isabella had known it was her time to go.

Exhaling slowly, she rose from the bed and opened Isabella's closet. There in neat order hung jeans, dresses, and tops. Antoinette caressed the clothes with her hands, putting them to her nose and inhaling her daughter's smell. Clothes her little Isabella would never wear. *What do I do with them?* Another tear fell down her face and she wiped it away. She was beginning to feel emotionally exhausted.

The last of the sun's rays peeked through the windows. Antoinette had wanted to begin packing, but she couldn't pull herself together. She also knew she couldn't leave this room like a shrine, either. She slumped back on the bed, fatigued. Maybe tomorrow, or maybe when Vito returned they could deal with it together.

CHAPTER 56

Feeling spent, Antoinette went to lie down on her bed. A memory of Isabella soothing her mind.

"Mommy, what's Heaven like?"

"Heaven, hmm...let me see. I believe it's what you think it is."

"What do you think it is?"

"For me," Antoinette said, adjusting Isabella on her lap, "I see rolling hills of green grass as far as the eye can see. The sky is blue without a cloud anywhere. The sun is bright and warm. The air smells like jasmine, and a warm breeze caresses my face. I stroll through tall grasses, each blade touching and massaging my legs like a million hands. I'm at peace and fully content."

"I like it, Mommy. I think Heaven is like being hugged by God all the time."

They giggled together.

Suddenly, a loud and persistent ringing sound startled her. She had fallen asleep. Antoinette jumped out of the bed. It was the phone. She reached across to her dresser, still dazed.

"Hello," she said heavily.

"Hi, sis."

"Salvatore. Wow. Hi."

"Were you sleeping? You sound out of it."

She shook her head. *Was I dreaming of Isabella?* "I was exhausted, so I laid down for a bit. What's up?"

"I'm just hanging out with Dad. Playing chess with him and some of his new friends here at the center."

"Good for you. How's he doing?"

"Fine. What about you?"

Antoinette took a deep breath. "Not so good."

"I can imagine. I'd like to stop by if it's convenient with you. Can we maybe get together tonight?"

She didn't want visitors. "Vito's out of town for work. He doesn't come back until tomorrow evening."

"So how about you and me? We could catch up."

She hesitated. "Oh. I guess that would be fine." She hadn't been alone with her brother in years.

"I'll tell you what. I'll pick you up at seven-thirty. I saw this restaurant near Dad's place I'd like to try."

"Okay. Sounds good. See you then." Antoinette hung up, thinking this was going to be very weird, spending time *alone* with her brother.

It took Antoinette over a half-hour to figure out what to wear. She tossed outfits on the bed like playing cards, settling on a pair of blue jeans, a beige knit top and a brown blazer. She was nervous, anxious, and somewhat uncomfortable about having dinner with her brother. After all, she was forty-seven years old, a school assistant, a survivor of her son's still birth, and daughter's premature death.

What are we going to talk about? What other life stories would she want to share with her brother—estranged brother, when her children were her whole life, and now she had *nothing*. Nothing left to give, and nothing left to show for.

Promptly at seven-thirty, Salvatore rang the doorbell.

Hesitantly, Antoinette opened the door.

"Hi." He wore silver slacks and a black turtle-neck.

"Hi."

She locked the door and they climbed the steps down from her porch.

Walking side by side, he asked, "Do you like steak?"

"Of course."

"Great. I was thinking of trying Spencer's Steakhouse. Want to go?"

"Sure. I believe Vito's been there with his boss. He said it was delicious."

"Good."

Salvatore opened the passenger door for her, and she slid into his rental car, a Ford Taurus. He got in and pulled out of the drive onto the street.

During the ride, conversation was cordial. They talked about bands they liked, types of food they preferred, and world news. Except for similarities around the eyes and nose, no one would guess they were even brother and sister.

Once they arrived at the restaurant they settled into a booth, and Salvatore ordered a bottle of Merlot. The ambiance was dark and cozy. Several fireplaces throughout the restaurant casted soft flickers of light and heat in the air. Antoinette was feeling more relaxed.

Her brother leaned all of his 6'4" frame over the table. Growing up, she remembered her dad saying Salvatore took after his father's side of the family. He resembled Frank's older brother, Ronnie.

"So, how are *you* doing?" Salvatore asked, squeezing her hand across the table.

Antoinette withdrew from his grip, and played with the stem of her wine glass. "Honestly? I'm lonely and tired. Saddened, shocked, and broken-hearted." She hesitated, looking up at her brother. "I was going to de-clutter her room today, but couldn't. It's not like I want to get rid of her. I feel anxious to get organized. It's hard to explain."

"Give it time, Antoinette."

Time. Why did I need 'time' for everything? It was over. The family life she dreamed about had disappeared.

"I don't know where to go from here."

"Have you and Vito talked about next steps?"

Antoinette almost wanted to laugh out loud. Vito had been avoiding the reality of their daughter's passing by putting off organizing her room entirely.

"No, we haven't talked about next steps since—" she struggled with using the word death, and avoided referring to her daughter by her first name. It was too personal. Maybe she was in denial.

Their Caesar salads arrived and she was grateful for the distraction to change the subject.

"You said Dad was doing well today?"

"Yeah."

"Did you guys catch up and talk?"

"What do you think?" He snickered.

"What did you talk about?"

He shifted in his chair. "We visited Mom at the cemetery and just chatted."

Antoinette sensed his discomfort on the topic. "You're being awfully vague."

Salvatore laughed. It was more like a snicker. "My whole purpose." He took a couple more bites of his salad, and pushed away his dish. "No, seriously, Dad yelled at me for a while. I listened. I was wrong not to come home to Mom's funeral, or visit more often throughout the years. She was a good woman, and a great mother to me. But, life for me has been a little complicated."

"Complicated? You're single. You travel. You have no worries."

Her brother averted his eyes from his sister. "My life *is* complicated. One day, I'll explain it to you, but not now."

"Why not now?"

He sighed. "Because it's not the right time."

"Is that the same load of shit you gave Dad today?" She was starting to get angry with him.

"I told him the truth. Everything I've been doing in my life. The 'why' for not keeping in touch. It was a good conversation." He smiled. "You know, Dad, he doesn't say much." Then, he lowered his voice. "But, before you think you can get our discussion out of him, think again. He's promised to take what I told him to the grave."

Alarmed, Antoinette tilted back in her chair. "It sounds serious."

She didn't know what was up with her brother. *Was he some criminal on the loose? Or, was he dealing with bad people?*

Salvatore folded his hands over his plate and took a deep breath. "Okay. Okay. You want some truth." He looked down. "I have three kids."

Antoinette almost spit out her wine. "*What*? Kids? *You* have *kids*. Why didn't you say anything?"

Her brother chuckled. "How do I bring up my children at my niece's funeral? I'm a lot more caring than you remember, sis."

She waved your hands. "Thank you. But tell me about your children? Are you married?"

Salvatore fidgeted with his napkin. "Umm... Was married. Their mother passed away...um...about six years ago." He pulled out his wallet and rested it on the table. Taking their picture out slowly, he passed it to his sister. "Here, let me show you a picture of them."

"I'm so sorry, Salvatore." Antoinette carefully took it from him. It showed a photo of two girls and a boy, roughly between the ages of eight and twelve. She coughed. The children were black.

He nodded, reading his sister's mind. "Yes, I have three *very beautiful* biracial children. Their mother was gorgeous. Lucky for them, they took after her."

She touched her heart. "How old are they? What are their names?"

He pointed to the picture and explained. "This one here, is Emily, she's my oldest at twelve years old. And," he chuckled, "my intellect. A straight-A, high-honors student, she loves reading books and singing Opera."

Antoinette observed Emily. She had straight black hair, light skin, and was very thin. "Wow. She's gorgeous."

Salvatore smiled. "I know. I have to watch the boys with this one."

Next he pointed to his second child. "This little man of mine is Abraham. He's nine and the middle child. He's my sports kid." Shaking his head he continued. "Every time I come back from a trip, we have to go out and play basketball. He's quick, too. His idol is Kobe Bryant."

She observed his only son. He was dark, handsome, and lanky. His eyes like his father were bright with curiosity. He was going to be tall like his dad, too, she thought.

"And then, my baby girl, Audrey. She's eight." Salvatore grinned. "She's my little lover girl. Always hugging me and kissing me."

"She's exotic looking," Antoinette commented, noticing her curls, round face, and piercing black eyes.

"She does look exotic," Salvatore nodded. "She's great. The only thing is she's been diagnosed with a slight learning disability."

"Oh no," she responded.

Her brother shook his head. "No, it's not a big deal. She's behind almost a year from the other kids. I have her in afterschool special programs. She's doing great."

"They're beautiful, big brother." Antoinette handed over the picture.

Salvatore smiled, taking the photo and putting it back into his wallet. "Thank you. I love them all very much."

Their steaks and potatoes came. While Salvatore dove into his meal, she picked at her food still trying to find her appetite and assimilate the news of her brother's children. She had so many questions regarding his family. *What was his wife's name? What was she like? How did she die? How has he survived being a single father to his three children? Why hadn't they connected sooner?* The list in her mind was extensive, but as she gazed at him, she sensed he was still hurting and didn't want to broach the subject at the moment. *Maybe later?*

She forced herself to eat, taking one bite at a time, deciding to change the subject—a more personal one to her. She needed closure. All her anger from the last day she had seen him when she was a teenager came flooding back. She wanted to yell and scream at him. He had left her alone so many years ago.

She was going to be an adult about this, so she calmly asked, "Tell me something. Why did you leave, Salvatore? I missed you terribly when you left. You have no idea what you did to me. I was traumatized for years."

He paused with fork in hand. "I had to. I was confused, got involved with some bad people. Did some dangerous drugs. I was afraid I'd get destructive. I needed to find myself or else I'd be trouble to Mom and Dad. Then, when I got on track, it was awkward to return. I left so abruptly, so I stayed away." He looked her in the eyes. "I'm sorry I had to do that to you. It was cowardly of me. I'm ashamed of my past behavior."

"Did you know Mom kept your room the way you left it, for years? Waiting for you to return."

"No, but Dad told me today."

Antoinette tried to see through Salvatore and figure him out, but couldn't. They never had anything in common. She didn't want to assume anything about his private life, and he was being very careful not to disclose anything. "Any regrets?"

"A few. Never coming home to see Mom and Dad, not saying goodbye to Mom at her funeral, and of course, meeting Isabella."

Hearing her daughter's name aloud made Antoinette's heart ache. "Are you happy, Salvatore? In Portland?"

"Yes, I'm living the life I want to live. I'm truly content."

"But, now you are raising three children by yourself. It has to be hard?"

Salvatore coughed and poured more wine into Antoinette's glass and then his own.

"Antoinette, I can't say enough how truly sorry I am for not being in your life. Though the timing for which I came back isn't the best, I'd like us to get to know one another better. Which brings me to my next question."

He had avoided her question about his children. Antoinette was a little suspicious as to why, but let it pass. She put down her fork and knife, not sure what "next" was going to be. "You've surprised me once already. What now?"

After taking a gulp of wine and dabbing his mouth with a napkin he said, "My job takes me all over the world. I am away fifteen or more days a month. I enjoy it, but it's a lot of time away from my family. I have a nanny who takes care of the kids. When I'm home, I try to spend time with them, but my other love, selfishly enough, is boating."

Antoinette laughed. So this was the big surprise, her brother whom she remembered would never go near the water on their few summer vacations to the Lake, was an avid boater.

"You're kidding? Boating? You?" she pointed.

"Why, yes. See how I've changed. For your information, I do boat racing. Up in Michigan, California, on the Gulf, you name it."

The waiter came to check on them. Salvatore nodded and ordered up another bottle of wine.

She leaned in. "You never cease to amaze me. What a surprise."

The waiter came back and refilled both glasses. Salvatore took another drink. "That's not the surprise."

She couldn't take it anymore. She had learned her brother had children, his wife was dead, and he's an avid boater who participates in boat racing across the U.S. *Now what?* She took a sip of wine and braced herself for the next news.

He rested back in his chair. "Because I travel so much, my biggest concern is my children and their well-being. Sure, I have Paula, my nanny who takes care of them; she does a great job, but she's elderly and not family."

A cold chill ran down her spine. "What are you asking me, Salvatore?"

He took her hand. "My job keeps me away from the kids. It's my reality, I have to travel. The other thing, as I said, is boat races. It's my vice and my addiction. And frankly, that keeps me away, too."

"I still don't understand."

"I want my kids to be taken care of if something ever did happen to me."

Antoinette touched his arm. "Are you sick or something?"

"No, no. But, I'd like to name you and Vito as the legal guardians of my children."

Her heart fluttered. Her brother *was* caring. She nodded. "Yes, of course.

Although I hope it never comes to that. I'm sure you're a great father, but I'd love to. I'm sure Vito would agree. Yes, yes. I will talk to him about it. What do we have to do?"

He relaxed back in his chair. "Thank you so much, sis. It means a lot to me that you'd be willing to do this. I also feel better knowing I have family support. I'll have my lawyer draw up the paperwork and send it off for you and Vito to sign."

She reached for his hands and held them. "Now, let's not worry about you leaving us, okay?"

A huge burden lifted. Antoinette felt like she was floating on air because of the reconnection with her brother. Her eyes welled up. She had been hoping one day things could be rekindled with him. Alone without her brother all these years, a hole had been left open within her heart, and now it could close.

Salvatore smiled.

"I'm glad you've come back. You are welcome here anytime. Mom would be proud of you." Antoinette forced a grin, thinking of her daughter. "Isabella would have adored you."

He squeezed her hands across the table. "Thank you for your forgiving, kind words."

It was her turn to request something from her brother. "So, when do we meet your darling children?"

Salvatore pulled out a little black calendar and set it aside on the table. Pointing to it, he said, "Yes. We'll have to schedule something before we leave here tonight. But for now, I have another priority?"

"Oh no. I'm afraid," Antoinette laughed.

He laughed with her, lifting a short menu off the table. "How about dessert?"

She wiped her brow. "Phew. Now we're talking, big brother."

CHAPTER 57

Thursday afternoon Vito entered Cleveland Hopkins International Airport. He had finished his training early, and was able to move up his flight reservation. It was a quarter to one, and his flight didn't leave until two-thirty. He walked up to the United Airlines check-in counter and took out his wallet. Slipping out from behind his driver's license, a picture of Isabella fell to the counter.

"What a beautiful little girl. Your daughter?" asked the clerk.

Vito swiftly picked it up and jammed it back into his wallet. "Yes."

"Lovely."

"Thank you," he whispered back. He hoped the woman wouldn't ask any more questions as she assigned his seat and took his luggage.

Vito meandered to his gate, picking up a coffee, and browsing the boutiques. At the gate, he sat waiting in a chair and stared out the window. It was a gray sky. Chicago was expected to get cold weather. The last two days were busy; he had no time to think, nor time to worry about anything. It was business as usual, but the loneliness and loss of Isabella wasn't far away from his thoughts and his heart.

He had called Antoinette the night before. She and Salvatore went out to dinner. His wife had sounded happy. He was glad for her. It had been a struggle for his wife to be estranged from her brother for all these years. Like his dad and him.

She told him they patched up their relationship and about their new inherited nieces and nephew. He was shocked to hear about his new extended family, and was looking forward to catching up with her when he got home.

Vito pulled out his wallet and took out Isabella's picture again. It was last year's picture from school. She was smiling from ear to ear, her long blondish curls accenting her rosy-cheeked face. She looked so cute and alive. *Alive*, he thought. Isabella would have been alive, if not for the accident. *I miss you, baby. Did I give you everything a father should have given his child?*

He wondered if she knew how much he loved her, despite how much he hated that she had a limb deficiency. He knew in his heart he couldn't change how he viewed his daughter's handicap sometimes. He willed himself constantly to not think of her leg, but it bugged him no less. He despised himself for being so selfish.

He pondered on how Antoinette had fared these last couple of days. Vito thought of Isabella's room. He knew Antoinette was itching to empty it out, but he didn't want to do anything. The thought of going through all her stuff was too painful for him. He wanted to preserve the room forever with his daughter's memory.

Sliding the picture back in his wallet, and putting it back in back pocket, Vito took a sip of his coffee. He should call Antoinette; let her know he was at the airport and would be home around four instead of seven.

Taking out his cell, he dialed home. The phone rang and rang with no answer until the voicemail went on. It beeped after the standard message.

"It's me. I'm at the airport. Got an earlier flight. Boarding soon. Will be home around four. Bye."

He clicked off.

Vito then laid his head back on the seat, and closed his eyes. He thought back to the first time Isabella took her first steps with her prosthesis, and how it was quite a challenge to get her to the fitting at Proven Prosthetics. He remembered the times she said she talked to Jesus and how alarmed he and Antoinette had been. They, *he*, should have embraced the spiritual gift she had. He remembered the family picture she drew for them. He was getting choked up recalling all these things about his daughter. They had been a family. And now, where would their life take them?

Shaking his head and opening his eyes to erase the memories, he noticed a family walk past him—a husband, wife, and a little girl probably around four years old. She wore her hair up in two ponytails, and she carried a stuffed animal in one arm. The little girl waved at him. Vito forced a smile and waved back at her.

God, I'll never understand your timing.

He got up and trekked to the window. His plane was there and they started boarding. He waited for his seat number to be called. Taking a deep breath, he sighed. It was back to reality when he arrived home.

CHAPTER 58

It was before eleven on a Thursday morning. Antoinette decided to get out and head to the library before her husband came home from his Ohio trip that night. She did an online search for parents coping with the death of their children. There were over ten million hits on search words for "coping," "loss," and "bereavement".

She then asked the librarian for help in finding specific books on that particular subject. After going through a stack of ten self-help books, Antoinette sat in a lounge chair with three of them, and began flipping through the pages.

What she was going through—those lonely thoughts, saddened feelings, exhaustion and low energy, clouded mind—were all normal, even though every loss was unique from one person to another. She wasn't sure how Vito was coping; they weren't communicating their feelings to each other.

All the books shared a common position. With time, the anguish of the loss would fade, even if the pain was still there. The memories of Isabella they shared would be with them forever, but slowly they needed to learn to live again and get used to a life without her.

Reading the books comforted Antoinette. She reflected on the ideas of the books until she realized the time—she'd been at the library over three hours. Her mind in a flutter, she bolted out of the door. Tonight, she'd talk to Vito. They needed to empty the room, move on, and restore their marriage. *They had too.*

Once outside, it started to rain. Not a shower, nor a drizzle, but a steady, refreshing, cold rain.

Going back to work was another issue. After agonizing over it, she notified the principal the other morning, and had let him know her decision. In the last couple of weeks of being home, Antoinette felt she couldn't go back to teaching at McKinnley Elementary—her daughter's school. The memories, the pain, it would be too hard to walk by her classroom every day knowing she wasn't there anymore. One day, after giving herself time to grieve appropriately, she could go to another school or, do corporate teaching.

Shaking off droplets of water from her jacket, Antoinette lumbered into the deserted house. She was getting used to the emptiness. But, once inside, anxiety and nervousness took hold of her mind, and she spontaneously decided to start packing Isabella's room herself. It couldn't wait, even if Vito told her they'd do it together. *Besides, he was very busy at work; I could get a head start.*

With a little courage, Antoinette plodded up the stairs, entering her daughter's room. She hesitated for a few minutes standing in the doorway, thinking of her baby. Taking a deep breath, she stepped in.

Antoinette got as far as the bed and slumped down. At first she couldn't move, and just stared at the wall in front of her. But then, she started picking up items. Soon, she was sniffling and wiping away the tears, as she carefully managed to box and label all of Isabella's beloved books. Then, she moved to the chest and did the same with its contents. After a couple of hours, she had packed three boxes. Carrying them one by one down the stairs, she stacked the boxes against the wall. With the third box in hand, Antoinette met Vito at the foot of the stairs.

"Hi. You're here already?" she said cautiously, squinting toward the hallway clock.

"It's four. Didn't you hear the message? What's going on?" Vito said, eyeing her suspiciously.

"I didn't hear—I'm cleaning."

He grabbed the box from her arms and threw it to the floor. It hit the hardwood with a loud thud. "Why are you doing this?"

"Because I had to, and you won't."

"No. Leave it," Vito shouted.

"Listen, I went to the library today and reviewed books about child loss," Antoinette said gently. "We can't freeze time. We need to move on."

"This is your fault," he said, pointing a finger at her.

"*My* fault? How is this my fault?"

"It's…your fault…she's dead!"

"She was hit by a car. This isn't my doing," Antoinette replied, moving passed him toward the kitchen.

He followed. "No, you're the one who said it was okay to go to Lizzy's. I didn't want her to go, but you let it happen."

She faced him. "For your information, I don't recall *you* telling her no."

"She was asking you, not me," he pointed again.

"And what are you, some stranger? You're her father! You could have said something, but you didn't. Do you know how hard this has been for me?"

"Oh, and it hasn't been for *me*?" he blasted back. "I've had to get up each day and earn a living while you spend all your time with her. This is all that's left," he said, pointing to the boxes on the floor. "We have to remember her, and you want to take it all away."

"It was *you* who insisted I stay home and raise Isabella. Vito, don't you get it?" she said, waving her arms. "I'm reminded each and every day of our loss, every moment I'm in this God-forsaken house."

Her husband was in her face. "What do you want to do? Get rid of her altogether? Like she never happened?"

"No, Vito. The reality is, she's dead, but I want to live like she is here in my heart," she said, touching to her chest. "I can't bring her back, I can't bring Devon back, and I can't bring my mother back. And neither can you."

"We should have had more children."

"*What*? Like that's going to erase the pain of Isabella? Lose one child, but you still have others, so it doesn't count?" She cringed. "Why didn't we adopt? Oh wait, I remember. It was 'I don't want to adopt because they aren't my blood,' bullshit."

"You're always right, and I'm always wrong. Go ahead," he said, and threw up his hands. "Pack her up and get rid of my daughter."

That was the final straw. Antoinette moved out of his way. "Sometimes, I hate you." Grabbing her keys off the kitchen counter she headed for the side door.

"I hate you, too!" Vito shouted back.

Once outside, she fumbled with the keys inside the car, and then pulled out of the drive. At first, she drove aimlessly around their neighborhood. A steady shower turned into a freezing rain. Her heart beat rapidly, as tears streamed down her face. *"Damn you,"* she pounded the steering wheel. "Why is he such an ass?"

The wipers moved in a rhythmic pace across the windshield. The air was cold in the car. Cranking up the heat full-blast, she hadn't even thought to put on her jacket.

Antoinette saw a familiar street down a ways. She knew where to go. Making a quick right turn, she headed toward her destination.

Going slowly on Featherherst Drive she saw the gates were still open at the Lincoln Memorial Cemetery. Driving through the curving road just before the street ended, Antoinette pulled off to the right side and got out. The freezing rain quickly turned to accumulating snow, and it swished under her sneakers. The icy flakes hit her face but she didn't care.

Antoinette passed several rows of headstones, not daring to look at the names. Something about cemeteries gave her the creeps. She hadn't been back since Isabella's funeral service.

There, in an open clearing beneath an oak tree a little ways from Devon's grave, she came up to Isabella's gravestone. Dusting off the accumulating snow, the inscription read, *Isabella, Our Rose*. A granite statue of an angel stood cradling a heart. Within the heart, covered by glass, she and Vito had inserted a picture of their daughter sitting on her bench in the rose garden. It was taken shortly before her death.

Antoinette knelt beside the grave. Her jeans were soon soaked from the snow. She shivered, pushing wet hair away from her face. She ran her hands around the gravestone and touched the inscribed writing. She began to breathe rapidly, fighting the anguish inside until she couldn't take it anymore. The tears let loose like a broken dam.

"Why did you have to go?" Antoinette sobbed. "I *miss* you so much. You were my life. I want you back. Come back." She fell to the ground pounding the grass-covered snow with her fists. "What am I to do?"

Looking up through the night sky, she wailed, "God. Why her and not me? Why have You done this?" With her fists clenched and voice hoarse, she shouted, "Bring her back."

"Antoinette, stop! Stop!"

Startled, she turned. Vito stood behind her. He had on his wool coat; hands in his pockets, eyes bloodshot from crying. White fluffy snow still fell from the sky.

Turning away from him, Antoinette collapsed on the ground. "I loved you so much."

Suddenly, he was beside her. "I loved her, too, just as much as you."

They held each other and sobbed. He caressed and cradled her face, kissing it tenderly through the tears.

"I'm so sorry. I'm not strong. I feel so much pain. That day of her death constantly plays in my mind," Vito whispered, embracing her, his own tears streaming down his cheeks. "I couldn't even save her. Fathers are supposed to protect their daughters, and I didn't. I'm such a failure."

"I'm sorry too," Antoinette whispered. "Let's not fight."

"I don't want to fight with you ever. I've been unfair to you, blaming you for everything, and to Isabella, thinking about her handicap. I've been a coward. I'm scared. Scared we can't get through this. I can't lose you, too." Rivulets of tears fell down his cheeks, his body shook uncontrollably.

"You won't," she said, raising her head to look at her husband, touching his face, the face that had made her smile all these years.

They hugged and faced the gravestone. It glistened with the sparkling snow collecting on it. Together, they touched and caressed their beautiful little girl in the picture. They remained there for some time, no longer feeling the icy snow on their skin.

After a while, Vito turned to her, "You're all wet." Helping her up, he sighed. "Come on, we have some more packing to do."

"I know," she replied, still dazed.

"Look at me," he said. Their eyes met. "I know Isabella will be in our hearts."

"Yes," Antoinette nodded, falling into his arms.

They walked arm and arm toward their cars. She glanced over his shoulder to look at Isabella's grave blurring in the falling snow. She stopped, thinking she saw something.

Vito paused, "What is it?"

Antoinette shook herself, unsure of what she saw. "Nothing. I'm just cold."

"Let's get you home."

***

A week later, Antoinette roamed the house. Isabella's room had been straightened out. Every box filled, carefully labeled and placed down in another corner of the basement. Her toys and books had been packed and delivered to the children's ward at Greenwood Memorial Hospital.

The porcelain nativity figurines remained behind the closed door of Isabella's room on the bare table—the only connection to their deceased daughter. It was a reminder of her life, and Antoinette couldn't part with it.

At the end of that week, Cheryl and Connor popped over. They hovered around the doorway.

"Hi. How's Lizzy?"

"She's not sleeping very well," Cheryl lamented. "Our pediatrician suggested we should have her see a counselor."

Antoinette nodded. "It might be a good thing for her. This has been a trauma to her as well."

"She's been taking things pretty hard. How are you guys holding up?"

"We're getting by, one step at a time. Want to come in for some coffee?"

Her friend backed away from the door. "We need to go. Connor needs to eat. Next time."

"Sure. Thank you for stopping by."

After they left, Antoinette closed the door and steadied herself on the wood frame. She let the tears roll down her cheeks. She cried not only for her loss, but for the loss of Lizzy's innocent spirit. *Will the image of that day ever leave my mind or even Lizzy's?*

CHAPTER 59

December

Thanksgiving came and went. Antoinette and her husband never did help Father Robert with the Thanksgiving delivery. Vito had been totally against it—against anything to do with the church, so rather than start another fight she called their priest and declined his offer.

Shopping malls and stores were filled with Christmas music. Antoinette had grown to love this time of year ever since Isabella had been born. She loved spoiling her with new clothes and toys. This year, there wouldn't be any gifts under the tree for her; ever.

Feeling a little sentimental, Antoinette decided she would buy toys for needy children, something to make herself feel purposeful. Then, suddenly, it hit her. Why not get gifts for her nieces and nephew! Isabella would have agreed. But before she did anything, she'd run it past Vito and see what he thought.

For now, there was a more pressing matter to attend to—the guardianship of her brother's children. It took her several weeks to get up the courage to tell her husband about it. So much had happened. She and Salvatore had been talking on the phone quite a bit since his visit. He had prepared all the paperwork for their signatures and had sent them over.

She had received them in the mail on December 16th, Vito's forty-seventh birthday. *What a surprise gift, this shall be. I will tell him tonight.* So, Antoinette cooked him his favorite meal of baked elbow pasta with sun-dried tomatoes, green peas and red peppers. Her dinner choice had pleased him. She was glad to do something nice for him. After supper, as they retreated to the den for a drink, she took out the envelope and handed it to him.

"Here."

"What is it?"

"Open it." Antoinette was both scared and excited. *Lord, let him be happy about this.*

She sat next to him twisting her wedding band. There were three pages and he spent a few minutes going over each page. She couldn't tell his expression as he flipped through the pages, his brow often furrowed when he was concentrating.

He was silent as he put the pages back in the envelope, finished his drink, and put the empty glass on the coffee table.

"So, I'm assuming this isn't news to you, just me."

She nodded. "I've known for several weeks now. I've been waiting for a good time to discuss it. We've been a little distracted. I got the packet today from Salvatore."

He laid back his head against the couch. She was waiting for a tantrum or an outburst, but rather he said, "Okay. Will we get to meet these kids someday? I hate to be legal guardians to three children whom I've never met."

Antoinette coughed. Stunned, it took her a moment to compose herself. "Are you fine with this?"

"Absolutely," Vito whispered.

"And yes, we are planning some sort of get together. Salvatore wants to come back to Chicago with the kids."

"Good." He stood up, taking the papers with him. "I'm going in the kitchen. I'll sign the papers and you can send them back to your brother."

She watched as he walked out. "Sure. Thank you." Shaking her head, she thought, what just happened? Could it be her husband was this agreeable? Grinning, she thought, *I'll take this response anytime.*

Antoinette called after him, as he exited the den. "I was thinking, it's Christmas and all, about the kids…you know…" She shrugged. "Presents?"

Vito nodded his head. "Do what you feel is appropriate. I'm good with it."

An excitement was building inside her. Her husband was actually okay with guardianship and Christmas presents. This felt good. She ran out of the room to call her brother and find out what Emily, Abraham, and Audrey needed. She was going Christmas shopping tomorrow!

CHAPTER 60

Christmas Day morning. After much pleading from Antoinette, Vito reluctantly agreed to go to mass with her. He hadn't gone since Isabella's funeral, and frankly with the way life had been going for them, Vito's faith was at an all-time low. The tragic death of his daughter was a huge blow to his understanding of God's ways. He often questioned if a God existed at all.

The church was crowded; all the pews filled. He and Antoinette chose to stand in the back. Their only other option was the dreaded "mother's room," which only would have reminded them of their loss.

It was hot and stuffy in the church. He kept looking at his wife knowing she got claustrophobic. He didn't want her fainting like she did when she was pregnant.

After some time, she whispered to him that she was stepping out and would wait for him in the foyer. He nodded, but then decided to follow her out.

"Ah, much better," Antoinette said, unbuttoning her coat." Then she turned. Vito was right behind her. "Why didn't you stay? You didn't have to come out with me."

"Oh no," he replied. "I don't want you having another blackout, and then we get stuck in Father Robert's office. No way."

His wife laughed, "Too funny."

They sat on one of the benches in the foyer and listened over the intercom to the remainder of the liturgy.

"After mass, we should go," he said. *I want to be out of here before the old priest sees us.*

"Why don't we say hello to Father Robert?"

"Do we have to? That priest never minds his own business."

She nudged him. "We should at least wish him a Merry Christmas, don't you think? It would be rude if he saw us and we didn't greet him."

He huffed for a bit, but then realized there was no harm by saying hello.

After the mass, they waited patiently as the last of the parishioners bid their goodbyes. Father Robert, upon seeing them, happily hugged Vito and Antoinette.

"I'm so glad to see you. Merry Christmas."

"You too, Father. What a nice mass," Antoinette said. "We heard from the foyer. Sorry, I couldn't stand in there. I was feeling a little crowded."

"We were at full capacity today, eh? What a glorious day it is. I'm glad you came out here," he chuckled. "I do remember your little fainting episode." Father Robert then motioned them to take a seat on the bench, "Come. Come over here and sit. I'll be right back."

After a few minutes he emerged from the Sacristy sporting a black clergy shirt with a high-banded white collar, and black slacks. He fumbled with his back pocket and pulled out a piece of paper from his trousers.

"Here," he motioned to Vito to take the slip of paper from his hand. "I've been saving this, hoping to see you two. I know you don't need my help with anything, but I have this flyer for you."

Vito cautiously opened up the pamphlet, wondering what other homework Father Robert had up his sleeve for them. But it wasn't homework. It was an invitation to attend a session for parents of deceased children.

"Father," he began.

The priest held up his hand. "If you feel like going, go. If you don't, then don't. I recommend it, though. They're good people, and they've helped a lot of families. You're both going to be okay."

"We're—" Vito nodded at Antoinette for confirmation. "It's taking—"

The priest lovingly held him by the shoulders. "I know, son, I know."

Vito weakly took the invite, stuffing the pamphlet into his pocket. They stayed a little longer with Father Robert, making small talk before departing.

On the drive home Vito observed a quietness about his wife. He looked in the rearview mirror—a big mistake.

Who am I kidding?

As he turned onto Trevor Lane, he noted every house had cars in their driveways except theirs. They had invited Antoinette's dad, Frank, over for dinner but he had opted to go to his friend. He had told his daughter over the phone in the morning, "Christmas is just another day." He wasn't in a celebratory mood... Something about losing his beloved wife and granddaughter, and feeling abandoned by the holiday.

Vito's parents went to their home in North Carolina for the holidays. They had invited him and Antoinette to join them, but he had no desire to go anywhere, either. Cheryl and Lee went to their cousins. So, it was just them two, all alone. It was ironic. Had they gone backwards? He never realized how much Isabella had filled their home, and with her not around anymore—everything was empty again. He couldn't comprehend it. One moment they were a family, the next, lonely people living under the same roof.

They changed their clothes. In the kitchen, Vito opened a bottle of wine. He laid the cork and wine opener on the counter next to the pamphlet Father Robert had given them. While Antoinette heated up two frozen dinners, he perused the details and session dates.

He felt his wife's eyes on him.

"You don't want to go to this, do you?" *Please, please say no, I can't take anymore sessions, ever.*

She shook her head. "No, we don't have to if you don't like." Then, she continued with their dinner preparations.

Vito smiled. "Thank you." He tossed the pamphlet in the garbage can.

He then brought up two small table trays from the basement, set them up in the den; they sat side by side watching football on TV, avoiding any conversation.

Through the front window, he noticed a light snow began to fall, cascading slowly and softly to the ground as if it had no hurry. The flakes were big and fluffy, the kind Isabella would have loved to stick out her tongue and catch in her mouth.

His throat felt dry. His wife picked at her food, and stared at the TV. He was not hungry anymore, but rather gazed to the window again, observing the peaceful, rhythmic descent of the snowflakes.

Grabbing his wife's hand and kissing it, he questioned whether peace would ever surround them once more after all that had happened.

God, please help us. We have to make it.

CHAPTER 61

October, 2010. One year after Isabella's death.

"Antoinette," Vito called from the driveway. It was Saturday, after one in the afternoon, and they had a far drive ahead of them.

"I'm coming!" she shouted from inside.

Leaning next to the car, he watched her come out through the side door. Antoinette wore faded blue jeans and a burgundy-colored cotton blouse. She had gained some weight back, not looking rail-thin as she had before. Her shoulder-length hair was dyed a chestnut color, and her face sported enough makeup to give her a glow about her he hadn't seen in a quite some time. His wife was restored to her old self.

She came out. "Okay… *Shit.* I forgot something else. Hold on." She ran back in.

He laughed to himself, thinking about what Father Robert had told him a couple of months back about restoration. They had been sitting outside on the patio near Isabella's rose garden, which was in full bloom. It was a Thursday, and the priest had come over for dinner. Antoinette was in the kitchen preparing their meal.

Father Robert had commented on the beautiful roses, and Vito shared with him how he and his wife talked to them each day. Something their little girl had taught them.

The priest then cleared his throat, "You like artwork?"

"What do you mean?"

"Have you ever been to an art gallery with Antoinette?"

Vito rubbed his chin. The idea of spending any time in an art gallery was like being in solitary confinement. He desired no part of art or understood artistic appeal. He was a black and white kind of guy. He'd rather watch sports on TV.

"No. Not my kind of thing."

"Understood. However, what's interesting about art galleries are the intrinsic details to the paintings. It's painstaking to paint, but what's more fascinating, is the effort and patience it takes to restore old paintings to their original state."

Vito shook his head. Father Robert was talking in parables as he always did. Sometimes he wondered if he was actually Jesus in disguise.

"Father, forgive me but I have no idea what you're talking about. Can you dummy it down for me, please?"

The priest laughed out loud, his belly bobbing up and down. "Why sure. Listen carefully. This is important. You'll know what I mean when it happens."

Vito shrugged.

"You've been through trials, you and Antoinette. When you first get married, your life is like a brand new painting. The oils are fresh and the color vibrant. Over time, the colors in the painting fade—the elements may affect it: dust, sun, etc.—like the trials you and Antoinette endured. Your marriage," Father Robert paused, "is like an antique painting that has been weathered. Now your job is to restore it to its original state. Restore your marriage, okay. Wash away the elements, so the oils can become vibrant and shiny."

Vito reflected on the last year since his daughter's death. It had been a bumpy ride. Despite being cordial to one another and sharing the grief over the loss of Isabella, his relationship to his wife had slumped and broken down once more. He had felt distant from Antoinette for a while, as if they didn't have anything in common. After all they'd been through in their marriage, the one true thing that had kept them together had been their daughter, and she had left them. They needed to transition from grief to gratitude.

Out of nowhere he heard, "Earth to Vito."

He blinked. "Huh?"

"Did you put the bags in the trunk?"

"Yup. Been waiting here for you. What took you so long?"

"I had to put some things away and lock up."

"You know the highway is going to be jammed getting down into the city. I don't feel like sitting in traffic all afternoon."

"Relax," she offered, getting into the passenger seat.

He pulled out of the drive and they saw Cheryl, Lizzy and Connor outside on their front lawn. He and Antoinette waved as they drove by.

As if reading his mind, his wife said, "Remind me this week to follow up with Cheryl and see how things are going with Lizzy."

He nodded. "I know. I don't know what to do. I feel awkward. Lee has been distant. He just waves when I drive by, but that's it. Everything's changed."

"I know what you mean. I miss talking with Cheryl and the kids, but what's there to talk about now."

Vito squeezed his wife's hand. It was their nineteenth wedding anniversary.

A few days earlier it was the first year anniversary of Isabella's death, and they had visited the cemetery.

Today, he wanted to distract their minds. He was taking Father Robert's advice. Their marriage needed renewal... Restoration. He had planned a weekend getaway with his wife. They needed to spend more time together, and move on.

As he drove, he recalled his morning's decision to stop at the cemetery, even though they had gone earlier in the week. Antoinette had no idea of his plans. He sped faster down Trevor Lane.

"Hey, Mario Andretti, the city is not going anywhere. Slow down."

He didn't look or respond but made a sharp right, and headed to the cemetery.

"Where are you going?"

"To visit our daughter, again."

"Oh."

He gazed at his wife, his palms sweating. "Do you mind?"

She smiled. "No. I was hoping you would."

A beautiful October day, the leaves were in their prime colors—red, gold and orange. They accented the streets like a mirage with the sun shining.

They drove through the cemetery gates and followed the road down a couple of winding curves, passing a few parked cars. Near the end of the path, Vito parked the car. He climbed out, opened the trunk, and pulled out a bouquet of red roses and two smaller-sized bouquets.

He came around to her side and grabbed her hand.

"They're beautiful!" Antoinette exclaimed.

They made a couple of stops before going to Isabella's grave. One was to visit little Devon, whom they never had gotten to know. He laid one of the smaller bouquets on the little grave. Then he and Antoinette treaded to his mother-in-law's grave, where he carefully placed the other bouquet.

Together, husband and wife trudged to a growing oak tree near where Isabella was buried. Vito positioned the final bouquet on the granite gravestone. He sat down on the grass. It was dry. Crunchy leaves were scattered about. Vito gazed up at the tree. Soon it'd be void of any leaves and winter would arrive. Together, they sat quietly in the afternoon sunlight. Not a sound could be heard except the occasional chirping bird.

Deep in his thoughts, Vito talked with his daughter.

Hi, Isabella. It's Daddy. How are you, princess? Your mother and I miss you. We're going to the city today. Remember how you liked going to the city? What fun we had going to the zoo, the museum, and the beach? I love you, baby.

He continued staring at the grave. The wind picked up a little, the oak tree began to rustle, and a few more dead leaves fell around them. Then, everything quieted down. He knew their little girl had been there with them. Silently, they gathered themselves and walked back to the car.

***

The city was crowded as usual. Vito turned off Michigan Avenue onto Huron Street and into the valet portal of the Centennial Hotel. They checked in and took the elevators to the fifth floor. They had a corner room overlooking Michigan Avenue. They observed the streets below; people with shopping bags, taxis and cars everywhere, causing all sorts of traffic jams.

They unpacked their bags and went out across the street to Oak Street beach for a stroll. It was very windy near Lake Michigan, and a little chilly, but there were still bikers and runners on the walkway. Vito and Antoinette didn't say much, but held hands as they walked. At times, he stole glances at his wife. She was beautiful to him, after all these years together.

She caught him staring. "What?"

He grinned shyly. "I'm glad we're here."

"So am I."

They wandered taking in the view, and then headed back to the hotel to take showers. Vito ordered a bottle of champagne and a bowl of fresh strawberries.

They sat on a couch with their robes on enjoying the strawberries and a little bubbly. Their eyes met. *I miss her. I miss her touch, her smell, her breath. Would she take me?*

He took her glass and his and put them down on the table, then undid her robe. It fell to the sides of the couch. He stared at her exposed breasts and stomach—nervous to touch her flesh like it was forbidden fruit. Then, taking her face in his hands, he raised it to meet his and drew his lips to hers. Her lips were wet and soft.

Vito couldn't believe the emotional surge and desire electrically shooting throughout his body. It had been months since they'd made love.

He gently picked Antoinette up and carried her to the bed. He climbed over her, kissing and letting his hands explore her breasts and body as she moaned. He could feel his wife's response as she trembled beneath him. His body shook and ached for her. He wanted her and wanted her now.

She quickly removed his robe, throwing it onto the carpet, wrapped her legs around his lower back and pulled him down hard. Soon he entered her. They began rocking together, kissing, feeling the intensity of their desire, with a forceful passion that hadn't existed in years. Like old lovers, their souls entwined together in desperate need for one another. Until, they both cried out in satisfaction.

As they held one another, Vito teased, "Man, was this overdue."

"You're telling me," Antoinette said heavily.

After some rest, they found each other again. This time slower, as comes anything with practice and familiarity to the outcome. When their desires had been satisfied they lay spent on the bed.

A few minutes later, his wife peeked at the clock on the night stand. "Don't we have reservations at ten?"

"Hmm...," he mumbled, closing his eyes.

"It's almost nine-thirty. Get up," she said, sitting up. "I'm starving."

Vito turned over. "Let's wait a bit." He didn't care about food; all he wanted to do was rest.

Antoinette jokingly shoved him off the bed. "No, let's get going. You worked me into this appetite, now feed me!"

They quickly dressed and strutted down Rush Street, a popular stretch filled with boutiques, restaurants, pubs and shops. They entered Helen's, a famous seafood and oyster bar.

People stood everywhere around the host desk. The air smelled like spicy perfume, garlic, and beer. A band playing in one corner giving the place a club-like energy.

They waited for quite some time. Vito was starting to get inpatient when the hostess seated them almost an hour later.

At the dinner table, Vito and Antoinette feasted on oysters, crab cakes and couple of bottles of Chianti. Taking a bite of a crab cake, Vito remembered how Isabella loved them.

He set his fork down, "Do you think about her?"

Antoinette wiped her mouth. "Are you kidding? Every day."

He took a sip of wine. "Sometimes I can't believe she's not with us."

"It's been a tough year," Antoinette said, sitting back. "I feel empty on some days, and others, I try to remember all the great times we had—it makes me happy to think of the good times."

Vito ran a hand through his hair. He had started feeling a burning sensation in his stomach. He wished it wasn't the wine. He already had several glasses worth. "I know I never express myself, but I hurt...hurt a lot knowing I don't have children anymore."

"I understand. I miss mothering my little Isabella."

He refilled their wine glasses. They had had a special day so far, and talking about his deceased daughter wasn't going to bring her back, but he was glad he brought it up. Isabella would have enjoyed spending the day downtown.

Grabbing his wife's hand in his own, he said, "Let's toast, shall we? To our beautiful daughter whom we'll never forget. To Isabella."

"To Isabella," Antoinette repeated.

They clinked their glasses.

He remembered their first date a few days after their initial introduction at

Antoinette's friend's party. They decided to meet for breakfast at Max and Eileen's Pancake House. He had some time in the morning before heading to clinics, and she had a free period from school. Vito remembered waiting nervously in the entrance of the restaurant, and seeing her come out of her car. She glided across the parking lot, oblivious to anyone watching her—carefree and young. She sported a silly grin on her face.

Upon seeing him stare at her through the glass doors, she stuck out her tongue. He laughed at her silliness, and at that moment, he knew he couldn't ever let her go.

Antoinette caught his gaze. She took a sip of wine. "Earth to Vito. Earth to Vito. Come in Vito… What's going on? You look like you're in outer space."

Vito laughed and shook his head. "No, just taking in the view. You look great, you know." He squeezed her hand. "I love you."

She responded, "Thank you. I love you very much. I've never stopped loving you."

His eyes stung. He swallowed, "I know. You're an amazing woman. I don't deserve you."

The waiter came with dessert menus. Vito ordered them two chocolate covered strawberries and two espressos.

Leaving the restaurant a little while later, he had a good buzz going on. Antoinette was a little giddy. Hand-in-hand they strolled down Rush Street and people-watched. When they passed a store corridor, he pulled his wife toward him. They stood there locked in a kiss, until he and Antoinette breathlessly pushed themselves apart.

With only a couple of blocks to go back to the hotel, he took her hand and they hurried around people wandering along the shops. Giggling all the way up the elevator, and skipping to their room, he barely unlocked the door with the key card before he grabbed his wife and threw her back on the bed.

***

The next afternoon, they enjoyed a content drive home. However, as they turned on their street, Vito noticed Cheryl and Lee outside with Connor and Lizzy.

"Should we—"

"Yes, let's."

He pulled over on the side of the street in front of the Starkweather's home and rolled down the window.

"Hi guys."

Lee shuffled over to the window, "How are you?"

"We're doing okay, Lee. How are you guys?"

"Eh, rough waters here and there, but we're working on it."

Vito sensed the Starkweathers' challenges with Lizzy. He and Antoinette were concerned on how the child was doing. The shock of Isabella's death had terribly affected her. He hadn't seen her out playing outside much anymore, only Connor. They heard she had been having nightmares of that day for a while, and was seeing a psychiatrist.

Behind Lee, he saw Cheryl sitting on the grass with both children. He wanted to get together with them like they used to. He turned to Antoinette, who was staring at Lizzy. She nodded her head toward him.

"If you and the kids aren't doing anything later, want to come over? We could sit out back—have a beer or something?"

"Ah, thanks, but today is not a good day, if you know what I mean?"

He felt Antoinette's hand on his arm. "Sure. We understand. We should get going. Another time." He pulled away from the curve and waved at Cheryl who waved back.

"Wow, awkward." His wife sighed.

"Tell me about it."

"What should we do now?"

She smiled at him, mischievously, "I have an idea."

He pulled into the drive and Antoinette thrust open the car door as he barely came to a stop and rushed inside the house.

"Can't you wait until I stop?"

A moment later she was out the door, Isabella's nativity set in her hands wrapped in a plastic bag.

Walking out of the garage, he smiled, knowing his wife's intentions. Yet still his heart ached. He knew Isabella loved those nativity figurines so much, and now giving it away was also a confirmation of one less item to remind him of his beloved daughter.

"I think it might help Lizzy."

Vito kissed her forehead. "Great idea. But are you sure about this?"

She took a deep breath. "Yes, I think so. What about you?"

Vito reached for the bag, peeled the plastic away from the set and gazed at it for a moment. He closed his eyes, hoping what they were about to do would have made Isabella proud of them, and benefit Lizzy. He caressed each piece with his hand, "I am."

"Thank you." She started down the drive and stopped. He was still watching her.

"You want to come with and deliver this together?"

He nodded. "Yeah."

With her parent's permission, they found Lizzy sitting on the back stoop. Vito and Antoinette approached her cautiously. The little girl once plump was now thin. She smiled weakly when she saw them.

"Hi Lizzy. What are you doing?" Antoinette asked.

Lizzy shrugged. "Nothing."

He winked. "Mind if we sit with you?"
Lizzy nodded.
They squeezed next to the little girl.
With Lizzy looking off in the distance, Vito said, "We have something for you. We thought you might like it." He motioned to Antoinette who pulled out the nativity set.
Lizzy turned and her eyes widened and watered. "For *me*? I don't know if I can…"
"Yes, honey, you can have it," Vito urged.
Antoinette laughed. "Isabella would have liked you to have it. You might want to put it on display, even if Christmas isn't for a couple months away. Isabella had this set out all year. The best part is that it brought her closer to the Lord, and she held onto that faith right until the end."
Lizzy took the set from Antoinette's hands and held it to her chest. "Wow. Thank you."
Vito said, "Now take care of the set for us, okay?"
"Yes, sir."
Vito and Antoinette hugged Lizzy, and then left her holding the precious gift that was their remembrance of Isabella. Walking quietly across the street and into their house, they unloaded their luggage.
Later, he found his wife in the kitchen taking dishes out of the dishwasher and putting them away. He strolled over to his wife and pulled her close.
"This weekend was perfect with you. Despite everything we've been through, I'm glad *we're* back. What you did this afternoon for Lizzy was terrific."
"Thanks. I think it was the best thing we could have done. I pray she gets better."
"Me, too."
"You know, seeing Cheryl and Lee like that hurts my heart. Our home is not the same anymore." Antoinette sighed.
"I understand. I keep praying all will be good with us." He took his wife in his arms and held her tightly.

CHAPTER 62

Monday morning, the next day, while clearing the cups and dishes, the phone rang. The caller ID showed an out of state call. Antoinette's heart jumped hoping it was her brother, the world traveler. She and Vito played a game every time he phoned. Where was Salvatore now?

"Hello."

"Mrs. Libero?"

"Yes, this is she," Antoinette answered, cradling the phone in her left ear, while she emptied out the dishwasher.

"Hi. I'm Dan Rezner, Salvatore's lawyer in Portland."

She nodded nonchalantly, "Okay."

"I'm afraid I have some bad news. Your brother was in a terrible boating accident and has...well... Salvatore has passed." He hesitated. "I'm so very sorry for your loss, and for sharing this news."

"Oh my God!" The phone dropped and Antoinette fell to the floor sobbing.

It took her almost an hour to compose herself after crying over the news of her brother's death. She had been estranged from Salvatore all these years, and it wasn't until last year at *her* daughter's funeral did they reconnect. Since then, they talked at least once a week. It was such a shock to lose him now. They had even become legal guardians to Salvatore's three children, and she and Vito were finally going to meet Emily, Abraham, and Audrey this Saturday.

With her brother's work schedule and her and Vito's own issues to iron out, a year had quickly past. She had spoken to him just a week ago for the final plans of their upcoming visit, remembering their phone conversation.

"Hello sis, how are you?"

"We're okay. How are you guys? Got everything planned?"

"Yes. I was calling to give you the details of our flight."

"We are so excited to meet the gang," Antoinette said, getting a paper and pen.

Salvatore chuckled. "They love the gift baskets you recently sent. Thanks for your thoughtfulness. They're just as thrilled to meet you, and to visit a big city like Chicago."

"My pleasure. I can't wait either," she said smiling. "So, what you got for us?"

"We arrive in Chicago at O'Hare Airport next Saturday at 4:59 p.m., on United Airlines flight 7712."

"Okay. Sounds good."

Salvatore coughed. "I'll also email you the full itinerary."

"Thank you." She took a breath. "So, any more boating in the works for you?"

"That was the other thing." He whistled through the receiver. "I'm leaving tomorrow for a few days in Michigan. There's a boat race in Bayview Mackinac. It starts on Lake Huron and ends at Mackinac Island. It's supposed to be one of the most scenic boat races ever. I can't miss it."

"Wow," Antoinette was surprised. "Then, you're going back to Portland getting the kids, and coming here? That's a lot of traveling."

Salvatore laughed. "Oh, it's no problem. I'm used to all sorts of travel. Besides, I got to get my clothes and organize the house."

"A lot to do in a short period of time, eh?"

"Don't worry, sis. This is my life—work and boating. You very well can't keep me away from boat racing."

"Don't I know it? Be careful."

It had been his last race. Her brother died doing what he loved. Still shocked, she called her husband and told him about her brother. She asked him to get her father and come home as soon as he could. By early afternoon, he and her dad arrived.

Upon entering the kitchen, Frank fell in her arms, crying like a child. "My son. My *only* son."

They stood in an embrace, while Vito sat at the table trying to make sense of it all.

Frank released his daughter, and wiped his tears. "Is that woman going to get the children?"

Vito reeled, "What woman?"

Antoinette already knew the details. After hanging up on the lawyer, he had called back a little while later to explain about the birthmother of her brother's three children.

"His wife, Nadeesh," she replied.

"I thought she was dead," Vito fumed.

"So did I, until I found out today she might be alive somewhere."

Vito glared at his father-in-law. "You knew about this and never said anything to us?"

Frank nodded. "He made me promise not to say anything to anyone."

"Why?"

Antoinette remembered her conversation with her brother, a year earlier, the night they went to dinner. Salvatore said he and Dad had ironed out their issues and he had confessed the whole truth of his life, and Frank promised not to repeat it.

Her father sat down at the kitchen table, fatigued. "Because he didn't want to burden anyone with his troubles." He motioned to her for a glass of water. "Let me tell you his story."

For the next half-hour, Frank recounted what his son had told him.

On one of his business trips to South Africa, Salvatore met an African woman by the name of Nadeesh at a bar one night. It was love at first sight. She confessed she was a victim of sexual trafficking. To help her get out of the country, he took her to Portland and married her. This all happened in a matter of three weeks.

Over the next several years, he and Nadeesh conceived three children together. He worked and traveled and she stayed home with the children. But after some time, when he'd return home, he'd find alcohol and drugs around. On one occasion, he found his wife with another man.

Salvatore said his wife became a different person. She'd forget to change a diaper on one of the children, or leave them in the car when she went grocery shopping. So, he hired a nanny named Paula Miller to help her. Then, Nadeesh would be away for days on end. It was not a good situation.

In order to protect the kids, Salvatore had her agree to give him full legal custody of them, and in return all she wanted was an undisclosed amount of money. Salvatore was heartbroken. He had loved Nadeesh so much. She asked him to choose between her or the children. He chose the children. She left and never returned, and that was six years ago. Salvatore admitted to Frank that he had a private investigator working on the case trying to locate Nadeesh, as he still wanted to help her.

When her father was finished, Antoinette was beside herself. She could only imagine the anguish and suffering her brother had endured; wondering if at first his wife would hurt his children while he worked. And then, searching for her because he loved her despite what she put him through. No wonder he had asked her and Vito to be the guardians of his children. He hadn't wanted to take the chance of Nadeesh coming back and fighting to get custody of them.

Antoinette circled over to her husband, who sat dumbfounded.

"We have to adopt these kids. We are now their legal guardians. They are my brother's flesh and blood."

"*What?* Are you nuts? You want to adopt them? They're black for God's sake!" Vito yelled, getting up from his chair.

"They're biracial, you idiot," she shouted back.

"Okay you two, cut it out," Frank said.

Pacing the kitchen, her husband remarked, "Dad, stay out of this, please."

Frank rose from the table, doing the sign of the cross and shuffled out, going into the den.

"Come on. Are you really serious? Isabella's been gone a year, and now you want to jump into an instant family. We're not the Brady Bunch. What if this Nadeesh comes around?"

"We have to call our lawyer and see if we can locate her. Cover all our bases. According to Mr. Rezner, there are no indications of any family history." Antoinette crossed his path. "Besides, where's your compassion? My brother named us as his children's guardians. We signed the papers last year, did you forget?"

"I didn't think he'd die." He folded his arms. "We didn't adopt an infant when we couldn't have kids years ago, and now you want to take on older children? This is crazy! Stop being Mother Theresa."

Her heart began to pound. Antoinette's face was on fire. She picked up one of the kitchen chairs and slammed it to the floor. The back of the chair cracked in half.

Frank hurried back into the kitchen, "Antoinette, be careful."

Vito's face went white. "What's gotten into you?"

Pointing a finger to his face, she blurted, "I've been a damn good wife to you. You didn't want to adopt, and I obliged because I loved you. We lost a son, and then we had beautiful Isabella, and she's gone too. You and I have carried a lot of crosses during our marriage. I don't want to grow old and be by ourselves. I already had that void with my brother not being around. Everything that I have ever loved is dead. That's my truth. A piece of me is with Devon and Isabella. I wanted more children, but they never came. We are given this gift… This opportunity to provide a home for these three kids, for my brother, and all you are thinking about is yourself. You're a real ass."

She clenched her fists, breathing heavy. Her husband stared at her. She knew he was hesitating, probably contemplating his next words. Everything was calculated with Vito. When he spouted out his suppressed emotions, his stubbornness came out, causing many fights between them. She took a couple more deep breaths to calm down, and waited.

Finally speaking softly, he said, "Okay, Antoinette. I get it. What do you want to do next?"

CHAPTER 63

That evening, after a few conversations with their own lawyer, Vito and his wife had a conference call with Dan Rezner from Portland to gather additional information. Sitting side by side on the couch in the den, he had rigged up a speaker phone for the three of them to converse.

"Hello Mr. and Mrs. Libero. Thank you for speaking with me."

"Yes. It's good we connected," Vito said. "We have some questions."

"Oh yes, I'm sure. I'm all ears."

"Let's begin," Antoinette said holding a pad and pen in her hands.

Mr. Rezner coughed. "By the way, let me express my condolences again. I'm terribly sorry. Your brother was not only a great client, but he was also my friend."

"Thank you," she replied. "I'm still trying to come to terms with his sudden death."

"Yes, I can—"

"So, where's the mother?" Vito intervened, not wasting any time with the lawyer.

His wife shot him a dirty look.

He held up his hand.

"Um..." A cough came through the receiver. "Right...My law office did a preliminary search for her here in Portland. It doesn't appear as if she's here in this state. But, that doesn't mean we shouldn't continue and try to locate her."

"We contacted our lawyer and he's going to be starting the process from this end," Vito stated.

"Good. We need to make sure we've done a search to show the court our due diligence for adoption if Mrs. DeSalvo is not found," Mr. Rezner replied. "Did your lawyer talk to you about filing papers for legal custody?"

Antoinette said, "Yes. We need to go to the Daley Center downtown."

"Where are the children now?" Vito asked.

"With the Nanny. Mrs. Miller or Paula. She lives four blocks away from his home. She's been their nanny the last six years."

"What do we need to do to get the children?"

"Come to Portland and pick them up before they are placed with the state. While the paperwork is being processed and the birthmother is being located, you'll have temporary custody of the children."

Vito rubbed his eyes. He was exhausted. It had been a rough day as it was with work, then this news of his deceased brother-in-law, and now going through these next steps with three new children. "How long can all this 'paperwork stuff' take?"

"Weeks. Months. Sometime longer."

He crossed his arms, looking over at his wife. "We know nothing about these kids or what they are like? Or better yet, if they'll like us. We were supposed to meet them for the first time this coming weekend."

Dan Rezner paused over the phone. "Yes, I realize the shock. This will be—"

Vito cutoff the lawyer again, needing to get it off his chest. "Last year we lost our only daughter. I've never been much in favor for adopting. My wife can attest to that. It's just overwhelming with what we've had to go through."

"I'm sorry to hear about *your* loss."

He pondered the situation for a moment. This is what Antoinette had wanted all along, a home filled with children. What about him? He had finally grown into his role of fatherhood, and then… Would this close his void for Isabella? *How could I ever love another child, other than my beloved baby girl?*

He had fought hard with his wife regarding adoption too. They were by themselves; that was their reality. He took a deep breath. *What did we have to lose?*

"Let's proceed." He turned to his wife. "Don't you say?"

"Yes," Antoinette replied, a smile spreading across her face.

"We'll be in touch as soon as we come to Portland, Mr. Rezner."

CHAPTER 64

The next few days were a whirlwind for Vito and his wife. They did some quick home renovation. First, rearranging Isabella's old room to be the girls' room for Emily and Audrey, and then converting their spare bedroom into a boy's room reserved for Abraham.

They met with their lawyer and filed the appropriate paperwork with the court at the Daley Center, as well as started an additional search for Nadeesh, the birthmother.

His wife also had several conversations with their nanny, Paula. A grandmother to five grandchildren, Paula loved babysitting Salvatore's kids. She had assured Antoinette that she was taking good care of the kids, and would provide them with whatever information she and Vito needed about each of them.

Vito and Antoinette also learned about Salvatore's desire to be cremated. He had included that in his will. That was done by the hospital his body was sent to, and handled by the Rezner Law office. What remained was a memorial service. Paula informed the Liberos that she and the kids would wait for them to do a proper service.

***

They landed at the Portland International Airport at four-thirty Sunday afternoon. The temperature was in the fifties. Vito had rented a van and they drove through the streets of Portland as misty rain began to fall. The windshield wipers squeaked back and forth. Antoinette turned on the heat and defogger as he drove.

As they followed the map and directions to Paula's home where the kids were staying, Vito was getting anxious. This was more than a coincidence he and his wife were being placed in. He was concerned about the children, and how they were dealing with the loss of their father. *How can I help them transition to their new life? What would Isabella think of all this?* He was worried. Then, he remembered a conversation he had with his daughter before her death about the subject of worrying.

She came to him one night after watching a TV show. He was in his den, reviewing numbers and making calculations.

"Daddy, you have a minute?"

He put down his papers and gazed at his pajama-dressed princess. She wore a concerned look on her face. "Sure, come here. What's wrong?"

She shuffled over to her father's side and hugged him. He hugged her back. "What's the matter? Are you okay?"

Her eyes misty, she asked, "Daddy, why do grown-ups always worry? Is that what's going to happen to me when I grow up? Worry all the time."

Vito squeezed Isabella again. "Where did you get that from?"

"A show on TV. They said when you are old your life is all about worrying. Is that true?"

He caressed her blond-haired head, not sure how to begin to answer the question. She had a point for a little girl.

"Oh, kiddo. Grown-ups always worry because they want to control everything."

He smiled thinking about his daughter's response. *She giggled, and then cocked her head. "Grown-ups are silly, Daddy. Don't they know they can call on Jesus for help?"*

Antoinette stared at him. "What are you thinking about?"

"Isabella. What she'd think of this situation?"

She reached over and touched his hand. "She'd love it. I wish she were here."

They made a couple of turns and then into a subdivision called Columbus Creek. Turning on Redwood Drive, they approached address 2357. It was a beige brick ranch with attached garage. Three bicycles blocked the garage. The front door was open.

Vito turned into the drive and shut off the car. Shaking inside, he grabbed Antoinette's hand.

"Are you nervous?"

She shrugged her shoulders. "A little."

He stumbled, "Me too."

They got out of the van and reached the front door. About to ring the doorbell, he stopped.

She looked at him. "What is it?"

He shook his head. There were countless questions still unanswered. How many more deaths could their marriage endure? He suspected that his brother-in-law had prepared for his children's future, given his risky boating excursions. It still didn't make him feel any better, though. There would be a lot of additional expenses. He knew his wife was hurting, too. She had become so happy connecting back with her brother.

"I'm so sorry for all this. I know how much you needed your brother back in your life—this void you carried with you. I—"

Her eyes full of tears, she whispered, "I know, it sucks. But, I have you to lean on."

Vito let out a deep breath then gently kissed Antoinette on the lips. "We'll make it work."

When he backed away, six eyes stared at them through the screen door. Startled, he waved. A short awkward silence followed as the kids and he and his wife eyed each other.

The silence was broken by Paula's sweet southern voice as she appeared behind the children hobbling toward the door, wearing a floral-patterned house dress and apron.

"Now, now, kids, it ain't polite to stare at company. Move out of the way."

The kids parted and Paula reached for the screen door handle. "I'm so sorry, darlings. Come on in." She escorted them inside.

They stood from tallest to smallest.

"Mr. and Mrs. Libero, this is Abraham, Emily and Audrey."

They politely said hello. Their faces carried a solemn expression, a realization more apparent in their demeanor, now that they were there. Vito forced a smile. *These kids will need a lot of time to adjust.* Antoinette then reached over and gave them each a hug. He followed his wife's lead, their return embraces stiff.

The Liberos spent the next hour hearing Paula recount stories about each of the children and the mischief they created for her on a daily basis. She kept it light considering the circumstances. The children laughed. It broke the ice.

Emily asked questions about the Opera House, and the music festivals at Grant Park. She was the talkative one. Mature beyond her age, she presented a confident demeanor.

Abraham seemed the joker. Already asking about the Chicago Bulls and smooth-talking Vito into taking him to a few games. He, of course, was thrilled for the attention.

Audrey on the other hand, was the quietest. In her own world, she doodled in a scrapbook while everyone else socialized.

What might have been an awkward and tense night of introductions and getting to know one another turned better than Vito had expected. The kids had warmed up to them. He left feeling pretty good.

The plan was to stay in Portland for a few days, connect with Dan Rezner, hang out with the kids, and have a memorial service for his brother-in-law. From there, they'd bid good bye to Paula, pack up the kids and fly back to Chicago.

***

The next morning the Liberos had several things to do. First, they picked up Paula while the kids were in school. She took them to visit Salvatore's home.

It was a two-story white split-level with a one car garage, and narrow driveway. It was in pristine condition.

"My goodness!" Antoinette remarked. "It's so immaculate and clean. With three kids, how is that even possible?"

The older woman laughed. "Bet you didn't know your brother was a neat freak. He knew how to take care of things and…" her voice cracked. "People as well."

They toured inside. White leather couches with a large screen TV occupied the living room. The kitchen was spacious with stainless steel appliances, and a long, rustic, picnic table with bench seating for up to ten people. Upstairs, there were three bedrooms, each child had his/her own room—decorated to their own liking. Salvatore's master room had a fireplace in the sitting area, and a canopy-type king-size bed.

One thing that was consistent throughout the house was the many portraits of Salvatore's wife, Nadeesh. There were pictures with her and the children, and several with Salvatore and her together through the years. Nadeesh was a very attractive woman, light green eyes, straight shoulder-length black hair, and flawless brown skin.

Vito couldn't help but stare at the woman's pictures.

"She's beautiful, isn't she?" Paula remarked as they walked about.

He nodded.

"No wonder his children are so gorgeous. They take after her," Antoinette said.

He was curious. "Who took all these photos? The photos are amazing."

"Salvatore," Paula replied. "He told me that he had taken photography lessons at one time. Enjoyed the art so much he went out and bought one of those really expensive cameras."

It was apparent to Vito that his brother-in-law was still madly in love with Nadeesh. Looking over at Antoinette as they strutted down the drive, he could tell his wife had come to that same conclusion.

Later, after dropping Paula back off at home, he and his wife stopped at the Rezner Law office to see if there were any new developments on Nadeesh's whereabouts. Dan Rezner confirmed he had none. However, he had some news on Salvatore's house to share. He told them per his will, the house would be put up for sale; this was already being handled by the law office. If and when it was sold, half of the money would go to Paula, his "partner" in helping him raise the children. The other half was going into the children's trust funds.

Vito couldn't believe how organized his brother-in-law had been. "Salvatore thought of everything, didn't he?"

His wife nodded, "I guess it goes to show how deeply he cared for his children and Paula. He seemed like an amazing father and friend. I could see a lot of that coming out now that we were talking."

"I wish we would have had more time with him."

After school that same day, before the sun began to set, the kids, Paula, and Antoinette and Vito drove to the Tom McCall Waterfront Park near downtown Portland and parked their cars. Together, they walked across to the middle of the Hawthorne Bridge, overlooking the Willamette River. It was Salvatore's request that his ashes be strewn over the river from the bridge.

Paula informed them that Salvatore drove through the bridge on a regular basis, and often came to take pictures of the bridge. He loved it so much because of its design and historical beauty. Originally constructed in 1910, the Hawthorne Bridge was the oldest operating vertical lift bridge in the United States.

Quietly, each of his children said something about their father. Abraham went first.

He smiled at everyone, but then sniffled. It was evident to Vito as the only male sibling, he wanted to be strong. "Okay, Dad. The sun is setting. I know you liked to see the sunset from a boat. We're here now as you wished for us to do." Abraham coughed. "I love you. I thank you for teaching me how to play basketball. I will…make you proud."

Antoinette wiped a tear from her eyes.

Abraham nodded toward his sisters. Emily nodded and straightened up.

"Daddy, you reminded me all the time that I was beautiful. I will always believe that because you made me beautiful." She lowered her head. "I miss you so much…"

The older woman began to cry.

Vito noticed more tears fell down Antoinette's face. His heart jerked. How he wished his wife and her brother had reconnected years earlier. She had had so little time with him. He hugged her shoulders.

It was little Audrey's turn next. She looked at everyone. "He was the coolest Papa, ever." And that was all she said.

Paula waved her arms, declining to say any words as she sobbed. Antoinette felt the same. Vito let go of his wife and took out a small silver urn from a plastic bag and opened it.

As cars bustled by, he opened the cap of the urn and little by little emptied Salvatore's ashes over the river. The ashes floated in the air and like a flock of geese, descended quietly and smoothly into the river. They hovered over the railings, watching as the last of the ashes fell into the water. Then, making the sign of the cross, they all trekked back to the cars.

It was a somber ride back to Paula's house. Vito held onto his wife's hand as he drove.

That night in the hotel room, Vito tossed and turned in the bed unable to sleep. He rose quietly not to disturb his wife, and walked over to the window.

Their room faced a twenty-four hour gas station and food mart. The sound of cars coming and going were also keeping him up. He sat on the ledge of the windowsill. Anxiety was taking over. He needed reassurance that the kids would be fine. He was scared he couldn't match up to the expectation that his brother-in-law had set in place. They were his responsibility now. Vito bowed his head and began to pray.

Heavenly Father, I don't normally pray, but I think this warrants a conversation with You. Tomorrow we leave Portland and head home with three children. I need you, Lord. Help me to direct the children in a way that will please You. Help me to become a good role model for them. But most importantly, let us become a family. You allowed this to happen in our lives, and so I will try to honor You by this grace given to us. Amen.

Vito sat there for a few more minutes hoping to feel something different, but he didn't. Instead, he headed back to bed where he slept soundly until daylight the next morning.

***

Gathering their luggage from the claim area at the O'Hare airport, they took a train that stopped at a long-term parking lot. Cautiously, all five of them then piled into the Libero's car and headed to the suburbs. As Vito drove, he observed the children through the rearview mirror. They sat wide-eyed in the back seat looking through the window, taking in their new surroundings.

As they pulled into the drive forty-minutes later, Cheryl, Lee, Lizzy, Connor, Antoinette's dad, and Vito's parents all waited inside for them. One by one, they stepped through the side door into the kitchen where their family and friends stood smiling. He closed the door behind him and turned to the kids.

Looking at all three of them, with anticipation and a nervousness of having an instant family, he announced, "Welcome home, we're glad you're here."

At first the children nodded and stood stiffly in the kitchen for a minute taking in their new surroundings, while the rest of the family and friends continued to stare at the newcomers. Vito suddenly got scared at the kid's reaction and put his arm around his wife about to ask her what to do, anything to break the ice when Abraham sneezed. A few seconds of silence followed until Frank emerged from behind Leonard.

"God bless you, child. My goodness. We're all staring at one another like we're window shopping."

Everyone chuckled.

He took the boy by his shoulders and said, "Do you know sneezing is a sign of good luck when you move into a new home?"

The boy lowered his eyes, looking a little hesitant.

"Nice one, Frank," Vito snorted.

"It is." He pointed to the other children. "We're extremely happy to have you here."

The kids then grinned back, and the rest of the family chimed in and circled the children, doing introductions and giving them hugs.

Vito exhaled deeply. A weight had lifted. His wife beamed at him. They had made a good decision. They had a family. *He* had a family.

CHAPTER 65

October, 2011. One year after adoption.

Antoinette stood in the flower department of their local grocer. Holding two bouquets of red roses in each hand, she scanned them, not sure which one to choose.

"Mom?"

She turned and gazed into the dark-eyes of her adoptive son, Abraham, grinning at being called mom. It had been an intense adoption process, but she and Vito had eventually been able to legally adopt her brother's children, after months of searching for their birthmother who was never located.

"Yes, my little man. What do you have there?"

Abraham held a bouquet of red roses. "I think *these* are perfect for Isabella. What do you think?"

Antoinette studied her bouquets and then at Abraham's bouquet. His dozen red roses were much nicer. She put hers down. "I love them. I think Isabella will, too. Thank you."

"You're welcome."

She looked around. "Where are the girls?"

"Emily and Audrey are with Dad and Grandpa Frank by the magazines and books. Should I go get them?"

"No. We'll go find them together. We should be leaving soon, anyway. I have what I need here. Ready?"

"Yes."

Antoinette put her arm around Abraham and they started for the magazine aisle. They could hear giggling from two aisles over. She shook her head; her father and Vito were probably cracking jokes at the pictures in the magazines. She was happy. She and her family were doing well. It had been a year of many adjustments, but the children had thrived. All in school, their grades were above average. Even Audrey, who attended a special education class twice a week for her learning disability was doing great.

As she and Abraham roamed through the store, he was telling her of a project his science teacher had assigned to them. "Your father can help you with that. Science isn't my strong point."

They had almost reached the end of an aisle, when Antoinette heard someone calling, trying to get her attention.

"Ma'am? Excuse me, ma'am?"

She watched as a slightly heavy-set woman looking to be in her thirties, approached her.

"I'm sorry to intrude. Are you by chance—Mrs. Libero?"

Antoinette pulled her son around, staring at the woman. "Yes and...who are you?"

"You probably won't remember me, but I saw you and I had to stop. I'm...Angela Green. I'm an EMT at Greenwood Memorial Hospital."

She blinked—the same hospital where Isabella was born. She didn't know why her name rang a bell. She couldn't place it. *Where did I see that name before? It sounded familiar.*

"This is going to sound strange, like I said... I'm sorry, but I had to stop you. I was there at the accident—"

Antoinette took a deep breath. She recalled the nametag of this woman who helped her up while Isabella lay on the ground. That day had changed her life forever.

"Oh." The memories flooded her mind. She turned to Abraham. "Ah... Why don't you round up the gang; tell them we'll be leaving soon."

"Sure, Mom." Abraham skipped away.

Angela leaned in and spoke, "I know this is awkward, but I am glad I saw you. From time to time I think of you and your husband, and what you went through."

Confused, she asked, "Why? You don't even know us."

"I know it sounds weird, but I lost my little sister, years ago to a car accident. I guess I have never forgiven myself. When that day happened to you, it brought back many painful memories for me. I am still so sorry for your loss."

Shocked, Antoinette was speechless. It had been two years since Isabella's death. So much had happened. She had a new family, and though she missed her child, it didn't hurt as much. Time was the healer, and so was love. Today was her daughter's two-year anniversary and they were all going to the cemetery, her dad, and her in-laws, Rosa and Leonard. It was ironic she'd run into this woman, here, and on this day of all days.

She touched the woman on her arm. "Thank you. Thank you for your thoughts. Today is the actual two-year anniversary. We were just heading to the cemetery."

"Oh, my!" Angela said, her face reddening. "I'm so sorry."

"It's okay. I'm sorry for you losing your sister." She stumbled forward and hugged the woman.

They separated and stood there a moment in silence before Antoinette heard Vito calling her. She turned as he approached.

"Are you ready? The kids want to go. Your father promised them ice cream afterwards."

Antoinette nodded her head, "I'm ready." She saw Vito look from her to the woman, as if expecting an introduction. "This is Angela Green. She's an EMT. She was…the day of—" She couldn't get any more words out.

"Oh. Hi." Her husband smiled, waving his arm.

"Hi."

Umm… It was nice to meet you, Angela." She held out her hand and they shook.

"Yes."

"We should go," Vito said.

"There they are," Frank yelled.

Antoinette turned and saw Emily, Audrey, and Abraham following their grandfather, as the group made their way toward them.

"What cemetery?"

She gazed back at Angela. Was this woman serious? She didn't want an intrusion. This would cause confusion to the kids.

"I'm sorry. I'm not saying now," Angela said holding up her hand. "Another time, I'd like to pay my respects. If you don't mind?"

"Sure. It's the Lincoln Memorial Cemetery, on—"

"Yes, I know where it is." The woman shuffled her feet. "I should be going. Can I give you my card?" She reached in her pocket and extended her arm. "Maybe we can go out for coffee some time? Talk more."

Antoinette stared at her. Somehow, their tragedy had affected this woman. She took the card. "Sure. Take care of yourself."

Vito put his arm around her. "We need to go."

She nodded to Angela and watched her walk away down the aisle in the opposite direction.

"Who was that?" Frank asked.

"Nobody," she said, putting the card in her purse.

"Dad. Start going. We'll meet up at the checkout."

"Suit yourself. Kids, we're leaving," Frank gruffed.

Antoinette then felt her husband take her hand and move her down the aisle quickly.

"Vito! Why are you in such a hurry?"

His face had paled.

"What? What is it?"

His eyes had moistened. "Remember that night of the accident when we had everyone over and I told you I went for a walk."

Antoinette nodded, remembering his parents and her father were there all night with them.

"I walked to the Paradise Bar and had a couple of drinks." He hesitated.

"While I was there, this Angela woman came in," he pointed down the aisle where they had spoken.

"So?" She was unsure where her husband was going with this story.

"She was drinking. The bartender knew her pretty well. Anyhow," he took a deep breath. "I overheard her tell the bartender her younger sister was killed by a car accident. She was pretty devastated about our loss because it reminded her so much of her own experience."

Antoinette stood motionless. It was now making sense why Angela felt compelled to visit Isabella at the cemetery. "My gosh. That's what she just told me. This is terrible."

Vito nodded. "I know. I'm sorry for never telling you about that night. It's...we had so many things going on. Maybe...maybe since she gave you her card you can call her and go out for coffee. I think she'd appreciate it."

She nodded. "What a great idea."

She heard her name called again.

"Are we ready to go?" Frank shouted.

Antoinette waved. "Yes, yes, we're coming." She and her husband reached the kids. "And, what's this I hear we're going for ice cream?"

"Yay!" Audrey, Emily, and Abraham yelled.

She nudged her father. "Nice going, Grandpa."

"*What?* Tell me you don't want ice cream."

Vito said, "I want ice cream."

Antoinette grinned. "Why not. Where's my bouquet? You have it Abraham?"

Abraham held the red roses high. "Yes, ma'am."

EPILOGUE: MANY YEARS LATER - THE FINAL ROUND

"Sometimes blessings come full circle much later than when you wanted them. In other cases, during the most unexpected times of your life. Everything is possible through Christ. The fulfillment of your life plans are always God's plans."

—From Antoinette Libero's Sticky Notes

CHAPTER 66

It was April around eleven in the morning on Good Friday. Earlier, it had been dreary with heavy clouds hanging low in the sky, but now the sun was peeking out. It would rain later. It always did on Good Friday.

Vito looked outside through the kitchen sliding door. "I'm going out for a bit." He turned on his heels and exited.

Antoinette was washing the breakfast dishes in the sink. "Get your hat while you're at it. It's windy out there."

He returned with a blue zip-up jacket and a black baseball hat.

She wiped her hands with a dish towel and walked over to him while he zipped up his jacket and adjusted his cap.

"Here," she said, lifting the collar around his neck. "We don't want you catching a cold, now do we?"

Vito smiled. He loved the way she fussed over him. She had been good to him even after all these years—forty-one years of marriage.

She patted his shoulders. "There. You're all set, dear."

He gave her a peck on the cheek. "I love you, you know that?"

Antoinette smiled back, revealing a lined face with youthful brown eyes that never lost its sparkle. "I do, silly. I love you very much."

He walked ahead and started opening the sliding door.

"You want some tea? I'll bring it out there for you."

"Okay."

Once outside, he walked onto their rectangular deck, straightening a large brown flower pot against the railings, and then stepped down four more steps onto the patio.

It was a little windy. The air was around fifty degrees and smelled of wet soil and worms. Vito wandered around the patio, hands in his pocket unsure what to do with himself. He felt restless and distracted. He entered their detached garage through the side door. His work bench was full of tools that needed to be organized and put away. He shook his head, marching out.

"Forget that."

In their backyard stood two large oak trees on each side of the lawn. He remembered years ago when they bought the house, how the trees was so much smaller, and thinner. Now, their trunks were thick, round, and their dense bark scaly. They used to be straight and firm. Not anymore. The one tree near the garage had its branches extended over the roof. Its back stooped over with its height. In some ways, as Vito eyed it, it too, like himself had aged and grown old.

He was seventy years old and retired for five years. He and Antoinette spent their days alone, together. Their three adopted children, Emily, Abraham, and Audrey, now adults, had moved out. It was quiet for the most part, but he liked it. He was content.

After working nearly thirty-two years in pharmaceutical sales, he was proud to say he had provided his family with a roof over their heads, and food on the table. What more could he ask for? He and his wife had their health, but more importantly, they had each other.

Vito picked up a few branches and looked at the sliding door. Antoinette's back was to him. She was talking on the phone again, probably with one of the kids. He shook his head. They called and chatted with their mother at least an hour every day. Laughing to himself, he thought, *what on earth could they possibly talk about every single day?*

Throwing the branches in the recycle bag, he moseyed over to the rose bush garden. The roses were beginning to bud, and the growing flowers spiraled up against the latticework. They did so every spring since Isabella's death.

I need to prune them soon.

It made him happy to see roses, as they were a constant reminder of his beautiful daughter who changed him into the father he became.

He grabbed a chair and slowly slid in it facing the garden, his back turned away from the deck and sliding door. The wind swirled around him flapping at his jacket collar, but he didn't feel the cold. Instead his body felt achy and tight, especially his arms and lower back.

"Oh, boy," he groaned, thinking of his parents, Rosa and Leonard. His father had constantly complained about his body hurting all the time and often attributed it to old age. He understood what his dad meant now. He was *old*.

He missed his parents and thought of them from time to time. They were no longer with him anymore. They had a tragic death and passed away suddenly seventeen years ago. They had been driving on one of the highways ten miles from their Charlotte condo when a semi-truck hit them straight on. It had been devastating. Although tremendously heartbroken, Vito was glad they at least died together. He was also grateful for having the opportunity to rekindle his relationship with his father when he was alive, as they got to spend a lot of time together watching old western movies and reminiscing about life joys.

The thought of his parents put him in a nostalgic mood, and Vito pulled out his wallet, taking out two pictures. One was a recent photo taken this past Christmas with the kids and Antoinette—his family. A family that almost hadn't been because of his stubbornness. But his lovely wife, convinced, or better yet, threatened him if he didn't go through with the adoption. She was definitely the stronger of the two of them.

Emily, Abraham, and Audrey had grown up—well-mannered, respectful, and purposeful. He attributed their drive and tenacity to make something of themselves from their father, his brother-in-law, Salvatore. A man who loved his kids and risk-taking all in the same moment. But, their compassion and gentleness he knew they learned from their adoptive mother, his wife.

The kids had turned out fine. Antoinette often reminded him that he did well with them. Teaching the kids how to drive, helping them find part-time jobs while they were in high school, and college hunting. Those were his strengths. The emotional stuff, like relationship issues, he left to his wife. With Emily and Audrey though, he did his best to counsel them on the "bad boys". He grinned. They had listened to him after all, and were currently in healthy relationships.

His finger massaged over the faces of his kids and then rested on his wife's face. There had been a time when he thought he didn't love Antoinette. But Isabella had changed all that. She came into their lives like a beacon of light, flooding them with her radiance; and guiding them back like lost ships at sea to each other.

Vito sighed. Antoinette was his true love. She never gave up on him or their relationship. She helped him give up alcohol and most importantly, find God. His mentor, confidant, and friend. It had taken almost a lifetime for him to realize that his stubbornness had been his *enemy.* And when he did surrender and let go of the "enemy," his heart opened, love walked in, and stayed there.

Since renewing his Catholic faith twenty years earlier, he had gotten involved with the Eucharist ministry and Usher ministry, as well as participated in Bible studies at Our Lady Catholic Community Church. Though Father Robert O'Malley, former pastor and friend, had left the earth and went to his new home in Heaven, Vito loved the fellowship of other Christians and the peace and joy it brought him to serve his Father.

He studied the picture of his wife again and smiled, suddenly choking up as a tear ran down his cheek. He rubbed it away. *Thank you, God, for her.*

He then gazed at the second picture. It was a picture of Isabella. A school picture yellowed and frayed at the edges from all the years of carrying it in his wallet. She had been seven years old when that picture was taken. Her long blondish hair couldn't hide her big, round hazel eyes and warm smile. She was smart, cute, and pure.

If there was anything he regretted the most in his life, was all the negative thoughts and feelings he had had about Isabella's condition when she was alive. It was the only demon he continued to carry in his heart after all these years. He tried to redeem himself with the other children, but it still felt like he had missed the opportunity the first time around.

"Sweetie, I'm so sorry. I hope you can forgive me," he whispered.

The wind picked up and a voice spoke softly in his ears. "You have been forgiven."

Startled, Vito sat up in his chair. There was no one around. He turned toward the sliding door. Antoinette was still talking on the phone. So much for his tea.

The pictures fell to the ground and he bent down to reach them, picking them up. A sharp pain riveted through his chest. "Ouch." He sat back and rubbed at his jacket.

He took a deep breath but it was constricted and suffocating, as if a heavy iron was on top of his chest pressing down.

"It's time..." a voice said.

Vito shook his head, gasping for air. "No...Lord... Not now, please."

He tried breathing in and out, but it was difficult and he began to gasp for air.

"Surrender, Daddy, and come home."

"Isabella?" He tried to get up from the chair, but couldn't. Both hands went cold as he clutched the pictures.

"Let go."

Vito stared down at the photos again. His eyes welled until they were blurry and he couldn't see. Then closing his eyes, he let more tears stream down his face. It was time to surrender. This time, to Jesus.

"Antoinette—" he whispered and then slumped in his chair.

CHAPTER 67

A light wind was coming from the east on a beautiful June afternoon. The sun was bright and shining. Its rays warmed Antoinette's face as she swayed back and forth in her old blue rocking chair on the front porch of her home on Trevor Lane. The smell of summer was around the corner. Today was her seventy-second birthday.

Closing her eyes, she silently recited a prayer of gratitude: *Lord, today, as you know, it is my birthday. I thank you every day for the blessings in my life, the people who have shared my life, but most importantly, the ever strong bond and relationship that I've come to know, through knowing You. In Jesus name I pray. Amen.*

This gratitude prayer was a ritual she did every day. She came to learn it through her good friend and pastor, Father Robert O'Malley, many years ago.

Father O'Malley had retired ten years ago at the ripe age of seventy-nine. He returned to his small seaside town of Newcastle in Northern Ireland's County Down where his family roots were. He said on many occasions, "I can't wait to retire. I will finally be able to drink a beer in the darn afternoon without being disturbed."

Six months into his retirement in the Irish land, they received word from their new pastor, Father John Doherty that Father Robert had passed. He collapsed from a bar stool while drinking a beer at one of the local pubs. He had only two requests which were found in a note in his wallet: to be cremated, which is unorthodox for a Catholic priest, and the other, was to have his ashes strewn over Slieve Donard, one of the tallest of the Mourne Mountains overlooking the Irish coast.

Antoinette could well imagine the uproar in the small town of eight thousand people about his cremation. With much pleading, his only surviving sibling, Mary, convinced the local church of granting her brother's wishes. Two young, newly appointed priests made the climb up Slieve Donard and cast his ashes across the horizon.

Back in Chicago, more than a thousand friends and parishioners, past and present, attended a mass dedicated to him. As Isabella would have said, "He's with Jesus now." Antoinette missed him every day. She knew though, she'd see him soon.

She suddenly thought of her father, Frank. He had a full life, one where he waited patiently for God to come and take him away so he could be with his beloved wife, Martha. He died peacefully in bed at his retirement condo, at the age of eighty-eight, seven years after her mother. He was also with Jesus.

Holding two envelopes in her wrinkled hands, Antoinette slowly opened the first. Taking her time reading the card; it was signed *Angela Green*, who now worked for Holy Name Hospitals for Children as the director of public affairs. Angela was a strong advocate for providing excellent medical services for children born with spinal and limb deficiency. She kept her updated with the latest news on healthcare for children. From the time their paths had crossed at the grocery store two years after Isabella's passing, a friendship had emerged between them, and they stayed in touch. Antoinette smiled. Angela had never forgotten her birthday.

Carefully, she placed the first envelope on top of the porch table, and opened the second heavier envelope; the address was from Nebraska. There were two small hearts drawn on the back of the envelope. Two pictures fell into her lap. The first one was a picture of Lizzy, her husband, Ron, and her daughter, Isabella, and son, Steven. A professionally done picture, probably taken at Sears or JC Penny. They were all smiling. The second picture was of eight year old Isabella, and six year old Steven. They were sitting cross-legged, side by side, on a lawn. Isabella was holding the nativity set with the figurines she and Vito had given her mother many years earlier.

Antoinette's heart warmed inside. Lizzy had become a loving woman. She moved away several years ago from Chicago to pursue a special education career after her mother Cheryl died. In the process, she met Ron, and they married. She was currently a full-time mom. Life had turned for the better for Lizzy. However, there was a time when they had almost lost her, too.

When Isabella passed, her best friend had changed. The Liberos didn't see much of Lizzy after that. She was in and out of therapy. The trauma of losing her only true friend affected her for many years. In high school, she surrounded herself with a bad crowd and experimented with alcohol. Antoinette and Cheryl still talked then, but it had become awkward. Cheryl often complained how bad Lizzy's behavior had changed. Her grades suffered. She and her husband, Lee, had tried everything; counseling and therapy sessions, as well as sending their daughter off to a private school. Nothing worked.

When Lizzy was seventeen, Antoinette received an urgent call from Cheryl. They were at Greenwood Memorial Hospital and asked if she and Vito could come there for support. Lizzy had tried committing suicide by slitting her wrists with a pocket knife during one of the free periods at school.

Going into Lizzy's hospital room, Antoinette noticed her wrists were wrapped with gauze and her arms strapped to the bed in case she tried to hurt herself again. She gently unbuckled the straps. With her hands released, the girl immediately covered her eyes and began crying.

"I'm so sorry," she whispered, through her tears. "I should be dead, not Isabella."

"Hey, hey..." Antoinette coaxed. "I never blamed you. It wasn't your fault, Lizzy. Stop harboring this pain inside of yourself." Taking her into her arms, she continued, "Isabella wouldn't want to see you like this. She loved you so much, Lizzy. She wouldn't want you to be hurting. It's okay to be alive."

"How?" Lizzy cried on, her voice muffled by Antoinette's shoulder.

She pulled away, staring the younger girl in the eye. "You must. Isabella will live on in your memory, forever. You have a prosperous life ahead of you. Do something with it. Honor her through the choices you make."

"Then why was Isabella's life cut short?"

Antoinette shrugged. "Because God had told her it was time to go. You see, we don't know when it will be our time. We need to go and live life to the fullest every day, and be ready to embrace it, when it happens. This is not the way for you to go. It is not the way Isabella wants to see her best friend. Besides," she stroked her hair, "someone has to take good care of the nativity figurines. Vito and I gave it to you to keep it safe. Can you do that for us?"

"Sure," Lizzy replied, wiping her face.

Antoinette kidded her, "You do still have it, don't you?"

Lizzy perked up. "Yes, of course. It's in my room on a table; set up the way...Isabella had it."

She smiled. "Thank you for taking care of it for us. Now get better so you can go on home. Your mom and dad and brother love you so much, and need you to be well."

They embraced and Antoinette stayed in her room that night until she fell asleep. Holding her was like holding Isabella. She could feel her daughter's presence in that hospital room, grateful for the grace and love surrounding them.

It took Lizzy almost a full year to recover. Their relationship blossomed into a close friendship. Now, their conversations were centered on parenting, and the joys of life that filled their cups each day.

Inserting the card back into the envelope, Antoinette closed her eyes, taking it all in. She was startled by the sound of a car. Looking up, she realized an SUV had gone over the speed bump in the street. *Jerk!* Didn't he see the speed bump? That speed bump was named by the neighborhood children, "The Isabella Bump." It was put in three years after Isabella died, and after another car accident with one of the neighboring children, who thankfully the injuries hadn't been fatal.

Antoinette got up from her rocker. Taking the envelopes, she shuffled around the house, taking slow steps to the backyard, to the rose garden. She had a full rose garden, tall and flowery, each shoot containing a blossoming rose. For the past twenty-five years, they had been blooming against the wooden fence on the left side of the property near their patio. She had a stone carving of Isabella's face cemented into their patio. Stopping and staring at her daughter's picture, she thought to herself, Isabella would have been thirty-two years old today. Her little rose. She used to call her that all the time.

"You're my little rose."

"Mommy, what are roses?"

"They are flowers with velvet petals. They come in all colors, red, fluffy pink, pearl white, or soft yellow. They are the most beautiful flowers ever."

"Can I have a red rose?"

"You sure can."

"I'd like that, Mommy, very much."

She was a beautiful, strong and curious young child. A child taken away too soon before her time. But when she had been alive, it was the best gift Antoinette could ever have asked for. Isabella taught her that in order for love to flourish, one needed to give it away freely, without reservation and expectation. This helped her marriage come full circle.

Next to Isabella's picture was a stone carving of Vito's face, her beloved husband.

"Lucky bastard," she had said between tears when she found him that morning two years ago when he had gone to the Lord. "You get to see Isabella before me."

In her mind, she heard Vito's voice. "We'll be waiting for you. Write a book about us, Devon… Isabella… Our kids."

"I will, darling."

Vito was buried the day after Easter Sunday. She missed him so much.

Her life had been prosperous. It hadn't always been easy, but she was grateful for her blessings. Together, husband and wife learned love was much deeper than the things they didn't have. Most importantly, they learned to surrender their expectations of each other.

She recalled a time when Vito asked Father Robert, "Does love come full-circle when you learn to surrender your expectations?" The priest responded, "Son, for you to ask me that question, can only mean to me you are surrendering."

Twenty-four years ago luck turned when she and Vito adopted three beautiful children. Her brother, Salvatore's children. In an instant, they had a family—a family Isabella would have wanted with a brother and two sisters.

Emily had been thirteen years old at the time. She was now thirty-seven, married to a hardworking man, a pharmacist, and she a stay-at-home mother of two children, living in Atlanta, Georgia. Her family was doing well.

Abraham was ten years old at the time of the adoption. He was the most divine child ever. Very respectful and loving. He dreamed of becoming an actor. At age twenty, he left home and went to California. He had landed spots in a few soap opera stints here and there, but they weren't substantial. Antoinette and Vito knew financially he was trying to make ends meet. They tried wiring him money every so often, but he had refused it. He finally landed a tiny role in a TV sitcom and began to do well. Recently, he had received a small role opposite a bigger named actor in a new movie. He was now thirty-four years old, single, and living in Los Angeles. Antoinette was proud of his persistence to never to give up.

Lastly, little Audrey was nine at the time. Educationally, Audrey struggled a lot. She had a learning disability. She and Vito had put her in after-school programs, and as the years passed, she progressed. She graduated with a Masters of Education. She currently was living in downtown Chicago and taught at DePaul University. She recently turned thirty-three years old and had a fiancé named Logan. For years, she has done all the grocery shopping every week for Antoinette.

Their father, Salvatore, would have been proud of how his children turned out. She wished he could see them now. They never did find their birthmother, and the kids never went searching for her either.

It had been great hearing from Emily and Abraham earlier today, wishing her a happy birthday. Tonight, she and Audrey had plans. She and Logan were taking her out to dinner.

As for her, when the children had gotten older, Antoinette went back to teaching high school, her first love. The students had changed, but the issues were the same. She had retired five years ago.

And Antoinette had recently wrote a book. A memoir of her life with Vito and all their children. It was titled: *A Circle of Roses*. She finished it last year, after years of writing down bits and pieces of ideas on notepads and sticky notes. She researched and found a great agent, Lori Lyndon, who shopped it to all the top New York publishing houses. Lori had called yesterday to inform her two publishers were seriously considering her novel.

Sitting on the bench across the rose garden, Antoinette looked up at the sky.

"Did you hear, Vito? My book about our life is going to be published. I did it… I wish you were here to celebrate with me. I miss you and Isabella so very much… I hope you guys are well. Save some fun for me when I come see you."

She closed her eyes, heavy with fatigue. Folding her hands in her lap, Antoinette took a calm, deep breath.

"Relationships have three phases. First there is the bliss period…feeling on top of the world. Like rock stars you're at the summit. Then, circumstances happen, which I call the 'cross'…those troubling times…we've all been

there... And finally, resurrection, coming up for air, breathing again, standing on top of your mountain...ready for new beginnings...joyfully surrendering..."

She smiled, thinking what Father Robert used to say about marriage and family—how a wedding ring symbolized the events of two people's lives, which were very circular. He used to say, "We end where we began."

In the distance, Antoinette heard music and faint voices... What's that? It's familiar. She nodded gently. Is it Vito and Isabella giggling?

"Happy Birthday to you. Happy Birthday to you. Happy Birthday to Mommy. Happy Birthday to you..."

ABOUT THE AUTHOR

Chiara Talluto is an avid reader, philanthropist, conservative, and energetic outdoors-type who dreams of owning a Harley and one day riding across the country feeling the wind whip across her face and tangling all of her brown hair. But until then, she is content on being a stay-at-home mom raising her two active young daughters and practicing wife to her wonderful and supportive husband.

Love's Perfect Surrender is Chiara's debut novel. Currently, she is hard at work on her second novel, as well as penning short stories that somehow cross her mind and must be put into words. When she's not writing, you can find her reading, writing in her journal, and playing mommy to her kids. Her motto: *Live, laugh, and cry.*

ACKNOWLEDGEMENTS

It has been said that the loneliest place is at the top of one's success. The loneliest place I've ever experienced has been sitting at the keyboard staring at a blank computer screen; waiting for inspiration on the right words, and the right sentences for my characters. I couldn't have completed this novel, nine years in the making, without the support and help of many people.

My writer's group friends: The Schaumburg Scribes at the Schaumburg Public Library. I have loved and cherished your life stories and critiques along the way. You've helped me become a better writer.

My beta-readers: Ann Marie Barry, Wendy Rue Sable, and Helen Osterman. Thank you for your honest feedback, ongoing support, and friendship.

My editor and friend, Brittiany Koren from Written Dreams Editorial Services. Your constructive feedback has helped me achieve my lifelong goal. Thank you for being the wheels to my dreams.

Eddie Vincent from ENC Graphic Services, thank you for your creative direction on my book cover. It's exactly what I wanted.

Lara Hunter from Book Technologies, thank you for your making my story look like a real book, both on print and digital.

Logan Stefonek from Stefonek Design and Illustration, thank you for designing the rose for the interior of the book. It's perfect.

To my parents, Anna and Giovanni. I'm proud to be your daughter.

My husband, Joe. My anchor, my love and my knight in shining armor. Thank you for sharing your life with me and being a great father to our little blessings, our babies, Ava and Stella.

Lastly, thanks to YOU, the reader for choosing this book. Enjoy!